The G.G. Garth TETRALOGY

For Taufiq
The New improved edition for your library shelves.
with love from your pal,
Ghia D
aka ggarth
12/5/2021

Jumpmaster Press
Birmingham, AL

Copyright Notice

The G.G. Garth Tetralogy, a collection by G.G. Garth:
Nightmare Matinee; *Driven to Kill!*; *Bad Dog: A Vampire's Canine*; *Party Till You Scream!*. These G.G. Garth titles were first published in 1994 and 1995 by Bantam, Doubleday, Dell, New York, NY, Bantam Starfire imprint.

Cover Artist: James Hislope
Author photo credit: Peter Mellekas

Library Cataloging Data

Names: G.G. Garth, Ghia Szwed-Truesdale

Title: *The G.G. Garth Tetralogy*: *Nightmare Matinee*; *Driven to Kill!*; *Bad Dog: A Vampire's Canine*; *Party Till You Scream!*

5.5 in. × 8.5 in. (13.97 cm × 21.59 cm)

Description: Jumpmaster Press™ digital eBook edition | Jumpmaster Press™ Trade paperback edition | Alabama: Jumpmaster Press™, 2018. P.O Box 1774 Alabaster, AL 35007 info@jumpmasterpress.com

Summary: A four book collection of G.G. Garth's classic tales of bone-shilling horror: *Nightmare Matinee, Driven to Kill!, Bad Dog: A Vampire's Canine, Party Till You Scream!*

ISBN-13: 978-1-949184-80-8 (eBook) | 978-1-949184-42-6 (paperback) |

1. Good Versus Evil 2. Young Adult Fiction 3. Thriller 4. Magic Realism 5. Myths and Legends 6. Horror 7. Vintage Pre-Internet

Printed in the United States of America

For more information: twitter.com/GGGarth; pph.me/GhiaWrite; https://www.facebook.com/ggarth1; GGGarthProductions.com

The G.G. Garth TETRALOGY

Author Note

This book is dedicated to Jacqueline Urra, and Kathy Squires, my original Editor at Bantam Starfire to whom I remain indebted for having taken a chance—back in the early 1990s—on my first four Young Adult novels: *NIGHTMARE MATINEE, DRIVEN TO KILL!, BAD DOG: A VAMPIRE'S CANINE,* and *PARTY TILL YOU SCREAM!* Titles ending in an exclamation mark—you knew—had to be campy good fun. Back then, I wrote to delight my young nieces, Kirian, Meredith, and Alysha, and nephew, Jake, who are now very fine adults. So, despite *The Horn Book Review's* 1994 concern that the YA horror genre foretold the demise of a generation's character, my thrillers did not warp *them.* In fact an outpouring of praise came from the likes of *New York Newsday, Rocky Mountain News, The Indianapolis Star, Cranston Herald,* Boston's *ABC* affiliate *WCVB-TV Channel 5,* and *The World of Fandom's* "Shelves of Doom". Fan mail deluged me from teens *and* Goths in their 20s and 30s. Fellow horror authors like Christopher Golden and John Peel extolled my tongue-in-cheek humor and science-based granularity as *educational.* Ultimately, my four zany stories survived as collectible cult classics.

In 2020, as we together slog through the pandemic polyfecta, pre-internet thrillers remind us of a time when you could not just ping Mom and say, "Come get me!" Back then we had to save ourselves—so too, today, amidst heightened local and global challenges. Yet, we still have a chance to turn things around, for which I am deeply thankful. I am grateful for many things in our amazing life. Not the least of which is the opportunity to adapt my vintage pre-cellphone tales to a 21st century attention span. And, I'm happy to include in my dedication, newest family additions, grandnephew Solomon and grandniece Ania, and my own cherished children, Alden and Jack: Already, they're better writers than I. Endless gratitude goes to my family and friends, and to my namesake. *Slasher kisses,* as ever, to Adam Novak. Special thanks to my childhood bestie, Tacia Breshears for facilitating the re-publication of my novels. Deepest gratitude to my Publishers, Gene Rowley and Kyle Hannah and their team at Jumpmaster Press. Thank you for championing my vintage pre-internet yarns. Here's to prosperity and joy for all in 2021!

—G.G. Garth

Table of Contents

Nightmare Matinee

Originally published by Bantam Books' Bantam Starfire, a division of Bantam Doubleday Dell Group, Inc. New York, NY, 1994

1

The Modern Unabridged How-to-Spell Book lay open on an oak desk in Eastridge. A page of the *grimoire* fluttered in the moonlight as another victim of avarice fell prey to the words on page 66. In the cozy home office, the book sighed in relief as a woman's soul fed the nefarious book.

Page 66, *Spell Instructions*, read like a chat with a weird old friend:

Before the moonful night, chant these words several times over the object that is to be given to the person or persons you wish to enchant:

Borum, borum, borum
Moon pulls water, light opens eyes.
Hormones churn and boil.
Receptor cells toil to kill all decision-making powers.
Spoil, spoil, spoil.
Victim mine, do my will.
Borum, borum, borum

Now, remember, the human body is 88 percent water. And you know the moon creates tides on our great oceans. Well, think of what it does to tiny little humans. The *grimoire* concluded with,

Keep in mind, when casting your spell, you must be very specific about the desired result. Otherwise, these spells have a way of getting out of hand. We mean, be careful what you wish for, you might get it.

"That'll take care of *you*, you little monsters," the woman muttered smugly to herself. Her cold words reverberated against the cover of the indifferent *grimoire* as her hands closed the shadowed pages and slipped the still-warm movie reels back into their metal cases.

2

A night at the movies alone with Katrina Phillips was a thought rarely far from any Westlake boy's mind. Deliciously dangerous; aesthetically very pleasing—deadly combination. None got a second chance, yet.

Since sixth grade, Aaron Sedgewood's fantasy began with that precisely: Katrina Phillips. Tonight, after half a decade, Aaron's wish was coming true: his first date with Katrina. Together they would watch the new 3-D horror movie at the run-down old theater that had just been reopened under new management. The new flick was released–coincidentally, it seemed–at the full moon and played throughout the remainder of the lunar cycle. Unbeknownst to Aaron and Katrina and the other students from Westlake High School who saw it, once viewed, the movie immediately began to change their lives. Six days it had played, and by 6:06 p.m. of Friday the 13th there was no turning back. Sixes aligned and ignited the insidious power of the movie's spell from page 66 of the *Modern Unabridged How to Spell Book.*

The movie was an invective brew of stardust, celluloid, and lunatic magic. Like Katrina Phillips, it was potentially tragic, and definitely addictive. Aaron was hooked on both Katrina and the movie.

Inside the shabby theater, a leprechaun-faced old man handed the teenagers two pairs of 3-D glasses and two hologram cards that served as movie tickets. Every matinee and night the movie ran, a different card with another hologram fright face was used.

"Collectibles!" Aaron smiled, peering at the face of the scaly-finned monster from the Black Lagoon. "You want my collection, Katrina. They'll be worth something, someday," he said. Katrina was nonplussed.

"Swag," she replied flatly.

In the dim light Aaron and Katrina took their seats in the dank old movie theater. A rattlesnake sound from behind them made Aaron and Katrina turn around to see Bear Henkel shaking a box of iridescent marbles impatiently. Soon the entire theater echoed with the glassy chatter of more movie merchandise as the other Westlake classmates joined Bear's chant demanding the movie begin. The occasional marble fell to the cement floor and skittered under the seats, adding to the clattering noise.

Finally bone-shaped letters spelling *Coming soon on Blockbuster home video* crawled slowly after the movie title *Still Life: The Best of the Worst.* Aaron nonchalantly leaned back as if to address Bear Henkel, but really in order to casually place an arm around Katrina Phillips' shoulders. Then, he turned to her with a handsome smile and a rakish wink.

Hasn't bitten my arm off yet, he thought with relief, eyeing her. Katrina ignored his move, examining the cardboard carton that contained her collection of marbles with the hologram horror characters inside. Along with popcorn and sodas, and the ticket of course, Aaron had purchased the hologram horror marbles for Katrina at the concession stand. One side panel of the marble box read: *Printed on recycled paper by adults in U.S.A., not in China by children who should be in school.* The other side of the box delivered a health warning.

"Aaron, can you believe these marbles are *hazardous to your health*?" Katrina scoffed.

"Yeah. My little sister died from marble inhalation. She hid'em up her nose and ended up choking on'em. My dad tried to vacuum them out, but it was too late. Don't worry, Katrina, I can handle it. I was too young to know her. My mother told me about it when I grew up."

Katrina laughed politely, unsure if Aaron was telling the truth or just trying to get her to laugh, and with that, their date was off to a stalling start.

Some years earlier, Katrina Persephone Phillips appeared in Aaron Sedgewood's class when her parents moved back to Westlake. She never spoke to Aaron until Friday night. *Talk about delayed gratification*, Aaron thought. Rumor had it Katrina was thoughtless—impatient. But Aaron was rendered blind by her *way*, not to mention a face that he, as an artist, considered perfect. *I'll risk it.*

And so he took a chance. Aaron had not expected Katrina's kind answer to his invitation to the movie. He'd drawn a three-dimensional treasure map on heavy paper, including the spooky old movie house on Green Street. To create the full 3-D effect, he outlined the edifice in dots of green and red and enclosed a pair of 3-D glasses. Inside the flap of paper he printed the proposed date and time, a big green-and-red-dotted question mark, his name–outlined in green and red dots–and

Répondez s'il vous plait. In parenthesis he added, *The favor of a reply is requested.* He hoped that she would appreciate his brand of old folks' formality.

The same day Aaron had slipped his 3-D movie invitation through the air vent in Katrina's locker, she palmed him back a tidy folded purple note. She had looked Aaron in the eye, then walked quickly away from where he leaned against the lockers with his best friend, Dan Pritcher. She left both boys stunned.

Katrina wrote her response in lavender ink; it read, "*Yes. I'll meet you at the...*" Instead of writing the word *theater*, she too, illustrated the dark, hunkered building, gargoyles and all, leaving out the 3-D effects.

Despite Katrina's encouraging reply, Aaron tried not to appear too enthusiastic about the date. Since he started taking Intro to Psych class, Aaron began to think more and more about his image. *My persona won't look good if I have to try too hard,* he thought.

Earlier that night Aaron conveniently did not mention to his mother that he was actually going on a *date*. That way, Mrs. Sedgewood could not pry and Aaron would not feel so guilty leaving her alone again.

"I'm just going to go see my favorite movie again with Dan," he told his mother a half-truth.

Aaron's mother had squinted at him through the clear solution in her martini glass.

"You know, Mom, it's that film Dad's girlfriend worked on," he reminded.

Aaron's spirit withdrew from his mother right on schedule: Thankfully, she had not responded with her usual guilt-inducing tirade. She had about reached her liquid limit.

"Well, have a nice weekend, Mother." Aaron forced a smile that barely adhered to his face as he headed for the front door.

"Tuck in your shirt, dear. You're too good to appear a Philistine. Even if it is merely a vile horror movie you're going to see..." Her voice pitched abrasively. "I still can't fathom what you see in such trash. Life is sufficiently terrifying already!" She had chased her words with a gulp of martini.

Without discussion or argument Aaron had tucked in his stiff-pressed button-down plaid shirt. When his back was to Mrs. Sedgewood, he'd unbuttoned the top few buttons to show off his proud new chest hairs. *Dad didn't have chest hair until his twenties. I'm lucky!*

"Don't forget your father's picking you up tonight, Aaron," said Mrs. Sedgewood, slurring. "He called. Said you knew where to meet him. We're supposed to get another downpour like we've had all week, so bring your slicker, darling."

Aaron didn't answer for fear his mother's behavior would change again with her next gulp from her martini glass. He stepped out the front door, looking forward to his weekend freedom, and most especially, to his first date with Katrina Phillips.

3

Gaggles of red-necked turkey vultures circled Westlake's toxic waste dump whose backland abutted the rear of the old theater. One bird picked at a nondescript lump amid the rubble. Another pecked him in an effort to preserve the fetid meat for himself.

As they filed out through the theater lobby, behind Aaron and Katrina, hideous, deformed ghouls glared from a streaked glass poster encasement. At first glance it was a Technicolor collage of gore. Recognizable to Aaron were Dracula, Freddy Krueger, Jason, Frankenstein, a benign-looking werewolf, Dr. Jekyll and Mr. Hyde, several witches, the Fly, the Phantom, the Creature from the Black Lagoon, and some winged monkeys. A poster tag line read "*A montage of the crème de la créme of horror movies.*"

Ahead of Aaron, Katrina pushed through the crowd of students to get outside. There they stood under the faded orange marquee. On it was the movie title, *Still Life: The Best of the Worst*. Its black block letters were skewed, barely pinned to the marquee.

Aaron's eyes adjusted quickly to the brighter light. The cooler air cleared the lingering essence of sour dairy and sulfur that had slightly irritated his nostrils during the movie. He hoped his breath didn't still reek from his recent tonsillectomy. He cupped a hand over his face, sniffed, and grimaced.

Aaron happily ushered Katrina past the other moviegoers. His prize was not only within arm's reach, he was touching her shoulders. Mark Stiger and Bear Henkel scuttled by the other students who dribbled out. Inside, Bear accidentally knocked Frankie Marcel against the concession stand's sharp metal corner.

"Hey, watch it, Bear! Jerk! You ruined my good white polo shirt," Frankie shouted, rubbing his ribs. Large drops of blood seeped through the white cotton. Frankie ran up the worn carpeted steps toward the *Men's Room* sign for cold water and a paper towel.

"Where y'going, kid?" A scratchy voice came from atop the stairwell.

"Boys' room, sir," Frankie replied as he wafted passed the old ticket taker's pall of cigar smoke.

"Don't be too long in there," rasped the old man. "We gotta close up for the night." The gnome-faced man descended to the lobby.

"Hi Bear! Hey Mark!, said Aaron outside the theater. "See you guys Monday in art!" *That's right, guys, I'm with her,* Aaron thought as he paused a bit longer to be sure all the guys saw him with Katrina. He felt a rush of adrenaline inside. With the launch of the new monster movie, the old theater was quickly becoming a popular hangout again—after only six days.

The full moon was on its way out, its deadly deed done. A slow explosion pulsed in every boy and girl who had seen the new movie, even once.

"Look out!" Mark Stiger suddenly bolted out, gripping his stomach. He rushed around the corner of the theater toward the bike rack. Several students peeked and giggled, holding their nose as mark threw up violently out by the bicycles alongside the theater.

"Must've been the greasy popcorn," Aaron joked, and then turned to the old woman in the ticket sales booth who was rapping incessantly on the window. She stared at Aaron, strip-searching his face.

That old bat sure is consistent, thought Aaron. Every time he'd come to see this movie, she had reacted the same way.

"Boy! Boy! How'd you like it *this* time?"

"Great, ma'am, just great, thanks. Except that Wolfman in the flick still looks more like a *terrier* man. Not very convincing!" Aaron waved good-by.

She rapped again, more insistent.

"What about the girl? What did *she* think?"

"Ask her," Aaron replied, laughing.

Katrina faced the old woman at the ticket window squarely and respectfully, and opened her mouth to speak. The old woman wrinkled her hairy upper lip like a horse eating and pushed aside the remaining stack of hologram cards on the counter. Craning her neck, she took a thorough survey of the Katrina's face.

"When did *she* first see the movie, boy? Sunday? Monday?"

Although he despised being called "boy," Aaron smiled politely and shrugged.

He wanted to look at Katrina's perfect face again as soon as possible. After all, for 120 minutes they had just sat in darkness, gawking at history's most despicable characters.

The small, ancient woman trained her bloodshot eyes on Katrina. A shudder of repulsion passed through the old woman on seeing Katrina's right eye. In it was movement at the outer corner, a fleshy green tendril or tentacle, the old woman wasn't sure which.

"Godfrey!" she yelled, then her weathered hand yanked the heavy red velvet curtains closed between the young couple and herself causing a spray of hologram movie tickets to dance and click against the Plexiglas.

Katrina giggled at the flamboyant hag and turned away.

"Gosh, what's her problem?" said Aaron.

"Probably doesn't approve of your taste in women, Aaron." Katrina glanced over her left shoulder at him and pursed her lips flirtatiously, then stopped to rub the irritation in her right eye.

"My sentiments exactly, Katrina. You read my mind. We must be ESP-ing," said Aaron, "Maybe the old lady's a Gypsy or a soothsayer?"

"This is Westlake, Aaron. We don't have Gypsies and soothsayers here."

"Yeah, but did you check out her garb? Weird stuff! All those tacky, shiny yellow ruffles. Every single time I've come, she's worn the gaudiest clothes. I'm surprised she doesn't wear the red velvet curtains from that ticket booth. She can't possibly be from New England to dress like that!"

Katrina broke in. "My mother has an outfit just like hers in lime green. She got it at a designer boutique in the city. *Haute couture* is very expensive, you know. I heard that the old lady's one of those eccentric Hollywood producers?"

Aaron threw his head back and nearly howled, laughing. "On drugs! And hiding out incognito as a ticket sales person for a B horror movie in Westlake! I doubt it!"

"Talk about 'unsolved mysteries'!" replied Katrina pertly.

The rubber sole of Aaron's high-top Air Jordan's scuffed on the sidewalk, and he bumped into Katrina from behind. All the while he had forced himself to either close his eyes or just not look at his beautiful classmate. *Delayed gratification is a major drag, but I can't let on yet how much I like her. Bad for my image if I start staring at her like every other guy!*

He looked at the starry sky and easily pictured Katrina's face in detail. Each feature on her face struck him as perfect, each independent of the others. The way her nostrils curved, the space between her chin and smooth bottom lip, her brow. He wished he'd brought his sketch pad.

Aaron was in love. Well, if it wasn't love, it sure was right up there with the feelings he had when watching his favorite team win or selecting the black 1968 Mustang convertible his father promised him for his sixteenth birthday that was coming up. Of course, it's true, he still barely knew Katrina.

"Great flick! Movie really grows on you, huh, Katrina?" He trailed directly behind her, so he still could not see her face as she spoke.

"I like how they spliced the different monster scenes together from all those movies and mixed them with the new film footage. But those 3-D glasses kill my eyes. One green lens and one red messes with my vision."

"Mine too, a little," Aaron agreed. "But it's so cool how they make it different every time you go."

"I wonder how they do that," Katrina said thoughtfully. "You're an artist, Aaron, I bet you can figure it out."

"I'll find out. My dad's girlfriend worked on this movie. She can probably tell me."

"That's so cool, Aaron."

Her enthusiasm inspired him to capitalize on the opportunity to book another date.

"We'll just have to see it together again and see how it changes... Hey, look at the stars, Katrina. Don't they seem really clear tonight? I've never seen them this clearly before. Wow."

Katrina found his enthusiasm amusing. "I can hardly see past the streetlamps. I wonder what Mr. Breen would say about that!" Her self-deprecating laugh referred to Wednesday's Psychology class chapter on subliminal meaning and symbolism. Katrina rubbed her eyes. They itched. Her vision was impaired by a fine yeast-mold web that sprouted on the surface of her eyeballs. She kept rubbing.

"You okay?"

"Yeah, thanks," replied Katrina. "Just pollen, or—*ouch*!"

"Here, let me help you," he offered, and put his arm around her.

"You're trying to be romantic, aren't you, Aaron?" Katrina smirked and pressed closer to him. Another zing scampered up his smooth, muscular arm and jabbed a sweet dagger into his heart. He didn't know how to respond. This was all new.

"*Owww,*" murmured Katrina again, dipping her head to rub a fat, pulsing irritation in her eye. "I've got—must be my contact lens." Her long, silky hair fell across her face as she fiddled dexterously with her right lens.

Her hair just goes on forever, thought Aaron.

"I got those disposable colored lenses this week. I'm still getting used to them, I guess."

"You mean to tell me your eyes aren't really that shade?" he teased about her lavender contact lenses.

"Oh, these are just enhancers. *They enhances my vision while they enhances my chances*."

"Katrina! Is that Mae West you're imitating!" *I am liking this goddess too much!*

Nodding, Katrina laughed, then glanced several times at herself in the window of the defunct J. J. Newberry's department store. She strained to see her reflection. *What was in her eye?*

"Good call." Katrina's voice wafted up from beneath her tent of heavy hair as she made final adjustments to her lens.

"I can't believe you've heard of Mae West!" said Aaron, daring to place his athletic hands on her shoulders. "And I'm the Creature from the Black Lagoon!" he droned in fun.

"You can't make up your mind who you are, can you, Aaron?"

As if she expected his embrace, Katrina reached behind her to slip her fingers through Aaron's belt loops on either side of his hips. And there they stood.

This is all right. She's all right! He thought, and he gazed at the texture of her luxuriant long hair.

Aaron had never actually *been* with a girl, *per se*, although he told his best friend, Dan, he had some close calls. Katrina laughed and stumbled on the tops of Aaron's inflatable sneakers. His elbows poked out clumsily as he held Katrina. He cradled her close to him in a gentlemanly fashion when another sluggish jab stung Katrina's right eye. She pulled away from him. She feared it was a nervous twitch and grew afraid that Aaron would see the distortion in her looks. *Vanity is sanity*, was her motto.

"Aaron, it's late. I should be heading home." Her voice sounded different all of a sudden. Tense. Twangy. Her hands recoiled to her right eye as she felt again the thick irritation there move erratically.

Maybe I've been too forward? thought Aaron.

"Would you like anything before I walk you home?" he asked tentatively, still face-to-face with every lustrous strand of hair on the back of her head.

Nervous laughter yanked Katrina's throat as the yeast-mold web spidered down the back of it. She forced a cheery voice. "You're so funny, Aaron. Everything's closed in Westlake at this hour. Besides, *the early bird catches the worm.*"

"You mean *the early worm gets eaten!*"

"You're very funny, Aaron, but I've got to go. Now."

She sounds really tweaked.

He thought of the old Blues Brothers skit from *Saturday Night Live. What'd I do t'tick you off this time, baaaybeh?* She did have that reputation for being mercurial. The *B.S.F., Brutally Severed Friendship*, was rumored to be her trademark among the boy's who'd tried, or *B.W.T.'s*. All got hacked. No one was immune. Aaron remained hopeful. *Maybe she has what it takes to like a cool, creative guy like me.* The others she dumped were *not the sharpest tools,* as Aaron recalled.

"Did I offend you, Katrina? I hope I—was I too forward?" He gave her the benefit of the doubt even though she had initiated the hand-holding. "You can tell me, okay?" He waited several seconds, and scratched at the nettlesome chest hairs through his plaid shirt. *Would it be better to just end it now and spare myself?—like Mother always advises. "Enterprise* to Katrina?"

In the plate-glass window of the closed-out J. J. Newberry's on the corner, Katrina saw a row of budding trees that shielded the white lamplight. Her own reflection stared at her from the *EVERYTHING MUST GO* sign painted inside on the glass. Queasiness sprang about in her intestines on seeing herself. The fat pulse she had sensed in her eye minutes before slithered beneath her skin to the Marilyn Monroe beauty mark next to her top lip. Katrina gaped at the glass; her palm went flat against the dull, thumping pain in her cheek. Her thin pointer finger ventured to touch her beauty mark. For the briefest seconds the brown sphere seemed to surge up from where it belonged on her face as if something were straining to escape from under her skin. Then it began to wriggle. But, it wasn't her beauty mark. It was a fleshy greenish tentacle. A strangled scream caught hold of Katrina's lungs. Hands on her face, Katrina turned her back to Aaron and pulled frantically at the tiny writhing piece of flesh. Her chest expanded sharply, then collapsed with the weight of anxious dread as she exhaled in despair with a scream.

"Oh, my God, it's disgusting! A worm, a stinky worm. It's on me...*Yuck!*" She was breathless.

"Must have fallen from the tree. Let's get out from under these trees!"

Katrina ran away from the harsh shadows of tree-lined Main Street around the corner to High Street, where there were neither trees nor streetlights.

Unnerved by her outburst, Aaron became a statue. His chest hairs stood straight. In two shallow breaths he caught up with Katrina and put an arm around her.

"Hey, Katie! Katrina, what's up?" She shook him off and kept running. "Come on, girl, you're giving me a wild case of the willies!"

In front of Katrina's house, Aaron caught hold of her shoulder and gently forced her chin to face him.

"You scared me, Katrina!"

His quick clarity of vision struck him as peculiar. But finally he could take a good long look at the goddess's face. A dark, irregular line threaded down to Katrina's chin like a wet newt tail. Its source: the Marilyn Monroe beauty mark. He smudged it with his thumb.

"Wow, Katie, you're bleeding! What was that thing that bit you?"

Katrina's stared back at him, her eyes tired and hollowed. "I'm fine."

"Oh, wow. What's with you? You look like you saw an ax murderer. Talk to me."

"I better go inside, Aaron. I don't feel very well." Her monotone trembled. Katrina *knew*: the worm had come from inside her head.

"Come on, it was just one of those green moth worms that chews the buds on the trees this time of year. Like in the biology lab specimen jars. Just fell out of the tree on you. You gotta give the thing credit. It's got great taste—" Aaron reined in his words, watching in disbelief as Katrina's healthy skin shriveled slightly.

At that moment the blood in Katrina's veins thickened and slowed. Her heart strained harder to move blood through her body. The water in her blood separated itself from the plasma and platelets and was flowing unnaturally toward her stomach. Her tissues bulged and strained with fluid weight. Water gathered *en masse* outside the wet, gristly lining of her stomach cavity. A barrage of water hit her gut like a liquid fist, tearing through a weak spot of its lining to mix with torrential bile injections. The weak spot in her stomach was the harbinger of an ulcer. Tonight the ulcer was forced to fruition.

Katrina plunged over the curb onto her lawn to vomit.

"Oh, wow. Katrina. I'll get your parents." He fanned his nose. The stench matched that of roadkill.

Heaving, her voice scraped, "No! Mom'll think I'm drunk."

"Drunk? Like *inebriated* drunk? Oh, be real, we had sodas. They'd be crazy to even think—"

"No. Go home, Aaron. Just go home." She retched again. Her sandpaper voice scratched, "Please go."

"I'll wait until you get inside at least, okay?"

Hunched, she crawled away from him up the steep lawn to the porch steps. Katrina reminded him of crippled Christina, the subject of the Andrew Wyeth oil painting he had chosen to reproduce for extra credit in art class.

Katrina's deepened voice slapped Aaron's gaze away. "Go, Aaron, please, just leave. Dammit, leave! Quickly! Hide! Before my fath—" Katrina cried softly. She refused to turn her face again to Aaron.

A large silhouette behind the beveled door glass snapped on the porch light. Yeast-mold webbing that had sprouted abundantly out of Katrina's right eye and spread down her neck and chest to her navel, now laced cross her lower back. Its brittle sound heightened her nausea.

"Go. Now! Or I'm dead meat. Mom thinks—" She heaved. "I went—" —and again— "...to the movies with... Correy... after her cheerleading practice."

Coriander Preston—the cheerleading captain and high honors student—got under the skin of only one person at Westlake High: Aaron. His dislike for Coriander began with her name. The wound was fresh. She'd lured him in, gained his trust, flattered his artwork, then claimed she just wanted to be friends. Aaron had felt humiliated. *Who would name a kid after a spice seed anyway?*

Inside Katrina's house, Mr. Phillips' big hand turned the doorknob.

Despite Aaron's humiliation, lately, he couldn't seem to escape Coriander. She frequented Aaron's favorite movie. Every single time, there was Coriander Preston buying Gummi Bears and smiling insipidly. In fact, it was Aaron who first took Coriander to see *Still Life* at Saturday's matinee. But Coriander had dumped Aaron right at the concession stand and gone to sit with jock Billy Carlyle. Tonight, for a change, Coriander Preston had not gone to the film.

"Go, Aaron, please!" begged Katrina.

Into the shadows, Aaron dragged his rubber soles away from Katrina as the front door of the Phillips house swung open.

"Katie?" The baritone wasn't angry. Her father sounded concerned.

Aaron debated whether to step forward and defend Katrina, or trust her judgement and leave. She knew her own parents. She would know how to handle them best. *Wouldn't she? Or was she "pulling a Coriander"? Did Katrina just stage the whole thing to get rid of me so she wouldn't have to kiss me good night? Nah, too elaborate. But, then again, she has been hanging around with Correy Preston. Guilt by association? They can't all be like that! Can they?*

"Dammit, Katie!" came the baritone again, stronger. A burly arm in a starched shirt reached down to pluck Katrina from the top step as if she were a pup. "You look horrible! Worse than usual! What the hell have you been doing with yourself?"

Worse than usual. Worse...than usual? What could her father mean by that? She was indisputably the best-looking girl in Art class. In the entire school!

The burly man closed the door carefully. The porch light extinguished and Aaron's eyes adjusted quickly.

In the darkness, Aaron pondered. It was true Katrina didn't look so swell after having a corpulent green worm attach itself to her magnificent face.

But why had her face bled? Had she scratched herself with those pretty French-manicured nails of hers to remove it? Was it some carnivorous worm that clung to human flesh with serrated teeth, a suction-cup mouth like the bloodsucker I got on my butt cheek last August at the Rust Pond swimming hole?

He was about to leave, when the front door opened again. Porch light slivered the night.

From within the house a stern female voice was shouting, "Get up to your room, young lady!"

Katrina's father stood on the porch. "Who's out there? I know you're out there, kid! I suggest you come forward and show yourself."

...if Mother finds out—He'll call her up—She'll embarrass me. And she'll want to know all about the romance.

Aaron was mute, but held his ground in the shadows. He thought he was out of sight, far enough from the porch light. But he was not out of throwing range.

"Aaaagh!" Aaron yelped as one of the geraniums in terra-cotta planters that lined the front porch grazed Aaron's jawbone and shattered on the tarmac behind him.

Potting soil and shards of terra cotta skidded into the underbrush. In the darkness, Aaron could see the mangled red geranium and its green leaves strewn, corpselike in the street. *Weird I can see it*, he thought.

"You stay away from my daughter, you hear me? You little coward! Afraid to show yourself! I know you're out there! You can't fool me, *kid*."

That was *twice* Mr. Phillips had called Aaron "kid." The front door slammed.

He tried to kill me! Aaron thought. His emotions began a tumbling act. *Katrina Phillips's father tried to kill me! With a potted geranium!*

Aaron's eyes focused on the limp red geranium on the ground. Although his hands still shook, Aaron wanted to comfort Katrina with them, tell her father what really happened.

Maybe the Golden Delight on the popcorn had been rancid and that was all the trouble? Mark Stiger threw up, and some other kids had been complaining they didn't feel so hot either.

To calm his fears, Aaron thought positive thoughts, as his mother recommended when her mood was good.

A lot of good it did her.

Aaron was sad at the thought of his mom who, by now, was probably passed out fully dressed and drooling undigested liquor on the paisley sofa. He displaced the ugly thought with memories of his mother back when she was smiley and fun. Even that hurt, because he missed his mother—the way she was *before*. So, he switched his thoughts to his own personal Katrina channel.

I'll see Katrina on Monday morning at school. I'll pass by her locker—after the second bell, so I don't seem too eager—and see if she's okay. Another handmade invitation might be in order too. Or a pop-up get-well card.

He stood a moment longer before Katrina's dark Victorian house that was crowded on either side by fir tree sentinels. He flinched; bloated drops of rain spattered on his cheeks and brow.

Katrina's lawn caught his eye; fat green worms wriggled though the matted spring grass in all directions. Dozens lumbered over the cluster of hologram scare marbles that had spilled from Katrina's abandoned gift box. Hundreds of green blobs emanated from the dark spot on the grass where Katrina had become ill; worms burrowed out of sight into the lawn.

She lost her marbles, thought Aaron, too shocked by the sight of worms to catch his own pun.

A police siren sounded far away. Adrenaline surged through his limbs. His instincts signaled warnings in a code he could not yet interpret. He ran down High Street toward the theater at the end of Green Street. His case of the creeps waned the farther he got from the Phillips' house.

Aaron concerned himself with getting his black mountain bike to his dad's house out at Eastridge. Engrossed as he was in Katrina, he had forgotten about the arrangement to meet his father at the theater.

Aaron prized the weekends with his dad. *He's a lot like me,* Aaron liked to tell himself. Plus Mr. Sedgewood had lots of cool bachelor toys: a Harley, a rider mower, a six-foot model of a World War I fighter plane his father and he were constructing together. Tonight, Aaron anticipated, the two of them would work on the model plane until one or two in the morning, chowing down on junk food while listening to loud music. Maybe some oldies. His dad liked the Beatles a lot. Eric Clapton was pretty good too. Tomorrow he could sleep late. Then his father's girlfriend would serve a breakfast of waffles, jam, Nutella, and hot chocolate. Aaron's father provided freedom, even from packing clothes. His dad procured a second set of everything.

Absent-minded, Aaron spun the combination lock that bound the chain of his bike to the chipped red rack in the alley next to the mottled theater.

He chuckled to himself, thinking about his favorite movie. It melded the most frightening scenes from all the monster and serial killer movies he had ever watched or heard of. There were even a few characters with whom he was not familiar: Norman Bates and Mother

Bates, for example. He would have to find out which movie they came from and rent the video cassette from Blockbuster Saturday at his dad's. He suspected his dad's girlfriend would know the title since she worked in the movie industry. Aaron thought she was just the coolest because she could explain all the special effects and film editing procedures to him.

Aaron contemplated the movie's benign Wolfman, who resembled a wire-haired terrier more than your basic Wolfman should. He laughed and missed one digit in the lock's combination.

"Do over," he mumbled, and spun the combination lock dial again as raindrops obscured it. "Oops!" He tried a third time."

Aaron replayed the first scene in his head, recalling the clumsy, handsome teenage protagonist named Skeet. Skeet reminded Aaron of the famous comedian Steve Martin. Already, Aaron knew many of the lines by heart; they engrossed him so much that he was unaware he had begun to say the lines aloud. Parroting Skeet's comical intonations, he laughed aloud to himself in the dark wet alley beside the theater.

"'*One thousand and one do's and don'ts of horror movies. Yes, folks, some common pointers, simple do's and don'ts for the next time you find yourself in a scary movie,*'" he said aloud, and laughed.

"'*...First off, you arrive home in your car and all the house lights are off,*'" Aaron quoted the movie matter-of-factly. "'*You know you left on the lights so your home would appear inhabited—to ward off intruders. Trust immediately that something is afoot. That is to say, something is DEAD WRONG!*'"

The combination lock popped at last and Aaron began wrapping the chain around the crossbar of his black 10-speed mountain bike.

"*...Do ask yourself, 'Are my car doors locked?' If not, lock them now. Then cock your ear...*" Which Aaron did mockingly but heard only the impact of rain on the theater roof. "'*What kind of music do you hear playing in the background? Do you detect a suspenseful beat? If so, drive away, before any of these possible, maximally gross, horrific scenarios happens to you at your vehicle...*'"

Aaron tilted the handlebars up and prepared to mount the sturdy bike. His voice trailed off as he grew uncomfortably wet from the spring rain. He thought of Katrina. *I should've said something to that jerk, her father. What could've happened to her? That creep tried to kill me.* Aaron shuddered, reflecting on the geranium pot that caused his jaw to bleed.

At that moment the wind shifted and carried a wisp of the foul smell of unwashed teeth. The briefest sensation was potent. Aaron balked at the stench. A heavy cloudburst snuffed out the odor. The loud downpour washed all aromas to the ground and into a leaf-stuffed gutter. It was then Aaron noticed his front tire was flat; a long slice ran one third the circumference of the tire. He groaned in frustration.

Just then, headlights wheeled up to the theater. The lights disoriented him and he experienced a sudden flash of double vision. It faded as fast as it came. Aaron blinked, blind and defenseless for a few seconds.

4

Billy Carlyle was about ready to call Coriander Preston, but the six-foot team captain was feeling very ill. Plus it was the dead of night.

It's probably her fault I got this, he thought. *I better not have mono or some weird disease from making out with her at the movies the other night.*

Meanwhile, the willowy cheerleading squad head lay still. It hurt to move.

I should've known he'd carry every illness known to Westlake, and now I've got one of'em, Coriander thought miserably.

The two teenagers in Westlake did not think twice before they pinned the tail of guilt on the other's donkey. Vengeful and shallow, they were a veritable cliché of each other. And now their skin and facial structure began to look alike, too.

They grew slightly more hideous as the stormy Friday night neared an overcast dawn. Only their hair color—which matched—would not change markedly, though it was already matted with sour greasy hair oil and sulfurous perspiration

Out in Eastridge, one page of the *Modern Unabridged How-to-Spell Book* fluttered mercilessly: More victims, more souls to energize its indifferent pages.

In Westlake, Dan Pritcher's spiny hand flexed to his face when he heard the late-night news. In the cozy den at the Pritcher's home, Dan sat on the Persian carpet listening to the local broadcaster deliver a report from the courthouse parking lot. Dan was stunned.

"Westlake high school athlete, Mark Stiger, sixteen, died at the Southgate municipal parking lot outside the courthouse this evening. According to Miss Clarissa Hawthorne, eighty, a witness and native of Westlake, the teenager crouched and flapped his arms. 'It was like he thought he had wings up there,' she stated.

"According to Miss Hawthorne, before Mark Stiger's suicidal leap, the boy screamed, 'I'll get you, my pretty.' Miss Hawthorne remains at the hospital for treatment of trauma and a bruise, because the boy's hand struck her arm just before he hit the ground. Autopsy reports will soon determine if there are signs of drug use."

Dan glanced around to be sure his parents were still out of earshot before he sniffled and wiped away the pools of tears that collected between the hollows of his ocular bones and glasses. On the black telephone on the coffee table, he dialed Aaron's number at Mr. Sedgewood's out in Eastridge. To wait any longer to tell Aaron would reduce Dan's fingernails to chawed stumps. There was no answer in Eastridge, only the answering machine.

"Danny, who're you calling at this hour, dear?" Mrs. Pritcher's kind face poked into the TV room. Dan tried to tell his mother, but he was speechless. His chin slackened and trembled.

"Darling, what's wrong?"

The local Saturday newspaper printed somewhere in the sopping blackness of Westlake. By midnight, the autopsy was a front-page headline:

Drug-free Suicide of Westlake Teen

5

The do's and don'ts of horror movies scrolled through Katrina's mind like a Basic computer directory. *What about when you're the monster?* She wondered in calm disbelief, staring into the wide mirror of her lavender bathroom. *The movie doesn't say anything about when you're the one mutating.* Seeing her own reflection silenced her crying.

Katrina's father still banged on the locked door to her bedroom, staggering over his own words. "Who was the boy, Katrina? Who was he? What were you damned kids up to? What did he do to you? Get you drunk?

Over the crack of thunder and solid din of rain on the slate roof, she could barely hear him. A welt the size of her father's hand raised her left cheek, and her face and throat writhed with movement. The repulsive, tickling sensation drowned out the pain from Mr. Phillip's heavy-handed slap.

Katrina had never thought herself beautiful before, let alone relatively attractive, since her parents were a constant reminder that she was uninteresting. But now she looked from the mirror to the sterling silver-framed black and white photograph of herself on the dresser across the bedroom, then back at the mirror. Physical evidence of her former beauty made her want her old face back.

I'm not so uninteresting after all.

"Go away, Daddy," she cried with difficulty, and spat another green worm into the lavender basin. "I'm all right, okay? I promise I haven't been drinking. Okay? I just want to shower and go to bed."

She couldn't very well tell him *he* was the one who was drunk without risking another blow.

"Herbert, you leave that girl alone, she's not well." Katrina's mother stood outside the door now too. "Katrina, let me in," cooed Mrs. Phillips. "Is it your—?"

"No, Mom, I'm fine, I just don't feel well." Plus, she knew if she opened the door for her mother, her father would barge in and the family brawl would continue in her only private space.

Katrina heard a door slam, then her father crowed, "You shut up, you—" followed by the sound of impact. Mrs. Philips said no more for the night.

Normally Katrina would open the door to save her mother from abuse, but she couldn't bring herself to spar with her drunken parents. Not this time. It was hard enough to contend with her own problem. And how would she explain her face being laced with green worms, especially after her parents' usual *scotch-with-scotch-with-dinner-on-the-side*? Whatever reason she gave they would say it was her fault, that she probably deserved it. Katrina braced her oak desk chair under the bedroom doorknob in case he got more out of control.

"Good night, Daddy. Good night, Mom. Sleep well," she sang tremulously.

Returning to her bathroom to slather a washcloth with liquid soap, she hoped that the frothy water would remove the worms embedded in her tender skin. The first pass with the terry-cloth wad took with it one worm and several layers of epidermis. As she rinsed the cloth under the tap, she thought of the time her dog had heartworm and was cured by some medicine. Did her parents still have any of the prescription left in the downstairs medicine chest? She wasn't sure she was willing to take that risk. The medicine had killed her dog right after the cure.

Katrina stopped rubbing her face when her cheekbone itself poked through a flap of infiltrated flesh. Quickly she tried to replace the thick flap of skin over the bone, but it would not stay put. The skin's collagen layer had been sucked thin by the worms and had lost its integrity and firmness. With the bone's exposure to the air, a fresh clump of worms spewed into the gap between the writhing patch, which would not lay still under her hand.

She squealed in panic. Tears of desperation overran her cheeks; saline burned in the small open wounds. The green worm that extended from her beauty mark stuck out farther and farther, as if attempting to slurp her tears. Frantically, Katrina yanked that worm by its cold-blind head. But the farther she pulled it out, the longer it reached, like the root of a poison ivy vine.

Oh, God, are these things growing longer under my skin?

Still holding the cloth to her cheek, she reached beneath the lavender toilet's water tank lid. There was her five-shot stash: A glass whiskey flask displaced eight ounces of tank water. Over the years, she had noticed her parents do the same trick so neither could accuse the other of day-drinking.

One-handed, she rinsed the plain brown glass flask under the tap and drank urgently. She had refilled it from her parents' liquor cabinet five days before, so it was nearly full. During that week, she had felt the desire to drink from it only after the fight with her parents about going to watch Coriander Preston's cheerleading practice Friday evening. Even though they were normally three sheets to the wind and absorbed with arguing amongst themselves, somehow they remained present enough to spot when Katrina was lying.

I can't take this any longer, I can't look at myself. Her face was molten with worms, and she was desperate. Splashes of the amber liquid dribbled across Katrina's face; she could not swallow fast enough. Accidentally a stream of whiskey bathed the wiggly green worm that extended from her beauty mark.

Katrina felt the worm recoil from the whiskey and withdraw back into her skin. *Interesting.* She leaned her head back to drink from the flask again and watched in the mirror as another worm disappeared into her face, escaping the burn of the whiskey. This gave her an idea.

She sucked down the fiery potion, which she believed would give her the fortitude to look again in the mirror. The alcohol temporarily neutralized the pain under her skin. She rinsed her face carefully with the cold water, taking care to hold shut the loose, loathsome skin flap over her cheekbone.

With cotton balls plucked from the etched-glass bowl on her vanity, she blotted whiskey on the worms that stuck out of her face, throat, and around her eyes.

Acid rain, thought Katrina as she blotted. *The booze is like acid rain to them.*

All the worms retracted into her face, quitting their grotesque dance. She took the last swig from the flask, anticipating it would be enough to wash away braver stragglers rerouting their retreat inside her.

The house was quiet. Exhausted and sweaty, Katrina felt helpless and drunk. The burning sensation from the whiskey suspended her worries artificially. She disrobed and sat on the floor of the lavender tub under a warm shower and cried. Then, she began to giggle insanely. She checked herself. "I sound deranged," she said aloud to no one. Shaking her head, she closed her eyes. "I'm not *dead* meat," she murmured at her hopeless situation, "I'm lunch meat, a cold cut. I am what you call worm food. I am..."

Her chin nodded on her knees until her father's persistent knocking woke her. She slammed the spigot shut before it overran the tub.

"I'm just going to sleep, Daddy. Good night." Katrina flicked off her bedroom lamp, then saw the band of light under her door brighten as Mr. Phillips shuffled away down the hall, mumbling epithets.

As much as she feared her father's temper, Katrina felt sorry for him; he seemed lost and pathetic since he'd lost his job. That forced them to move to Westlake from the capitol. That's when Mr. Phillips stayed home 24/7. Katrina's mother made no sense out of it, explaining only that *Daddy's not working for a while.*

Until the move, Katrina had never seen so much of her father, so, at first, she was excited that he'd be home all the time. Traveling, negotiating, *doing business*—he had always been very active. All of a sudden he had to just stay at home and, as her mother put it, keep a low profile and some *blahty-blah* about being caught in political crossfire. For the purposes of Katrina's school administration records, Katrina had been instructed by her mother to say he was on sabbatical from his job as a government advisor. To Katrina the definitions meant a prematurely retired, active alcoholic. Katrina felt as if she and her parents were hiding out like bandits. She wished they would just be a normal family again.

Katrina pulled out an oversize lavender cotton t-shirt from her chest of drawers and glanced again at the mirror.

"Sleeping? You monsters." Drunk words crept out as she examined the wormholes and pockmarks on her brow and cheeks and around her eyes.

Her skin lay still.

As she adjusted the t-shirt on her shoulders, a single pang of movement under the skin of her clavicle stung. Immediately she picked up the flask of whiskey and held it upside down over the collar bone. She waited. The few remaining drops of liquor struck—enough to cause the worm to burrow deeper into her flesh to escape the alcohol flame.

At least I don't have to look at you.

A sun-sleepy-lizard movement surged up the right side of her throat; she felt deeply sickened and angry. She was too drunk and exhausted to be frightened. There was no more whiskey in the flask. But she knew there was rubbing alcohol in the cupboard under the sink, and she knew *not* to drink that.

"I'll give it a try on the outside." With a drenched wad of cotton balls she slathered the skin of her face, throat, chest, and arms. For a time, stillness ruled.

She felt drained, but she could feel the faintest tickle inside her esophagus. She wanted to gag, yet tried not to for fear of a replay of the evening's experience. *It seems the only way to keep these living nightmares down is with alcohol.* She would need another supply of whiskey from her parents' liquor cabinet—fast.

To wait until Monday morning would be suicide. The smelly green parasites would remain dormant for only a short time. Jagged snores came through the wall. *Maybe I can make a run for it.* She opened her door and peered both ways.

5

Rain masked the license plate of the car. Aaron squinted. He could not see the vehicle behind the headlights.

"Quick! Throw your bike in the back," Mr. Sedgewood hollered out the window of his Land Rover.

"Great timing, Dad! Some scumbag slashed my tire."

"Can you believe this weather?" Mr. Sedgewood said as he examined Aaron's tire. "Not a drop all the way back from the city. Until Westlake, then *whooosh*. Weird, they said, rain only within a five-mile radius of Westlake."

Soaked through to his new chest hair, Aaron was glad to see his father. Aaron mimicked a monologue from *Still Life: The Best of the Worst*, while he stowed the bike in the car. His father warmed up the engine. And, Aaron broke into an impersonation of Skeet, "'*Should you choose not to leave the premises, be prepared for any of the following, and remember, stay in your car, I repeat...*'"

"Aaron, you about ready, son?" Mr. Sedgewood's rich, friendly voice was dulled within the heavy car walls as Aaron slammed reached up for the back hatch. "Don't slam the back hatch!"

Aaron couldn't hear and he slammed the back hatch then dawdled in the black rain toward the passenger side door.

"'*Tip numero uno, Option (A) monster throws self at you, breaking car window.*'" With a thud, Aaron threw himself dramatically against the big car.

"Aaron, c'mon. Pizza's getting cold." Aaron pressed his face flat against the passenger window. Mr. Sedgewood reached over and opened the latch. "Get in, my man. Lucinda would be proud to hear you quoting the movie she worked on."

Aaron climbed up and shook his wet feet out the open door. "Where *is* your girlfriend, Dad? I thought you said she'd visit again this weekend. She up at the house?"

"Lucinda left this morning for the city. Had to take care of some business."

"Again! It's Friday night! I never get to see her." Aaron faked a sulk.

"You like her a lot, don't you, son?" Aaron nodded agreement as his father explained Lucinda's absence. "The entertainment business is a very social one. She had to go to a schmooze party with her colleagues."

"What does she do again exactly?"

"She's a continuity editor for films and she also helped produce *Still Life the Best of the Worst*. She invested her entire life savings in it. So if it does well in the theaters, she'll make a lot of money."

"Well, I've seen it every day since it opened, so she's making a lot of money off me already. Well, off *you* and Mom! Nearly everybody in school's seen it as often as I have. Except Dan. And you."

"I saw it before Lucinda did the final editing on it, before she sent it down to the theater. I liked it well enough."

Aaron could tell his father did not really like it, so he spewed another movie quote: "*At this point, ask yourself, 'Will I make it alive from car to house? Did I bring a flashlight?'*"

"Eat your pizza, son..." Mr. Sedgewood slid the warm cardboard box onto Aaron's lap and drove on. "Seems like your mother's not feeding you. You're looking thin, Aaron. She's still too wrapped up in herself. Is she still going to the AA meetings?"

Aaron shook his head and kept eating. His father left it alone.

"Hey, what the heck happened to your jaw?"

"Nothing, Dad. I'm okay," Aaron said, wiping his wound with the back of his sleeve. *More importantly,* Aaron wondered, *is Katrina okay?*

6

By 11:58 Friday night Dan felt silly calling Mr. Sedgewood's house to track down Aaron. Mark Stiger was already dead, so what could Dan actually *do*? It was too late to save the day. But Dan felt he had failed Mark by not detecting suicidal signs sooner.

"Go ahead and call him, Danny. You need to talk to a friend right now." Mrs. Pritcher hugged her son again and left the kitchen to tell her husband the terrible news. She closed the door to give Dan privacy.

Dan cringed when he heard Mr. Sedgewood's rich voice.

"Yeah? Aaron, turn that down! Hello?" The B-52s whacked out *Love Shack* in the background. Aaron plucked an air guitar near the bass speaker that obliterated his father's voice.

Dan spoke quickly in case Mr. Sedgewood was angry about the late call, "Sorry to bother you so late, Mr. Sedgewood. This is Dan Pritcher, Aaron's friend. May I speak to him just for a minute, please?"

"Sure, buddy, hang on a sec, Dan. Aaron! Phone!"

Aaron hoped it was Katrina Phillips calling him, but he remembered there was no way she could have gotten his dad's unlisted number.

"When're you going to join us for a weekend, Dan?"

"Thank you, sir, I'd like that. Any time's good."

"No need for you boys to wait till you get your license. You can come on out here and drive around on the property. Practice. Aaron did tonight. I let him drive right out to the cliffs to watch the lightning hitting Westlake. What a show! Not a drop of rain up here, but, boy did we see some action over the valley. Pretty bizarre stuff. Never saw it like that before! Oh, here's Aaron, Champ, nice talking with you, Dan!" Mr. Sedgewood passed the phone receiver to Aaron.

"Dan, hi!"

"Aaron, it's me, Dan. Wow, your dad talks a lot."

"I know."

"Oh," said Dan.

"Dad, Dan says you talk a lot." Aaron laughed and play-punched his father in the shoulder. "So, what's up, Dan?"

Dan was silent.

Aaron prompted Dan jovially, "Dan, hi, it's me, Aaron. You just called me to see what I'm up to at midnight? ...Hello?"

Dan opened his mouth to speak and had to stifle a sob. He faked a horrendous cough.

"Dan, are you all right, man? Choke on a chicken bone?"

"Did you listen to the news tonight, Aaron?"

"Nope. Was there a special on hay fever? Heck no, man, I was out holding hands with the goddess. Until she got sick on me."

Silence again.

"Dan? What, did I miss something better on *Nightline?*"

It required focus for Dan to utter the splintery news.

"You're not going to believe this, Aaron. Mark Stiger jumped off the courthouse roof tonight. He's dead." No time elapsed for Aaron to formulate a coherent reply before Dan rushed on breathlessly, "He committed suicide!" By muted TV light Dan cried openly behind his glasses.

"I just saw him at the movies tonight. He got sick on—" startled by the news, Aaron choked. "Oh, man, I'm sorry, I forgot Mark's your cousin."

7

Before Aaron left Eastridge Sunday night, he roved each room of his father's house. That was his habit. He liked nosing through his dad's stuff.

One of the book-lined rooms upstairs had special appeal to Aaron. On the oak desk was a wood-framed photograph of a horse hurdling a hedge. On its back, a rider crouched in an English saddle, poised perfectly for the jump. Aaron eyed the rider and determined it was a woman. Her face was obscured by a shadow cast by her black helmet brim. All his life Aaron had seen shots like it lying around the house, most of his expert equestrienne mother and sometimes of her prize-winning dressage and hunter jumper students. He was astonished his father would have one of his mother's photographs still lying around.

Aaron felt displaced as he found unfamiliar belongings cluttering the oak desk, which, incidentally, Aaron never used yet felt he owned. He poked through the unwelcome stack of notes and paperback books. Glancing through the pile of open books, he noticed a heading in one of them that he thought read *Warning spell to binder*. It made no sense but had a good rhythm to it. He jammed on his air guitar, repeating the four meaningless words, then continued to forage through the pile. *Whose stuff was this?* It didn't seem like his dad's usual, *Seven Habits of Highly Successful People*, that his father considered as essential as studying the Bible.

Off the top of the pile on the oak desk, a manila envelope spilled tattered video splicing tape and film scraps. He figured those belonged to Lucinda. Aaron picked up a segment of film and held it up to the light. *Looks like it's from Still Life: Best of the Worst*, Aaron thought excitedly.

Pale white words outlined in pale red dots were barely visible across the bottom of each tiny frame. Aaron's eyes narrowed to a squint, but he still couldn't make out the words. *Must be subtitles for the overseas market*, Aaron decided, stuffing one of the film segments into his shirt pocket.

"There you are, Aaron! Been looking all over the house for you. Time to go back to your mom's."

"Dad, what's all this stuff on my desk?"

A flicker of uncertainty shadowed Mr. Sedgewood's face. "Well, it looks like it's some project Lucinda's been working on. Leave it alone, son. She probably has it in a special order." He led the boy away from the oak desk.

In my study! Aaron thought, annoyed. He craned his neck to see over his dad's arm. In that moment, that open *warning spell to binder* book slid off the top of the pile and folded itself shut. *Weird*, thought Aaron. The gold lettering on the red cover caught Aaron's eye and he did a triple take.

"*The Modern Unabridged How-to-Spell Book?*" Aaron laughed. "Dad, that's stupid, why don't they just call it a *dictionary*? *How to spell...*"

"Just one of those new terms, I guess," his father said absent-mindedly, taking no notice of the book. He snapped off the lamp and ushered Aaron out of the home office.

Even without the light, Aaron was surprised at how well he could see as he glanced back. It seemed his permanently dilated pupils took in every available scrap of light. He glanced again at the wood-framed photograph. "Dad, how come you've still got one of Mom's photos? Doesn't Lucinda mind?"

"Oh, that's a shot of Lucinda. She's an accomplished equestrienne like your mother."

"Too bad I can't see her face in it. She's a babe, Dad! Good choice!"

"Glad you approve, son. Looks like Lucinda might move in with us sometime soon. How would you feel about that?"

Aaron wasn't so sure.

8

Coriander Preston and Billy Carlyle tried every excuse to convince their respective parents to let them stay home from school. Although the inflammation subsided mildly as the moon waned, they both thought they looked worse than they had on Friday night. And neither Billy nor Coriander wanted to be seen in public after the changes that occurred to their respective faces over the weekend.

The Prestons insisted their eldest child go to school. There was the championship game that afternoon and the varsity cheerleading captain simply could not be absent. The *Boston Globe* sports editor was expected. His photographer might get some nice photographs of their daughter. It would be such wonderful exposure for the family, and excellent for her college apps in a few years. "Don't disappoint us, Coriander!"

The Carlyles would not listen to Billy's pleas either. Their eldest was bounced out the door by 7:45 a.m., and on his way to school. Certainly the team captain could not miss the championship either.

To Coriander's and Billy's astonishment, the Prestons and the Carlyles had not noticed the oblong protrusion that—over the weekend—grew to deform their foreheads. Nor had their family members seemed to notice the mild stench of curdled milk emanating from their armpits and breath. But, then, their families had not yet seen *Still Life: The Best of the Worst.* Coriander pushed her bangs down over her eyes; Billy wore a baseball cap.

At 7:30 a.m., Katrina Phillips swilled whiskey from her brown flask and zipped the bottle into the bottom security pouch of her purse. She hollered good-bye to the housekeeper and backed into her bedroom for a moment to eat a glom of toothpaste and compose her balance before darting toward the staircase. She had waited to open her bedroom door until her parents left for tennis, and had not anticipated the housekeeper would already be making their bed upstairs.

Katrina had succeeded in staying out of view all weekend, averting her head if spoken to and letting her hair fall like a shield over the writhing worms.

"Hold on, hold on, Katie," the housekeeper suddenly yelled from the opposite end of the oak-paneled hall. "Don't you go until I give you a proper fare-thee-well." The plump old bottle-blonde stumped after

Katrina. "Why, isn't that a handsome hat, my dear! But you shouldn't cover your pretty face."

Katrina tried to smile as she tugged on the veil of the pillbox hat she had filched from her mother, and backed toward the banister. The black veil extended past her chin to meet the rim of her lavender cotton turtleneck. Katrina was hopeful her face would not be too noticeable through the veil. Her classmates might accuse her of over-dressing, but at least they would not see the pockmarks and lesions left by the worms, nor the swelling left by Mr. Phillips's hand.

"I've really got to run, Mrs. Fortworth," Katrina said, backing down the wide stairwell.

"Oh, come, Katie. You've got time for your weekly hug."

"No, really," Katrina stammered. "I'm late for school. I—I'll see you next week, Mrs. Fortworth!"

Katrina leapt down the stairs and slipped as she fled out the front door.

Mrs. Fortworth noted Katrina's unusual behavior and the vaguest scent of liquor in the air at the top of the stairs. Dolefully the housekeeper shook her head. *Katrina's toxic parents are contagious*, she thought.

At school the police had cordoned off the locker to the left of Katrina's. Its door stood open; they searched it. Although steeped in whiskey, by 8:10 a.m. she was still capable of wondering why the police were searching Mark Stiger's locker. She hadn't seen the news.

"*Excusemeplease.*" Katrina wobbled past the two police officers while adjusting her denim skirt.

"Nice hat you got, miss." One officer glanced up.

The second bell rang as Katrina aimed her tiny key at her padlock's blurry double. Thalia Pollocks and Coriander Preston scurried past in matching floral dresses on their way to homeroom.

"Hurry up, Katrina!" Katrina did not turn to acknowledge the far-off echo of Correy's voice.

"You want some help, miss?" asked Officer Nancy Fieldstone, kindly.

"Sure." With a delirious catlike grin Katrina fell back against the locker, and dangled key.

"Can't be too difficult." Officer Fieldstone opened the padlock easily.

"Thanksverymuch."

"No problem." Then Officer Fieldstone leaned in toward Katrina and sniffed. "Miss, is there a reason you smell like alcohol?"

Katrina giggled. "A reason?" She could think only of the truth and how unbelievable it would sound if she tried to explain that she had figured out the secret to keeping the worms from boring out through her pores and making her look like Medusa with a thousand tiny snakes sprouting out of her head.

Patiently, Officer Fieldstone stood back and observed Katrina who giggled again.

"Istotreatmyacne. That'swhy Ihaveto... wearthisdumb veilhat... tohidemyacne." Katrina smiled sweetly at the officer and turned to the shelf inside her locker where she rested her hat brim and stared in at the metal floor for a long time trying to catch her equilibrium. Slowly she bent over to pick up a red card that fell out of her locker. A yellow paper sun with blue goggle eyes and a paper cigar leapt up when she opened it. She recognized the handwriting. *Get well soon, Katrina. From your friend, Aaron Sedgewood.*

"Get wormed soon, Katrina," she said aloud, and tittered.

The PA system crackled and sounded a thunderclap when the principal's breath hit the microphone. Over the weekend it had been vandalized—hacked at with a butcher's knife—so the principal's attempt to announce the notices failed.

"Hey, shouldn't you be in class?" asked a second officer. Katrina's head bobbled in agreement.

"*What'reyoudoinginMark'slocker*?"

"I think this girl's drunk." Officer Fieldstone tapped her partner, bent inside the dead boy's locker.

"Was he a friend of yours, miss?" the officer asked sympathetically.

Over the loudspeaker, the principal's harsh voice lamely blotted out homeroom conversations. *"Good morning... appears to be broken... vandalized... over... weekend... nouncements... please wait in your homeroom... orning notices will be typed up and delivered to each homeroom... sorry for the del..."* In Katrina's drunkenness the announcement sounded nonsensical. Her high-pitched laugh brought both police officers to her side.

9

Restless to learn more about the Stiger suicide, Mr. Breen strode out of homeroom into the corridor to wait for a student council member to deliver the notices. He watched a few girls race to homeroom swapping 3-D hologram cards with monster faces on them. Students who had seen the movie two times in a single day had doubles to trade.

Mark Stiger's seat was empty. And Frankie Marcel in his signature white polo shirt, was absent. *His impeccable attendance record is ruined*, Mr. Breen noted on the roster incredulously.

"Shhhh, quiet, please!" the teacher implored his students. "And Mr. Carlyle, kindly remove your cap indoors, like the gentleman you are." Students snorted.

When Katrina stumbled past escorted, Mr. Breen closed the door so his class would not see. The police guided Katrina toward the principal's office, each holding Katrina up by an arm when she swerved or stumbled. Her lavender purse dangled from her neck. One drunk hand fiddled with the red card from Aaron, and she giggled oddly.

"Back inside, please," Mr. Breen instructed Coriander, Billy, and the other students who sneaked up to the homeroom threshold to watch. "If you feel the need to gawk at someone unusual, look in a mirror."

Billy and Coriander each felt their foreheads to check the oblong protrusions were covered. Nervously, two *brows* shot each other a knowing glance.

"...Every individual is unique and different," Mr. Breen continued as he closed the classroom door. "That goes for each and every one of you. Unique. Different. No two the same."

Mr. Breen saw no protrusions; he was simply taking the opportunity to share snippets from his Introduction to Psychology class lecture.

Dan Pritcher passed Katrina and the blue uniforms on his way to deliver the announcement to homeroom teachers. He'd offered to help out, especially since the notice pertained to his deceased cousin.

"Thank you, Dan," Mr. Breen said, pulling a page from the top of the pile of photocopies. "I'm sorry to hear about your cousin, sorry for your loss."

Dan nodded mechanically, and noticed Billy Carlyle haranguing Coriander, tugging at the back of her shirt. She struck at Billy's shoulder with her notebook, but he deflected the blow.

"You're the ugliest person in the world," Billy gurgled.

Coriander spat back, "You are, Billy."

Billy's actions ceased in the ray of Dan's somber gaze, allowing Coriander to hit Billy square in the face with a notebook.

Coriander laughed. "Thanks, Danny!" She waved flirtatiously at Dan.

"All right now. That's enough, Miss Preston," Mr. Breen warned.

"That's *Ms.* to you," she grumbled under her breath.

"And, Mr. Carlyle, again, your cap," he added before he closed the door and stepped into the hall. "Dan?"

"Sorry, Mr. Breen. I'll leave now. I just spaced out for a sec."

"No, Dan, it's okay," murmured Mr. Breen, "I understand you've endured a terrible loss. Please come see me if you'd like to talk about it. When you're ready, my hours are posted outside the guidance office."

"*Guidance* office? Yes, uhm. I'll do that," Dan droned. But the boy had no intention of having his head shrunk. He could deal with it alone, he thought. He was determined he could make the guilt pangs go away by himself. Nodding good-bye, he headed toward another homeroom with the stack of notices.

Mr. Breen reentered homeroom and shot a glance at Billy Carlyle who slumped and pulled his cap down over his brow.

Mr. Breen straightened against the back of his chair and cleared his throat. Whispering stopped completely as he read.

"'*A most unfortunate incident occurred on Friday evening. Mark Stiger committed suicide. Memorial services to honor our friend and schoolmate will be held tomorrow afternoon at 2:00 p.m. Afternoon classes will be canceled. For students wishing to attend the service, a school bus will be provided. The Stiger family requests that no flowers be sent. Instead, they have asked that contributions be donated in Mark's name to the Jimmy Fund because Mark loved movies...*'"

Two flights up in Aaron Sedgewood's homeroom the reading finished. Several students stared to cry when Mr. Hamm hid his tears in a handkerchief. Aaron turned to the window and stared past the river and across town to where the toxic waste dump and the back of the theater were visible. Against the overcast sky, red-necked turkey vultures swooped the town dump. The reality of Mark Stiger's suicide finally penetrated Aaron's well-wrapped emotions. He did not attempt to stop his tears from spilling over.

Sniffling in the room continued anew, mixed with anxious laughter when Bear Henkel blurted out, "Haaaa. I don't get it."

“What don’t you get, Bear? Mark’s dead!” Goose bumps covered Aaron’s muscular body when his outburst resonated in the room. And Aaron sensed Bear was weirder than usual.

“You mean Hamm was serious?” Bear cracked his knuckles and stuck his face forward in disbelief. The warning bell sputtered and rang over the vandalized PA system. The students filed out of class into a vague sulfurous mist that crept through the stagnant hall air. Bear cracked his knuckles and shoved his hands into his trouser pockets and manipulated the batch of scare marbles that glowed between the layers of denim. In his other pocket, his fingernails scraped a gray whetstone. His eyes gleamed with dementia.

10

On the back of the black mountain bike with the new front tire, Dan rode home with Aaron for lunch as planned. Still in shock that morning, Dan had forgotten to ride his own bike and instead had walked to school. The inevitable mayhem in the cafeteria would have been intolerable for Dan so he was relieved to be going to lunch at Aaron's. Already classes were unbearable.

"Mother?" Aaron hollered as they entered the hall. Mrs. Sedgewood did not answer. The boys heard *clip clop clip clop*.

"Dan, wait here a second." Aaron jogged through the main floor of the house. No mother. In the kitchen Aaron checked the sink. A martini glass contained a Spanish olive. He sniffed the glass, then flicked the olive into the compost bin next to two other olives. He rinsed and dried the glass, returning it to the cabinet.

"Okay, Pritch. It's safe," Aaron called out.

Mrs. Sedgewood was visible through the back bay window. She was out by the stables with the horses and her lunch-hour dressage students.

Aaron nuked the grilled provolone and tomato sandwiches she had left prepared in the refrigerator, and shared a bottle of Gatorade with Dan.

"Did Bear know anything more about Mark?"

"Guess not. Said he threw up by the bikes and ran off, yelling crazy stuff. But that's what I don't get. The coroner didn't find any trace of alcohol or drugs."

Standing as they ate, the boys were comfortably silent through the meal. The familiar clip of hooves out back clunked in the spring-warm kitchen air. Mrs. Sedgewood's luncheon table looked as pristine when the boys left as when they arrived.

"Wait, before we leave I gotta show you something cool." Aaron ran to his room and retrieved the segment of film he had found on the oak desk at his father's on Sunday. The boys stood outside by the bicycle to examine it.

"See, it looks like a scene from *Still Life*. I recognize Skeet, the main character. But it's got white writing at the base of each frame."

Dan squinted, holding it to the overcast sky for more light. "Looks like a subtitle to me."

"I guess they're going to show it in another country."

Dan's eyes danced. "Or it's a subliminal message!"

"Can you read any of it?"

"Too tiny, I need a magnifying glass."

"You got one? I don't."

Dan enjoyed the intrigue. "Yeah, I'll decipher it tonight."

"Cool! Bet this little clip of film will be worth money if *Still Life* catches on!"

The boys made their way back to school, with Dan in somewhat better spirits now.

"So, Aaron, I saw the daughter of the man who wants to kill you," he joked.

"Where?"

The bike swerved as Aaron scanned the sidewalk for Katrina.

"Delivering the principal's notice. This morning."

"Oh." Aaron was disappointed.

"She said hi to me."

"Yeah? How'd she look?"

"How d'you think she looked, Sedge? Great. Had on a black hat with a veil... in mourning for my cousin."

Aaron smiled, thinking of Katrina, and scratched the annoying chest hair that increased threefold since Friday night at the movie.

"It was kind of weird though, Sedge. She was with those two cops who were searching Mark's locker before the bell."

"Maybe they wanted to ask her some questions since hers was right next to his?"

"When I got down the hall, both lockers were still wide open.

"Both of'em?" Aaron was alarmed. "Katrina's too?"

"What does *both* mean, Sedge?"

"Did you notice anything out of the ordinary in her locker?"

"I wouldn't know what to look for *out of the ordinary* in her locker, Sedge."

"No, I mean, did you see, like..." Aaron hedged, shy to admit he had given Katrina another card so soon after the first one. "Dan, did you notice anything like a red card, sort of a big red card?"

"Oh, you mean like the one she was shredding into the wastebasket?" Dan chided.

"You're kidding?" Aaron swerved the bike as he turned to look Dan in the eye.

"Hey! I'm joking. She clutched it to her breast Aaron, as the cops led her away," Dan said melodramatically, and the two friends laughed together for the first time since the news of Mark's death.

By the time Billy Carlyle's study hall hour slid onto the clock, his bangs were matted with perspiration and oil covered his brow. He felt alternately sluggish and aggressive; the chemical change wrought havoc in him. Across the hall, Aaron and Dan milled like specters.

"Seen her yet, Dan?" Aaron whispered.

"I heard she went home sick. The principal's secretary tells me everything."

"Good to have a best bud who's a suck-up."

"No prob."

Dan caught sight of the small window in the parallel study hall door. Through it, over by the high windows, slouched Billy.

"Look at that goon. He was harassing Correy this morning," Dan growled.

"Who? Oh!" Aaron saw Billy flipping through *Sports Illustrated.* "Looks pretty ugly," Aaron smirked. "Did she beat him up or something? Look at his face, Dan. Wow, he gets uglier the longer I look at him."

But Dan saw nothing but the same old Billy Carlyle he whom he loathed.

The second bell rang.

"Men! It's time for your favorite class. Social studies!" Mr. Hamm beckoned. "Come along! Men! Don't break my heart now. Now!"

Dan and Aaron reluctantly crossed the hall to social studies class.

"Pew!" Aaron wafted the air. "Dan, was that you?" he whispered just as Coriander Preston rushed by. The foul stench seemed to come from her.

Dan smelled nothing. "Hi, Correy," Dan said softly.

She didn't notice.

Aaron glanced at Coriander. He laughed aloud, "Nice perfume, Correy."

"Buzz off, Sedgewood," replied Coriander.

Aaron poked Dan. "Look at her face! It's got that lump like Billy's. Did they go parking and get confused? Looks like the only banging they did was with their heads on the dashboard."

Dan pushed Aaron into class in an attempt to silence him, and held Coriander's gaze.

"Man, what a stink! Whee-ew!" Aaron continued, sending Coriander a smug wink that said *I was never interested in you anyway in case you were wondering.*

"Sour grapes, Sedge, she dumped you, move on," said Dan who noticed nothing out of the ordinary—no stench, no deformed brow bone. In fact, Dan would have been content to take in the sight of Coriander Preston all day.

Later that afternoon, shouts of support sounded across the playing field for the Westlake High School team.

Mr. Hamm ran back and forth, coaching and yelling at the team. "Come on, men! Kill'em."

From the bleachers Aaron and Dan watched the frenzied field solemnly. The crowd's zeal grew fervent as halftime neared.

A *Boston Globe* photographer ran back and forth, yelling, "Move it!"

Cheerleaders danced in the field. Dan noticed that Coriander was uncharacteristically clumsy. At halftime Aaron scanned the bleachers for a black-veiled hat, hoping Katrina had rallied and returned for the championship.

The game ended without overtime. Billy Carlyle and his team charged the sidelines, shouting. "Coach Hamm! Coach Hamm!" The Westlake High team won by a greater margin than usual: 56 to zero. Dan and Aaron ambled over to congratulate the team.

"Sedgewoooood," yelled Mr. Hamm, "you should be on this team, darn you."

"Thank you, Mr. Hamm." Aaron's loner grin told him, *Yeah, right, thanks anyway.*

As the team disbanded, Billy Carlyle came face-to-face with Aaron. The two boys glared at each other. For a moment Aaron's boyhood fears clambered into his eyes for all to see. *Damn, if I show how scared I am, he'll kill me. I've gotta be convincing, gotta look convincing. I am not a wimp!* Aaron puffed his chest at Billy aggressively. *This is the creep who stole my date!*

"You're ugly," Billy growled, "and so pathetic."

"You're uglier," Aaron retorted. "Is that your new look, Carlyle?"

"Hey, hey, you men." Mr. Hamm inserted himself between them. "Men! Men! Nothing a nutritious meal can't settle? Hey, hey, hey! Men! Hey! Cut it out, both of you!"

Brawny Mr. Breen approached the scene. "If you feel the need to fight, I am sure it's nothing that can't be resolved through discussion. Lads! Use your words," he said, raising the pitch of his ever-calm voice.

Aaron backed off first.

"Keep out of this, Breen-jerk!" sniped Billy. Hearing Billy grunt words, primitive anger disgorged in Aaron's gut. Aaron catapulted onto Billy full throttle.

As he pummeled Billy, Aaron's own superhuman strength amazed him.

"Get off me, you crazy psycho!" Billy grunted.

Skinny Dan wanted to pull Aaron off Billy.

"It's just not right to perpetuate violence!" yelled Dan.

Then, on second thought, Dan leapt on Billy's back with the delicacy of a praying mantis. Billy flicked Dan off him. Dan hit the field two yards away with the wind knocked out of him. Hamm and Breen tried physically to separate Aaron and Billy.

Over a dull roll of thunder Mr. Breen shouted, "We can resolve this through discussion! We *can* resolve this!" Mr. Breen nearly screamed the second time when a violent blast of lightning was followed by a thunderous cloudburst. His savage cry triggered the release of clenched teeth and fists. The sky disgorged and a deluge served to disengage the boys' vehement embrace.

"Apologize to Mr. Breen," yelled Aaron, breathless, stepping away from Billy. "I said apologize, Carlyle!"

Lightning reflected in Aaron's colossal pupils. Burnt ozone and ferrous perspiration hung between the boys. Thunder was immediate.

"I'm sorry, Mr. Breen..." Billy groused reluctantly. "I'm not afraid of you, Sedgewood. And I've got the power to hurt you, too, if I want, you psycho nut job."

"I don't think so, Carlyle, ugly rat-bastard."

"*Language*, Mr. Sedgewood," cautioned Mr. Breen.

Stealthily Aaron backed up, his eyes hard fixed on his opponent.

"Let's get out of here," Dan begged, dusting himself off. "What's your problem, man? You just flew off the handle for no reason."

Leaden spring rain drowned Westlake for hours. In the quiet art room in the basement of the high school, Dan watched Aaron apply the final touches to his extra-credit project. The *Christina* reproduction was due before spring break, and that morning Aaron had been too distracted by the talk of Mark's death to work on it.

"So, you want to go see it? It'll clear your mind," said Aaron through teeth clamped around a spare paintbrush as he slung a sultry curve of pure beige around the rump of canvas Christina. Aaron admired his version of the original painting.

"Naw, I have to edit articles for the school paper."

"But, Dan I feel like out of respect for Mark we've *got* to go." After a pensive moment dabbing Christina's fisted right hand, Aaron continued. "Mark was the one who turned me on to *Still Life: The Best of the Worst.* Said he'd seen it a buncha times the day it opened. Hey, Dan, turn back to the Wyeth page, would you?" Aaron stroked the brush again on the woman's hand. "Dan!"

"Sorry." Dan obeyed. "I keep spacing out thinking about my cousin."

"I totally understand, man," said Aaron. Then, suddenly Aaron pulled away from his reproduction and stared at the photo of the original in the art book. "Jeez, I never noticed she's and old lady. Check this out, Dan. I thought she was a babe. But she's a hag-dog, look at her hand. Man, it's *antique.*"

Dan gazed at the book and shrugged. "Sometimes things are not as they appear, Aaron."

11

The man with the handle-bar moustache handed the woman a receipt.

"Sorry, ma'am. Can't do nothin' to rush it. Been waitin' for a shipment. Leave it. I'll call you when it's ready. About two weeks."

She thanked him and turned to leave as large teenage boy blocked her way.

"I need to replace my tube as soon as possible," said the husky boy, nervously as he pulling a front tire rim out of a huge Westlake High wrestling team duffel bag.

The bicycle repairman gestured for the boy to move over so the lady could depart, then he examined the tire.

"Looks like more'n a tube, fella. Looks like the entire tire's been took off. You're gonna have t'wait just like everybody else, two weeks. Leave your home phone number and a five-dollar deposit."

The beefy youth scribbled his number on an oil-smeared pad and anxiously headed for the door of Westlake Greasy Wheel.

"And a deposit, kid! Five little ones, right here." A black-oiled index finger gestured toward the till. The boy rummaged awkwardly for his money. With it, he pulled out a few scare marbles that skidded across the raw wood floor. He rushed away.

"Hey, I need your name, kid," the handlebar mustache called after him, ready to write next to the phone number.

"Bear, er, Robert, er Bob Henkel," he shouted back, nearly splitting a seam with nervous tension as he squeezed his fingernails against the smooth whetstone in his other pocket. Bear left the shop and ran off to the old movie house. He didn't want to be late. He had already purchased his hologram horror card, just in case, before heading to the bike repair shop. Perspiration gathered in the creases of his hands. He *had* to see the movie again, get a fix. Slashing tires was just not doing it for him. In a fit he had even forced himself to slash his *own* bike tire to keep himself from giving in to the bloodlust to cut human flesh. He realized his little brothers and sisters weren't safe if he stayed at home. *And really,* Bear reasoned, *that was a good excuse to see Still Life: The Best of the Worst one more time.*

Checking tickets at the door to the theater, the bald, leprechaun-faced old man flicked his cigar into a smelly ash receptacle by the door. Glancing at Bear's vampire hologram card, he handed over a pair of green-and-red 3-D lenses.

"Back again, young fella?" the old man said in a faint whisper. Bear's thick throat constricted, he swallowed hard. He could not wait another moment to see the movie again. He craved it so much that after the first run he hid under the seats of the theater on the cold cement floor to watch the second showing.

By the time Bear came out of *Still Life: The Best of the Worst* that night, he felt no lasting relief. He needed much bigger thrills than the B-rate horror movie to satiate his ravenous desire to slice. He needed to feel the cutting of something softer than rubber tires. He envisioned soft living flesh. It wasn't personal, and he knew it was wrong. *But I want it,* he thought, frenzied.

On Bear's way to the curb outside the theater, the flashy old woman at the sales booth took a thorough look at the thick-necked boy and shook her head. She saw the demented glare in his crimson eyes. Bear felt the old woman stare at him.

"Boy! Come back here and let me take a look at you," the old woman cawed.

Bear jogged away in a burst of panic, pushing Aaron out of his way. Aaron saw the wild-horse glint in Bear's eyes flash sharp, like a butcher's carving blade. "You all right, Bear?" Aaron jogged toward Bear to catch up.

"Hey, Bear-man, I'm talking to you!" Aaron quickened his pace, but Bear ran faster. In his haste, Bear dropped his duffel bag. It clanked and split open on impact—out rolled an oval plastic mask. Aaron watched Bear desperately scoop up the contents of his bag and race away.

Weirdo, thought Aaron, and turned back to the theater.

"Boy!" the crone screeched.

Aaron sauntered up to the ticket booth, digging at the annoying family of black hair that had spread to the back of his shoulders and biceps. Tufts splayed over his collar like a small Edwardian fringe.

"Yes, ma'am?" Aaron found it difficult not to laugh at the flamboyant old lady who tonight had traded in her shiny yellow ruffles for a tight-fitting white-sequined turtleneck sweater.

"If he's a friend of yours, you'd best keep an eye on that boy. Got it? He's not well. Not well." She disappeared in one yank of the heavy red velvet curtain.

Another weirdo, thought Aaron. Perplexed, he unlocked his bicycle before heading home.

Frankie Marcel peered out the attic window of the theater at Aaron.

"*Bzzzzzzzzt*!" said Frankie, trying to speak. But only one sound came out. And it came out as, "*Bzzzzzzzzzzzzzt*!"

Frankie found refuge in the attic once his vocal cords had begun to change. He realized he ruined his perfect attendance record at school, but he knew he couldn't emerge in public now. Were it not for his signature white polo shirt, no one would have been able to identify him.

Frankie was hungry. The last of the desiccated insect husks on the window sill were entwined in dust. A remnant dustball clung to his face. He wondered what was happening to him. Frankie wasn't himself anymore. In fact, he wasn't a boy at all.

"*Bzzzzzzt*!"

Aaron never heard Frankie's cry for help from the theater window high above the bike rack.

12

In the TV room after dinner, Dan set his pen on the table and gazed at submissions for *The Westlake Tornado*. To concentrate on editing was grueling. Dan felt so sad about his cousin's suicide. The satire column that was Mark's would be replaced by his eulogy which Dan began to write.

"Danny, can you help me with my bike?" Josephine, his nine-year-old sister, interrupted him politely.

"I can, but not now, Josie." Dan's attention remained on the eulogy.

"But, Danny, my tires are flat." Josie whined a little, her cuteness fading as she was not getting her way instantly.

"I'll do it later, I have to do this now."

"Nooo, do it now, *pleeeeze*."

"Can't Dad do it?"

"Nope," Josephine smiled hopefully.

"Shouldn't you be in bed by now?"

"Nope. Mom said I can stay up now that it's daylight savings."

"How'd you get two flats, Josie?"

"I don't know. But I didn't do it. They're cut."

"What do you mean, *cut*?"

"Both of'em." Josie thrust out her pointy cleft chin.

Dan sighed and tousled Josephine's ringlets. "Okay. Show me."

Reluctantly, he followed Josephine out to the garage. Night had settled into the dense fog that cloaked the Pritchers' yard. Dan examined the pink rubber. A slash ran one third the circumference of each tire. Dan's suspicions hatched as he recalled what had happened to Aaron's bike tire.

"Have you noticed anyone weird around here lately?"

"Nope. Only a nice man in a hockey uniform when I came out to play just now. But he was real nice. He waved at me and said hi and everything. He was sort of jogging in place and then he ran away from me."

"Who was it? Someone from my grade? Did he know you?"

"I don't know. He didn't say he did."

"Well, what did he look like?"

"I don't know."

"But you saw him?"

"*Mmmm-hmm.*"

"Any distinguishing marks?"

"Not really. He was just a plain old hockey player."

"Hockey season's over." Dan's gaze settled on his own bicycle and drifted out beyond the garage door to the primrose hedge by the stone wall where twigs rustled back and forth. Then he saw that both their bikes had been vandalized. Dan's had the same length slice on the front and rear tire.

"But I want you to fix it now. Please."

"Mom will have to take us down to the Greasy Wheel after school, Josie. Let's go inside now."

Dan was never so gruff with his little sister. Normally he would have made every effort to indulge her harmless whims. But something shiny was parting an opening in the primrose hedge by the stone wall. In his panic, Dan caught a glimpse of a hockey goalie's mask gaping at them.

"Inside! Now!"

Josephine pouted. The bushes rustled. The mask and the blade disappeared. Footsteps thudded away through the fog, over the embankment toward the main road. Protectively Dan pushed Josephine into the house.

"Now, you listen to me, Josie. Next time you see anyone in the yard, just come inside and get me..." She nodded agreement. "That guy's a psycho. Whoever he is."

"How do you know that, Danny?"

"Josie, a normal person would not go around *off season* in a suit and mask with a huge meat cleaver like that."

Josephine smiled up at her brother in secure agreement.

While Dan had always refused to go to horror movies, from the advertisements he was familiar with a character from a popular slasher movie. The character dressed like their tire-slashing vandal who was clearly getting his kicks by copycatting. Dan's brain began computing the strange variables, mixing and matching, trying to solve the petty crime before it could grow lethal. Josephine started energetically toward her mother's art studio upstairs.

"Mom! Mom! There's a psycho slasher outside!" the little girl hollered.

In the TV room, Dan dialed 911 on the rotary phone, then depressed the button before the dial rotated back to zero. Instead, he called Aaron.

13

Mrs. Fortworth waited with Katrina until 10:00 p.m. The Phillipses were late returning from the club.

"Please, don't tell them, Mrs. Fortworth," begged Katrina from her lacquered lavender canopy bed. "They'll never understand!"

Katrina rubbed her temples, trying to ease her hangover. The car engine gunned up the steep driveway. Katrina dove under the sheets. "I'm pretending I'm asleep."

"Well, Katrina, how shall I explain why I'm still here at this hour?"

"Just say I came home sick from school. And you stayed with me because you were worried. Can't you just say that? This once? They'll pay you extra."

"I don't care about the money, Katrina, I care about *you*. If the principal calls them directly, it's out of my hands. You realize that. And, Katrina, I'll lose my job. Do you want that?"

"Oh, *please,* Mrs. Fortworth. It's a first offense and the principal thinks you'll discuss it with my parents. Please!" implored Katrina. "And can you please write me a note? And sign it?"

Mrs. Fortworth kissed Katrina's forehead and pulled the pastel sheets up to frame the girl's face.

"All right," the housekeeper conceded, "On two conditions. You must promise me you'll stop with the liquor. And you must talk to your guidance counselor at school about your father hitting you."

"Breen? I can't talk to him, he's so formal."

"You choose, dear. But there's no reason for this kind of behavior, and you *can* do something about it while you're still young. Before you grow accustomed to the pattern of abuse. When you're my age, I do *not* want you to feel like you're right at home in an abusive relationship." Mrs. Fortworth gently cupped Katrina's swollen face. "Getting hit should not *feel like home*. You are a beautiful child, and I don't mean because you have a pretty face. No one has a right to misuse his authority like that. No one, Katrina." The gentle woman smiled earnestly. "Promise me you will do as I ask."

Just then, Mr. Phillips slammed the front door. He and Mrs. Phillips were bickering. Katrina's ulcer stung with a fierce injection of bile.

"I promise you, Mrs. Fortworth."

A few minutes later Katrina pressed her ear to the doorjamb, listening to the housekeeper chat with the Phillipses.

"Well, here, let me give you fifty dollars extra for your time," the baritone voice slurred.

"That's not necessary, Mr. Phillips. Thank you. She's got a common illness. Nothing that can't be cured with loving attention."

Mrs. Fortworth let herself out the back door. Katrina scampered into bed with her purse as footsteps ascended. Under the covers Katrina unzipped her purse. Aaron's crumpled card fell out when she removed the whiskey flask. She heard another row starting between her parents as they walked to their bedroom.

Here goes, thought Katrina. *I hope they kill each other so I can go live with Mrs. Fortworth.* Her parents' brawl continued in the master bedroom. A door slammed open then slammed shut. Katrina took a safe-measure swig from the whiskey flask and stuffed it back inside the secret zipper compartment in the bottom of her purse. Aaron's card lay next to her face on the pillow. She smoothed out the damage she had done to it while sitting in the principal's office that morning.

She would have to control her drinking enough to be able to function at school, yet she still needed to keep the horrid worms at bay. She wondered which was worse, the hangover that slammed inside her skull and tormented her digestive system, or the worms that once again began to writhe within her.

14

Outside Katrina's second-story window, a fir tree branch began to dip and bounce under the weight of the shadowed male who clung to it. Fir needles tickled her screen.

Vulnerably close to the window, Katrina's hand drooped over the edge of her mattress, gripping Aaron's get-well card with sleep-atrophied fingers.

The strong tree limb moved like a slow-motion trampoline, every few seconds bringing the human shadow level with her windowsill. The young man grasped the window lip to steady himself. From the darkness his eyes virtually glowed against the screen; through the night fog the waning moon's final rays shed light that reflected in his retinas. He spotted the photograph on Katrina's dresser and the red card in her grasp.

Katrina heard stirring. She squinted through her thicket of eyelashes and saw a human shadow fall across her arm in the dim light.

Oh, great, she thought, *now this.*

She was afraid to scream—afraid to move. Her parents would blame her and then she would get hell. Unless this night prowler killed her first. *Which option's worse? If I die now, I'll never have to deal with them again. Why couldn't this sick-o have gone to their window instead?*

Breathing outside her window grew audible.

"Katrina? Thank God I got the right window!"

In the dim light it was easy for him to recognize her lithe arm and his get-well card.

"What are you doing here, Aaron?" Katrina sat up.

"A simple thank-you-for-the-card would be nice, but I guess I can't expect immediate gratification in every aspect of my life," he joked.

"*Shh*! Are you crazy?" she demanded. "My father'll kill us both."

"Yeah, he nearly did me the other night."

"What do you want?"

Her question stymied him. *Wasn't it clear? Maybe she was just really a weird girl without a clue.* Then again, maybe he was making a total fool of himself.

"Aaron, for God's sake, you'll kill yourself pulling stunts like this!"

She began to unlatch the screen, when they heard her father's voice approaching in the hallway: The man who had called Aaron "*kid*" one time too many.

"He's coming. Aaron, what do you want? Please, leave!" Her open palm pressed against the screen desperately, silently signaling Aaron to hasten his departure. Aaron just grinned at her and pressed his hand flat against the screen opposite hers. Hers was cold; his warmed it. He considered challenging the cretin who had tried to kill him with a terra cotta geranium pot, but he decided he wasn't in the most advantageous position to do so—being two flights up, out on the end of a tree limb as he was.

Finally Aaron spoke. "Just wanted to make sure you're okay, Katrina. Didn't see you all day, you know. I bought you another box of scare marbles since you, *ummm*, lost yours." They giggled.

"Go!" She glanced at her bedroom door as the strip of hall light at its base was broken by her father's feet.

Aaron left the cardboard box of hologram marbles on the window ledge. Then he slid off the branch and dangled for a moment, getting his bearings in the night. The last eight feet into the shadows was a painless drop. Thick fir boughs sprang back gently outside Katrina's window, once, twice, three times. The fourth time, movement was ever so slight before the tree decided to keep their secret.

"What's going on in here?" Mr. Phillips struck the light switch as he barged in, popping the lock of the hollow door.

But Katrina's breathing was steady, practiced, convincing. To her father, she appeared sound asleep. Inside, she glowed with delight at Aaron's bravery. Several worms writhed in pain. And one died.

15

Katrina waved to Aaron from the other end of the pink and gray hall on her way to homeroom. Was it the cafeteria stench in the air ducts that had been following him? He couldn't tell and quickly forgot about it as he wandered awkwardly toward his goddess. Everyone was watching them, but Aaron was oblivious.

"Did you lose weight, Aaron?" A deliriously charming smile shone behind Katrina's black veil.

"No. Did you?" He thought she was lanker than usual, too skinny, unhealthy. Almost cadaverous.

"See you at lunch?"

"Uhm. Sure..." Aaron was caught off guard. "See you at lunch, Katrina." A hot wave of excitement welled in him.

"Great, I'll save you a table."

And she was gone. He remembered too late that he had planned to go home for lunch.

Mother'll drink if I don't show. But, like Dad says, it's not my problem. I've got to get on with my own life, even if she wants to refuse every form of help, and poison herself.

Dan had witnessed the infatuated exchange. "So, Sedge?" he pried.

Aaron's black eyebrows vaulted in triumph. He clapped Dan on the back, knocking the wind out of him with a hairy hand. Dan sputtered. Aaron adjusted his necktie, worn out of respect for the dead boy's memorial service that day, and tucked the ruff of neck hair inside his white button down collar.

"You been lifting weights or what, Sedge?"

"Sorry, Pritch. Hey, you don't think Katrina's got one of those eating disorders, do you? Like we read about in Breen's psychology class?"

"Well," Dan answered, "watch what she eats at lunch. Logical?"

"Yeah, but don't some girls throw up their food?"

"If they're bulimic. If they have anorexia they just starve themselves to death."

"Got it."

"Ruins the teeth too, stomach acids coming up. Takes a few years... probably die of starvation before the teeth go."

"Jeez!" Aaron noted.

"That's if she doesn't kill herself with proteolysis." Dan answered Aaron's bewildered stare, "That's what happens when you starve yourself. Basically, your body digests itself—to death. The ketones are the digested proteins that cause the bad breath. You'd better review your notes before the midterm next week, bud."

"*Digested to death!*" Aaron pondered. "Do you smell it too, Dan?"

"What?"

"The smell of pro-tee-whatever, the ketones?"

"No. I'm just saying, *ketosis happens*." Dan scowled. *Aaron sure is acting weird.*

"How d'you know all this stuff, then?" Aaron asked. "You're not even *in* Psych class."

"I borrowed Coriander Preston's notes."

"Why?"

Dan smirked mischievously. "It was easier than asking her on a date."

"Sly dog, Pritch!"

"She couldn't very well say *no* to my quest for greater knowledge."

"What kind of messed-up *persona* wants to starve herself to death, Dan?"

"Beats me," Dan confessed. "I wish my metabolism would permit me to keep weight *on*. By the look of it, Sedge, you're becoming like me. Skin and bones."

"And hair," Aaron added. "But, personally, I prefer a girl with a bit of flesh."

"Personally," Dan confided, "I myself would prefer *any* girl I could get. With a brain of course. Let's take Coriander Preston, for instance."

"Let's not," said Aaron. The boys chuckled in unison. Still, secretly Dan hoped to get Coriander to like him.

The white polo shirt was absent again from Mr. Breen's homeroom. Missing Persons had been notified about Frankie Marcel.

At lunch the cafeteria was still abuzz with talk of Mark Stiger's impending funeral service and rumors of why so many other kids were absent.

"Did you bang your forehead, Correy? No offense, but you look awful," Katrina remarked bluntly, imagining she and Coriander shared a common bond of abusive parents. "You okay?"

"Oh, no, I mean, yeah." Correy fluffed her bangs over her protruding brow bone and changed the subject. "You going to the memorial service for Mark?"

The two girls placed their trays at a center table.

"Yes. Are you?"

"I don't know. He was sort of a weirdo."

"Well, I'm going. Save those two seats, Correy, would you?" Katrina didn't skip a beat.

"For whom?"

"Aaron Sedgewood and Dan Pritcher."

"Sloppy seconds! Katrina, really?"

"Oh, there they are." Katrina ignored Coriander's cruel remark and stood to wave at the boys. From the other side of the cafeteria the boys waded through the crowd of hungry students. Dan peered over his gold rims past Aaron at Coriander and grew shy at the thought of eating at the same table with her.

"You want to sit with *them*? What's *with* you, Katrina?" Coriander had just overstepped Katrina's tolerance level for stupid attitudes. Katrina glanced sharply at Coriander through the black net of her pillbox hat, ignored her, and quietly positioned her milk carton under the table and poured into it whiskey from the flask in her purse. Katrina's silence ensnared Coriander's curiosity, and by the time Aaron and Dan arrived with their trays, Coriander had not yet raised her eyes from Katrina's face.

"Correy," Katrina began with no emotion. "The sight of you is making me sick. Would you please leave the table, or I'll puke."

Dan's heart sank. Coriander's hand flew to her bangs to adjust them over the obvious protrusion. Katrina noticed Coriander's hand had enlarged and sprouted a tuft of spindly rot-gray hairs. She watched the laggard growth in awe. Aaron noticed too, and looked to Dan for a reaction. Dan shrugged at the girls' spat. Apart from the harsh words, he noticed nothing out of the ordinary. He was concentrating on appearing casual in front of Coriander.

"Jeez, Correy, you're starting to look like Billy. What's happening to you?" Aaron remarked snidely.

Humiliated, angry, and scared, Coriander dropped her plastic dessert spoon and fluffed her bangs again to conceal the increasing proportions of her brow bone. Then she shoved her heinous hands into the pockets of her blue blazer. Katrina turned to Aaron and Dan.

"Sit down! I saved you guys seats."

"Thanks, Katrina. But we don't want to interrupt anything," Dan said politely.

"Oh, don't worry." Katrina smiled sweetly at Aaron. "Coriander was just leaving. She's not feeling well suddenly."

Coriander stood and issued a rebuttal to Katrina, but all Aaron and Katrina heard was vulgar grunting. In frustration, Coriander's oversize tufted hands took on a life of their own. Just as Thalia Pollocks walked by, Correy pushed Thalia and her tray aside, causing a milk carton to fly from the tray toward Katrina's black veil as Thalia was knocked violently to the tile floor.

Aaron instinctively protected Katrina from the airborne milk carton. He caught it in mid-air and presented it to Katrina gallantly as a gush of a soft pumpkin hitting the floor drew their attention back to Thalia. Blood seeped from Thalia's head over the black and white tiles. Coriander Preston ran from the dining hall, her hands cleared the way for her with superhuman strength, knocking students onto lunch tables, into food-spewed trash bins, and walls.

"Call an ambulance," Dan instructed. His temples pulsed in panic, but he himself was unable to move. "Katrina, go! Aaron! Somebody! Get help!"

Katrina braced her stomach for the agony her ulcer would endure and sucked down half her whiskey-and milk potion, then aimed for the exit hall where the pay phone booth was.

Later that day, students rubbernecked as they boarded the school bus for Mark's memorial service. In the bus, Dan, Aaron, and Katrina sat together as lights from two ambulances flashed in the circular driveway of Westlake High School. The ambulance containing Thalia screamed out of the school parking lot. The principal gesticulated aggressively and shouted while several medical attendants fastened Coriander into a straitjacket. She kicked and drooled between gory screams. One attendant thrust a hypodermic needle into the soft back of her knee while another white-clad woman held her thigh before stowing her gently in the second ambulance.

"There goes Bonehead. She didn't want to come to the service anyway." Katrina's words left a hurt lump in Dan's heart. Katrina called out the open window of the school bus. "You gonna behave like a human being now, Correy?"

"You're next, Katrina," screamed Coriander before succumbing to the sedative.

There must have been over one hundred mourners at the memorial service for Mark, the suicide victim.

Aaron nudged Katrina. "Look who's here." A larger, hairier gray hand smoothed bangs over an ever more misshapen brow bone a few rows ahead of them in the church. "To the left."

Katrina smirked at Aaron and said, "The ugly bone-head."

"She may be a bonehead," Dan agreed, "but she's not ugly. I think Correy's not bad-looking." He peered around, looking hopefully for Coriander, but he did not see her. "Where *is* Correy?" Dan whispered thinking, *That's impossible. They wouldn't have released her so soon.* Dan continued craning his neck, hoping to see the face of which he was secretly so fond.

"There she is," Katrina said.

"Uglier than hell," Aaron agreed.

Dan looked around for Correy's lean form. "Where is she?"

"Right there." Katrina pointed discreetly with her chin.

"Where?"

"Oh, for God's sake, Dan, what's your vision?"

"But I don't see her," said Dan, "and I'm far-sighted."

Aaron leaned past Katrina, who sat between him and Dan. "Dan, look right over there. The one with the Franken face."

"Right there!" Katrina snapped.

Dan weaved his head back and forth. "Billy's blocking my view. I can't see past him."

Katrina grew impatient with Dan. "Count with me, Dan. Third aisle from the front, fourth seat in from the far left. Right there!"

Dan counted back three and in four, and there sat Billy.

"Yeah, I see scum bag Carlyle. Not Coriander!

"No, it's Correy!"

"But we're referring to the same seat, Katrina!"

Mourners turned and glared; the three quieted down. Seeing them after the ceremony, the Frankenstein-faced Billy Carlyle ran out. Stumped by the disagreement, Katrina, Aaron, and Dan left the bizarre discrepancy alone for the time being. Mark's funeral was not the place to discuss it.

Although the rest of the afternoon was free, Dan turned down Aaron's invitation to join Katrina and him at *Still Life: The Best of the Worst*. After Mark's memorial service, Dan just wanted to be alone. He thought it strange that Aaron wanted to go again, especially after his cousin's memorial service. Dan wondered about the film segment and remembered his promise to Aaron to examine it with a magnifying glass. The tiny lettering at the base of the film scrap seemed intensely unimportant just then. His heart ached.

Aaron and Katrina arrived for the matinee and stumbled in the nebulous light to their seats. Half the seats were taken. The ticket sales dame and the cigar-puffing old man were at the back of the theater where they often stood like disfigured sculpture. A trickle of suspicion reflected through Aaron's subconscious when he saw the ancients again.

The film was already rolling and the narrator, Skeet, roved an eerie Victorian house like a news reporter.

"Looks like your house, Katrina," Aaron whispered as they sat down in the old cracked green leather seats.

A "*shhhush!*" lanced them sharply from a few rows back.

Aaron glanced around at the audience. There was an indistinct misshapenness to each person's head and posture. He rubbed his eyes and turned to the screen.

Confidently, Aaron put his arm around Katrina and gently gripped her lavender-cotton-covered shoulder. With his other hand, he loosened his necktie and opened the collar button of his shirt. To his alarm, the voluminous hairs that surrounded his neck seemed to have intentions of their own. They poked out, each in a different direction; he tried to tuck them in with his spare hand but had to re-button his top button to control them. Katrina made eyes at him and patted his chest.

"Pretty impressive, Aaron," she teased.

Aaron appeared self-assured, but he could not concentrate on the movie. Having single-handedly tucked in the hairs that grew like weeds all the way around his neck, he considered how he would go about kissing Katrina. What was stopping him?

What if she rejects me? What if she noticed my neck hairs, too, and thinks they're gross? He pictured her face in his mind and zeroed in on her lips. Katrina gazed blankly at the movie screen.

Is she thinking what I'm thinking? Aaron agonized in cool silence.

The comical protagonist, Skeet, spoke directly to the audience from the silver screen as Aaron massaged Katrina's shoulder with his strong, hairy hand. *How to boldly go where no Westlake boy has gone before... if the lady doesn't protest*, thought Aaron.

Skeet's voice bled into Aaron's thoughts. "*Cobwebs. Lots and lots of cobwebs. DON'T shrink away, and DON'T shine your flashlight directly into them. You won't be able to see through. DO duck down and angle the light for best visibility.*"

The face of Dr. Frankenstein's monster jeered behind the cobwebs.

In tandem, Aaron and Katrina turned to each other to whisper.

"That looks like Correy."

"That looks like Billy."

But when they turned on the last syllable, their lips met through the fine black netting of Katrina's pillbox hat. Aaron lifted the black veil slowly and pressed his not-too-moist mouth to Katrina's.

Cool! It's really happening! All Aaron's doubts about whether Katrina liked him dissipated. The long years of adoration were well worth the long, long, tender kiss.

Feeling Aaron's warm breath and virile lips on her own, Katrina's brain suddenly released a hormone into her blood that killed several of the vulnerable new worm larvae inside her brain where they gestated.

In the foreground the movie rolled on. *"You may encounter a dead relative, loved one, or stranger in any of the following positions. It's the slain look, very dull, but quite in fashion."*

Behind Skeet a corpse fell forward with a thud onto a desk. A scream from the soundtrack tore Aaron and Katrina apart; their infinite moment was over. The wave of healthy pleasure Katrina felt in her heart and body frightened her. She unzipped her purse and removed the whiskey flask. Katrina had every intention to extinguish the forceful, unfamiliar feelings that sluiced through her. Her stomach muscles clenched, anticipating the burn with which her ulcer would respond to the whiskey.

"Hey, what's that?" Aaron whispered.

"Want some?" She offered him a swig. Aaron took the flask and raised it to his nose. Katrina assumed he would share her vice. The passion that soaked Aaron's soul withered with the first whiff from the bottle. He thought of his own mother's drool blending with the paisley pattern of the velveteen couch.

"What're you doing with this, Katrina?"

"It's for my sore throat." Her small laugh was cut short by Aaron's look of disdain.

"You don't need this crap, Katrina?"

Katrina reached for the flask, but Aaron pulled it back out of her reach.

"You don't really drink this junk, do you?" Aaron gave her one last chance to lie to him. Angry sweat crept between his hand and her bottle.

"No, of course not, Aaron, not normally but—Give it to me!" Katrina grabbed for the flask with a desperate reflex. Aaron yanked it away. The flask slipped in the slick sweat of his hand and smashed on the concrete floor. The aroma of whiskey cleared the musty, damp-leather air.

"Oh, God, Aaron, what did you do?" She knew that without her whiskey, only minutes lay between her and the arousal of the worms. Aaron raked his torso and arms; hair suddenly blanketed his body.

He tried to control the anger in his voice the way his dad did. "Let's just watch the movie, Katrina."

He resumed the firm grip on her tense shoulder, his glazed stare on the screen. He felt Katrina fidgeting. *I think we've just had out first fight,* Aaron thought, disheartened.

On the screen, the hideous Face of Death from *Tales from the Crypt* knocked at the front door and waited for Skeet to answer. Katrina glanced over at Aaron to see if he recognized the likeness between the Crypt Keeper and herself. Aaron's brows still knitted in a frown. When Katrina looked back at the screen, the ghoulish face of death seemed to single out Katrina and stare directly at her. Then it winked a repulsive, crusty eye and cackled before the camera angle changed and zoomed to a close up of Skeet. Suddenly on the screen, all the horror characters whose key fright scenes from their best movies played bit parts throughout *Still Life* converged on Skeet, looking their most frightening.

"*Off script!*" screamed Skeet in terror. "Dudes, that's not in the script! You're not supposed to attack me! Help!"

"Weird, that scene wasn't in it the last time we..." Aaron frowned.

Katrina's mind swelled with worm regeneration and her brain hurt. She did not recall the winking scene the last time she saw the monster movie either. Nor had Skeet been converged upon by the entourage of ghouls. What was amiss? Had it actually winked at *her*? Singled her out? She glanced at the geometric pattern on the face of her lavender Swatch. The movie would not be over in time. She felt the harbinger of the ascension of the green worms: Her throat tickled. She had kept them at bay for ninety-six hours and now it was as if the slimy critters wanted to make up for lost time. It was as if the worms knew she had become defenseless without her fluid ammunition. They imbibed her fear, suckled her stressful waves of cortisol. And grew. And slithered. The surface of her skin prickled delicately. It wasn't just her panic. Through her epidermis the web of yeast-mold rot spread again.

Aaron turned to her with the look of disapproval his father used to cast on Mrs. Sedgewood for drinking too much booze. When Katrina's visage came into focus within a fraction of a second, it was not her peerless countenance Aaron anticipated. Katrina appeared gaunt and horribly flawed. One chubby green worm reached from the Marilyn Monroe beauty mark to loop through the black veil netting as if climbing the ropes on an obstacle course. Several worms played on the gymnasium of exposed cartilage and bone that now comprised Katrina's face. A flap of desiccated flesh drooped over Katrina's jaw past the edge of her veil. And, instead of alcohol, a rancorous stench of putrid meat repelled Aaron as the worms chewed and Katrina's body digested itself in front of him.

"Aghhh!" he wheezed, leaping from his seat.

"What's wrong with you, Aaron?" Katrina sputtered, not realizing how quickly the transformation had overtaken her this time. Yeast mold blurred her vision.

"Shhhhh, you two!"

With a skeletal hand Katrina felt her face permeated by worms. She tried to scream, but her vocal cords gave out as a writhing mass hastened to block her air passage.

"Will you two shut up!" hissed an Elvira look-alike.

Aaron backed away from Katrina toward the aisle; he tripped on someone's feet and glanced around at the complainers and saw more ghouls. Hideous. Everywhere. The theater was full of mutant human flesh. A perfect mirror, the screen was populated with their celluloid twins. Panicked, Aaron ran out, pushing aside the enfeebled crones who still stood at the back of the theater. Katrina was left to handle the crisis on her own. *As usual,* she thought as she suppressed her gag reflex and flicked away a green worm.

As Aaron ran in the fading afternoon light, his brain tried to retrieve his honed vision of Katrina. Lovely Katrina in braids, Katrina in a ponytail, Katrina with her hair down, but so serious, always serious. Then the face of death superimposed itself over the purity of her beauty. His mind's gruesome 3-D projector would not shut down.

Katrina gave up trying to breathe She felt the new generation of worms form a squirming ball that blocked her throat. She accepted that she would now die of green worm inhalation just as four old feet scuttled to the middle row toward Katrina. Four eyes squinted to ascertain the problem.

"Move aside, boys," the old woman instructed the students who blocked the aisle, too engrossed in the movie to notice Katrina's plight. "Move aside, children."

The ancients ignored the ghoulish aspect of the grumbling youths; a sole witness' knuckles cracked audibly in the balcony. It was Bear Henkel.

The old man leaned over Katrina to administer mouth-to-mouth resuscitation. Katina's eyes opened to withered, smoke-browned lips, and the stench of cigar breath. She couldn't scream. For lack of air, she had grown so weak that she could not even push away the scrawny, gnarled hands that gripped her head and face. In her delirium she stared at the ancient man and tried to see disguised in his wrinkles his original features. His kind eyes regarded her with compassion. What might he *really* have looked like as a boy? she wondered. Or had the craggy face just become more and more itself, more a reflection of the true soul within the flesh, more so than possible with a youth? Her thoughts blacked out for a few seconds.

"She seems to think she's the wormy one," observed the ticket sales hag.

"Maybe she's choking on one of the marbles?" rasped the tar-coated voice.

"Darling, perhaps the Heimlich would be more effective. She seems to think she's choking on—" Her electric-green *lamé* tunic shimmered in the caliginous, silvery light cast by the movie projector.

It took both of the ancients to hoist the skinny girl and position her over a bolted theater seat for the Heimlich thrust to her solar plexus.

"Oh, my, what a miserable predicament, darling!

"Just look at this dear girl. A pity. They *were* rather an adorable couple, don't you think, dear?"

"Like we used to be, sugar-lips," rasped the old man, suddenly releasing Katrina when a hologram bullet from the balcony pelted his tight, shiny bald head. The face of death hologram in its tiny glass globe bounced and rolled. In the same moment, Katrina watched the ball of worms from her throat as it jettisoned to the floor in front of her, like a warring mass of miniature snakes. She gasped for air, a balloon imploding.

"Hey!" The old man rubbed his skull and tried to cry out, but, as usual, his voice just creaked from sixty years of smoking.

"Shhhhhh! Be quiet!" said a Dracula look-alike.

Free from the old man's grasp, Katrina ran out of the theater. *Oh my God, those old coots tried to kill me!*

Bear ducked behind the balcony to eavesdrop on the theater managers' conversation. Although Bear thought it might be crucial to alert someone to what he overheard, he could not pull himself away from the addictive movie and so he sat through to the end. He was dying to find out whether Skeet would get killed this time. The movie had changed in small ways on every viewing, as if someone was re-editing it each night. Or was it spellbound by the *How to Spell Book*? At tonight's showing of *Still Life: The Best of the Worst*, it looked like Skeet was cornered by doom in the Victorian house, surrounded by all the ghouls. At every turn, Skeet was attacked and nearly killed. Bear's fingernails scraped tensely against his whetstone.

Up front on the screen, the retinue of ghouls gnawed and chipped away at the door. Skeet spoke faster as he cowered from the impending threat. He backed himself into a corner of the basement, screaming to the audience for help. His usual mock fear now became real.

In apprehension, some of the student viewers turned their heads away, averting their gaze, not wishing to see the demise of their favorite character. Others' eyes adhered to the climax. When the movie ended, an uproarious response of shaking marbles arose from the audience. A dismembered Skeet close up remained on the screen as the credits rolled and zombies fed.

16

By the time Mr. Breen marched into Introduction to Psychology class on Wednesday afternoon, Aaron was baffled that his best friend still was not agreeing with him. Dan believed Aaron and Bear and the rest of the Westlake students were experimenting with hallucinogenic drugs.

"Sedge, what you're describing is biologically impossible," assured Dan. "Unless..."

"But I *saw* it with my own eyes, man. She's a ghoul like that thing on that creep show on TV."

"Never saw it," Dan stated with a superior tone. *Aaron should know better.*

"And look at everyone else." Aaron gestured to bony, rotted corpses, vampires, werewolves, and phantoms passing in the hall. But Dan just shrugged.

"Master Sedgewood, would you kindly take your seat so I can commence," said Mr. Breen placidly.

"I think those weird old people have something to do with it. The way they look at us every time we go. It's like they *know* something," Aaron continued.

"Sedgewood, please!" Mr. Breen reiterated.

"Dan, look, the room's full of'em. Breen can't see us either, it's so weird. And Frankie Marcel's still missing and—"

"Sedgewood! I am starting to write *one* demerit!"

Aaron backed into class, leaving Dan expressionless in the hall. Then it fused in Dan's head what Aaron was saying. Dan recalled what Bear had said the night before in a frenzied midnight visit—about Mark's death being unnatural. *I'll have to speak to Mr. Breen about this mass hysteria syndrome phenomenon,* thought Dan. *It must have something to do with that film.*

Aaron entered class gagging on rank death decay.

Mr. Breen was saying, "Billy, I'm glad to see you've elected to leave your cap at home today."

Billy hadn't bothered with a disguise. Everyone who knew *knew*, and that was that.

"Holy cow!" Aaron thrust open a window and hung his head out for fresh air.

The faces in the classroom—Billy, Correy, Bear, and several others—were recognizable only as their counterparts in the movie. Katrina looked only half cadaverous today. And she reeked of whiskey breath that angered Aaron.

"Sit down, please!" Mr. Breen tapped a desk impatiently with a pink demerit slip.

The newly initiated students looked inquisitively at one another, blinking, disbelieving, then believing for lack of an alternative. Those who had seen *Still Life: The Best of the Worst* bore witness to one another's true personality metamorphosing through their skin: Mirror images of their equals in the movie. Those who had not seen the movie looked normal and did not detect anything out of the ordinary. They weren't grossed out by the stench, they weren't grimacing at the Fraken twins, Correy and Billy, with their matching, huge, hairy gray hands and block heads. Nor did they notice Bear's shots of crimson and chartreuse dementia in his eyes. Nor Fred Holliston's new widow's peak, vampiric fangs, and sunken eyes. None of the teen decay fazed them; they were blind to it.

"Oh, great. Someone else with an eating disorder," Katrina said as she slapped away vampire Fred, who was advancing on her neck.

Billy forced a grunt. "Sure stinks in here."

"You're the one who stinks, Carlyle," said Aaron brusquely from across the room.

"Let us not start again, gentlemen. Monday's incident sufficed. Today is Wednesday, a new day... Who has read the chapter on ethology?"

Coriander raised her hairy gray hand with newfound confidence, and Mr. Breen nodded. "Good to see you back at school. Feeling better, Miss Preston?"

She smiled insipidly, muttering, "*Ms.* not Miss."

"I see they let you out of the looney bin, Correy," Billy gurgled. He almost sounded happy to see his twin.

"Today we're going to discuss ethology, the study of behavior from a biological standpoint, or how the chemicals in your body—and those you choose to put into your body—affect your brain and thus your behavior. I am an ethologist. Not ornithologist, not ethnologist, but ethologist. An ethologist, that's how I like to think of myself."

Billy mocked the teacher loud enough for the class to hear. "I like to think of him as Gangrene Breen."

"Shut up, Billy," Katrina hissed from behind the black veil as Mr. Breen rambled on.

"Trying to hide something with that hat, Katrina? Did Sedgewood do *that* to you? Hah, I'm surprised you let him near you."

"Face it, Bonehead," Katina snapped. "You're a—."

Aaron overheard the exchange and leapt from his seat toward Billy. His tongue flailed against his teeth, and he tasted blood. He wiped his mouth, and a red smear graced his hairy forearm. His teeth were stiletto sharp.

This isn't happening! Aaron thought frantically.

"Hey, Sedge..." Billy Carlyle grunted, "can't control yourself, huh? What're you Wolfman, Dr. Jekyll, or Mr. Hyde?"

"Eat puke and die, Carlyle," Aaron fired back. His face twitched to contain his rage and his new set of sharp teeth.

"That's it! You're both in big trouble—" Mr. Breen started.

To Aaron's alarm, the twitch in his face persisted to a throb; his face became elastic. It hurt; he heard his nose reshape itself into a hairy canine snout. His eyes ached and his body prickled with nettles of hair. He felt angry at the world, especially at Billy Carlyle, sitting over there like a brick-head. Malice sizzled in Aaron's brain, escaping through his synovial fluid into his spine that channeled it throughout his tissues and bloodstream.

"Aaron..." whispered Katrina. "What's happening to you?"

Once again everything in Aaron's normal world flummoxed as he looked around the room freckled with ghouls.

Billy laughed. "Yo, Dogface!"

Aaron snarled at Billy and struck at him. Billy blocked. Deep, deep inside himself, Aaron was afraid. He was afraid that he had lost control forever. He heard words from his own mouth. But it was another voice, another *persona. What am I, possessed?* He did not recognize his own behavior. *Why do I want to dismember this guy?* From slow motion to fast forward, the room became a lunatic's metronome.

Katrina's face of death leered at Aaron. "You've changed, Aaron. You've got it too!" She pulled her chair a safe distance away.

As his anger swelled, Aaron's endocrine system caused him to mutate into a lupine creature with claws that grew—painfully—from his fingertips.

"Aggghhhhh!" He gripped his hands as the nails grew.

"Oh, Aaron, I'm so sorry for you." The high-pitched hissing came again from his once-upon-a-time dream girl. "You're the Terrier Man, Aaron!"

Mr. Breen burst back into the room with the principal. "I don't know what's gotten into these boys," he was saying.

A low, bilious growl rumbled inside Aaron. *What did Katrina mean, I've got it too? Something off the wall's going on here. Got us seeing things. But Breen's not clueing in!*

"You're all blind!" he suddenly shouted.

He then screamed, his mouth open wide and he cut loose into a howl. The class shrank back. Mr. Breen's voice was distant. Aaron's energy condensed and expanded. He was losing power, fainting. He stumbled in a last attempt to throw himself at Billy. Aaron faded as he slipped down a wet, lightless tunnel in his head, his spirit rewinding down his spine to his tailbone and into nothingness. The stench in Aaron's nostrils was sweet, cloyingly pleasant in the moment his consciousness tipped over the edge, cascading farther into an abyss. A soft thump sounded as Aaron's face of hair hit the floor.

"Is he on drugs?" asked the principal.

17

Deathly groggy with a tugging ache between his lungs, Aaron awoke face-to-face with a grinning woman. As his eyes focused, her features seemed intimately familiar.

"Hello, Aaron." Her dulcet voice bordered on saccharine.

"You're not my mother. I want my mother!" *Does she think she's my fairy godmother with a voice like that?* The thought accelerated through his mind as his brain began to function. Slowly he raised his head. He did recognize the room. It was his Eastridge bedroom. Crickets and frogs chirruped and purled in the darkness outside.

"Aaron, your father will be home from work in a little while. He had to catch up today since he missed three days looking after you, you little monster. I told him I'd stay with you today since your fever's come down some.

"Where's my mom? Who are you?"

"I'm Lucinda, honey, remember me?" The attractive lady became a bit awkward when Aaron showed no recognition. "I, uhm, I'm your dad's fiancée. Oh, gosh, I guess I should've let *him* tell you we're getting married soon. I'm sorry."

"Are you a drunk like my mother?" The harsh, garbled words weren't Aaron's, although they came from his mouth. *Not again! What am I saying to this woman? This is Lucinda!*

"No, dear, no, I'm not." She was taken aback but held her ground. "You've had a tough time with your mom, huh?"

How would she know?

Aaron tried rubbing sleep from his eyes, and cut his cheek.

"Ahhhhhh!" he screamed, seeing that werewolf claws and hair still adorned his fingers.

Lucinda jumped up from Aaron's bedside. "What on earth? What is it, Aaron?" she demanded with a tarnished smile.

"Don't you see it? Can't you see my hands? It's still happening." Aaron sat up, shouting, kicking up the blue and green plaid sheets.

"Lie down, Aaron. You've got it bad again. Lie down, please!" Lucinda yelled right back at him.

Aaron tried to get out of bed, but he was strapped in at the waist.

"What the heck is this? What're you trying to do to me? Where's my father? Did you kill him? Somebody help *meeee*!" Aaron could think only of the movie *Misery* which he'd seen four times on home video.

"Aaron, stop it. We had to tie you in, honey. You're a danger to yourself." The flustered woman began to cry, as if she felt responsible. She acted as if she didn't know what to do or how much she should tell Aaron about what had happened. "You were a danger to yourself, honey, and to people around you. We had to have the doctor come and sedate you. You've been incoherent since Wednesday. It's the fever."

Wednesday? Oh, gosh, I've been like this for how long?

Time was running out for himself and his classmates, and he knew it. A pang of longing for the movie's Wolfman felt like starvation. His peculiar resemblance to the creature he'd nicknamed Terrier Man now felt like a blood bond. Aaron tore the buttons off his sweat-drenched nightshirt to check the density of his body hair.

"Aaron, please," Lucinda begged nervously, "Keep your clothes on!"

She backed away from him. Aaron pushed up his hair-bloated sleeves and watched its growth. He touched the stilettos in his mouth; his lupine finger pad sliced against them. He sucked the blood and liked it. Hungrily he eyed Lucinda, who observed him from a safe distance.

Aaron's mind rewound the events that led up to his last memory. Lines from *Still Life: The Best of the Worst* careened in his mind around the image of Katrina's beautiful lips. *Will I ever be able to do that again? She's so gross now.*

To Lucinda's relief, Aaron lay back, closing his glassy eyes as he tried to piece together his bizarre predicament.

"Aaron, this might help. Someone's here to see you," said Lucinda sweetly and tiptoed out of the bedroom.

Soon, a quick tap on the door frame brought the welcome sight of Aaron's best friend. Dan shut the door behind him and approached the bed waving the length of film he'd been assigned to research.

"Hey, man, how's it going? You look like crap. Better not be contagious."

"I'm still sick, Dan," admitted Aaron. "Keep a safe distance. I don't want to hurt you. I wanted to rip Lucinda to shreds though."

"You just have a fever, man. Look what I've got. Remember this, Aaron? I think we're onto something! It's not a subtitle–it's a subliminal message!" Dan spoke very fast, he was so excited. "It says, '*I have to see this movie every day or I'll die.*' Bet I know why you're addicted! I asked Breen about it, and he said subliminal messaging in commercials and films was outlawed decades ago because it was used to manipulate mass audiences to do things that otherwise would never have occurred to them to do. Even Coca-Cola and Kentucky Fried Chicken used to use subliminal messaging. And it looks like whoever edited these subliminal messages into your favorite movie wants people to get addicted to it so they'll see it again and again. So the filmmakers will make more money from the repeated viewing."

"Mouthful!" replied Aaron, gesturing to get to the point.

Dan took a breath. "Get this, Tuesday night Bear came to me totally wigged out and started emptying his pockets and handing me stuff, like this whetstone and these crazy marbles. I couldn't really understand him, he was so hysterical, and then he raced off. But first he said something about Katrina choking and you running out of the theater. Katrina confirmed it. And Bear said he thought the old people would do to all of us what they tried to do to Katrina, and to my cousin Mark, and Bear said that *he* was next and thought *he* was going to die or kill someone."

"Oxygen!" urged Aaron.

"Yup, getting to it." Dan inhaled fast. "Then he said some guy named Skip or Pete was in some Victorian house and got killed by monsters... Do you know anything about this, Aaron?"

"Skeet, in the movie," Aaron corrected. "Skeet got killed?! Damn!"

"Bear said Skeet shouldn't have been killed by the ghouls, that it never was that way before, or something, and that it was *their* fault, I mean the old theater managers' fault. He said he overheard their conversation after Katrina left the theater 'cause she was choking. Bear said he hit the old creep in the head with one of these scare marbles. You realize, Aaron, these hologram marbles are geometric impossibilities."

"What're you getting at, Dan?"

Dan removed several hologram marbles from his pocket to show Aaron. "It's because of these weird marbles that I got to the bottom of this," Dan said in conclusion.

"You didn't believe me?"

"No offense, Aaron, but, apart from that scrap of film you found, the marbles are the only visible proof that what you're saying might have some truth to it. The reason is logical: These hologram marbles are a geometric impossibility." Aaron gawked at Dan, awaiting a more comprehensive explanation. "You see, I went to the Public Library to see how a hologram is made, because I thought you had to have a flat surface to have a hologram. Turns out I was right, as usual."

"And here I thought *I* was at the top of the food chain?"

Dan ignored him. "You have to split an image, a photograph of a thing or a person on, like, movie film, then project it in two laser beams onto a flat surface. But the two lasers have to reflect off special lenses and the lower one has to refract through an anamorphic lens—"

"Cut to the chase, Dan!"

"Right. An anamorphic lens is, basically, a *squeezing* lens that condenses the image. You know how the 3-D glasses split the images and over-lap them to give the *depth.* Well, the 3-D glasses are sort of the *manual* version of a hologram. Compared to the hologram, which sort of does it *for* your eyes. Ready-made. But still it doesn't explain how they got holograms *into* these marbles. A marble is a sphere. There are no flat surfaces in a marble. And when I broke one of the scare marbles open, you know what happened, Aaron?"

"Surprise me before I fall asleep."

"Watch this, Aaron!" Dan smashed one of the marbles containing the Crypt Keeper from *Tales of the Crypt.* The boys watched in amazement as the image inside the hologram marble escaped like a living being, then evaporated into thin air.

"Cool!" Aaron wanted to break another one.

"The iridescent hologram ghost blew my mind. So... that's when I went to the Public Library."

"And those old people were selling the scare marbles to us!" Aaron scratched at his hairs. "But that doesn't mean they're responsible for them or for the movie existing."

"Yes, it does, because Breen read in *People Magazine* about a Helga and a Godfrey Horror. Their pseudonyms."

Aaron recognized their names. "Yeah, famous Hollywood directors."

"Yes. They are responsible for the worldwide distribution of *Still Life,* and those two old people at the theater look just like the people in the magazine. I checked it out. Though mind you, Aaron, if it weren't to save your life, I'd probably never have made a point of flipping through said publication."

"Worldwide distribution!?" Aaron sat up in bed as the possible consequences struck him. "Get Lucinda. She worked on the film—she must know these people. She can help us!"

"But Aaron, didn't you find this segment of film here at your desk that *she* invaded? She must know about the subliminal messaging used in the movie to make kids addicted to it," Dan cautioned.

"Come on, Dan. She's cool. I'm sure *she* has nothing to do with getting kids addicted and turning them in to monsters. She's gonna marry my dad, Pritch!"

"And you're dumb enough to believe that makes her a safe bet, Aaron?"

"She can help us catch those two old freaks!"

Just then Dan sensed someone behind him and turned around to see that Lucinda had gently opened Aaron's bedroom door. Dan flinched at the sight of the grinning woman.

Crap, how long's she been listening? Dan wondered.

Lucinda gave Dan a reassuring smile and the two boys explained the problem.

"Dan, I'm so proud of you!" murmured Lucinda softly. "I just found the subliminal messaging myself and I'm gathering evidence against my bosses. Subliminal messaging was outlawed in 1958 to protect consumers in America, England, and Australia. Give me back the film segment and I'll make sure it gets into the right hands. I have a meeting with Helga and Godfrey here this evening. They're coming by after the theater shuts down. I'll make sure your dad is here and we'll confront them."

"You mean you believe us?" asked Aaron.

"You don't think this is mass hysteria?" probed Dan.

"Of course I believe you. I know these people and I know they're dangerous. They'd do anything to make a buck from their movies."

"Wow..." Aaron felt relieved she believed them and could do something about their plight. Inexplicably, however, once again Aaron suddenly became filled with rage toward Lucinda.

"You b—, Lucinda!" He caught his breath. "Oh, my God, I still can't control myself! Dan, you talk to her. Tell her I'm sorry."

"Stay with him, will you, Dan?" Lucinda gracefully lifted the film strip from Dan's fingers. "I want to put this in a safe place. I won't be long."

"Stop her, she's evil! What'd you do with my dad!" blurted Aaron. "Crap, Dan, tell her I'm sorry, my mouth's got a mind of its own." Aaron could not control his instinctive rage.

"It's okay," purred Lucinda, "I understand. It's just the fever making Aaron delirious. I'll be back in a while. Stay here with him, okay, Dan? Keep him calm."

Eager to see Aaron, Katrina dropped her bike at the base of the expansive Eastridge lawn and bounded through the front door of Mr. Sedgewood's house. The screen door was shut but the inner door stood wide open. Following the sound of a conversation, she trotted up the stairs and listened. Katrina was happy to hear the voices of Aaron and Dan talking to a woman. On the second floor landing, Katrina decided to stop in the washroom she passed on her way down the hall toward the bedroom from which the voices echoed. She felt she looked awful and tried to make the best of her wormy appearance. She had tried to give up on the whiskey as a de-wormer. But still relied on tiny sips to keep the atrocious vermin at bay.

Just as Katrina was closing the bathroom door, Lucinda was opening Aaron's door onto what appeared to be an empty hallway.

Closing the bedroom door behind her, Lucinda hissed, "Little monsters!"

Unseen Katrina overheard Lucinda's mirthless tone and watched through the door jamb as the woman strode down the hall toward the book-lined study at the other end of the hall. Stealthily, Katrina followed in silence and stood outside the room to listen while Lucinda placed a call from the rotary phone on the desk.

"Helga? Hi there, it's Lucinda. I got your messages." Katrina watched through the door jamb as Lucinda lit a match and set it to the film strip she had taken from Dan for so-called *safe keeping*.

But I overheard her promise to keep that filmstrip safe! thought Katrina.

"Great, thanks, Helga. I understand your concern. There've been some problems with the reel... I understand completely... Of course I believe you. Sounds completely crazy, but I believe you. Look, why don't you and Godfrey bring the film reels out to Eastridge tonight and we'll have some drinks and take a look at it?... Super. I'm sure I can fix it... Yes, I promise it's nothing to slow the worldwide release of the movie! See you soon!"

Lucinda hung up the black rotary phone receiver and patted *The Modern Unabridged How-to-Spell Book* that fluttered indifferently on the desk in front of her. Katrina saw the book moving and fluttering of its own volition, and she shivered in fear. Katrina knew now that Lucinda had to be up to no good. She ducked back against the wall as Lucinda glanced behind her at the wastebasket.

"Hmmm. Now, there's an idea!" Lucinda's beautiful face cracked into a wicked, leering smile as she whispered the words so delicately, Katrina could barely hear her. Katrina watched as Lucinda melted the film strip over the waste basket, then let the molten plastic cool down with a few breaths from Lucinda's lips. She tucked it inside the pages of *The Modern Unabridged How-to-Spell Book* and slammed the book shut before she strode into the hallway and down the stairwell to let herself out the front door. All the way, until Lucinda was out of the house, Katrina heard Lucinda cackle about the demise of the "*little monsters*".

Just then, the *How to Spell Book* burped.

18

Cautiously, Katrina sneaked into Aaron's room.

"...so it seems to be some form of mass hysteria induced by sleep deprivation resulting in self-destruction," Dan was explaining to Aaron. "The victims don't enjoy REM sleep, so they can't process their daily problems and so they go crazy, becoming paranoid and having delusions of themselves as horrible creatures from their worst nightmares, which in turn—"

"It's not mass hysteria, Dan!" Katrina cut him short.

"But I've been researching it, and—"

"It's that woman who just left here."

"No, it's not, she's going to help us," said Dan. "Aaron—?"

"That's Dad's girlfriend Lucinda," concurred Aaron.

"*Fiancée!*" corrected Dan.

"Whatever you say, guys, but can you explain this?"

Katrina held up *The Modern Unabridged How-to-Spell Book* that fluttered and sighed in her hands.

Dan gasped. "What the heck is that?"

"And check this out." Katrina opened the book to show the boys the melted lump of film that was now partially digested by the book. "I watched that lady burn it and stash it inside this book. Then, this thing burped! Didn't you?" She petted the big book and it sighed happily.

"Are you on drugs, Katrina?" asked Dan knowingly.

"Bite me, Dan, my body is my temple," she snapped back. "Listen, Lucinda is in on it with those creepy old geezers. They're trying to infect the world with that addictive movie so they can get rich and famous."

"They're already rich and famous, Katrina," alerted lock-jaw Dan. "I am chagrined to admit, I read it in *People Magazine*."

"Well, so they can get richer and famous-*er*—"

"Hey, that's the dictionary with the stupid title. *How to Spell*—" Aaron recognized the tome and laughed uproariously.

"Like hell it's a dictionary!" Dan said, watching the book flap and wheeze of its own accord.

"It's a witch's book, *that* witch, with a capital *B*. *And* it opened itself to a chapter called '*Spell Reversal*.'" Katrina set the heavy book on Aaron's bedcovers. There it lay twitching like a spastic animal. The boys stared at the flapping pages and then at Katrina.

"Well, call the police or something!"

"Seriously? We need a plan." Katrina rolled her eyes, and from under her left eye one a green worm slithered out onto her lap with a moist *flapppp*. She flicked it onto the hardwood floor with her middle finger. Stunned, it did not writhe for a few seconds, then it tried to burrow under the plaid area rug.

"That's really gross, Katrina!" moaned Aaron.

"What! Do you prefer I swallow it?" Katrina asked. Aaron chuckled.

"See that, Dan?" Aaron asked.

"What?"

"The worm on the floor." Katrina pointed. "It came off my face."

"Yeah, right. Let's get on with this." Dan was anxious.

Aaron sighed. "No one's gonna believe us, you realize. Even Dan still doesn't."

"I wish your father would hurry up and get home," Dan said.

"She's probably tied him up in the basement," said Katrina.

"You're right. We shouldn't *wait* for my Dad," said Aaron. "I need to trust my instincts on this one." *They got me Katrina,* he figured.

"I'll bet she's responsible for Mark's death too," Katrina added.

"But he didn't really have anything in common with the rest of us," Aaron said thoughtfully."

"*Except* that your cousin was in the theater when we were."

"*Except* that my cousin was self-destructive," Dan stated. "Intro to Psych notes—thank you very much, Coriander Preston!"

"What do you mean?" Aaron and Katrina asked defensively. "We're not self-destructive."

Dan continued quietly but firmly. "For starters *you* drinking yourself into oblivion, and *you* picking fights with people bigger than you. I'd say you both rate as self-destructive."

"Maybe," said Katrina, peeved Dan saw through her protective shield. "But I have to drink to keep the worms down. That's a fact. They'll devour me. And, so what if I'm a little drunk. I get by okay. As you can see by the worms crawling out of me, I've just about run out of my stash."

"You think you're suppressing your demons by drinking, Katrina. But you're just afraid to face your fears," said Dan analytically. "Textbook. There *are* no worms. I see Aaron's mother do it all the time. It's sad, and very common."

Katrina frowned.

Aaron defended his flesh and blood. "My mom survives, though."

"She's miserable, Aaron, ever since your father left her. That's not *living*! It's like the living *dead*."

"Like me," Katrina whispered in hot realization.

The truth rankled. Aaron couldn't reconcile the vivid memory of his happy, productive mother with the bitterly marinated woman she had become since his father left. A wave of loving compassion for his mother coursed through him and caused a few hairs to wither across his face, leaving bald patches.

"Agh," sighed Aaron, feeling the change.

"Okay, you guys," Katrina's semi-semi skull face contorted into a half-eaten smile. "Let's get on with this. What about Correy and Billy?"

"Can't tell'em apart!" said Aaron.

"Except she's a babe," Dan added. "And he's a massive drip."

"Oh, come off it, Dan! They both look like the Frankenstein monster in *Still Life: The Best of the Worst.*"

Katrina giggled coyly and gurgled up a long green worm. She gagged, covering her mouth, and pulled from her purse a small *Ball* canning jar. Its dark amber liquid sloshed as she unscrewed the lid to drink.

"You said you ran out of it!" said Aaron incredulously.

"Just about. I tried to *not* drink, I tried," she whimpered, "But now the worms are back, Aaron. And it hurts and I feel disgusting."

"Don't do it, Katrina, please," begged Aaron.

"I don't have a choice, Aaron." She lifted it to her lips to sip.

"You *have* a choice. I'll help you get through this." Aaron extended a disgusting paw to her starved arm. She held his hand with her exposed carpal bones of her rotting hands.

She trusted him. "I'd give you a kiss, but you look really terrible," said Katrina.

"Look who's talking," replied Aaron tenderly. Katrina's kind eyes spoke to Aaron, but on seeing the annelid movement of her face, his gaze boomeranged back to her eyes.

They laughed and gazed lovingly at each other. Katrina sat on the bed beside Aaron.

"Maybe I should wait outside," suggested Dan, uncomfortable with the heightened intimacy vibe in the room.

"No, just guard the door, Dan," said Aaron wrapping his hairy arms around Katrina. "In case Lucinda really is in on this scam thing, we don't want her clueing in to our plan."

"We don't have a plan, Aaron," said Katrina softly. "...yet."

"I wish your father would hurry up," Dan groaned. Katrina pulled away from Aaron's embrace to wrap up the problem solving.

"It's funny, Dan *acts* nerdy like Skeet but hasn't started to *look* like him."

"Who's Skeet? Oh, yeah, the, um..."

"Yeah, you know, the funny narrator in the movie!" said Katrina.

"I haven't seen it, Katrina!" said Dan belligerently.

"Why not? Everyone else has."

"*Baaa,*" Dan mocked her herd mentality, "Hey, lambie, I hate scary movies, Katrina, that's why," *Like I should have the same twisted taste in entertainment!*

"We started acting weird only since we saw the movie the first time," Katrina said.

"I get how the subliminal message makes us want to see the movie over and over," said Aaron. "But how did we start mutating?"

"What do you mean, *mutating*?" Dan thought Aaron and Katrina were becoming more demented by the minute.

"Dan, don't you see the hair on my face? And my claws? Hold my fingers."

"Keep dreamin', Sedge."

"No, come on, feel my fingers."

Reluctantly Dan reached for Aaron's fingers. Aaron guided Dan's hand to the long, sharp claws.

"Careful you don't cut him," Katrina cautioned. Dan squeezed Aaron's fingertips and then... Dan's fingers passed right through Aaron's talons.

"Whoa, it's a mirage, or... or a hologram," said Aaron, awestruck.

"Like when you look in 3-D glasses the 3-D effects are sort of a mirage." Katrina jumped in excitement and a piece of nose cartilage fell onto her collar and down her blouse. "That movie," she continued, "...it did something to our eyes and our brain. Allowed us to see in a weird way. And this creepy book must have the answer in its *Spell Reversal* chapter."

"Or perhaps," Dan assassinated her analysis with a highbrow tone, "it's something scientific, Katrina. Aaron, maybe your *Visual Magic* book explains it? The one you got on our Science Museum field trip in sixth grade." He searched Aaron's shelves and triumphantly held up the small red, yellow, and black book.

Page 21 of the picture book was covered with a flat spiral of green and red dots. As the book instructed, Aaron held up a pair of cardboard-framed 3-D glasses with the green lens over his left eye and the red lens over his right. The spiral stuck out from the page at him. Then, following the directions, he turned the glasses around so the red lens covered his left eye and the green his right. The spiral receded into the page away from Aaron.

"Pretty bizarre stuff. Check this out."

They tested a second 3-D illustration, this time of a toothy Tyrannosaurus Rex that seemed to stick its head out off the page at them. But when they inverted the glasses, the dinosaur's teeth seemed to tip inward into its mouth like shark teeth.

"It switches around how we see stuff. Sort of *inverted*, but real. Like the movie made what we saw real," Aaron said.

"Like it makes us see ourselves the way we really are—but *inverted*," Katrina said excitedly.

"*Inverse universe*," murmured Dan contemplatively.

"And it seems like some people mutate slower if they're not so messed up. Like you, Aaron, why did it take you nearly a week? For me, it took less time."

"What do you mean, Katrina?"

"Oh. Nothing ten years of intense psycho-therapy can't cure, I'm sure." Katrina joked, then grew serious and spoke truthfully, "My parents—both of them—are alcoholics. And my father hits me and my mother for sport." Katrina fiddled nervously with her purse. "I want to go live with our cleaning lady."

Aaron petted her emaciated hand. "You can live with me, Katrina."

She smiled at Aaron whose grin was still overgrown by dense black wiry hair. He looked gross, but she still found him so completely adorable. Katrina wondered if they would be stuck like this forever.

"I hate to say it, Katrina, you're really disgusting to look at. But I still like you. A lot."

Katrina knelt by his bed and placed a skeletal hand on his bushy chest.

"You're not exactly the hunk you were either, Aaron." She spoke tenderly.

Aaron held her bony shoulder with a hairy claw and pulled her hideous face toward him. They looked into each other's eyes and saw only the spirit of the person whom they cared for. Dan peered out the bedroom window, pretending he wasn't there, and wondering what Coriander Preston was up to. Thirty feet below, he saw Lucinda walk out to the barn, then watched her return to the house with two red gas cans. He thought nothing of it in that moment as he was still daydreaming about Coriander.

Katrina regarded Aaron and shook her head in amazement. "And we thought no one could tell what we're really like, Aaron."

"I love you, Katrina. I've always loved you. But now I really, really love you. Thanks for being my loyal friend."

Katrina leaned in toward Aaron's fur-face and pressed her half-decayed lips to his bristles. "I love you too, Aaron. You're a true friend." The brief peck on the mouth spurred them both to retreat cautiously. "How about we close our eyes," suggested Katrina, because in her heart she wanted so much to kiss him.

"Okay, careful of my teeth. I don't want to cut you, Katie. Unless, of course, your kind *wants* to taste blood."

"No, my kind doesn't eat at all."

They giggled and closed their smiling eyes. One kiss lead to another. The peck became a passionate embrace. Dan rolled his eyes uncomfortably. Katrina and Aaron kept their eyes closed, remembering their first kiss and recalling how it felt to be themselves at their physical best. The chemistry in their bodies changed as love flowed openly between their odious monster mouths. A sense of prettiness sprouted inside Katrina's medulla and spread through her endocrine system and her remaining flesh and organs. Behind closed eyelids she saw her world turn a royal shade of her favorite color.

"Do you know what a wonderful girl you are, Katrina?" Aaron pulled away for a moment to tell her. When he did so, he noticed she was looking better. Her face was growing back together. The flap of skin that hung from her jaw had sealed itself to her face, with no trace of scars or scabs.

"Hey, look at you, Katrina! How do you feel?"

"Great, better." She spoke softly, her eyes still closed, she continued to kiss him gently. Aaron kissed her passionately again, then pulled away to look at her face. "Now how do you feel?"

"Really wonderful!" Katrina's face was nearly normal and Aaron's fangs and much of his fur had sloughed off, leaving patches of scruff.

"I don't understand it, but this seems to be helping." He went to kiss her again.

"But, Aaron." Katrina pulled back half an inch from his face. "We can't walk around like this, our faces stuck together, I mean." She patted the strong features that had started to repossess his face and his receding canine snout.

"You're right, Katrina." Aaron drew her closer to him and wrapped her in his powerful, now-smooth arms and kissed her for a very long time, stroking her sumptuous hair.

"Aaron!" Katrina drew away reluctantly.

"Yes?" He kept kissing her mouth and smooth healed cheeks and throat.

"What're we going to do about this?"

"Oh." Aaron opened his eyes to behold his dream girl, "I see your point."

Outside, headlights folded into the hood of a yellow Porsche, and its beast engine trembled to a purr and shut down. Dan watched the two crones clamber out.

"They're here!"

"I think we can take'em, don't you, Dan?" With little regard for Dan's jaw-clenching discomfort, Katrina didn't wait for an answer, and continued to kiss Aaron. The last traces of Terrier Man disappeared.

Katrina giggled. "Potent stuff. Now, don't get mad, Aaron, until we figure this out completely, or you'll get all hairy again."

"That's okay, Katie, as long as you're around." He kissed her again.

"C'mon, you two! They're coming up here now!" Dan popped the romantic bubble.

"Okay, when I give you the signal, we'll all attack. Got that, Dan!"

Katrina stole a final kiss, closed Aaron's nightshirt over his smooth pectoral muscles, now completely devoid of hair. Aaron winked at Katrina so openly, one of the squirming last generation of worms exploded inside her solar plexus. The worm died, poisoned by the cortical sex hormones released in her endocrine system. She felt the worm burst, and she winced. Her cheeks flared with embarrassment.

"They're coming down the hall," whispered Dan peeking through the door jamb.

Katrina slid under the bed with the *How-to-Spell Book*.

"Untie my restraints while you're under there, Katie."

"Shut up!" Dan coughed. The bedroom door opened.

"Look who's here!" sang Lucinda. Helga and Godfrey smiled at the boys. "Allow me to present Helga and Godfrey Horror, the famous director-producer team who've overseen the test-marketing of *Still Life: The Best of the Worst* right here in little old Westlake in preparation for its global release. Aren't you boys excited?"

Dan and Aaron nodded politely. Dan shook hands with the elder couple after they awkwardly handed each other the tins containing the film reels. From her vantage point beneath Aaron's bed, Katrina could see a red velvet hem at Helga's ancient swollen ankles.

"They wanted to stay close to their baby—the *movie*—and actually see for themselves how the audience reacted to it. So they bought the old movie theater in Westlake, per *my* suggestion, and opened its doors for you kids."

"Like a giant focus group," said Helga with her sandpaper voice.

Lucinda continued introductions. "This is Dan, Aaron's friend, and Aaron, my fiancée's son. Dan, would you please set up these folding chairs for Helga and Godfrey? I'll just go grab snacks."

"We know *this* boy well enough," Helga said. "He's often at the movie."

"You're not feeling well, young fellow?" asked Godfrey.

"It's your movie!" said Aaron. "It's like our eyes've been opened. We can see our own flaws and other kids' too, but we can't control ourselves." Aaron was angry at himself for speaking so soon.

Dan backed him up. "Apparently, sir, they can see each other and themselves as these horrible characters, but no one else can see it. No one who hasn't seen the film."

"Like truth serum?" Lucinda added as she reappeared from the shadows with a huge bowl of SmartFood popcorn. "Frankly, if I were you, Helga, Godfrey, I'd be insulted at having my artistic integrity questioned. By children!" There was a callousness in Lucinda's inflection; it caused Aaron's fangs to grow back in.

"But you said you believed us." Dan protested.

Lucinda ignored him. "A boy like you, Dan, isn't mature enough to see a piece of art like *Still Life: The Best of the Worst*," said Lucinda, "But you sure do have one enviable fantasy life." Her words angered Aaron anew.

"Godfrey," whispered Helga. "Aaron's teeth. Like the movie, darling. It's a hologram. How miraculous, superimposed on his face. It's the strangeness we've been noticing about each of the children at the movie theater last week. Like that girl who thought she was choking on a ball of worms. The one you tried to save, Godfrey. At first we thought kids were coming in costume—dressing up for the show as their favorite character like folks do for re-runs of the cult classic *Rocky Horror Picture Show*. But then, we looked closer."

"Yes, it seemed as if the students' energy or their belief sustained the image of the thing and made it a real hologram," confirmed Godfrey. "But just a hallucination can't hurt a child, really. Apart from scaring."

"Pretty sure a lot of teenagers are traumatized by this," said Aaron. "One's dead. And one's gone missing."

"This kind of rubbish will interfere with the profits of the film." Lucinda turned toward the door.

Intending to attack Lucinda, Aaron leapt up on the bed but was too weak to stand. So he fell straight back down on his back.

"I'll fetch beverages. Godfrey, please go ahead and set up the first film reel. I'll be right back." Lucinda left the room.

Katrina kissed the *How to Spell Book* and whispered to it, "I'm leaving you hidden safely under the bed, but I'll come back for you." The book sighed happily. Katrina's was the first kindness the age-old book had ever experienced, given the historic lot of avaricious spell-casters using it to give them what they wanted, when they wanted it. Like an archive, the book had a long memory, and it recalled each of those users. Conversely, it would forever remember Katrina's protective kiss.

Katrina slid out from under the bed.

"Why, Godfrey, that's the young lady with the worm ball! What on earth's she doing under the bed?"

"Shhh." Katrina placed a finger to her lips. "Obviously you don't know what's going on. Lucinda's up to no good. She put some kind of curse on the movie or the theater. We have proof. Under the bed. I'm going to call the police. Be right back!"

Katrina dashed out the door into the hallway and slammed *smack* into Lucinda, spilling Coca-Colas.

"I guess we'll forgo the drinks. We won't really be needing them anyway. This won't take too long."

"You must be another of Aaron's little monster friends," mewled saccharine Lucinda. Katrina attempted to dart past Lucinda, but she was caught in the woman's strong arms. "Come and watch the movie with us."

As if the furnace turned on, a dull rumbling roar invaded the house. Lucinda pushed Katrina back into the room, locked the door, and pressed "Play". *"Coming soon to Blockbuster home video"* appeared on the screen and rekindled the deadly threat.

"I smell smoke!" yelled Katrina.

19

Mr. Sedgewood drove up the long driveway of his isolated home in Eastridge. Few windows where lit. Most drapes were drawn.

Must be asleep already, he thought.

A lavender bike lay edge of the grass. It gave him pause. He entered the house, but the light switch didn't work. In the darkness it hit him:

Smoke.

"Lucinda? Honey? Aaron? *Aaron*!

The pall of smoke forced Mr. Sedgewood back outside. He ran around the house, seeking less treacherous access and saw flames shoot out of the chimney, then one bedroom window blew out, vomiting fire.

"Oh, God, no!" he coughed and ran for the satellite phone in his car.

"Smoke? You smell smoke? That must just be the popcorn I burned. Now, sit down, little girl, and watch the movie."

"She's nuts!" declared Katrina and bolted toward the door as Lucinda snapped a small derringer from her trousers and pointed it at Katrina.

"I don't think I need to bore you by saying 'nobody move,' do I?" Lucinda lit a cigarette and took a drag. She then tossed it, lit, into the trash.

"Lucinda, be reasonable." Frail, shriveled old Helga stood firm.

"Reasonable? Hell, I'm reasonable. I'm not going to get arrested and ruin my career because you all know too much, so I've taken prophylactic measures."

"What good will killing all of us do?" implored Geoffrey.

"Why don't you do it in reverse order? You already ruined your life, so leave us out of it!" Katrina snarked.

Sparing his dry throat, Godfrey nodded his support to Katrina.

"Shut up, little girl, little girly-girl, *monster*." Long-festered stress caused Lucinda's mind to fissure and crack.

Katrina remembered the magic book and stooped under the bed to reach for it. "What'll happen if this burns, Lucinda?" Katrina held her voice steady behind the magic book as she backed toward the window.

"Give me that," the deranged woman squealed, grabbing Katrina by the hair with one hand and the book with the other. Still gripping her gun, she seized the *grimoire*. It moaned in despair. "My little bookie, bookie, book, my pet book, my magic book. It'll just burn up with you silly little monsters." Lucinda turned and grabbed the door handle to escape, but her flesh seared. "*Aggghhh!*" Already the door knob was searing hot from flames engulfing the hallway.

"You misused your authority, Lucinda," said Helga. "You have taken a classical art form and trashed it. For what?" The old woman approached Lucinda who blocked the door. "And now you want to ruin these young lives too. Let the children go! If they are believed, so be it, the rumors will help promote the film."

"Helga, back off! Don't come near me, or I'll have to shoot one of them. You know I keep my promises."

Lucinda intended to make a run for it. She tore pages from the *grimoire* to place over the sizzling doorknob and opened the door. Flames and smoke rushed in at her, scorching her hair and face.

"Aaron? Aaron! Lucinda? Are you there? Answer me, goddammit! Aaron!" Shards of glass sprayed the room as Aaron's father smashed the far window to get inside. Smoke obscured Mr. Sedgewood's vision as he bashed the wooden crosspieces out of the window frame with the butt of a rifle he kept in his Land Rover. Katrina grabbed at the magic book in Lucinda's hands as the evil woman prepared to escape through the flames.

"Dad?!" Aaron was almost too weak to answer.

"Get the hell out now. The whole house is going down!"

Helga and Godfrey passed Aaron through the window.

"He's still very sick. You'll have to carry him." They followed. The room was engulfed in a glowing mass of choking smoke.

"Dan, Katrina, come on," Helga yelled, descending.

Quickly, Dan approached the window. "Run, Katrina, hurry. we can't wait any longer, I'm—" He retched from the smoke and heat that baked his lungs.

"But the nice book!" Katrina screamed. "She's—"

"I've got it!" Dan lied to motivate Katrina to just get out before they asphyxiated. He pulled her through the open window after him and steadied her feet on the ladder. Down they climbed.

"Where is it, Dan?" Katrina tried to yell down at him as they neared the lawn, but her voice was hobbled by the heat and smoke. The fire's roaring turbine drowned out other sounds.

"What?" Dan yelled.

"The book? Where's the book?"

"Just leave it, Katrina. It'll burn with her."

"No, I promised it—" Katrina stopped herself then explained in a way Dan would understand, "We need it, or we'll never turn that curse around."

Dan grabbed her ankle. "Don't even think of going back in there, Katrina. You'll die."

One kick was enough to throw Dan's hand off her leg. Katrina scrambled back up the ladder and into the flames.

"Katrina! Nooo! Mr. Sedgewood, I've gotta go after her!"

"No, Dan, get down here, I'll go," yelled Mr. Sedgewood.

Clambering back inside Aaron's burning bedroom, Katrina minced around patches of flame that ravaged her shins. She saw Lucinda in the far corner, clutching the *How to Spell Book* to her chest and rocking like a shell-shocked child. A chunk of wall fell through the charred floorboards blocking the line of sight between the two females. Katrina leapt off to the side as her long hair went up in a spray of embers. She swatted a crisped bald patch but kept her aim on the madwoman. Lucinda's lips moved; she was having a conversation with herself; Katrina could not hear her voice over the ripping flames.

"Give me the book, Lucinda!" Katrina reached for the magic tome. Deftly Lucinda swiped Katrina's ear and pulled her face in close. Her demonic eyes gnawed away Katrina's bravado.

"No."

"Yes!" Katrina jabbed a knee into the woman's face and rolled with her just as that portion of the floor fell away.

"Let go!" shouted Katrina.

In one violent motion, Katrina yanked the magic book away from Lucinda. Pages ripped as Lucinda tried to hold on. She stuffed them into her mouth as if she were starving, and chewed obscenely. Katrina was forced by the extreme heat to run. As she dashed back toward the open window with the remains of the grateful magic book tight under her left arm, Katrina tripped. She nearly fell through the broken floor just as a hand grabbed her right arm. She screamed.

Was it Lucinda?

"Katrina, where's Lucinda?" Mr. Sedgewood yanked Katrina and the *grimoire* to the safety of the ladder. He then climbed back inside to search for his broken paramour.

Lucinda whined beyond the huge flaming hole in the floor. Fire bursts sprang up between them like hellfire. A ball of saliva-wet pages was clutched in Lucinda's seared hands.

"Lucinda, let me help you," Mr. Sedgewood pleaded.

"Forget about us, stupid." She stared through him, disinterested. A wall of smoke obscured her grotesque smile as the floorboards under Mr. Sedgewood's feet gave way. He leapt for the windowsill and pulled himself up over the edge. The wall of the house tilted inward as he clattered down the ladder. The haunting cry of fire trucks neared.

"Get back!" Mr. Sedgewood stumbled away from the house and across the lawn to join the others.

"Is she dead?" Katrina asked expectantly.

"She couldn't be anything but dread," Dan wheezed.

"'*Ding-dong...*'" murmured Katrina stroking the wheezing magic book protectively, as it began cooing in her embrace.

Mr. Sedgewood was silent as he led them away from danger. He didn't understand... yet.

Epilogue

Dan and Coriander reached the center lunch table in the sparsely populated cafeteria.

"Eat up!" Dan smirked as he set down his tray and flamboyantly began shuffling an entire set of the hologram collector cards on the table in front of Aaron.

"Hey Katrina, nice haircut," said Coriander smugly. "The seared look."

"From Sears." Katrina joked.

Upon hearing her voice, Aaron looked up from his milk carton that bore photos of the missing prom couple under the words "*Have You Seen Me*" on the side of the carton.

Aaron reached for Dan's monster cards.

Dan's hand clamped over the deck. "No, those are *mine*! Correy gave'em to me." As he tussled Aaron for the cards, Dan accidentally dropped his newspaper on the lunch table.

"You look great, Correy!" Katrina replied cautiously.

"Thanks to Danny." A big smile graced Coriander's lips. She put her arm over Dan's shoulder. "He can be very convincing when it comes to matters of life and death."

Dan shifted uneasily. He wasn't used to having what he wished.

"Too bad about Billy." Aaron's tone was shaded in politeness.

"Maybe he'll learn to love too," Coriander said.

"Himself, preferably." The others glanced at Katrina for her lack of empathy. "I mean it!" Katrina defended. "I mean *himself*. If I didn't, I know I'd still be a club member of the *Still Life* walking dead in the state mental hospital with him. At least he's alive, for God's sake."

Their judge-y looks softened in agreement.

"Does anyone know what happened to Bear?"

"MIA since last week."

"Didn't get any answer on his home phone." For a minute they were silent with melancholy.

"Bear was a good kid," murmured Aaron.

"The police found Frankie Marcel's body," ventured Dan. "I didn't have the heart to read the article yet." Dan took the responsibility to turn the subject away from Frankie's death. "How's your mother, Aaron?"

"Not totally cooled off yet since Dad came to the house. Storming around making him suffer a bit. She told me she's secretly glad his house burned down because he's gotta stay with us for now. But she made me promise not to tell Dad that she likes the idea of him staying. Doesn't mean they'll get back together, but at least they're trying to help each other for a change. And instead of ignoring Mom, I'm going to help her too."

"And the old people?" asked Coriander. "Danny told me they shuttered the movie until they figure out how to *disenchant* it. But how come nothing ever happened to *them*? They saw the movie! Didn't they get addicted to it, too, like us?"

"You know what I think!" Katrina explained, "I think they'd grown to be so much themselves that they couldn't mutate like us. They're totally formed, like fossils. And we're still young so we're still forming ourselves."

"Plus, the old geezers are still in love," added Aaron giving Katrina a loving nuzzle. A stray remnant patch of fur fell away.

"Aaron, can you *not* do that at the lunch table?" said Coriander, completely grossed out.

"You know what I think? I think that the remaining hair and fangs will subside the longer we feel love for ourselves and each other. Soon, all signs will be gone."

"Like an inoculation for chicken pox?" asked Dan.

"Exactly," Aaron confirmed, "Once you've had it, you're safe."

"Probably a placebo," Dan scoffed and stood to go.

Aaron shrugged. "Leaving so soon?"

"Off to see Breen. You know..." Dan lowered his eyes. "...for Mark's sake."

"I'm booking time with Breen today too," Katrina announced proudly. "I feel much better already, knowing that I'm able to talk about hard topics. Even my parents are considering family therapy. And they promised to go to Alcoholics Anonymous together." Katrina smirked. "Probably only because our cleaning lady threatened to report them."

"For what?" asked Coriander.

"Well, my dad for hitting me and my mom for enabling him. They're both booze-hounds," said Katrina matter-of-factly.

"Katrina," exclaimed Coriander with genuine compassion for a change, "Why didn't you ask for help sooner?"

"I didn't know it's child abuse until Mrs. Fortworth explained it to me."

"Welcome to the new normal," Coriander added with a kind smile.

"Thanks, Correy, I decided if they still behave badly, I'll figure out how to use what remains of the *How to Spell Book* on them."

Just then, a face of death hologram marble skittered across their lunch table and bounced off Katrina's tray onto the tile floor with a clack. The four friends glanced up and were greeted by a familiar—but relaxed—"*Haaaaa.*"

"Bear! You look like hell, man," exclaimed Aaron jumping up to give him a man-hug.

Bear was hardly recognizable: gaunt from worry.

"It was horrible," exclaimed Bear. "I nearly killed someone." Bear hesitated, "I nearly killed *me.*"

As the last of the Westlake High students filed out of the cafeteria to return to class, Katrina sat staring at the missing prom couple's black and white photograph on the side of her milk carton. Aaron slid over next to her, pushing Dan's forgotten newspaper aside.

"Aaron, why'd you lie to our friends?" asked Katrina, incredulous. He was silent. "Don't pretend you don't know what I'm talking about! Why'd you lie?"

Still, Aaron said nothing.

"You know it's *not* like a chicken pox inoculation." Katrina's exasperation grew. "All we know is that it's temporary and it comes back if we don't make out all the time. For all you know, Aaron, we could be dead at the next full moon! We still have all those active receptor cells in our system."

Earnestly Aaron stared into Katrina's eyes for a long time before he replied.

"So they'd have hope... Katie, at least... until Helga's parapsychologist witch doctor people figure out an antidote." Between them the silence was vast. "And who knows," Aaron added, "maybe Dan's right, maybe it's like a placebo, and if we believe it enough, it'll work."

Aaron gave Katrina a loving kiss. She couldn't resist him. As Aaron moved in closer to embrace Katrina, his elbow brushed Dan's newspaper onto the floor. Its headline faced the cafeteria tiles,

Eastridge Firefighters Report: Mystery Unsolved
—Arsonist Remains at Large

Driven to Kill!

Originally published by Bantam Books' Bantam Starfire, a division of
Bantam Doubleday Dell Group, Inc. New York, NY, 1994

1

Aaron Sedgewood licked his bowl of pasta salad and stood.

"That's bad manners, Aaron, but you're forgiven," said Mrs. Phillips with a smile.

"Great cook, Mrs. Phillips!" Still chewing, he grabbed his *Westlake High School* sweat shirt and winked at his pretty girlfriend, Katrina Phillips.

"Chilled worms are the greatest. Thanks for dinner, ladies."

"No trouble, Aaron. Anytime." Replied Katrina's mother, standing to clear the table.

"Thanks for letting us test out the menu for the Halloween dance, Mom."

Aaron's expression turned mischievous. "I think we'll need to work on the bloody eyeball soup though. I'm not so sure I like peeled green grapes and tepid tomato sauce together."

"We'll try apple cider as a broth then," Mrs. Phillips suggested, lifting a plate of thin crisped cheese strips. "Diluted with mango juice, and a dash of cinnamon."

"Mmm, fried flesh strips!" Katrina plucked another baked Parmesan strip from the plate before her mother covered it.

"It's fun to test new recipes," said Mrs. Phillips. "I love cooking experiments."

"It's only because Dad's gone that she lets us do the cooking here," Katrina remarked. "Ever since that prom couple disappeared last spring, Mom's afraid to be home alone."

Mrs. Phillips was silent for a bit before she spoke. "I hope you get your car fixed soon, Aaron. That's a long bicycle trip for you to make at this hour. You've got a bike light and reflectors?" Aaron nodded. "And it's chilly, Aaron. Dan and Correy were wise to take off before the sun set."

"*Wise* and *Smart*!" declared Aaron, dramatically holding up a bag of *Wise Chips* and *SmartFood Popcorn*. "Dan just wanted to drive his new Honda. Plus I wouldn't have passed up the opportunity to stare a little longer at the most gorgeous girl in school and her matching mother."

Mrs. Phillips smiled and blushed.

"Mom, it's not about *you*. It's about *me*," Katrina scolded and rolled her eyes, muttering, "Suck-up, Aaron!"

Smirking, Aaron grabbed a handful of licorice bats and backed out toward the entry hallway.

"Ignore him, Mom. Aaron specializes in Advanced Groveling," said Katrina.

"I'm happy to drive you, Aaron. Good practice for Katrina, too," Mrs. Phillips suggested as she followed the teenagers to the foyer where Aaron's windbreaker hung.

"You'll let me drive, Mom? I haven't got my driver's permit yet.

"I'm considering it, Katie," said Mrs. Phillips.

"Don't worry, Mrs. Phillips. I got around on a bicycle for years. I'll be fine."

"I'll walk you down the hill at least. To the end of High Street."

"Just don't stop for strangers, you two. I feel so uneasy with the rumors of a serial killer in our area."

"Dan Pritcher thinks the Triborough area is like the Bermuda Triangle," Katrina announced. "Starting with that prom couple last spring, then the North Andover murder. Next thing you know, he'll strike in Westlake again."

"Yes," reflected Mrs. Phillips, frowning at her daughter's enthusiasm about a serial killer, as if he were a New England Patriots football celebrity, "Dan was on quite a rip about that earlier."

"Everyone at school thinks they eloped," Aaron added.

"Plus their bodies weren't found," added Katrina, "so there's no proof of foul play."

"No body, no crime," mused Aaron.

"Don't be long, Katrina. Please." Her mother glanced out the beveled window in the front door at the darkness before turning to kiss her daughter's cheek.

"I'll only be ten minutes, Ma. Just to the end of High Street... and," Katrina wheedled, "...to the beginning of Prospect Park."

"Mom, there's no proof the killer killed Westlake High School students yet. I'm keeping score!"

"Don't be vulgar, Katrina."

"Oh, Mom," Katrina sighed. "I love you so much, you're cute when you worry."

"Any of us could be next, Katrina. You never know with that sort of degenerate. And take a sweater. It's nippy out..."

"Halloween's coming!" Katrina finished her mother's sentence, "*...to a theater near you!*"

"Harvest moon's not 'til *after* Halloween this year. The *Farmer's Almanac* says so!" snarked Aaron.

"That's not what Farmer Brownell predicts for this year," noted Mrs. Phillips. "His column in the paper predicts freezing rain on Halloween and possibly snow. You'll want to dress accordingly for your Halloween party."

"Mom, do you really believe that ancient coot?"

"*Language*, Katrina, show some respect for your elders. Someday you'll appreciate the old man's wisdom." Mrs. Phillips turned to retrieve Aaron's windbreaker.

Katrina rolled her eyes and launched her killer eyebrow behind her mother's back. When Mrs. Phillips turned back around, Katrina smiled sweetly. Her mother seemed so tired tonight.

"Leave the rest of the ghoul food, Mom. I'll pack it up and share it at school tomorrow."

Aaron hoisted his knapsack onto the credenza in the vestibule.

"I nearly forgot, Katie." He pulled out what appeared to be a collapsed tangle of wood blocks with hinges and joints and a wire hook at one end. "Surprise!"

"Kindling?" Katrina guessed.

"I made it in wood shop for you."

Curious, Katrina reached for the contraption and unfolded the hinged segments.

"Smells nice."

"It's a skeleton, made of wood!"

"Mom, smell it."

Mrs. Phillips did and smiled. "Mmm. Fragrant! Cedar!"

"...blocks to...?" Katrina ventured.

"Cedar blocks to keep moths from eating your woolens, Katrina," advised her mother.

"It's a hanger," Aaron explained, pointing out a top hook in the pinkish-brown wooden skull head. "For Halloween."

"Yeah, so, it's a hanger for Halloween? I don't get it," replied Katrina flatly.

"Katrina, it's a very thoughtful gift." Mrs. Phillips examined Aaron's handiwork. "A hanger made of cedar for your closet!"

"The wood blocks are jointed like bones, and see, the skull swivels..."

"No offense, Aaron, but why would I want to hang a *skeleton* in my *closet*?"

"Cause *everyone's got one*, Katrina." Aaron waited for her to laugh. He tried again. "*Everyone's got one...* Get it? Everyone's got a *skeleton* in the *closet*, Katrina. So you should too. A *skeleton* in your *closet*. *Everyone's got a skeleton in their closet.*"

"It's an old saying, Katrina." Mrs. Phillips laughed uproariously at the idiom. "Well, you kids're too young yet to have any skeletons in *your* closet."

"But now's as good a time as any to start?" Katrina joked, and stared blankly at the morbid gadget.

"How clever—cedar keeps moths off your woolens, and it truly is a skeleton *in* the closet." Mrs. Phillips kept on giggling. "Two birds, one stone, delivers a laugh, keeps moths at bay, and hangs your finest pashmina."

"I thought it up myself. Now everyone's making'em for their parents."

"Thank you Aaron," Katrina said politely, handing the cedar hanger to her mother before her mother could wax eloquent again. "We'd better go, Aaron."

"Ten minutes," cautioned Mrs. Phillips. "And be careful."

"Mom, what could *possibly* happen in ten minutes?"

Katrina's question was about to be answered... in under nine minutes, in fact.

The streetlamps winked on, illuminating a *missing persons* poster featuring last spring's *MIA PROM COUPLE* that read *HAVE YOU SEEN US?* Aaron pointed at the poster of the handsome couple and nudged Katrina.

"We could elope like they did, Katie."

Stumped for a clever retort, Katrina smiled a cat-canary smile at the idea. As they walked down High Street, Aaron hugged Katrina's shoulders with a strong arm. His other hand guided his black ten-speed.

"It might frost tonight," he justified his hasty embrace, mimicking Mrs. Phillips' frequent warnings.

Katrina snuggled closer to his hard chest. He stopped for a moment to retrieve something from his jacket pocket.

"*Eeew*. How can you eat those things, Aaron?"

He popped another candy bat in his mouth.

"I love licorice."

"I hate licorice."

"Dutch people use it as a mood enhancer."

"Okay, I'll try it."

Black toothed, they chewed and walked in silence until they reached Prospect Park.

"I miss your long hair, Katrina," said Aaron, turning to face her. "Are you gonna grow it out?"

Katrina balked at Aaron's lack of tact. She flicked her shoulder-length hair in his face as her pretty upper lip drew back involuntarily into a snarl.

"What happened to *Advanced Groveling*, Aaron? Coriander Preston has nice long hair, maybe you should go out with *her*!"

"Coriander Preston is going steady with my best friend."

"Aaron! That's your *reason*?"

"*Shhh*, Katrina, I'm teasing you! I like you the way you are. You know that." Aaron kissed her tenderly on the lips. "Besides, you're beautiful, Katrina, I worship you. You're a goddess. I was just saying..."

"Yes?" Katrina whispered, "That I'm wicked smart." She nestled so close he felt her breath escape near his mouth. It smoked in the night chill. Katrina was irresistible to Aaron. He could have held her all night right there at the edge of Prospect Park.

Deliberately he glanced away to break the electric charge zinging back and forth between them. He knew he'd better head home.

"School tomorrow. You should probably head back. Go," he said softly, "I'll wait until you get to your mailbox." Aaron gestured protectively, pushing her away from the burrow she'd created inside his jacket. "See you tomorrow at your locker. And bring me some of that worm food for lunch."

"You can have all the candied bats! See you." She took a few steps and blew him a foggy kiss. *Aaron,* she thought, *is the cutest.*

From the darkness in Prospect Park they heard something cry, too near for comfort but too far to determine what it was. Maybe an animal. Rabbits made that sound when the coyotes got them. Then there was another cry. Unmistakably human, gravelly, and desperate.

"Help me, oh my God!" it shrieked.

A thump and rustle in the bushes sent Katrina straight back into Aaron's protective embrace. A car door slammed. An engine revved and exploded in a frenzy of ignition. The grinding of pebbles and dirt under wheels shrilled through the air. Like a giant ghost engulfing them, road dust from the far side of Prospect Park wafted through the trees toward Katrina and Aaron. Dirt fog.

"You heard that, right?" Katrina strained to look down the tortuous path that led deep into the park. She could not see through the dense forest.

"Nnnnnope, I heard nothing. Let's get out of here and pretend we never came," whispered Aaron, pulling her by the hand. "I'll walk you back up to your house and your mom can drive me home."

"No, let's check it out, Aaron. Come on. Someone's hurt, sounds like need help."

"We should just leave and call the police, Katrina."

"You're no fun." Katrina broke his grip and darted playfully toward the thicket, then stopped. Her eyes twinkled at Aaron. "C'mon, Aaron. Chicken? Whoever it was obviously already drove away. We're safe."

"You're a nut, Katrina," Aaron said, hoping to call her bluff. "Katrina! Oh hell. Don't do that. Come back here. Katie!"

Aaron stumbled toward Katrina's footsteps and nearly tripped over her in the dappled darkness of Prospect Park. She was crouched next to a human heap on the ground. A woman.

"Crap. Wouldn't you know we'd find a body. Katrina, let's get out of here and call the police."

"She might still be alive," said Katrina breathlessly as she struggled to roll the bulky body on its back. "Give me a hand, Aaron."

"I—I don't think she's breathing, Katrina," stuttered Aaron, feeling the woman's wrist for a pulse.

Through the branches, splotches of light from a streetlamp scantily aided their vision. A trickle of metallic tinkling emanated from the old woman on the ground.

"Listen! Look, she's wearing a headset."

Aaron removed the clunky black headphones from the disheveled old woman's head. He pulled an earphone toward his ear, but the cord was hung up on something and did not reach. His hand traced the wire back to the collar of the old woman's ragged overcoat. *Maybe it's caught on a button.* But he discovered that the cord was laced twice 'round her neck.

"Double crap. Strangled!" groaned Aaron. His trembling hand unwound the cord of the headset from the wrinkly throat. A wheeze escaped the woman's blue lips and her eyes popped open as a shudder of death rippled through her body. Alarmed, Katrina fell backward onto the ground.

"She's alive! We can save her, can't we, Aaron? Pump her chest, shake her." Katrina lunged at the woman's face to perform CPR, but Aaron held her back.

"No," Aaron said cautiously, "No. No, she's not alive." When it was clear the old woman was already dead and the guttural death rattle wheeze had been her final utterance, Katrina slumped against Aaron and cried with him in the grizzled silence in the park. There was nothing they could do to bring her back to life; they felt powerless.

Katrina wiped the tears off her face. "What was she listening to?"
"What difference does it make?" Aaron whispered.
"Maybe the type of music is a clue. It might *mean* something."
"It just means she's dead."
Katrina lifted the headset to her ears. "Harpsichord."
"So what?"
Katrina shrugged and set the earphones daintily in place on the old woman's ears. "So what should we do now?"
"Call the police, like I said." Aaron helped Katrina to her feet and they headed briskly out of the park.

"Dead lady's in the woods," offered Aaron, introducing the subject as neatly as he knew how to the police officer, Nancy Fieldstone.
"Officer Fieldstone, what's going on?" Katrina blurted, her mind racing. "Is it part of the same pattern as the murders in North Andover and Eastridge? Do you think you can catch the serial killer? Do you think he'll stop killing people?"
"Killers don't *reform*, Katrina. They *reformulate*," Officer Fieldstone nonchalantly quoted the man who had influenced the young policewoman most since the death of her own mother at birth: Her father. "I just hope we can anticipate the killer's next move."
Katrina was stumped. What sort of gibberish was that?! *Killers don't reform; they reformulate?!* The high school sophomore had expected the pretty police officer to actually fill them in, give them the scoop. Instead, the kind officer wrapped Katrina and Aaron in heavy green wool blankets that itched, sat them down, and took their report at the edge of Prospect Park. A team of officials went in after the old woman's body. Red ambulance lights flashed intermittently between blue police cruiser lights. *Like Christmas in blue*, thought Katrina, going into shock.
"Looks like someone indulged her in one last, very expensive listening experience," a medic commented as he helped carry the corpse, now encased in a thick plastic body bag.
Katrina strained to listen in on Officer Fieldstone's comments to a detective. A medic gave the portable CD player to Officer Fieldstone who handed it to the detective. Music still whimpered from its twisted earphones.

"Here, Detective Fieldstone, have a listen," said Nancy Fieldstone cordially to her father. He was her boss; she'd agreed to shadow him for one year on one condition: No nepotism. She was far too proud and competent to require his help, or so she thought.

"What the heck kind of music is this?" Detective Fieldstone popped the CD.

"It's one of the Brandenburg Concerti. Classical," she explained, "It's beautiful music if your batteries are good, but these are among the undead."

"Thanks Officer, looks like that liberal arts education of yours is not going to waste fighting a life of crime after all."

"Dad, shut up," whispered Officer Fieldstone, "My colleagues won't respect me if you *go personal* on me." It was obvious they were related; she was the estrogen-enriched younger twin of her father. While she bore no resemblance to her belated mother, she did have her mother's high energy.

"Nepotism makes the world go round, Nancy," Detective Fieldstone whispered back.

"I found this, too, Detective," Officer Fieldstone said loud and clear so her fellow police officers could hear. She held up a battered cassette deck and worn-looking cassette of the Brandenburg Concerti. No one knew yet what to make of the evidence.

In a nearby town a man wrote in his diary. His pen pressed deep into the lined pages of a spiral notebook. His curly script resembled beautiful calligraphy:

Wretched woman. What an awful life she led. But I saved her from all that. Best possible way, too. I'm too tired tonight to go into every detail, but I must extol my own brilliance, immodest tho' I am. Oh, if only there were someone whom I could tell of my brilliance. Someone to appreciate my genius. It all goes unappreciated. This evening was too perfect for words. You see, Dear Diary and Confidant, it was the top-of-the-line portable CD player that did it. All top of the line, highest quality. Except the batteries. I figured she wouldn't need the long-lasting type. The sound on her old cassette deck was abysmal. Oh, yes, but she went out with a smile on her face. Thanks to me. Best customer service ever!

Around midnight Katrina awoke from a deeply troubled sleep. Evil images of bloated blue lips and popping eyes faded like phantoms from her mind as she stumbled sleepily toward her window. Still trembling as her vision focused, she realized that her bedroom window was open and she was reaching her bare arms out the window toward the fluffy limb of the pine tree. Shuddering, she shut the window and briefly considered running down the hall and getting into bed with her mother like when Katrina was little.

What did I dream about? Katrina struggled to grasp the fleeting quicksand dream. The harder she tried to reconstruct it in her memory, the quicker its shards melted away like hot glass in a bottomless swamp. Terror throbbed inside her and rankled her soul. And then she remembered the headset cord and the old woman and her last rasp of breath.

Katrina crept down the hall to her parents' room and slid in next to her mother in the king-size bed. Sleepily, Mrs. Phillips patted her daughter's head and went back to sleep mumbling, "It's okay, dear." Though her father was gone now, Katrina felt safer being with her mother. Even so she lay awake afraid to move. As morning light grayed the master suite, Katrina grew calm enough to let go of her stiffness and drift away into a sweet dram about Aaron.

2

Long shadows striped the floor of the art room in the basement of Westlake High School. At the drafting table two girls finalized the outline for the Halloween dance.

"Last night I had this dream, Correy," confided Katrina softly.

"Tell me the good parts first." Coriander Preston smirked and slid aside a folder marked *HALLOWEEN DANCE PLANS*. "I prefer my dessert before the main course." Coriander giggled and picked up a floor plan of the gymnasium and pretended to study it. Her superlong hair swished against the seat of her chair.

"If you think 'good' means to be scared to death, Correy," said Katrina, envying Coriander's long hair.

Coriander sketched out decorating designs for the Halloween dance as Katrina completed the tally for the dance budget and stuffed the totals sheet into a folder.

"Was it about Miss Chantal?" Coriander laughed. "With classical music?"

"Show some respect for the dead, Correy," groaned Katrina.

"Well, you know, she did spend her life roaming Westlake, listening to that worn-out cassette. I remember even when I was a kid seeing her carry that cracked, taped-together plastic cassette player around on Main Street, clutching it to herself and singing, '*Mine, mine, mine,*' in rhythm to the music."

Katrina groaned again. "That was before headphones."

"And, worse," Coriander continued, "with low batteries. It sounded weirder when I was a kid."

Everyone knew the sound of Miss Chantal on Main Street—That off-kilter noise. Katrina rubbed her face and tried to shed the depressing memory.

"Aaron's dad said Miss Chantal was *his* music teacher when *he* was in high school, that's how *old* she is. That was *before* Miss Chantal went mad." Then, the church had cared for her in the winter, and the quiet streets and waste bins of Westlake in summer, spring, and fall. Katrina stared off. "So sad..."

"Okay, Katrina, you're depressing. Enough Grim Reaper for one day," Coriander advised giddily, "She's deader'n dead, so let's move on... Show me the list."

Katrina removed a list from the Halloween dance folder entitled *GROSS FOOD FOR THE DANCE* and read, "*Roadkill delight–Limburger cheese and tinned skinned tomatoes; worms–pasta salad; coagulated blood–tomato aspic; apple cider–add rubbery candy worms and spiders to each cup; chocolate-covered ants; fried flayed flesh strips–baked cheese strips; bloody eyeball soup–peeled grapes in tomato sauce*. Did I miss anything?"

"Oh yeah," Coriander remembered, "Aaron said at lunch that he told you he wants V8 Juice instead of Marinara sauce for the eyeball soup. Okay? Got any other gross ideas for munchies for the dance, Katie?... Katrina? Hey, are you okay? Are you going to *cry*?

Katrina clicked her adding machine on and off and stared at it, avoiding Coriander's question.

"Katrina, I think that seeing Miss Chantal's body was too much for you. You ought to go see Mr. Breen. Let him shrink your head out of it. You're really sort of a nut case today."

Katrina thought incessantly of Officer Fieldstone's nonsensical comment, *Killers don't reform, they reformulate*. Finally, she forced herself to speak.

"Why would anyone want to kill a harmless old woman?" she asked tremulously.

"Hey, ladies! You forgot candied bats," Aaron said skidding up behind Katrina.

At the sound of Aaron's voice, Katrina wiped her eyes and sniffled. Under Aaron's arm was a poster roll, and he carried the *Westlake–Eastridge Yellow Pages*. He placed it on the drafting table and leaned over to kiss Katrina.

"Hey, gorgeous." Aaron's comforting voice yanked her back to reality. "Nightmares last night?"

Exhausted, Katrina gave a nod. "Yeah, about the dead bag lady."

"Well, I had a dream I was bodysurfing on a human wave around the inside of Foxboro Stadium." He pretended to fly around Katrina's chair. "I guess this means I'm still in shock, huh?"

Katrina wasn't listening.

Aaron tried to divert her attention, picking up the *Yellow Pages*.

"Check this out!" Aaron read from the *Yellow Pages* book, "'*Everything you need for your prom night is provided by our limousine service*,'" that's what the ad says." He pointed at the *Limousine* section of the directory. "I say we rent a limo from *this* company to take us to the Halloween dance. Their '*guaranteed plummy customer service*' will cheer us up."

"I like the sound of *plummy customer service*," replied Coriander.

"Why don't we just drive to the Halloween dance. After all, you painted your Mustang convertible a *plummy* shade of *Midnight Madness*. What better color for a Halloween dance!?"

"My car's been in the shop so much lately, Katrina, I can't count on it for the dance." Aaron repositioned the *Yellow Pages* on the drafting table for Katrina and Coriander to examine and got to work unrolling a poster. "Besides, see what they say in their ad, '*One-stop shopping. Totally personalized.*' Massively convenient!"

"Big advertisement," mused Katrina.

"Wow, a two-page spread!" exclaimed Coriander. They must do all right."

A shiver clawed its way up Katrina's backbone as the slightest autumnal chill kissed the air in the art room. She got up to shut the windows high along the ceiling of the basement classroom.

"So, you get your corsage, boutonniere, and everything through the limo company?" Coriander read. Not that we'll need anything but *dead* flowers for a Halloween dance."

"I bet the owner can get everything we need," confirmed Aaron.

"Costumes?" Katrina cocked an eyebrow.

"Well, no. But it says here, '*music, drinks, snacks, et. cetera*'."

"Sounds too easy." Katrina knitted her brow.

"You can never have it *too* easy." Aaron chuckled smugly.

Coriander glanced up from the *Gross Food* list. "You should know, Aaron. You who never had a summer job, unlike the rest of here us at *Westlake High and Dry School*."

"Oh come on, Correy, my father doesn't pay for *everything*. I'll use my savings to cover the limousine rental."

"Yeah, from your allowance. Brat," Coriander said flirtatiously.

Aaron smiled adorably. "Hey, better rich and bratty than broke and bratty. Plus, I muck the stables for my mom."

Katrina cast a disapproving eye at Coriander and sat down with the *Yellow Pages*.

"Their advertisement says they interview you beforehand to see what you like. They'll even match the color of the car and the flowers to the girl's dress."

"Cool!" Coriander enthused. "You could match your lipstick and nail polish to the dress and the car."

"That sounds tacky, Correy," sneered Katrina.

"Well, Chameleon Limousines it is. Let's '*Call Bob McGhoul for a personalized interview*,'" said Aaron.

"Stupid name!" Coriander read over their shoulder.

"Which? *Chameleon* or *McGhoul*?" asked Katrina.

"Look who's talking, *Coriander Spice Seed Preston.*" Aaron smirked. "I'll call and make an appointment with *Bob*. You and Dan want to go in on it with us? We'll get a giant tacky super stretch limo, and drive around like prom. But scary."

"Sure, why not," said Coriander, packing up her drawings and lists. "If we can get Dan to go. He's so worried about that stupid serial killer that he always leaves my house before dark."

"As if serial killers *only* kill at night!" Katrina laughed.

"Even now that Dan's got his new Honda. He's no fun at all anymore."

"He'll come," Aaron said. "when he sees my poster I drew for the Halloween dance." Aaron taped down its curled edges to the table, his hands speckled with bright poster paints.

Westlake High School
Weird Logic Halloween Dance
Come As You're Not
(Don't come if you must come as you are!)

"Oh, Aaron! It's *purrrrfect,*" Coriander gushed. "For Dan especially."

Katrina shot her a hard glance. Coriander pushed the envelope of decorum with Aaron too often.

"I just adore the way you've combined the reds and yellows to create a real Halloween look." Coriander's effusion persisted like Gorilla Glue, "Exactly the look we're after, Aaron. Just what I envisioned. You read my mind!" Coriander's gaze trained resolutely on Aaron.

"Aaron only reads *my* mind, Corry," snapped Katrina irritably.

"Aaron reads m—"

"How massively surreal that you seem to know a lot about it, Coriander. Have you and Aaron been working *together* on this?"

"I *am* head of the decorating committee," Coriander bit back. "In addition to being Cheerleading Captain *and* Homecoming Queen! And Aaron came up with the concept for the poster. At lunch today. You were unavailable. Remember? At the nurse's office."

"Isn't it a great poster?!" asked Aaron, lost in the crossfire.

"Yes. It's great," Katrina confirmed tersely. "Aaron, everything you draw is great."

"You're so territorial, Katrina, and you know you don't need to be." Coriander's tone softened. "I hate it when you get like that."

"So what'll you go as, Katie?" asked Aaron, purposely changing the subject.

"I don't know. How about a princess? Lady Di," mumbled Katrina. "Poster says '*come as you're not, don't come as you are.*' I don't feel like going as a classy freak from the underworld this year."

"I'll go as an unpopular girl," Coriander decided. "I wonder what that's like."

Katrina and Aaron glanced at each other; Katrina's top lip curled involuntarily.

"And me, I'll go as Dracula, I guess. I don't know what else to go as," Aaron said.

"Well, maybe in the meantime we can come up with something else for you, Aaron. We've got time," said Coriander with a knowing smile.

"No, Correy, he can go as Dracula if he wants to," Katrina said insipiently.

"Whatever you say, Katrina. You're the queen," Aaron reassured her with a bright smile.

"What about me, Aaron?" Coriander pouted. "I'm queen, too!"

"Uhh, I guess," Aaron stammered. "but you'd have to get a dress to match Katrina's."

Katrina glowered again at Correy's open flirtation.

"Poacher," muttered Katrina.

"Wear something dishy, with cleavage." Coriander insisted, attempting to jar Katrina out of her little mood. Katrina rolled her eyes. Coriander giggled. "C'mon, Katrina. We'll check out the fabric store for costume cloth. My mother's an awesome seamstress. Remember, she did those alterations on my cheerleading uniform. You know how well *that* fits me."

"The whole school knows," teased Aaron.

Katrina shot him a look.

"We'll go tomorrow. I don't have cheerleading. And then the four of can go to Mr. McGhoul's Chameleon Limousines. Deal?"

3

Before dark that day, Bob McGhoul test-drove a new limousine. He had driven past the little girl's sign earlier:

50 cents for a cup of lemonade.

Only half a dollar!

So, he circled back to check out her customer service. Along the rural road, the little girl with the long braids guarded her lemonade stand. She had taken great care to position it just over the embankment so that drivers would see her sign. But the high embankment in front of her home put her house out of sight from the road. Her nearest neighbor was a quarter mile away.

The large red arrow on her sign brought the stretch limousine directly to her.

At last, a customer, she thought. *Should I say "May I help you?" or "What would you care for today?"* Her little palms sweated.

Dark tinted glass dropped away silently into the gray door, revealing a man's smiling face. A ponytail stuck out the back of his head. He dangled a one-dollar bill out his open window.

Better yet, thought the little girl, *he's a nice man who can obviously afford to shop here.* She beamed at him and shyly flipped one braid through the other, making a half knot over her flat chest. A golden autumn leaf swished in her button face and she swatted it away.

"Mighty late in the season to be enterprising with lemonade," said the man pleasantly. "I hear the weather's going to turn real soon." He squinted against a setting sun.

Her throat went dry with excitement. "People still drink lemonade." She was adamant, then conceded, "Even though no one's stopped today. Till you."

"Fifty cents? Prices have gone up since I had a lemonade stand. I was about your age. You nine? Ten?"

"Almost ten," she affirmed. "Well, nine and three fifths, actually. My big brother Dan helps me with fractions. I'm ahead of my class in math. But not Social Studies."

Smiling, Bob McGhoul opened his door and got out of the limousine, leaving the door wide open. By force of habit, he hit the power-lock button on the console inside the driver's-side door. All the doors bolted instantly with no more than a soft click.

The driver's door of the limousine hung open invitingly to a plush velvet interior that seemed to beckon the little girl. She wondered what it would be like to jump on the big seats and pet the smooth gray velvet. But she would have to move that bright red gym bag off the front seat and out of her way first.

Although he was not a huge man, Bob McGhoul towered over Josephine. When she noticed him watching her, Josephine took a step back. So, McGhoul leaned back against the rear door of the car and smiled reassuringly.

"So?" He grinned, creasing, and re-creasing the one-dollar bill held in his immaculate fingertips.

"Would you like to buy a cup of lemonade?" she asked hopefully.

"Sure, I'll take one."

The little girl went behind the stand and plucked a colorful paper Dixie Cup from a stack. She glanced up at the man, who still squinted against the sun.

"Why don't you wear sunglasses?" she asked.

"I like people to see my eyes, so they know I'm an honest man." He had not paused to think of the answer, so she believed him instantly.

Awkwardly, the nine-year-old poured lemonade from a large, heavy pitcher into the cup.

"Perfect. You didn't spill a drop," McGhoul said admiringly.

"I'm very good at what I do!" Proudly she offered up the cup to him.

As McGhoul sipped, Josephine glanced again inside the limousine. Its interior was so plush. *Like clouds*, she thought, *but that bulky red gym bag takes up too much space.*

McGhoul regarded the child intently. "Perfect customer service, young lady. Customer service! It'll make or break you in business."

"That'll be fifty cents, please." She smiled proudly, bobbing heel-toe, heel-toe.

"Okay." He dangled the one-dollar bill above her head. She reached for the dollar, but he did not release his grasp on the payment. For a few long, awkward seconds they both gripped the one-dollar bill. The little girl looked quizzically at him.

"Young lady, perfect customer service includes providing exact change." His friendly indignance caught her off guard. "What if you were to run off with my dollar? Presumably, *this* is your house? Exact change first, please."

Her expression changed to one of insecurity. "I'll have to check in my coin box." She released the greenback and darted under his arm, glancing inside the car at the red gym bag as she headed back to her table. She opened her makeshift cash box.

Josephine's bottom lip trembled as she realized she had no small change to give the man. He had already sipped away most of the lemonade in his paper cup. She couldn't very well ask for it back. Yet she absolutely did not want to give it away free.

"I haven't got any change," she admitted, ashamed, and a renegade tear crept down her pudgy little cheek.

"No change? Well... we can remedy that."

"We *can*?" Hopeful again, Josephine wiped away her tears.

"Sure. Come here." His kind smile coaxed her nearer to the open car door. Then Bob McGhoul's lips curled into a supercilious grin. "I always had exact change for my customers when I had a lemonade stand. This is an important lesson for you, young lady. Are you ready to learn it?"

She demurred at the reprimand. "Yes."

She watched him toss the last of the lemonade down his throat. He creased the paper cup with his fingernails. A stray drop soiled his fingers, and he wiped them on the little girl's white shirt collar. Bewildered, she waited for him to advise her on business. Another brilliant autumn leaf hung in the air between them, then tipped and fell precipitously to the ground.

Out of the corner of his eye, Bob McGhoul noticed a skinny teenage boy with a black mop of hair and gold wire-rim glasses lurching down over the lawn embankment toward the road.

"Josephine!" the teenage boy hollered. "Come get washed up for dinner!"

"Your brother the math whiz?"

"Yes. That's Danny. Just a minute, Danny!" Josephine Pritcher yelled back.

McGhoul tossed the paper cup onto the floor of his limousine and gently pushed the little girl out of his way. He got into the limousine and shut the door. He shifted into drive. All his moves were calm.

Josephine grew petulant. "You can't leave without paying me!"

"Oh, that's right. For the little entrepreneur who hasn't got exact change, here is half a dollar." McGhoul pointed at her sign. "It does say '*only half a dollar*.'"

He made a crease with his fingernails and tore the one-dollar bill in two. Josephine bit her pouting lip in disbelief as her profits were ripped up. The man pressed one half of the dollar bill into Josephine's palm.

As Dan Pritcher neared the lemonade stand, Bob McGhoul accelerated gently and drove away, patting the bright red gym bag lovingly.

"That'll teach her to improve her customer service," he murmured. His right hand reached into the red bag to caress its contents. "Ha! She'll never make that mistake again. It's a thankless job I do teaching others about customer service."

Humiliated, Josephine Pritcher shoved the half dollar bill into the pocket of her blue jeans and forced herself not to cry.

"Any sales today, Josie?" Dan asked.

Her sad voice betrayed the lump in her throat.

"Nah. That guy just wanted directions." Josephine hid her sniffles by pouring lemonade on the ground.

4

WELCOME TO BOB McGHOUL'S CHAMELEON LIMOUSINES blinked in multicolored rainbows of fluorescent light over a metal door with many locks and no windows.

Aaron rechecked his Swatch. "The guy said come at three thirty p.m."

"Well, it looks like he doesn't want anyone coming in his showroom when he's not there. Three, four, *five* locks!" Katrina counted. "Six, *seven*, holy cow! For what? To keep the limos from escaping?"

"To keep the dog from escaping!" Aaron yelped as he jumped away from the fence.

Next to the cinder block office building, a snarling Doberman faced them behind the chain-link. The property was encircled by the unsightly metal mesh crowned with razor wire.

"Quiet down, Cupcake," cooed Dan Pritcher, approaching the frothing canine. "I'm good with animals, so no worries, Correy." The Doberman charged the fence, fangs catching on metal. Dan leapt back. "Or, do whatever you please, big guy, as long as you do it on *that* side of the fence."

Coriander grabbed Dan's sleeve and tugged him toward the parking lot. "Danny, maybe we should stay away. This place gives me the creeps. Most car dealerships have a front window showcasing their amazing cars. This place is sealed up like a vault!"

"That *was* my idea, as I recall," said Dan. "It's safer to stay at home with the doors locked in this climate of serial killers."

Aaron pointed indiscreetly at a shadowed security camera mounted under the multicolored awning. "Guys, I definitely get the feeling we're being watched."

The four friends glanced at one another.

"Want to leave?" asked Dan.

"Guess so," said Aaron.

Shivering, Katrina kicked the door and leaned deliberately on the buzzer, then shouted into the camera, "I think it's pretty rude to get us all the way out here and make us wait outside in the cold!"

Aaron took her hand. "Katrina, cool it." They started back toward Aaron's black Mustang convertible. A sudden clunk and click of latches and bolts brought their attention back to the door.

"Kids, hold on!" cried a muffled voice through the heavy door. Finally it swung open. A good-looking man in his early forties with brown hair past his collar smiled at them.

Katrina was mortified and hoped he had not seen her bad behavior on the monitor.

"Hi, kids. Sorry about that. Come on in! Ten minutes over schedule. I was down back changing the tires on one of my cars. Sorry. I'm really, really sorry."

The good-looking man did a double take and stared at Katrina's face. He gawked for an impolite length of time before his smooth composure returned. After that, the man avoided looking at Katrina altogether. To Katrina, he seemed distracted.

"What was that all about?" Coriander whispered, jealous her own good looks had not received a second glance from the strapping gentleman. Katrina shrugged.

He had to have seen the fit I threw on the monitor. Katrina was embarrassed all over again.

"It must take you a long time to get the grease off your hands," Katrina offered, attempting to make amends. She noticed the man's hands were immaculate and perfectly manicured: not a trace of grease under the nails. He followed her gaze. "I mean, in your business... Sorry," Katrina mumbled. "never mind."

"That's okay. I didn't think you were being fresh. In my business you've got to keep your hands clean to keep the customers happy. I'm the owner, mechanic, salesman, and the main driver. So I wear these to keep the gunk off'em."

Bob McGhoul held up a pair of slick, soiled rubber surgery gloves for all to see. "I buy'em by the double dozen, boxed. They're disposable."

"Surgical gloves," remarked Dan. "Used by the medical profession."

"And criminals." The remark escaped Katrina's mouth.

Bob McGhoul smiled, forcing his gaze away from Katrina. "Come on inside, kids, and we'll go in the back where it's more comfortable. I'll show you the cars and we'll talk." The man gestured, waiving the four friends past him into the building. Aaron led the way.

"Nice guy," Aaron said. Dan nodded and pushed his glasses up on his narrow nose.

"I'll just lock up so we won't be disturbed," McGhoul said, tripping deadbolts with practiced ease.

"Do you get a lot of walk-ins, Mr. McGhoul?" Katrina scrutinized him, trying to catch his eye again. Fleetingly he met her gaze. Nodded. Smiled shyly. Then quickly averted his eyes again.

"I keep my cash register out here in that front room by the door, so you never know. Now, Young People, please, sit, enjoy some crackers with *pâté*. And we'll get started."

The four teenagers stared at the crackers and *pâté*.

"Go on, help yourselves. It's delicious," assured Bob McGhoul demonstrating by smearing a cracker with a knife-load of the grayish paste from a small jar on the coffee table. "Delicious!" he declared. "I can't go one single day without this excellent, excellent *pâté*!" McGhoul stuffed another heavily-laden cracker into his mouth. Politely, each teen palmed a cracker, but no one touched the *pâté*. "It's brain food. Makes you smarter!" Still no takers. "That's okay, um, I understand it's an acquired taste. Home-made, though, if you're feeling adventuresome... Or n*ot*..."

Relieving them of the awkwardness, a huge bearded man wearing amber-tinted glasses lumbered in from the back office eating an oversize candy bar and carrying a box of them under his arm.

"Mr. McGhoul, the students might prefer a candy bar instead of *adult food*." The bulky man's cumbrous feet scuffed the floor as he approached the teens. "*Aaaaggghhh!*" he wailed as he tripped on a bright red gym bag on the floor near a settee, scattering candy bars. The teenagers tried not to laugh, and scurried to help gather up the fallen sweets.

"He's like Paul Bunyan," whispered Katrina.

"Eat as many as you like." The large man recovered his balance. "I got a case." His words were muffled by a chocolate-coated tongue as he continued to chew. The students barely understood him.

They stared; no one but Aaron accepted the giant's imposing invitation. Although his eyes were virtually obscured by the amber lenses, Katrina could see he looked at her—intensely. That gave her the creeps.

What, is my face falling off today? she thought. *Maybe both of these dudes saw that movie last year.*

"Young People, this is Paul Reed, my night watchman," Bob McGhoul explained, and reached his hand into the box of oversize chocolate bars. "And, in addition to being a phenomenal chef..." McGhoul indicated the *pâté*. "...and host, Paul helps me with the cars, as well. Thanks for the snacks, Paul."

"You want me to put this gym bag away for you?" Paul offered nonchalantly.

"No, thank you," said McGhoul abruptly, turning his attention back to the teenagers.

"So no one else trips."

"No."

"Are you sure, Mr. McGhoul?" asked Paul, nevertheless reaching down to pick up the red gym bag. "I'd be more than happy to put it away for you, sir. You know, to kind of clean up around here."

"No, *really*, Paul, that's all right, I'll get it." Hastily, McGhoul recovered the large red bag from Paul's grip and stowed it under an official-looking desk. "Thank you, Paul. What you *could* do to be helpful is quickly dispose of any trash in the limousines before I give these young people a tour of the showroom."

Paul nodded and left through another office door that clicked shut behind him.

McGhoul looked chagrined. "Sorry, guys. I let Paul live here. Out back in the shed. He's sort of a loner. No family, I guess. I felt sorry for him. He does odd jobs for me. Very helpful guy, and thorough. Cleans up the place." McGhoul downed another cracker with *pâté* and immediately prepared another for himself. "Can't let this manna go to waste! Paul makes it fresh. He understands customer service, which as you know is really important to my business. Don't let him scare you off, okay, he's harmless. Nice guy, polite. So? Introductions?"

By then, the four teenagers had cast knowing glances at each other, like, let's get on with it.

"I'm Aaron. This is my best friend." Aaron pointed at Dan and continued to gnaw happily on a gargantuan chocolate bar.

"Dan Pritcher," Dan said as he extended his skinny hand to McGhoul. "My girlfriend, Coriander Preston..."

Coriander swished her super-long hair back and smiled charismatically and offered McGhoul her hand to shake. "I'm the cheerleading captain, and I was Homecoming Queen."

But Bob McGhoul did not shake Coriander's hand. His attention was elsewhere.

"But we call her Correy because it's just too weird to name someone after a spice seed." Aaron laughed. Coriander made a face at Aaron.

"And *this* is...?" asked McGhoul indicating Katrina.

"*Oh*. My girlfriend, Katrina Phillips." Aaron hugged her as she lifted a warning eyebrow at him for having neglected to introduce her in the first place.

McGhoul laughed, noting her reaction. "She's going to be a tough customer to please, I can tell. But I love a challenge. People so often settle for less, and that gets *pretty* boring for a man of my perfectionism. This'll be a refreshing change. Customer service is my forte."

"Great. This is gonna be fun," declared Aaron.

"I love providing service to teenagers especially. Prom's my favorite season. Here, have a seat. Sodas are in the mini fridge. Help yourself."

Plush gray velvet sofas looked inviting, like a good car seat. The essence of freshly sprayed Scotchgard hung in the room.

"And speaking of unusual names," he said, sitting at his desk, "mine's pronounced *McFoul*. The *g-h* in McGhoul is like the *g-h in 'enough.'"*

"*McFoul*?" Aaron was surprised.

"Dutch-Irish?" Dan surmised.

"I thought it was *McGhoooul*, like 'ghouls and goblins.'" Coriander laughed with a syrupy surplus of gaiety.

"Nope. It's *McF-o-w-l*, like chickens and ducks, or like Shakespeare's conundrum, *Fair is foul and foul is fair*."

"Guy quotes Shakespeare." Dan nodded approvingly at the literary reference. When he did so, his glasses slid down again.

"Well, that's just grand. Now let me show you my business."

The teenagers looked around at the glossy posters of elegant Porsches, Bentleys, Daimlers, Cadillacs, Rolls-Royce Corniches and Phantoms, Jaguars, Lincoln Continentals, and one breath-taking Mercedes Benz that adorned the clean white walls. Signed photo portraits of famous sports figures, actors, and politicians were hung prominently too. Some of them read, *To Bob, Thanks for the ride. With much appreciation*, or *Bob, you're the best driver ever. Kisses...*

"Do you know all these people?" Dan asked.

"Sure I do. They're my customers," McGhoul responded proudly.

Coriander was impressed. "Wow!"

On McGhoul's wall-of-fame, one black-and-white photograph, a Polaroid of a beautiful young woman, hung among the car posters and the glossy head shots. Unlike the other, formal photos, it was unsigned. Aaron stole a few glances at the pretty face, but was careful not to seem too obvious. Katrina might get jealous again.

"The posters are *nothing*. Wait till you see *this*." Bob pulled a cord and drew back a curtain to reveal black plate glass; beyond it, fluorescent lights flickered on in the vast showroom where every imaginable limousine came into view.

"Wow. Car Disneyland! Are all these yours?" marveled Aaron.

"Yep. We'll go out to the showroom in a little while and I'll show'em to you, each and every sexy car body.

"Hey, man, you're like a kid running a candy shop," Aaron noted.

"Limousines are my favorite hobby and my lifeblood."

"Your lifeblood?" Dan questioned, pushing his black hair out of his eyes and adjusting his glasses.

"They're my life. They sustain me. Limos and the customer service that goes with'em. I give the best possible customer service at any expense. If it weren't for my limousine business, heck, I'd be just another *schmo* loser."

"What's this over here?" Coriander wandered across to the far wall of McGhoul's tony office.

She studied a wall chart that looked like an endless semester schedule. The long chart was printed on Dot Matrix paper.

"I'm a real chart man," replied Bob affably, "And that, young lady, *that* is my preference chart. I'm big on spreadsheets. Love my Lotus! Never was one for taking notes, even in school." McGhoul silenced his nattering only with periodic bites of *pâté* cracker. "And letter writing, *forget it!* The more succinct, the better. Leaves me more time to devote to giving great customer service."

"So what does this chart actually *do*?"

"It gives a detailed account of who likes what," said McGhoul excitedly "What colors, sizes, shapes. What you like to eat and drink, what music you like to listen to. Every detail you tell me about yourself goes into a Macro and then onto a chart like that one. *Bingo, presto*, press one button and my computer just spits it out."

"What for?"

"Raw marketing data. It's a goldmine. Strictly about people who use limos. It has great value. Especially about young people. So I can create a long life for my business. Someday people will figure out how to drill and mine this data. Someday..." He trailed off realizing that the teenagers stared blankly at him. "Repeat customers, that's the name-of-the-game. Chances are, if you use my service now for a prom—or in your case, for your Halloween dance—when you get married, you'll come back to me for chauffeur service. Or you'll want me to be the designated driver whey you're old enough to trash yourselves on New Year's." McGhoul laughed at his own bad joke and bit zealously into another savory *pâté* cracker. "Or, for the cortege at your funeral."

"Okay! Got it," said Coriander. She'd moved on.

"So let me ask you to answer a few questions about yourselves, if each of you wouldn't mind filling out my scientifically-designed *Youth Preference Questionnaire*." Bob McGhoul handed a sheet to each. "And here's a big old pen you can keep. It's got my company logo on it."

Aaron examined the tiny illustration of a thorny reptile that dotted the *i's* in the word *Limousine* on the pen. And its long, spikey tail curled to form the letter "*C*" in *Chameleon*. As he filled in his name and address across the top of the questionnaire, he wiped the nib of the pen where a blob of black ink kept beading up.

"Cheap pens," the fine artist in Aaron commented to Dan.

Dan wiped the blobby nib of his own pen and examined the chameleon logo.

"Aaron," whispered Dan, "Do you recall in Social Studies class when we were reading about the Masai warriors in Kenya? The tribe that drinks cattle blood..."

"No."

"Well, to the Masai tribe the *chameleon* is the sign of death," Dan whispered, and he made mock-scary eyes at Aaron.

"Wooo," snarked Aaron and returned to gnawing on his pen as he read over the questions. "Let's see, my favorite entertainment personality? Joe Bob Briggs!"

"Who's that?" Dan asked.

"You wouldn't know him, since you don't like horror movies."

Dan had a flicker of recognition. "Oh yes, he's a social satirist who rates horror movies by how many heads roll."

"I'm impressed *you* know that." Aaron kept writing.

"Dan, do you always have to be such a geek?" Katrina asked. Dan gave her a snotty look.

"Please be sure to fill in the part about your favorite songs, so we can play them while we're driving around... *cruising*."

"You call this *scientific*?" Katrina muttered, "This is none of his business, Aaron, the stuff on here." Katrina said it just loud enough for McGhoul to hear. "Height, weight, and home address?! Why does he need to know my *weight*? I'm not filling it out!" Blushing, she folded her arms over her chest and slumped sullenly in her chair.

"Oh, Katrina, like you really need to worry about 'filling out' *anything*," Aaron attempted a compliment.

"I thought you got over your anorexia last spring, Katrina," Coriander needled her.

"Yeah, quit worrying about your body, Katie," Aaron blundered further into a derailed compliment, "Without it you'd be nothing." Aaron paused and thought for a moment then noticed Katrina's look of disdain. "I mean—I didn't mean it *that* way, Katie. I—"

"It's better if you fill it out," McGhoul interjected hopefully. "That way you'll get the best service possible. That's what my business is all about, individualized, personalized customer service. Plus it's for the future. There's no telling whether you and Aaron will still be together in a few years, say when you use the service for your wedding. And I'd sure hate to lose you as my customer," he mewled.

Embarrassed, Katrina stared at the page littered with questions. With her blobby *Chameleon Limousines* pen she filled in blanks as if it were a PSAT.

"And the address?" Dan asked, blinking behind his wire-rims.

"The address," began McGhoul, "is so I know where to fetch-and-step, *and* send the bill. And, I need to know whom to contact in the unlikely case of an emergency."

"Where to send the body," noted Aaron jokingly.

Dan grimaced and kept on writing.

"Say, Mr. McGhoul, is that a famous person?" Aaron asked casually, glancing again at the black-and-white Polaroid photograph on the wall. "She looks kinda like Katrina. Don't you think? Sort of. Hey, Katrina, maybe you guys're related?"

Dan, Coriander, and Katrina stared at the snapshot and made halfhearted noises of agreement.

"Hard to say, it's not a great photo," said Coriander about the pretty woman in the vintage 1960's photo.

"Famous person? Oh, that's my high school sweetheart. I graduated some decades ago. Now whenever you're ready, I'll take the questionnaires and we'll head out to the showroom."

"What happened to her?" asked Aaron, making conversation instead of chewing on the *Chameleon* pen.

"To whom?" Bob McGhoul asked.

"Did you marry her?" Aaron mused impishly, "Is she *Mrs. McGhoul*?"

Reverently, Bob McGhoul bowed his head and appeared forlorn.

"Brenda." He sighed then was quiet for a long, uncomfortable moment before he answered, "Brenda Caughin... died. Was murdered. On our prom night. Never caught the perp. Never found her remains. Only some of her clothes."

Aaron wished he had not asked McGhoul about Brenda Caughin. Deep down he thought it was funny her name sounded like *coffin*. To relieve his discomfort, Aaron was dying to laugh. Yet, he resisted what would have appeared a tawdry outburst given that the man had lost his loved one. *I must still be in shock from seeing Miss Chantal's dead body,* thought Aaron, *Poor Mr. McGhoul.*

5

At 3:30 p.m., Officer Nancy Fieldstone's Westlake beat took her to the Eastridge Bluff where she had not been since the previous night. By day, her favorite dense thicket did not cloak her as well as it often had by night, but she took the chance no licensed high schoolers would show up that early at the cliffs to make out. And the potheads hung out mostly under the covered bridge. Leaving her police cruiser in the parking lot, she sneaked into the bushes to relieve herself.

What the heck is this? she wondered when, in the underbrush, she happened to notice a wad of stuff. *A bag person must've camped out up here last night.*

Fieldstone kicked at a pile of trash and old clothes considering how her father the respected Detective Fieldstone would analyze this evidence. A brightly colored paper Dixie Cup creased exactly down the middle clung to her polished black leather shoe. She shook it off. A creased wrapper from a jumbo candy bar fluttered out of sight, as Officer Fieldstone picked up a badly soiled taffeta party dress. It appeared to be discolored by five dark brown blotches. She spread it on the ground.

Blood!?

Next to it, she shook out a black tuxedo, trousers, and a once-white dress shirt. Neither shoes nor undergarments appeared in the mix.

"*H-holy cow! M-matching* stab wounds!" The young officer glanced furtively around as she scooped up the clothing. *That prom couple last spring could not have run off and eloped, that's for sure—not with these knife holes in their clothes.*

She dropped the moldy heap and raced toward her cruiser, but then she stopped. Pacing, she considered what her father, the detective would do. When she regained her nerve, she retraced her steps to the decaying armful of fabric and placed it in the trunk of her cruiser. Then she floored it for the Westlake Police Department. *What's the connection? What's the connection to the other murders?* Nancy Fieldstone wondered. Had the nubie Officer not been so nervous when she stashed the bundle of wet fabric in her trunk, she might have examined the bloodstains more carefully. But she was over-eager to get back and show her father.

That night Westlake reporters broke the news confirming the bloody slaughter of the missing prom teens. The national wire services picked it up, and every town in the entire country heard the whole brutal story.

"This could scare the murderer out of hiding," Detective Fieldstone praised his daughter's work as they watched the news report over TV dinners, "Great job, Nancy!"

"You mean now that the serial killer knows we're hot on his tracks, we just wait for him to screw up, Dad?"

"Just one little blunder, pal, that's all we need," affirmed Detective Fieldstone.

6

Seldom impressed, Coriander exclaimed with heartfelt excitement, "Big banner!"

"And quite a commitment!" Dan noted.

Above the cars in the showroom of Chameleon Limousines a huge banner hung from the high ceiling. In the still air neon green tassels dangled from the lower hem.

Bob McGhoul of
Chameleon Limousines says,
"I'll give you the best
Customer service even
if it kills me."

"Yes, well, Paul Reed had that banner done up for me. He knows how much I value my customers." Bob McGhoul said as he led the teenagers toward the limousines. "Thoughtful guy. Thinks of everything. Good employee."

McGhoul opened the trunk of a shapely hunter green Daimler.

"So, you said everything we need for prom night is in the trunk?" Aaron asked. McGhoul smiled reassuringly.

"How much is all this going to cost us?" asked Dan.

"Depends on the car and how many hours we're out. I do ask for a fifty-percent deposit up front based on my estimate. That I'll give you in writing."

"Are all these classic cars?"

"Yes, everything on this side of the showroom is over forty years old, or based on an older design, like the Phantom. It's a new fiberglass model of the old Rolls-Royce Phantom."

"And those're all new ones?"

"Yes, the stretch limousines became popular later. Especially for the bigger basketball players. Not much leg room for those mutants in the older models."

"You rent to Celtics players? asked Aaron. Bob nodded. "Cool!"

"I service all the major New England cities. I get sports types, suits, you name it. Part-time drivers do some of the runs for me if I'm booked up with my most important customers."

"Hey, Aaron, there's a summer job for you," suggested Coriander. "Get you outta the barn."

"I require all my drivers to be twenty-one or older, with a clean record."

A set of four small tires stacked behind a white Jaguar caught Aaron's eye.

"Those don't fit on any of these cars, do they? They're so small."

"Good eye," McGhoul praised. "Those tires are spares for a little economy car I let Paul use for errands."

"What kind?" asked Dan.

"Honda Civic."

"Like mine," said Dan.

"I like to drive the Civic around town, too," McGhoul explained further. "Easier to park. It lets me blend in with my surroundings, you know, and not be flashy driving my limos around town!"

"Like a chameleon," observed Dan. "You blend in."

"Very good," said McGhoul approvingly. "Very observant."

Katrina drifted away from the group to look at the newer limousines on the far side of the showroom. Some of the luxurious vehicles seated as many as twelve people, others as few as four. The interiors gleamed with chrome and polished hardwood, dark leather and velvet.

"Say, what's in here?" Katrina opened the side door of the showroom.

"Hey, don't open that!" McGhoul yelled as the steel door swung shut behind Katrina and she disappeared.

McGhoul blanched.

"What's the matter?" Aaron asked as McGhoul sped across the showroom floor to the door at the far end.

"He looks worried as hell," remarked Aaron following him. "What's in there? What's wrong?" Aaron demanded, but received no answer. Dan and Coriander trailed them to the steel door.

The door dumped Katrina out back in the courtyard whose chain link fence was topped with Concertina wire. The cool autumn air refreshed her after breathing the scent of Scotchgard inside Chameleon Limousines. Late afternoon sun blinded her—squinting, disoriented.

Seems perfectly fine out here to me, thought Katrina. *I wonder why he said not to open the door. He's probably a heat miser, like Dad was.*

The sun's long rays were suddenly eclipsed by the lunging Doberman. Falling backward, Katrina screamed as the snapping jaws came within inches of her face.

"Halt, Iris!" Paul Reed commanded. His eyes were steely behind the amber-tinted glasses. Reed's large fist nimbly snatched the ferocious dog out of the air mid-leap. For such a big man, it was astounding how swiftly Paul could move. Katrina had not seen him come from *anywhere*; he was just suddenly *there.*

And, with that, Paul had saved Katrina's life.

The Doberman's snarl waned to a whimper. Paul set the dog down gently but did not release his grip on the loose skin of its neck. Still, the Doberman stood guard, never removing its gaze from Katrina.

The bearded man spoke sternly, "That's no way to treat a customer, now is it, Iris!" Paul Reed petted her snout. "Lie down!" Iris obeyed.

Katrina was still shaking when Bob McGhoul and her friends emerged from the showroom.

"You okay, Katrina!?"

"She's fine," Paul reassured them. "Sorry about Iris. She's a killing machine."

"He's sure proud of his dog," Aaron whispered as he hugged Katrina.

"I'll say," blubbered Katrina as she stood wobbly-legged.

"The training Iris received made her that way," Paul Reed explained. "If only I'd gotten her when she was a sweet pup. She's a rescue. Through her training she became *this.* Full of hatred and stealth. Apparently she was beaten and taunted into being a savage protector."

Coriander rolled her eyes. "Can we go now? I have to get to cheerleading practice... *Priorities*!"

Paul paid Coriander no mind. "Iris and I are a lot alike." Paul kissed the dog's face. Iris licked Paul briefly. It seemed to nearly break Paul's face to smile.

Coriander grimaced and a volley of glances shot among the others.

"Paul, did you have an opportunity to clean out all of the cars yet?" McGhoul asked cautiously.

Ignoring his boss, Paul Reed just kept petting the Doberman. All eyes on Paul, he finally spoke. "Yeah, I did it this morning," Paul muttered testily, avoiding eye contact with Bob McGhoul.

7

When Katrina arrived home from the Chameleon Limousines interview, she found a note Mrs. Phillips had left for her:
Gone Grocery Shopping. I love you, Mom.

Aaron stayed briefly for a snack, but he had to leave to get his Mustang repaired again. He kissed Katrina good-bye and waved as he started his engine.

"Your car sounds awful, Aaron," Katrina yelled as he backed down the Phillips's driveway.

He shouted over the Mustang's throaty rattle. "You sure you'll be okay alone till your mother gets home?"

"Oh, sure, I'm fine now. Really. I'm just overtired."

Katrina waved him away and trotted up the front porch steps. The screen door swatted shut and she closed the heavy beveled glass front door, watching Aaron drive off. She did not bother to lock up; her mother would be home soon from work. Her father had been gone about four months now. She stood alone in the rambling old Victorian front hall, then ambled back to the kitchen to forage.

As usual her mother had forgotten her shopping list on the counter by the wall phone. The local newspaper lay next to it. She grabbed a tall glass of Gatorade and wandered into the dining room, sipping. Beside the empty cracker bowl she and Aaron had shared, Katrina's Advanced Composition class homework lay strewn on the dining table. "*Know Yourself*" was the title Mr. Stroud had assigned for this week's essay. Katrina scribbled another paragraph in pencil, erased two sentences, rewrote them, and got up to refill her Cheez-It supply thinking, *My sheet of paper looks like a battlefield of Number 2 pencil lead and eraser rubber.* The double-hinged door between kitchen and dining room swung behind her like a loud paddle, spanking back and forth at the same time that the click of the front door blended in with ambient noise. Katrina did not hear the front door open.

Guess that's the last of the Cheez-It box. Bummed, she shook orange dust from the box into her bowl, wet her finger and licked it. She rooted around in the cupboard for another treat. A box of shortbreads caught her eye. As she set it on the counter, she noticed the newspaper next to her mother's forgotten shopping list. Katrina scanned the article about the late Miss Chantal. Then she gasped as she noticed a shorter column about Mr. Samson, the Triborough Cinema owner. His daughter, Patty Samson was in Katrina's Advanced Composition class, a senior this year, whom Katrina did not know well. But Katrina had always envied Patty. *She gets to see all the horror movies free.* But today, Katrina felt sorry for Patty.

The article said that Patty's father had been found dead in his own theater positioned with a jumbo tub of popcorn and a King Cola cup in his lap. Mr. Samson was a workaholic, according to his ex-wife, the article said. *What an undignified description,* thought Katrina. *A jumbo tub, King Cola, and a workaholic.*

She read further. A few theater-size candy bars were found tucked between his seat and the armrest. At first she couldn't imagine what was meant by "theater-size," but then she recalled the huge ones displayed in the glass cases at the fancy Triborough Cinema. The article said Mr. Samson died happy because he had a big smile on his face when they found him. *Cause of death: asphyxiation.* Apparently he suffocated on a mouthful of popcorn while watching a favorite movie. Katrina wondered if the two deaths were somehow related, Mr. Samson and Miss Chantal, both so close together, both asphyxiated. The hair on the back of Katrina's neck prickled; she presumed this was in response to the newspaper article. Katrina's instincts were clamoring to be heard; she ignored them.

Deep in thought, Katrina leaned against the wall by the magnetic knife rack that was bolted between the stove and the refrigerator. It displayed an array of knives of different lengths and widths, some serrated, others thin—all potentially dangerous, in the wrong hands. Katrina closed her eyes, pondering the sad news. As she did so, a man's eye peeked at her through the kitchen doorjamb gap. The man watched as her eyes fluttered open again and she turned to the kitchen counter. He watched as Katrina's pretty hand reach for one of the knives. He held his breath, watching, as she slit open the box of shortbreads.

She doesn't want to ruin her manicure, he thought.

When Katrina returned to the dining room through the swinging paddle door carrying a glass of juice and shortbreads, the autumn chill breezed in from the foyer. Katrina shivered. As she set down her comestibles on the dining table beside her homework, the man scuttled silently into the kitchen through the second door down the hall.

I'm sure I shut the front door. Puzzled, she padded down the hall to the front door. It stood open. She glanced outside at the trees that swayed in the wind.

I must not have latched it. She shut the door tightly against the breeze and tripped the dead bolt.

Katrina went back down the hall to the dining room where she resumed her homework at the table, poring over her "*Know Yourself*" essay draft. She started from the top to recapture her flow. As she nibbled at her snack, she held her pencil poised to write, but...

That's weird. Katrina stared at her "*Know Yourself*" essay and read aloud the last sentence on the page, which was written in black ballpoint pen: "*I know you better than you know.*" The handwriting matched Katrina's. She did a double-take. *I didn't write that.*

Katrina looked up to confirm that she was still alone. She tried to erase the ink with her pencil eraser, sighing when the thickly beaded black goo smudged a gash across the page. She would have to rewrite the entire essay. The Chameleon Limousines pen she had been given lay in her pencil case where she had placed it earlier. Yet she had written the rest of her essay draft in pencil.

"Aaron, you write the weirdest love notes!" She shouted, assuming he had let himself back in. "Nice attempt at forging my handwriting! Such an artist." Aaron did not reply. "Come out, come out wherever you are!" Katrina bent to look under the long tablecloth. "Aaron?" Aaron was not under the table. And he was not crouched down next to the sideboard. She searched. "I didn't even hear you come in, Aaron."

A floorboard creaked in the hallway. Across the hall, she leapt onto the couch in the parlor and shook the heavy curtains. There were no shoes below the drapes. She peaked behind the TV console.

By that time, the man had scoped out the kitchen. In case Aaron *had* actually returned, the man decided to leave. *If I stay, it'll probably scare the girl too much.* He did not want that. No. Girls did foolish things when they became scared–*all that screaming and thrashing!* He might have to kill her if she did. A wave of ambivalence then nostalgia overcame him. *But if I stay...,* he deliberated, *this could be our house together.*

"Aaron?" Again, Katrina hollered sweetly as she attempted to discover his hiding spot. "You do realize this means I have to rewrite that *entire* essay–thanks very much for wasting my time!"

Again, she heard the front door. *Unmistakably* the front door. She whirled around and tiptoed into the hall.

"Aaron! This isn't funny!" Again, the front door stood open. Chill wind greeted Katrina.

Dread filled her gut.

I locked that door. I just locked it, just now. She glanced around: No one. A dash up the stairs to the landing: No one. She looked out onto the front porch: No one. She flicked on the porch light: Darkness loomed beyond the glow of the lamp.

"Who's here?" Her voice quavered. *Aaron's never pulled a stunt like this.*

"Mom?" *I would've heard a car.* Panic rooted itself firmly in her heart. Tight prickles crept over her skin, and her eyes tingled and watered. *I'm alone and someone I don't know is in this house with me. I am alone...*

Her thoughts quickened to a solution: *Sheer bluff.*

"Ma! I'll help you with the groceries!" Katrina shouted at the top of her lungs to stave off the anxiety that wrenched and twisted her vocal-chords. "Be right there!" She knew her mother was not home yet. Then she noticed that the cellar door was ajar. *Not going down there!* she thought, alarmed.

Fake'em out, she told herself. *Get hold of yourself, get outside and make a run for it.* Katrina bolted back toward the front door. *If my bluff works... if I can just get out of the house, I'll be safe outside...*

Shattering the silence, the house phone rang. She froze.

She leapt for the phone, glancing behind her, *turning, turning, turning* so no one could blind-spot her. Stretching the telephone cord out into the hall, Katrina stood as close as possible to the safety of the open front door that let out onto freedom and infinite darkness.

Keep turning, keep turning...

Over the phone wire came a smooth voice, "Did I leave my Social Studies book there?"

"Aaron!?" barked Katrina. "How'd you get *there* so fast?"

"So fast? I've been sitting here waiting at the car mechanic since I left your house, Katie-cutie. Still waiting for my dad to come get me. He and my mom are at their counseling session. They might get back together..." Aaron jabbered on and on. Katrina heard none of it.

Look behind you, Katrina, behind you. She tried to whirl, but the phone cord was wound around her. She'd tied herself in place.

"You mean you *w-w-weren't* just here? Just now? You *d-d-didn't* just write on my essay?" she stammered, untangling herself from the telephone cord. Her throat felt thick and tense. Her delicate fingers flicked away tears.

Aaron laughed. "What're you talking about?"

A car horn beeped as Mrs. Phillips gunned it up the steep driveway to the portico off the kitchen.

"Never mind, I have to go help Mom unload groceries." Katrina was shouting.

She feared her own growing paranoia.

What's wrong with me? Maybe I did write it without realizing. Maybe my subconscious is at work, tricking me. I'm overtired. Who would let themselves into the house like that? Correy?... No, someone's here, I know I locked the door the second time.

"Hey, Katie," Aaron's happy voice sounded distant. "Guess what surprise I got you for Halloween."

Katrina was silent, listening to house noises, she had forgotten that Aaron was still on the line. She pressed the receiver against her head, holding it tightly in her white-knuckled fist.

"Well, I guess you're busy. I love you, Katie," Aaron said softly.

Without a *good-bye,* Katrina slammed the receiver down and sprinted out of the house not daring to look again behind her.

"Hi, Mom! Want help with the groceries?" Katrina was so loud the lump compressed out of her throat.

"That's a welcome *first,* darling. Thank you!" Mrs. Phillips looked tired.

Before Katrina dared re-enter the house, she waited for her mother to go inside. With an armload of brown paper bags, Katrina followed on her heels.

"Katrina, I told you to keep the cellar door shut, dear. Drafts! Heating bill!"

"Uhhh, sorry, Mom, but..."

Mrs. Phillips unpacked groceries on the counter and laughed at herself. "Ah! So *there's* my shopping list! Can't believe I forgot it again! Oh, Katie, I see you've added things to the list, thank you darling. Your handwriting looks so..." Mrs. Phillips examined the additions to her forgotten shopping list. "My gosh, Katrina, it's just like mine. Very good, sweet heart, your hand is truly *maturing.*" Her mother paused. "Not so *little girl loopy-loo* anymore..." Mrs. Phillips hugged her daughter. "I'm sorry I didn't even think to ask you if you needed anything else for the Halloween dance."

"Wha—?" Katrina had not added anything to the list.

"'*Princess needs push up bra, silk stockings, and garter.*'" Mrs. Phillips read as a bemused smile crept over her face. "Why, of course, every princess has to have the proper undergarments! No need to be embarrassed, Sweetie-pie, I'm your mother. I understand these things."

Katrina's mind flashed. Had Aaron written that as a joke before he left? Or *had* someone else actually been in the house? Who else but Aaron would call her *Princess*?

Katrina took the shopping list from her mother. Blobby blank ink again. Katrina flinched. How long had the intruder been in the house with her, watching her?

"It's just a joke, Ma. Aaron. Forget it." Katrina's mind reeled.

She bolted the door to the cellar and roved the house, yanking down the roller blinds against the darkness.

That night, Katrina turned in early, exhausted from processing too much fear: the intruder, the death of Miss Chantal and Mr. Samson, the canine attack—and, she thought, *probably Dan's paranoia about the Triborough murders was contagious too.*

Dead tired, she took out her lavender contact lenses in her lavender bathroom. Then she got in bed and lay back against the lavender floral fitted sheet and pulled her fat pillow down over her eyes to the bridge of her perfect nose, molding it to her lovely bone structure, shutting out the lamp glow from the front porch. Listless inertia paralyzed her limbs as sleep courted her into submission, and she crashed.

A sudden soft series of footsteps in the hallway broke through Katrina's crushing slumber. Too groggy to sit up, Katrina listened as the erratic stepping came again outside her door. Like small animals in a playful tussle, the unnatural sound was too gentle to be a ruckus, yet too erratic to be ignored.

Reluctantly, she sat up and peeled back her warm duvet comforter—even her hand ached for slumber. She couldn't tell how many hours had passed since she had fallen asleep and could not bring her alarm clock into focus when she looked around for it on the night table. Katrina opened the bedroom door but saw no one in the dimly lit hallway. *Unusual*, she thought, *someone moved the tiny night lamp to a different socket*. She did not recall noticing that when she went to bed. But after all, she'd been exhausted.

She padded down the hall to her parents' bedroom.

"Mom?"

The bed was made up with a comforter Katrina did not recognize. And there was no sign of her mother. Katrina peered in the open door of the adjoining bathroom. It too was dark, empty.

Where's Mom at this hour? Did she go back to work at the emergency room and leave me alone in the house? Katrina rubbed her eyes, fighting to keep them open. Exhausted, she wanted so much to lie down on her parents' bed and go back to sleep. Red numbers on her mom's bedside clock read *3:00 a.m.*

Mom must be downstairs reading late. Panic bristled through Katrina. The nagging question of the erratic ruckus goaded her back down the hall toward the landing. Then, she heard it again. *Downstairs*. There was a flicker of a shadow in the hall down there.

"Mom?" Barely able to get the word out, Katrina's sleep-heavy voice sounded more like a spastic grunt. She tried again: same grunt. She frowned and tiptoed down the stairs after the shadow.

Downstairs, the front door stood open, and Katrina saw snow. *Farmer Brownell's weather prediction was accurate after all,* she thought vaguely and shivered. Suddenly, Katrina sensed she was not alone; she was in danger. *From what? All was quiet. Where was the threat coming from?*

"Mom?!" Katrina tried again.

The shadow disappeared in a flicker of candlelight then reappeared in the murky darkness at the end of the hallway that led past the cellar door and on to the parlor. She entered the parlor.

Shoes under the drapes? Someone was behind the drapes. She approached. Someone was *there*, a stranger. A slightly familiar stranger, she sensed, but wasn't sure, and she was so infinitely fatigued, the thought of climbing back up the stairs to the safety of her bed was insurmountable. Before she could yank back the curtains, the stranger spoke.

"Snow. In October. Farmer Brownell *was* right. But *I know you better than you know."* The unmistakable words were those inked anonymously on her Advanced Composition homework earlier that evening. Again, the voice repeated the phrase, this time from the shadowed end of the hallway near the kitchen door.

Katrina whirled around. "Do I know you? Daddy? Is that you? Where's Mom?" Katrina begged, though she knew it could not possibly be her father. She yanked back the drapes and found more shoes. Her father's.

Suddenly she was back on the stairwell. She stepped down off the last step into the foyer, regretting the move as soon as her bare foot struck the cold floor. Immediately, she turned to face the gray silhouette of a man. He approached hastily. The nocturnal visitor was not breathing. It was not her father who came at her from the end of the dark hallway.

Katrina tried to scream. Nothing came out. Her throat seized up in groggy exhaustion. She longed to fall back to sleep but knew that if she were to survive she must run outside where it was safe. Run to a neighbor's house. Shuddering in the cold, she backed toward the open front door and tried to shout for help. Her throat constricted: Nothing. The man approached faster and faster it seemed—his face obscured in shadow. Outside, *out*! Into the night and snow Katrina ran, tumbling down the porch steps, scraping her leg, down the steep front lawn to High Street in her long lavender t-shirt and bare feet. Stumbling, tumbling, she landed on the sidewalk, aching from the fall and exhaustion. She looked up. Her home seemed so very far away.

And there he stood on the porch. Laughing quietly, he stepped down toward her. Where could she run? The world was asleep at three in the morning.

Then Katrina noticed her feet were no longer cold.

But it's snowing. My entire body is cold with fear but my feet are not cold, she thought.

Abruptly her throat released an enraged shout: "Get away from me!"

"Katrina? Katrina, darling?" Mrs. Phillips closed the front door and put her bathrobe around Katrina who was in a heap on the floor in the vestibule. "You fell down the stairs in your sleep, Katie. You opened the front door!" Mrs. Phillips was very worried.

Katrina looked around. No snow. Farmer Brownell was not right, not yet. She rubbed her bruised hip.

"Katrina, sleepwalking is very dangerous," Mrs. Phillips said gently, guiding her daughter upstairs to bed. "I think Miss Chantal's death has had a terrible effect on you. You must talk to your school counselor first thing tomorrow until I can get you an appointment with a doctor."

8

I have seen her. She is 15. Nearly identical to Brenda, a man wrote hard in a spiral notebook with blobbing black ink. *Like Brenda, she is discerning. She demands the finest customer service. To serve her will be pure pleasure. So many years I have dreamed of her. Now the time is come. Yippie!*

He pressed the pen deeply into the paper, his exclamation marks breaking through the page. He kissed his diary and he shut his eyes, imagining what serving Katrina would be like. He looked forward to recording every detail in his notebook. With the *Chameleon* logo pen, he retraced the title page of the diary:

A DIARY AND CUSTOMER SERVICE LOGBOOK

His sloping *A* with its deft crossbar danced on the page. The sinuous spine of the small *a* curved gracefully into a little curly tail. He dog-eared that day's page—it had been such a special day, after all—and he imagined every detail again.

Then he wrote:

P.S. On a side note, I gifted a very fine few bottles of wine to a most appreciative recipient and watched him savor it. Such glorious appreciation one rarely sees. I must remember to buy another glass, however, because I let him keep mine as a souvenir.

The man removed his glasses, but before he rubbed his eyes, he stripped off the surgical gloves from his hands and placed them between his mattress and box spring next to the secret diary.

Every day before the Halloween dance the fresh corpse of another murder victim was discovered. Katrina lost count.

Officer Nancy Fieldstone had gone to bring in the homeless wino for questioning in connection with Miss Chantal's murder. Instead, she found the man dead with an expensive champagne flute stuck in his mouth. The necks of a dozen empty bottles of red wine were clutched in the old man's gnarled fists. Each bottle was from a different year, yet all labeled *Liber Pater Graves.*

"*Serious God of Wine,*" Officer Fieldstone translated the label. "See Dad, that liberal arts education you paid for put to good use again."

"Looks like someone hosted a wine tasting party," her father muttered.

Officer Fieldstone placed her fingers on the stem of the crystal champagne flute and slowly slid it out of the wino's mouth. A cup of blood spilled out, and thick blackish goo leaked from the wino's purple stained lips.

"*Cause of death: asphyxiation,*" she logged in her police report and handed it to Detective Fieldstone.

"Nice work!" remarked her father proudly, "I trained you well."

A *sommelier* was brought in to identify the wine labels. Each bottle of *Liber Pater Graves* had been worth crazy money, in the thousands. *This plum,* the *sommelier* advised, was one of the finest red wine hybrids composed of Merlot and Cabernet Sauvignon grapes harvested in the Bordeaux region of France. The champagne flute, the expert advised them would be priced at about $110 per stem.

"But the culprit used the wrong glass!" the affronted *sommelier* explained to the detective and his daughter. "This red is a rare vintage. It has not only *legs,* it has *sheets*. They've insulted it by serving it in a champagne flute. It is an *outrage.*" The vintner continued to deride the serial killer's lack of erudition.

"The wrong glass?" Officer Fieldstone sneered in disbelief. "Seriously, buddy? I don't give a *sheet.*"

The *sommelier* sneered back. "It should have been served in a *Claret* glass. In England, we—"

"Look, Bub," Nancy Fieldstone didn't miss a beat. "We've got a serial killer on our hands, and you're takin' issue with the *wrong glass*?! Thank you for your time." She dismissed the *sommelier*. "*Sheet,* man!"

Her father smiled. "Now that's a *glass-half-empty* kind of guy." Detective Fieldstone was proud of his daughter. "Don't you see, kid?" Detective Fieldstone explained. "The champagne glass itself was not fissured. It had to have been placed *in* the wino's mouth after his death, and with considerable care."

Before Detective Fieldstone could point out the similarity to the deaths of Miss Chantal and Mr. Samson, Nancy Fieldstone nailed it, "*Glass-half-full! Full* customer service with a malicious twist!" She high-fived her father. "I'm on it, Dad!"

9

Aaron opened the passenger door to his Mustang.

"How's my best girl today?" he asked.

"*Only* girl, you mean." Sullen, Katrina looked overwrought.

"*Only* girl," Aaron corrected himself, and continued warily, "I'll drive till we get there, Katrina, in case we get stopped on the main road." In his black Mustang convertible they sped out toward Eastridge. "Fasten your vanity belt, Katie. I wouldn't want you ruining that face of yours if we have a crack-up."

Katrina rolled her eyes, then leaned her head back, relaxing. The cold wind rushed through her thick pullover and tossed her hair.

"Blast the heat please, Aaron." Katrina loved riding top-down.

Every day since the intruder incident, Katrina had thought about asking Aaron whether he had added that weird sentence to her Advanced Composition essay or the syrupy note about the *Princess* lingerie on her mother's shopping list. Ultimately, she had decided against it. The lingerie subject was way too private. And for that matter, so was the "*Know Yourself*" essay. *Better to let it slide and opt for a more upbeat topic. But what?* Instead she shifted the conversation to her recent recurrent nightmare and decided that that was a safe enough subject.

"Aaron, I've been having this same nightmare every night for weeks. It nearly scares me to death."

"About Miss Chantal still?"

"Worse. I'm wearing this perfect prom dress, like the one Coriander's mother is making for me. It's fuchsia velvet with a huge crinoline that makes me float. I really float in the dream. And I can't wait for you to see me in it."

"Does it show any cleavage?"

"Aaron!" She glowered. "*Priorities!*"

"Just kidding. Go on," he urged as he stepped on the gas and they sped out of Westlake toward, gaining elevation as they approached the Eastridge cliffs.

"So I float down the hill to the road and look back at my house. Mom *and* Dad are waving at me from the porch. They tell me to hurry or I'll miss my ride. When I turn back to face the road. I expect *you* to pick me up in the Mustang. But instead there's this fuchsia hearse. A fuchsia hearse parked right in front of my house!"

Aaron smiled. "What make?"

"Cadillac, I guess. It had that emblem. Why?"

"No reason. Go on."

"And it matches my dress!"

"So?"

"So that's tacky, Aaron."

"I think it sounds kind of cool. I mean, not for every day, but you know, for Halloween." He grinned.

"Can you imagine riding in a fuchsia hearse that matches your ball gown? Awful!"

"Katrina, first of all, I don't wear ball gowns, and secondly this nightmare's not sounding too scary. Unless the fashion police get in on the action." Aaron signaled left and turned up a winding road leading past Eastridge Bluff. At a discrete distance, a compact car followed the Mustang.

"Wait—Aaron, this nightmare gets massively creepy. The door of the hearse swings open and I try to get in and sit down. Instead, I have to squeeze in around a red coffin and *lie down next to it*. The lid of the coffin is open. Before I can look in the coffin the hearse door slams on the hem of my flowy velvet dress. Are you listening?"

"I'm fascinated. Keep going." Aaron hid a yawn as his Mustang drew nearer the desolate property owned by his father.

"...the driver starts laughing and laughing and hits the gas and I say, 'Hey, my dress,' and he won't turn around, and he won't stop. I can't see his face and he won't stop driving. He just says, 'Look in the coffin. Everything you need is in the coffin.' He has a gross giant mole on his neck right behind his right ear."

"What's in the red coffin?" Aaron asked.

"You, Aaron! Dead!"

Aaron winced at Katrina's shrill voice and welcomed a reason to change the subject. "We're here. You ready to drive?"

Isolated fields behind Mr. Sedgewood's old burnt-out house reached all the way out to the cliffs overlooking Westlake.

"Guess your dad's not gonna rebuild since he and your mom are getting back together."

Aaron smiled and nodded and drove on along the overgrown driveway toward the ruins. "My parents are gonna re-build here."

"You're moving away from Westlake?" Katrina was alarmed again.

Aaron sought to calm her. "A weekend country house. We can use it for parties, Katrina! *Party till you scream!*"

Finally, Katrina laughed. Together, they had a giggle fit, oblivious to the compact car lagging behind them which parked out of sight. A man emerged and hunkered down in the overgrown field grass, watching the teenagers.

"No better remedy for nightmares about fuchsia Cadillac hearses than a driving lesson in a black Mustang."

"This place gives me the creeps," Katrina said, glancing around, recalling the terrible incendiary last spring.

"Yeah, but at least here in the open field, you won't get caught driving without a learner's permit, and there's nothing to run into."

"Except *that.*" Katrina pointed at the charred skeleton of the derelict house.

"Just keep your eyes open, Katie, and use your head."

"Use my head." Katrina laughed nervously. "Are you sure it's okay for us to be out here?"

"Yes. Your mom even said it's okay."

"The grass is kind of high to drive in, don't you think, Aaron?"

"We'll try it. If it doesn't work, then at least I'll have you all to myself in a secluded spot."

"You're very humorous, Aaron."

"I'll tell you what. If you do well driving, Katie, I'll tell you the surprise I have for you for the night of the Halloween dance."

In the driver's seat, Katrina struggled with the standard shift and the clutch, and then she had trouble turning the steering wheel.

"I wish you had automatic steering."

"You mean power steering. But how do you think I get these great muscles?"

"Aaron, it's hard enough to shift the gears, let alone steer manually!"

"Come on, keep at it and I'll tell you your surprise," Aaron cajoled. "Hey, watch out! A car is a lethal weapon, Katie!"

"Sorry, *I, I, I* thought I saw a man over there."

Katrina glanced in her rearview mirror.

"Probably you saw *what's-her-name's* ghost." Aaron laughed.

"You mean your dad's—"

"Yup. With a capital *B*"

An hour passed and Katrina still did not have the hang of shifting and using the clutch. But steering was going better.

"Had enough?"

"I'm pooped! Now you have to tell me what my Halloween surprise is!" she demanded coyly.

But Aaron refused to divulge it no matter how many times she smooched him.

"Maybe after a few more lessons."

"Not fair, Aaron, tell me!"

"Nope." He kissed her, wrapping her in his arms.

She gave in willingly and kissed him back until the sun set and the desolate field made her too uneasy. Nearby, a car motor started up. Katrina looked nervously at Aaron.

"Let's go, Aaron, before we—"

"Get caught making out?"

"Before we find another body."

10

Of all the days for there *not* to be a murder, Halloween day passed, uneventfully with the exception of Farmer Brownell's natural death of plain old *old age* at 102. The local radio news said he died while writing his renowned "*Harvest Predictions*" column for the local paper. The coroner said "natural causes," but Officer Fieldstone and her detective father had to wonder. Farmer Brownell had promised frost and freezing rain for Friday night, but no one believed it. His grave was dug late that afternoon at Horizon View Cemetery while the ground was still soft. With his burial slated for the following week, the hole in the earth beckoned a stray black cat after a hapless vole. The vole, however, burrowed deeper into Farmer Brownell's grave, leaving the cat stuck and hungry.

Meanwhile, Westlake High School was wall-to-wall gory posters reproduced from Aaron's design for the *Weird Logic Halloween Dance*. Nearly everyone in the halls was discussing how they would come as they weren't and not as they were, as the posters directed.

School let out at lunch and sports were cancelled so students could get ready for the Halloween dance. After decorating the gym with the rest of the party committee, Katrina and Coriander walked together from school to Katrina's house. Coriander had brought her costume to school to get changed at Katrina's. The boys planned to meet them at the Phillips house before the dance.

"Any more nightmares?" Coriander asked.

"Same one I told you about—fuchsia hearse, matching ball gown. So *gauche*!" Excited about the Halloween party, Katrina made light of it.

"Laughing driver? Disgusting mole behind his ear?"

"That's the one." She wanted to forget and have fun with her friends. "Not to change the subject, Correy, but Aaron promised to have a surprise for me," said Katrina as they climbed the porch steps of the Victorian.

Smiling, Mrs. Phillips let them in. The girls blew past her and bounded up to Katrina's bedroom.

"Hello ladies?"

"Hi Mom!" Katrina yelled back.

"Hi Mrs. Phillips! Thank you for having me!"

"Correy, I can't wait to see what Aaron's surprise is. Mom!? Oh my God! Katrina yelled as she flung her books down in her room and ogled the beautiful ruby and diamond pendant displayed in a clear glass box that she found on her bed. "Mom, did Dad give this to you for your last anniversary or something?"

"Don't yell, dear," said her mother, ascending the stairs. "A messenger brought it for *you*. You just missed him. From Aaron?" Mrs. Phillips joined the girls in the bedroom.

"Must be." Katrina carefully lifted the heavy lid of the glass oblong. "Unless I've got a secret admirer I don't know about." She laughed.

"The glass box is sort of coffin-shaped, don't you think?" Coriander noted.

"Killjoy!" Katrina retorted.

"Let me see, honey. Oh, my heavens, that necklace is terrific. That Aaron certainly is attentive. You'll treasure this the rest of your life, darling."

"Even if you and Aaron *don't* stay together!" Coriander remarked jealously. "Like Mr. McGhoul said."

"Can I have my moment, Corry?" Katrina glowered at her friend.

"Sorry. What's the card say?"

Katrina looked. "No card."

"Well, from whom would it be besides Aaron?"

"No one, Mom. I just wish he'd made me one of his cool cards."

"Katrina! Be grateful," said her mother.

They laughed as Katrina tried on the pendant, heavy with diamonds and rubies set in rose gold in the shape of a heart. It hung stupendously into her *décolletage*.

"Not bad, not bad." Katrina thrust out her chest.

"Oh, Katrina, it's absolutely regal on you. The craftsmanship is breath-taking. Must be antique." Mrs. Phillips hugged her daughter. "I'll leave you girls to get dressed." Mrs. Phillips turned and closing the bedroom door behind her added, "I've got to prep for trick-or-treaters."

As Katrina pulled on her panty hose, she pinched her thighs and grimaced. Looking at herself sideways in the full-length mirror, she straightened her back and scrutinized her thin body in the scanty slip she wore.

"I wish I could suck in my thighs like I can my stomach," groaned Katrina.

"Oh will you give it a rest, Katrina!" Coriander scolded, "You're so lucky you were born smart. If you hate your thighs so much, do the *butt-rock walk* we do for cheerleading practice and you'll have thighs like mine in three weeks. Plus, you're pretty." Coriander watched Katrina primp in the mirror "Pretty girls get stuff like that necklace."

Splinters of light refracted off the pendant. The girls stared at it.

"Or they buy it themselves," Katrina said defensively. "And, Correy, you've got a great face. Plus, you have perfect thighs." Katrina tried to be supportive, as she glued on a false eyelash.

"Yeah. A *classic* face, my mother calls it. I hate that, when adults say, 'You've got *claaassic* features.' Like I just stepped out of a Greek mythology book. But you're really pretty, Katrina. You could get any guy you want."

"I've *got* the only guy I want. Plus, you're the one who won Homecoming Queen and class president and made the honor roll and cheerleading captain. I mean I'm the one here wearing your hand-me-down crown, Correy. The whole school's going to know it's yours." Katrina positioned Coriander's sparkling Homecoming tiara in her own hair. It looked cheap compared to the real vintage jewelry around Katrina's neck. "What else could you possibly want?"

"To look like you," Coriander responded matter-of-factly.

"What, so you can steal *my* boyfriend?" Katrina's humor fell flat. Correy shot her a wounded look.

"Katrina, don't *start*."

"Just kidding, Correy, sorry!" Katrina hugged her friend, then went back to the mirror to apply the other fake eyelash, "Anyway, I look like my *mother*." Katrina applied black mascara to her butterfly lashes.

"And your mother is gorgeous, Katie."

"Oh, give me a break. She has gray hairs. It's *character* that matters, anyway. And everyone at Westlake High knows you and I both have enough character to choke a horse."

The girls giggled at the truth. Coriander slipped into a gray jumper and mismatched knee socks, then put white powder all over her face. She painted circles under her eyes with pewter-tone eye shadow and made a crooked part in her hair.

Katrina regarded her fuchsia velvet ball gown hanging on her closet door on Aaron's cedar *skeleton-in-the-closet* hanger.

"What do you think, Correy?"

Coriander nodded approvingly. "Great hanger! I got one of those too. Pretty sure every girl at Westlake High now has one."

"Aaron—?" Katrina's cheery mood withered as she imagined that Aaron had made a cedar skeleton hanger for Coriander, *too*.

"No, dummy, Dan made me a *skeleton-in-the-closet* hanger in shop class. All the boys pirated Aaron's idea."

"Oh." Katrina felt ashamed and relieved.

"Aaron's so creative. I just love that necklace he gave you. Can I try it on before I get completely into my unpopular-girl costume."

Masking her reluctance, Katrina lay the fuchsia ball gown on the bed. Slowly, she unclasped the pendant and handed the brilliant bauble to Coriander. It shone in such contrast to Coriander's new gray look.

"Too bad he didn't give me matching earrings to go with the necklace," mused Katrina.

The girls laughed at Katrina's *silly-greedy* comment.

"Too *matchy-matchy,*" Coriander offered. The girls laughed harder than before. "But, you never know, Katrina, maybe earrings are coming too."

11

Aaron arrived in vampire costume, with Dan in tow as a bearded professor. Dan wore his usual gold wire-rims. A bow tie sealed the collar of his Oxford cloth shirt, and a tweed blazer, short plaid pants, and penny loafers with no socks finished off the ensemble.

"Like Albert Einstein," explained Dan, pointing at his bare ankles.

The stack of books Dan carried reached higher than the wire-haired gray wig skewed strangely on his head.

"Danny, the poster says to '*come as you're not*,' and you've come as you *are*," said Coriander as she came down the stairs. Aaron laughed. Dan did not. "And those," Coriander pointed at the stack of books, "are staying right here."

Setting them down on the console, Dan looked annoyed and sweaty. He unbuttoned his tweed blazer with one hand and wiped his brow.

"I like the way I am," retorted Dan. "Why would I want to *come as I'm not*?"

Drably clad Coriander escorted Dan into the parlor for snacks.

"You don't really *want* to carry around that arm-load of books all evening, *do* you, Danny?" Coriander was her most persuasive in a darkened corner of the parlor.

"But it's part of my costu—" Dan started to say before she shut him up with kisses.

"Hi, Aaron." Appearing weightless, Katrina floated elegantly down to the foyer to meet him in her fuchsia velvet ball gown. She twirled around in the hallway and held her head high to show off her beautifully adorned *décolletage*. Everything sparkled.

"Wow," said Aaron. "*Princess!*"

"Thank you, Aaron," she said softly as she hugged him close and kissed him carefully around the red lipstick that faked blood at the corners of his mouth. "You're not so bad yourself, Mr. Dracula. Despite your unoriginal costume! Love that bow tie. You look like a vampire lawyer."

"Yeah, well, I figure it's impossible to spill food on a bow tie."

"Or blood."

"The cape gets in my way. I feel like Zorro."

"Hey, where's our super stretch limousine?" Katrina asked looking over Aaron's shoulder to the street.

"Oh, I told him to drive around the block a few times. Nice necklace." Aaron changed the subject.

Katrina blushed, flustered. "I love it." Words to thank him for the stunning necklace failed her.

They heard Coriander's bloodcurdling scream from the parlor, followed by laughter from Dan and a wicked high-pitched cackle.

"It's just Mom," Katrina explained. "She dressed up scary so prowlers will think she's a kook and not dare break in."

Katrina kissed Aaron long and hard on the mouth until her mother came up behind her.

"Oh, hi, Mrs. Phillips, Katrina was just explaining CPR to me."

"*Mm-hm.* More like cardiac arrest!"

"Nice costume, Mrs. Phillips. I almost didn't recognize you. You look so..."

"Ugly?" Mrs. Phillips said merrily. "I like to scare the trick-or-treaters. It's half the fun."

Aaron gawked. He had never seen Mrs. Phillips look anything but supremely elegant. She had smeared her face with greenish-brown eye shadow and highlighted her eyes, nose, and mouth with purplish-red lipstick. Her graying hair was teased and haggy, her teeth blackened. A long hooded black cape dragged on the floor behind her, and she hunched over a lighted candle, grimacing.

"Looks great, Mom! Just don't burn your face."

"I can't wait for the doorbell to ring," Mrs. Phillips hooted, then drawled pretending to stir a cauldron, "*Nowww, my daaaughter, why don't you invite Aaron in with the others for Halloween cake before I turn you into a newt?* And turn down the TV while you're in the parlor, Katrina," she added as the doorbell rang, "I wouldn't want the screams from your horror movie to upstage me."

The bell rang.

Mrs. Phillips yanked open the front door and stuck her face toward the trick-or-treaters. Her candle illuminated her macabre visage from below.

Three piercing little screams came from a bunny, a shark, and a mini-witch on the front porch steps.

"*Come baaaack, I won't hurrrt you, little ones.*"

The bunny began to cry. The great white shark's mouth hung open in awe at the spectacle.

"Mrs. Phillips?!" the pretty blond mini-witch challenged her.

"Come on, have some candy," Mrs. Phillips loaded their candy bags.

"Wow, Katie," whispered Coriander. "Your mother's really twisted."

Dan interjected, "I think it's cool to see how far she can push those kids to get a reaction out of them."

The teenagers watched Mrs. Phillip's antics from the hallway, happily eating the Halloween cake she had made from scratch while an episode of *Still Life: The Best of the Worst*, finally serialized for TV, played in the background.

"You're so creative, Mrs. Phillip, a Halloween cake shaped like a freshly used butcher's knife," Dan commented.

"Well, you know, it seemed appropriate," replied Mrs. Phillips, closing the front door. "I view it as the kickoff off a new hobby."

"Baking or butchering?" Aaron asked, deadpan. Everyone laughed.

"Now we know who the real Triborough serial killer is!" Dan said, laughing at his own joke.

"Well, what do you say we head out?" Katrina prodded.

"Let me check and see if our chariot has arrived. Yeah, he's here. Katrina, I have to cover your eyes."

"Oh, no, Aaron, you didn't have him paint the superstretch limousine fuchsia to match my dress, did you?"

Aaron and Dan laughed perniciously.

"Just let me cover your eyes till we get to the car. Dan, you cover Correy's."

"Oh, wait! Newsflash! The *milk carton couple* interrupted that pathetic horror movie," said Dan, pointing at the TV.

A local news crew was interviewing two teenagers, a beaming boy and very pregnant girl.

"Oooh, look, they're so in love!" exclaimed Katrina, turning up the volume.

"Cripe! That's the missing couple on all the posters you see around town."

"The ones from prom night last spring?"

"Yeah! They're alive."

"I'm so relieved," said Katrina. "But wait, that's impossible. The papers just said they found their outfits with knife holes and bloodstains all over."

"Heck, I'd never even wear a tuxedo if you paid me," said the smiling boy on the TV," even to my own wedding... which was last spring."

"We eloped," the prom girl added.

"*Wed not dead!*" the announcer declared to the American public. "Upon their arrival home from their elopement last spring, the missing teens say they've returned to finish high school and get their diplomas.

Both teenagers were high honors students when they decided spontaneously on prom night last year to—"

"Wow!" said Aaron. "I'm relieved, I have to admit."

"Shhh," commanded Dan. "There's more."

"Hey, there's Detective Fieldstone!" Katrina waved at the television screen.

"Westlake forensics pathologist, Dr. Priestly van Swift, determined the stains were not bloodstains at all, but food coloring applied deliberately to the clothing."

"Hey, that's the father of Kenny," remarked Dan. "My science lab partner."

Detective Fieldstone then told a bold-faced lie on national TV. *It wouldn't be the first time in history a public figure had done that*, he wagered.

"So I calculated that, with the help of the news media," said Detective Fieldstone to the camera, "that we could bring the missing teenagers out of hiding by announcing that they were believed dead. Sure enough, we appealed to their good conscience and the kids came forward because they did not want an innocent person to get blamed for their murder. The eighteen-year-olds do owe us all an apology for the worry they have caused the residents of the Triborough region, and their families. But tonight we, at the Westlake Police Department, are simply happy to have the kids home safe and sound."

"Cool! Let's go have fun," said Katrina.

"This doesn't mean we're safe from the Bermuda Triangle Killer," cautioned Dan. "I mean, guys, there still have been rather a lot of dead people turning up lately! It's not like we're suddenly safe from—"

"...No curfew is being imposed in the Triborough area," the news announcer continued, "But police caution that no one should go out alone."

Katrina sighed with relief.

"So, we don't have to worry as long as we're at school or with Mr. McGhoul."

"As long as we're escorted, we're fine, Dan," Coriander agreed.

"Take a shawl, Katrina, it's going to frost," said Mrs. Phillips.

"No, Ma, I don't want to have to carry it."

"And I don't want you to carry your books, Danny," Coriander said, taking the stack from him as soon as he picked it up. "They're staying here." Coriander kissed Dan and whispered something in his ear. Dan conceded immediately, and hid a smirk.

When the doorbell sounded again, already, Aaron was guiding Katrina toward the front door, his hands over her eyes. Mrs. Phillips repeated her witchy *shtick* for a group of grade school girls in neckties, business suits, and wingtip shoes that were much too big for their feet.

"Hey, it's Josephine!" Dan barely recognized his little sister.

"Trick-or-treat!" yelled Josephine Pritcher and her friends at the top of their lungs.

"What on earth are you dressed as?" inquired Mrs. Phillips.

"Crooked businessmen," Josephine responded naturally. "I'm the boss."

"Hey, Danny, can we ride with you?" A tiny colleague of Josephine's asked.

"Sorry, no room," Dan replied.

"That's a really cool car you got," said Josephine's other little friend.

"*Shhh*, don't give it away!" said Aaron.

"Hey, Josie," Dan asked curiously, "what's that in your lapel? Doesn't look like a kerchief to me."

"Half a dollar bill," replied Josephine. "It's part of the businessman look." Josephine removed the torn dollar bill and held it up for Dan to examine.

"Why'd you rip a perfectly good dollar bill in half?" asked Katrina.

"I didn't." Josephine pointed at the limousine driver awaiting the teenagers, curbside. "He did."

"Time out," said Dan, "*Who?*" Dan went out onto the porch for a private sibling conference. Dan made his little sister explain what had happened on the day the limo man patronized her lemonade stand. "You should've told me, Josie."

"But it's so embarrassing," Josephine demurred.

"That's what sibs are for. No matter how embarrassed you are. Promise? Always tell me. Always ask for help!"

"Yeah, I guess so."

"He's just a jerk. Now go have fun and ignore the guy, okay? I'll deal with him."

"You can't beat him up, Danny, you're too skinny."

"Trust me," Dan assured, "I'll take care of it. Have fun, ad do not speak to him. You promise?"

"Promise!" replied Josephine, glancing over her shoulder at Bob McGhoul standing by his vehicle.

"Don't even give him the satisfaction of a second glance" instructed Dan. "Just pretend you don't even see him."

"Hey, come on! What's the holdup?" shouted Aaron.

"What's all the whispering?"

"Coming!" Dan acted calm, but inside he fumed. *How dare anyone take advantage of my kid sister?*

Shouting thanks for the Halloween goodies, the little girls trekked down the porch steps past the glowing jack-o'-lantern faces that Mrs. Phillips and Katrina had carved. Josephine led her team of white collar criminals down the steep lawn to High Street, and right past the driver of the hired car. When she turned around one last time to wave goodbye to Dan, McGhoul hastily turned his face away from her.

Following the little girls down the steps, Aaron kept his hands over Katrina's eyes all the way to the car.

"Oh, my heavens!" Katrina heard her mother gasp then chuckle.

"*Shhh*, don't tell her!" Aaron hollered back.

At the sidewalk, Aaron released Katrina, and shouted, "Surprise!"

There stood Bob McGhoul smiling gallantly in full chauffeur's livery. He bowed to Katrina and held open the door of a highly polished fuchsia hearse.

"Good evening," Bob McGhoul said, faking a scary Transylvanian accent.

"A hearse!" cried Katrina. "Is this some kind of nasty joke, Aaron?"

Deflated, Aaron mumbled, "I thought you'd think it was funny."

Everyone laughed except Katrina.

"Oh, come on, Katrina!" Coriander was still laughing. "It's our Halloween dance. *Weird Logic.* Lighten up. Let's go have fun."

Coriander was already allowing Bob McGhoul to help her into the hearse. Dan stepped in after Coriander and waggled a jar of Grey Poupon mustard he found on the seat.

"I am not setting foot in that hearse!"

"Katrina, look inside! The hearse has been converted. There are seats and plenty of room." Dan patted the silk brocade upholstered seat.

"You won't be sharing a seat with a *coffin*," said Bob McGhoul reassuringly.

"You told them about my nightmare!" Katrina accused Coriander and Aaron.

"It's not as if you were keeping it a big secret, Katie," piped Coriander from deep inside the hearse. "That's all you talked about for the last three weeks!"

"Come on, it's all in fun. Please, just get in," begged Aaron.

"You go, Aaron. I'll meet you at the high school," Katrina seethed.

"You gonna' *drive* yourself there?" jested Aaron, not meaning for it to sound anything but friendly.

"I'll *walk!*" Katrina retorted.

"No, you'll come with us. *Please*," Aaron pleaded. "It won't be any fun without you, Katrina."

"You call this fun? I call it perverse!"

"It's Halloween, Katrina! Not prom." Exasperated, Aaron got into the hearse without her. Katrina stood folding and unfolding her arms, trying to decide if she was being too theatrical.

Am I one of those hysterical types? She cringed at the thought.

"Nice necklace, *Princess*," whispered McGhoul as he stood nobly holding the door like a queen's footman. "Looks expensive. Looks like one I bought for a girl once. A long time ago. Hers had matching earrings. Looks great on you."

Bob McGhoul's smile was tender and honest. His whispers touched Katrina's heart.

"And, Katrina," McGhoul added whispering even lower. "This hearse hasn't squired a corpse..." He thought a moment before he continued, "...to a funeral in, *uhm*, decades."

His words sounded spontaneous. Unrehearsed. Katrina believed McGhoul was speaking the truth. And, in fact, he *was*. That is to say, every word that he uttered was accurate.

After many scant glances he ventured at her pretty face, he recognized that it was trust that grew in Katrina's eyes. Maybe Katrina even liked him a little, deep down. He was surprised. And happy.

"I promise to deliver the best customer service to you this evening."

"Thank you, Mr. McGhoul," said Katrina.

"Call me *Bob*," he whispered.

She did not.

Nevertheless, he offered his hand to assist her. To everyone's relief, Katrina accepted McGhoul's hand and stepped into the hearse without further argument. Aaron smiled broadly at Katrina. A smirk lurked on her lips. He darted in with a quick kiss. She wasn't ready to smile at Aaron, but she was, in fact, excited. Plus, she so totally adored him, so didn't want to wreck his fun.

"Are we ready for a *suuuuuper* road trip and a serious night of dancing the night away?"

"Okay, let's go." Katrina's tone was acquiescent, yet the smile on her fuchsia lips was irrepressible.

Bob McGhoul leaned inside the hearse. "Anything you need, you just tap on the Plexiglas divider. Only the best for my customers! Drinks are in the mini fridge under that seat. Custom-made cassettes are in those slots, to your left. You get to keep them—*if you survive Halloween night.*" McGhoul laughed an ominous fake-evil laugh that made the teens laugh a lot too.

In seconds, McGhoul was in the driver's seat. All doors locked automatically when he hit the button on his console. For a second the laughter stopped... then burst out again.

"This could be fun," mused Dan, getting into the spirit.

"A toast, a toast," Aaron said, opening a bottle of sparkling apple cider. He poured first for the girls. The frothing liquid bubbled up over Katrina's fingers and drizzled along her wrist.

"Cute, plastic champagne flutes," noted Katrina.

"Mine's glass," said Coriander. "*Chin-ching, beautiful ring.*" She tapped it with her fingernail.

"Yeah, my parents have this type. They're really expensive," Aaron added.

"Hey! How come I get the cheap plastic one?" demanded Katrina, dismayed.

"I'll swap you mine, Katie," offered Aaron.

"Ever the gentleman," remarked Coriander.

Normally, the attention Coriander paid to Aaron would have annoyed Katrina, but tonight she found herself deliciously above it all. Dan did not seem to notice it either. Then again, he never did.

The fuchsia hearse sped gracefully down High Street and took a left onto Main.

Bob McGhoul opened the slide vent in the divider to apologize for the single plastic champagne glass. "I may have broken one this evening, uh, when I was packing the hearse."

"She'll get over it, Bob," Aaron assured.

Aaron handed Dan Pink Floyd's *Dark Side of the Moon* cassette to insert into the cassette player. Dan cranked the volume. As they cruised slowly by the high school, Aaron waved at several classmates through his half-open window.

"Very cool, Sedgewood!" a football player hollered. Aaron raised his plastic champagne glass in salute.

"Jeez, I wish the windows would go down all the way," said Aaron, catching his elbow and spilling a bit of his bubbly drink. "Guess dead people and coffins never needed to reach out the window."

As they drove around Westlake, with their favorite music blaring, they waved at costumed friends who walked toward the high school like a lively cast from *Night of the Living Dead.* Periodically, Katrina glanced up at the clear divider separating the driver's compartment. Each time, Bob McGhoul's kindly eyes were in the rearview mirror. Katrina thought it very professional that he kept an eye on them. *He seems really nice,* she thought.

They drove slowly by another flock of costumed students. Two redheaded girls and a blonde wrapped up as mummies and wearing top hats separated themselves from the group and suddenly lay down in the road yards ahead of the fuchsia hearse.

"Hey! Get out of the road!" Bob McGhoul yelled, and beeped the horn. "Look at these morons."

"It's a stupid new trend," said Dan.

"That's what you kids do for kicks?"

"We don't," said Katrina.

McGhoul had to stomp the brakes to avoid hitting the three girls in the road.

"Brakes work!" Aaron snickered.

"Hey, girls!" yelled McGhoul, driving carefully up to them. "You like playin' chicken?" Giggling, the girls finally started to get out of the way. "You want to try something really dangerous?" McGhoul challenged them.

"Yeah!" they answered giddily.

"Yeah? Try stayin' alive until you're my age! That's a *real* game of chicken." He sped on shaking his head in disgust.

After forty-five more minutes of hilarity, Bob McGhoul opened the slide vent between the compartments.

"How you kids doing back there? Okay?"

"Great. Fine," all agreed.

"Good. What do you say we head you over to your Halloween dance?"

"In a while, in a while. We don't want to be the first ones to arrive, Bob, my man," Aaron said.

"Okay, I'm just going to swing by the gas station then and tank up. These big old cars are gas guzzlers. You don't mind, do you?"

"Do we have a choice?" Katrina asked, making fun.

"It's either that or we sit by the side of the road. Which do you prefer?" McGhoul gave Katrina a funny look in the rearview mirror, but she was smooching Aaron's ear.

"I wouldn't mind using the ladies' room, actually," admitted Coriander.

"Will you be okay for another ten minutes? Horizon View gas station here only takes cash. And I've got a credit card. So I'll drive back to the gas station by the high school."

"Fine with us."

On the way, they drove past Horizon View Cemetery and Horizon View Retirement Home. Aaron leaned out the window, raising his glass to an octogenarian who balanced a cane on the front step of the old people's home.

"Hey, how's it going?" Aaron yelled.

The old gentleman waved and craned his neck.

"Do you know him? Katrina asked.

"No. But he's all alone, so I figure he'd appreciate the wave. Probably thinks I'm a relative."

"Or the Grim Reaper on drugs," Dan added.

"You're weird, Aaron," Coriander said flatly.

"Wouldn't you want someone to wave at you if you were forced to live in the grammar school you went to when you were a kid? That's like hell before dying." Aaron said playfully.

"Grammar school?"

"My dad said that's the old grammar school, they converted. They use chalkboard erasers as door knockers and the wallpaper has printed on it a thousand times '*I will not talk in class.*'"

The girls laughed.

"You're kidding!" said Katrina.

"It could be very comforting, actually. Like being at home," said Coriander.

"More like being kept after school until you die," said Aaron.

"That old man might be the next victim," Dan suggested in a somber voice.

"Oh Dan, you're so droll." Coriander sipped at her *faux* champagne. "Such a cheery companion. I thought you were jazzed about this?" Then she tried kissing him to lift his spirits.

"I doubt it," Bob McGhoul interjected. "The old fellow looks like he's got everything he needs to keep him happy."

"Wait." Dan did a double take. "What?"

"Well, Dan, you suggested that maybe the old man would be the next victim." Bob McGhoul deliberated a few moments too long to seem believable. "But if you've been following the news coverage of the murders," he paused to choose his words carefully, "you'd have noticed that all the victims were *lacking something*."

"Yeah—*life*." Katrina and Aaron snickered.

"What do you mean they were *lacking something*?" Dan probed further. "Mr. McGhoul, the papers stopped giving the gory details because they didn't want to give the killer any jollies reading about himself."

"We must read different newspapers," McGhoul proposed. "*And* here we are at the gas station. Rest rooms, anyone?" McGhoul opened his window and turned off the ignition.

It was then that Katrina noticed the hem of her fuchsia ball gown was caught in the door, just like in her nightmare. Her eyes darted up at McGhoul's in the rearview mirror. She thought he saw her panic.

McGhoul must think I'm a head case. I'm not going to over react, my friends'll think I'm crazy—but what if they're trying to make me crazy? No, no, they're just having fun. I won't give them the satisfaction, I'll just pretend I don't notice that my hem is caught in the door of this matching fuchsia hearse, just like in my worst nightmare... Everything's just like my worst nightmare!

She recalled Aaron's face, dead, in the coffin in her dream; she couldn't bear the thought. She turned to kiss him passionately right on the mouth in front of Coriander and Dan, and Bob McGhoul whose eyes glowed incandescent with envy, in the rearview mirror. No one noticed.

"I'll be getting out now." Dan averted his eyes and opened the door, releasing the hem of Katrina's fuchsia velvet ball gown.

"OH! Let me get the door for you." Bob McGhoul bounded around to the side of the hearse.

Dan escorted Coriander to the ladies' room. She yanked him inside and shut the door behind them. Katrina and Aaron snuggled in the back seat as McGhoul ordered a full tank from the gas station attendant. Katrina was determined not to overreact again. She had to get a grip on her imagination. After all, the prom teens were back safe and sound, "*wed not dead*," so what did she have to worry about? It was time for fun. It was Halloween. The silliest holiday of the year. *Halloween,* she thought. *Anything could happen.*

"He's watching us kiss," Katrina whispered into Aaron's lips as he pulled away tenderly and caressed her lovely jaw.

"Who?" Aaron whispered back.

"Who else? *McFool!*" whispered Katrina.

"*Shhh*, Katie, he might hear you."

"Don't you think it's a little weird he's watching us kiss? Aaron?"

McGhoul glanced in the rearview mirror again before he paid the gas station attendant.

"Need a cash receipt, sir?" asked the attendant. McGhoul shook his head and glanced again in the rearview mirror to see if the students had overheard.

Katrina and Aaron were otherwise indisposed.

"Sir, if you would," said the pump attendant pocketing Bob's cash payment for the gasoline. "Please pull your—er, *car*—ahead so the next customer can tank up."

The hearse slowly pulled forward out of the way of the pumps.

"Did he just say 'cash receipt'? whispered Katrina.

Aaron pressed his finger to Katrina's lips. "*Shhh*, Katrina, he might be able to read your lips in the rearview mirror."

"Oh, you think so." Laughing flirtatiously, Katrina faced Bob McGhoul in the mirror. "Do you think he can make out what I am saying *now*? Think he can read lips *backwards in the mirror*?"

McGhoul instantly averted his eyes. Obviously, he had read her lips, and pretended to ignore her. As Bob McGhoul tapped a syncopated rhythm with a cleanly creased wrapper from a jumbo candy bar on his dashboard, the automatic windows slowly closed.

"Hey, we need air back here, Bob my man. We're steaming up the windows. Hello?" Aaron laughed.

McGhoul hit the gas so fast that the back door slammed shut. Power locks clicked decisively in place.

"Hey!" demanded Aaron as he and Katrina were dashed against the seat back.

Katrina's fears rushed back. "See, Aaron, I told you. I *told* you."

"One last loop around, one last loop around to make—your *nightmare* come true!" Bob McGhoul's tone was menacing. Katrina screamed. The fuchsia hearse ripped tire marks on the tarmac as McGhoul wheeled madly out of the gas station.

"The windows, Aaron, they're stuck." Katrina pounded on the glass. "We're locked in. He's power-locked the windows and the doors!"

12

Dan ran after the limousine shouting. By the time Coriander came out of the ladies' room, only skid marks remained.

"Idiots! I can't believe they ditched us!" Dan groused, "That limo guy's a jerk to go along with Sedgewood's little joke."

"Aren't you glad I made you leave your books?"

"I'm going to kill Sedgewood! I paid half for that car service!"

"Oh come on, Dan, they're just horsing around to scare us. C'mon, we'll meet them at the high school."

"Yes, if we don't get murdered on the way!"

"You're fun," cooed Coriander sarcastically. "Dan, c'mon, we can walk to the party from here with all the other kids heading over the bridge."

Just as Dan and Coriander reached the far lawn of the high school, they saw the fuchsia hearse speeding out of the school's crescent drive.

"They're probably already inside the dance," Dan snorted, "Jerks!"

"Do you truly care that we didn't arrive in the hearse and see everyone's reaction, Dan?"

Chagrined at the possibility that his girlfriend might think he actually *cared* what others thought, Dan sullenly replied, "No, not at all." And took her hand.

"We'll ride in it going home. Danny, no big deal."

"I want my half of the money back," muttered Dan.

"Frankly, Dan, I don't give a *dime*. Get it?" Coriander attempted to pry loose a laugh from him.

He still frowned and grumbled about the risk their livery driver had taken placing them in *potential* danger from the Triborough murderer.

As they entered the high school, the harrowing howl of wolves met them. Dan looked to Coriander for an explanation.

"It's the endangered species CD I got at the Boston Museum of Science gift shop. *Wolves Greatest Hits*. Good effect, huh? Wait till they play my *Baboons in Mating Season* CD!"

Dan did not laugh. Coriander was disappointed.

In the hallway, there was no sign of Aaron and Katrina. Inside the gymnasium two girls slam dancing in matching lime-green straightjackets blocked their view.

"Maybe they were abducted at the door by the Triborough Slasher," joked Coriander.

Still, Dan ignored her and continued to glower.

13

Over the din of Aaron and Katrina's yelling, Bob McGhoul waved his hand to calm them.

"Sedgewood," shouted McGhoul gently, "you did say you wanted to be alone with her. So now you're alone—Told you I'd work it out. Don't let me stand in your way. You can get out now if you want."

Flustered, Aaron shook his head. McGhoul peeled out of the high school driveway and sped toward the winding road to Eastridge.

"So you're not going to kill us?" Katrina demanded.

"Man, I tell you..." McGhoul did not address Katrina directly. "...your girlfriend has a colorful imagination. Doesn't she?" McGhoul laughed and patted the red gym bag on the seat beside him. "You can just pull that little velvet curtain over if you want privacy." Even the velvet curtain was fuchsia. Bob pointed over his shoulder at the right side of the divider. "Pull it."

"I get it." Aaron leaned forward and jerked the divider curtain shut. The hearse hurtled up Lake Shore Drive. "Thanks, man. Katrina, relax, he was just goofing on us. Come here." Aaron pulled her close.

Abruptly, Katrina withdrew and stared out the window. "Do you know where we're going, Aaron?"

"We're just going to drive around for a while. Alone."

"What, until we run out of gas?"

"No, we're going to park somewhere."

"*Park?* I'm not entirely comfortable with this, Aaron. I mean I love you and all that, but this guy is right here." Katrina stalled, feeling trapped.

In fact... she *was*. The car swerved gently, and they could feel the rumble of a dirt road beneath them. They both glanced nervously out the window.

"I don't know this road, Aaron," said Katrina, very much ill-at-ease.

"I do. So please just relax, Katie." Aaron patted her hand reassuringly. "It goes right along the lake out to the point. Come on, I just want to kiss you, okay? I don't have any more weird surprises in mind."

The car swerved gently again. "You know this road too, I suppose, right Aaron?" she asked in a gentler tone.

Aaron looked out the window.

"Yes, sure, this is the shortcut that leads from the point over to the back of Farmer Brownell's old place. I used to ride my minibike up here in middle school. It's an old logging road."

Aaron let his hand run up along Katrina's arm to her throat. She twitched slightly and kept staring out the window, watching the lake and the dark trees pass. Aaron's fingers ran delicately along the heavy chain of Katrina's new pendant to where it plunged into her *décolletage.*

To his surprise, Katrina slowly lay her head back against the seat, chin in the air, like a cat awaiting a stroke. She closed her eyes. Aaron resisted the temptation to take advantage of Katrina's low-cut ball gown. He sighed and traced her collarbone back up to her throat and jawline with his finger. Everything about Katrina made Aaron want to sketch her portrait, to trace every curve and angle of her being. Aaron leaned forward to retrace the same path with kisses.

Katrina relaxed into it. After several minutes, she sat up straight. "Stop that!"

"What? What's the matter?"

Recalcitrant, Katrina stared out the window again.

"Aaron, I don't recognize this road. Do you?"

"Sure I do," Aaron lied. "Sort of. Isn't it the one that..." Aaron drew back the fuchsia velvet curtain and tapped on the divider. "Hey, Bob, do you know this road? 'Cause I don't."

"Oh sure," McGhoul reassured him placidly.

"Where are you taking us, then?" Aaron tapped on the divider again. "Bob, my man, we don't know this route. We don't recognize this road. Are you sure you know where you're going?"

"Sure, of course I'm sure. I just said so, didn't I?" McGhoul laughed wildly.

"Then where are we going?" demanded Aaron.

"To a bone-yard," McGhoul replied seriously.

"I don't want to go to any bone-yard, Aaron!"

"He's just kidding around, Katie, like before, don't worry."

Bob McGhoul laughed insanely and swerved off the old dirt logging road, and down an unkempt path through the trees that lead into the back acre of a cemetery. Headstones and marble monuments flew past like ghostly specters.

"Aaron, I don't like this. I want to go back now. *Now!* Do you understand?"

"Uh, Bob my man..." Aaron's voice trembled slightly. "Would you mind taking us back now? We're ready for some dancing." Aaron tried to sound jovial. But he just sounded scared. "We're really social animals, you know... *Bob?*"

“He’s insane, Aaron, we’ve got to get out,” Katrina whispered, gripping Aaron’s arm when she caught sight of an open grave. A dump truck loaded with dirt was parked next to it, poised to pour; nearby stood a backhoe. Lopsided, a tombstone leaned against a tree to the left of the dark hole. As the hearse slowed abruptly for a sharp curve, Katrina read the headstone:

Farmer James Brownell
Predictor of frosts
Tho’ not his own permafrost
Halloween 1915 - Halloween 199__

Under normal conditions, she and Aaron would have joked about the epitaph, and pointed out that the stone-cutter had not finished carving the date. Recognizing the grave bolstered Katrina’s confidence slightly, but thought the sight of Farmer Brownell’s open grave terrified her.

“Horizon View Cemetery,” she whispered. “If we can just get the doors open, Aaron, I know the way from here to my dad’s grave over the hill. From there, I think I know the way to the road. Horizon View Retirement Home is just down the street. We can use their phone.”

“Yeah. *If.* It’s a gigundo cemetery on foot.”

They tried to pry the door open, but McGhoul controlled the master lock.

“Child-proof!” hollered McGhoul with a guttural lunatic’s laugh.

The driver swerved again around a granite mausoleum and bolted straight down another hill toward a dark patch of overhanging trees.

“The woods! We’re going to crash, Aaron!” screamed Katrina.

She braced herself for the jolt as the maniacal driver floored it and plunged furiously into the thicket of large oaks.

Then—nothing happened. Oak trees blurred past. The hearse plundered low bushes and thready saplings that screeched along the car’s underbelly and sides, scraping the fresh fuchsia paint job. High trees on either side cloaked the night sky.

“Oh, Aaron, he’s going to kill us! We’ll never find our way out!”

“That *would* be a logical progression,” McGhoul snarled.

“It’s an old logging road, Katrina. We’ll follow the path,” said Aaron, then mumbled, “If we can get out.”

“In the dark, Aaron?”

“How’re we doing back there?” McGhoul asked as if he really cared.

“You crazy bastard, let us go!”

“Not much chance of that, kid. It’s Halloween, remember, and I’m *maaaad. Maaaaad* about you.”

“I told you, Aaron. I told you!”

Zooming onward, it seemed like forever that they charged along the thicketed logging road at high speed MC'd by McGhoul's evil cackle. Miles and miles of nothing but thorny brambles and trees, and insanity. On and on into the night—would it ever end? Worse yet, would it all end prematurely—their lives with it?

Then the scraping of branches on metal ceased. Katrina and Aaron stopped screaming to listen. The fuchsia hearse burst out of the forest. McGhoul still laughed like a cannibal savoring human blood.

"Hey, it's the football field. It's the back of Westlake High!" Aaron's relief was epic.

"Oh, like he's really going to let us go free, Aaron," Katrina scoffed, in tears.

"You've got a point there, Katrina, since Aaron pre-paid me!"

"We've got no leverage." Aaron realized his fatal mistake.

The hearse zoomed up the grassy embankment toward the back of the high school and careened around the brick building to the front, where it screeched to a stop. The power locks snapped open. Immediately, Bob McGhoul was at their door to open it. He rolled out a fuchsia carpet twelve feet long and bowed graciously to Katrina and Aaron.

"I wish you a fun-filled Halloween dance!" he said.

"Cool," said Aaron, trying to sound completely unaffected by the adrenaline raging in his bloodstream, "I always wondered where that road led."

"Want a few shots of whiskey to calm your nerves?" asked McGhoul. "Stash of nips in the glove box."

"No, thanks, jerk!" snapped Katrina, visibly shaken.

"Aw, come on, you guys. You're no fun. Did I *deliver* or what?! You hired me for a Halloween adventure—and you got it. That's what you paid me for. To give you the best possible door-to-door customer service, *personalized to your dreams.* Quality service! This was an opportunity for me to provide you with quality service. Have you ever had better than *this*?"

"I didn't ask to be scared out of my wits." Katrina cried with relief and rubbed her eyes. Her fake lashes twisted like poisoned millipedes.

Gently, Bob McGhoul plucked them from her face and palmed them. "You look better without them, Katrina," said McGhoul softly.

"Stay away from me, weirdo! I did not want *this.*"

"No, but you wrote on your questionnaire in the entertainment section that you love to go to scary movies. You even quoted lines from that Academy Award Winner, what was it...*Nightmare Matinee*?"

"*Still Life: The Best of the Worst,*" Aaron corrected.

"Yeah, and Aaron told me about your nightmare, Katrina. What could be more surreal? More personalized? Come on, kids, do I look like the killer type? *Noooo*. So, go have fun at the dance. I'll be waiting right here when you get out."

McGhoul offered Katrina his hand to assist her to take a step onto the fuchsia carpet. She refused and strode hand-in-hand with Aaron along the runner. So, McGhoul ran forward.

"Queen's footman comin' through," he hollered to get through a huddled group of ghoulish smokers blocking the way. Bowing majestically McGhoul opened the high school door.

"Classy ghouls!" Bear Henkel shouted above other students' commenting on the style with which Aaron and Katrina had arrived.

"Sedgewood, you'll definitely win *best vehicle*, but you'll have to challenge *me* for *most original costume*." The remark floated up in a cloud of smoke from a member of the shadowed clique—another vampire.

Handsome McGhoul smiled enchantingly at Katrina as he straightened up. Nonchalant, she brushed past him. Even when he turned on the charm, and looked briefly, dazzling, into her eyes, she feigned indifference.

"Come on, Katrina, it's a Halloween dance! I had to give you a *little* scare," McGhoul crooned and offered his hand to help her up the steps into the entryway of the school. Something about him softened her heart. He was intrepid, and weird, and seemed to think of everything. Katrina could not resist smiling back, slightly. As she accepted his hand, she felt charged by a surge of adrenaline, and a hot little thrill passed through her. Her bare eyelashes fluttered at McGhoul. He smiled—thinking of his plan for her false eyelashes that he had tucked securely in his breast pocket.

Why's he being so flirtatious and charming all of a sudden? And stranger, why am I responding to it? She wondered.

McGhoul bowed again slavishly. Katrina turned to look back at him for the last time. Aaron had already gone on ahead. McGhoul smiled gallantly at her.

"I'll be waiting for you, Katrina."

He closed the school door behind her and, smugly, strolled back to the fuchsia hearse.

Inside Westlake High School gymnasium, a host of wraiths and phantoms danced to *The Monster Mash*. Red metallic streamers seemed to pour blood from the ceiling, dangling into a roiling sea of dry-ice mist under lit by green and pus-yellow light bulbs. Coriander had done a fine job as head of the decoration committee. Katrina and Aaron glanced around for her and Dan. Dangling corpses blocked their view; one had been disemboweled, spilling colorful autumn leaves into a pile on the floor of the gym. And Aaron's skeleton hanger knockoffs were made available at the cloak room.

"Hey, Aaron, nice posters!" Billy Carlyle shouted above the din.

"Thanks, man," hollered Aaron. "I see you came as you are."

"Is that a costume or is it really you?" Katrina teased Billy-as-Frankenstein.

Another flock of masqueraders advanced, forcing Aaron and Katrina onto the dance floor of the ghouls' paradise. The fluorescent skulls that Aaron had hand painted on the floor per Coriander's instruction were already well scuffed by the dancers.

"What are you *not,* Katrina?" asked a sophomore girl in a goat outfit.

Katrina laughed self-deprecatingly. "A princess."

Puzzled, the girl in the goat costume replied, "But you kind-of *are* already."

"And you're *not* a... goat?" Katrina asked.

"*Weird Logic,*" the girl quoted Aaron's poster and shrugged, jangling a string of tin cans that hung around her neck. Katrina noticed there were bite marks cut out of the cans, as if a goat had tried to eat them.

"Nice can, "Aaron joked, referring to the tin can necklace.

"I think we have to dance, Aaron, if we're going to stand here." Katrina brushed his cheek with her lips jostled by the crowd of dancing teenagers.

"Okay. Keep your eyes peeled for Dan and Correy."

"Bet they're ticked."

Jostled again by fanged and horned dancers who flailed claws and spiked tails, Katrina and Aaron were squished into a tight embrace between a hairy brown spider and a leper. Two swans danced to their right. To their left, a brown bear and a hippo.

"Party animals!" shouted Aaron. Katrina laughed.

"I keep feeling like something bad is about to happen," she shouted over Billy Idol's *White Wedding*.

"Well, we could take control of the situation and go under the bleachers and actually *be* bad, "Aaron shouted back.

"Very funny. Don't be disgusting, Aaron," Katrina said priggishly. "It's so dirty under there."

"You're such a *princess*, Katrina," he teased, pulling her into his arms again and nibbling her naked ear.

"Don't slobber; I value my hearing." She hugged him.

They slow-danced for a long time, enjoying the hollow echo of *Gregorian Chants*.

"Aaron, look, there's Bob *McFool*. I wish he'd quit looking at me the way he does. He stares like he *knows* me." The words rang in her head for a moment. Then she noticed McGhoul conversing with Officer Nancy Fieldstone who was patrolling near the double doors of the gymnasium. With his red gym bag slung over his shoulder he gesticulated wildly as he spoke to her.

"Bet he's telling her about our ride from hell," observed Aaron.

"Bet he's flirting with her." Katrina laughed.

"Nah, she's too young for him."

"Oh, and you'd know?" challenged Katrina.

"Yeah, I know. From my dad—when he and my mom were split up, he discovered that old dudes my dad's age got—"

Katrina wasn't interested. "Hey, maybe The Fieldstones will arrest *McFool*?"

"For what? Scaring us? After I paid him to?" Aaron joined in her laughter.

"We didn't pay him to scare us, Aaron?"

"Well, we sort of did. *I* sort of did. I asked him if he could come up with something extra special for the occasion to surprise us. He did. The guy even went out of his way and bought the old hearse and converted it so we could park our backsides in it for a few hours. It wasn't in his showroom when were there, remember?"

"Well, he's had fun at our expense. Look at him telling her all about our hilarious ride in the forest."

Bob McGhoul and Nancy Fieldstone were laughing incessantly.

"Man, dude's flirting his butt off! Aaron laughed. "Good luck, dude."

Even with the weighty red gym bag hanging pendulously off his shoulder as he spoke, with each big gesture, the young policewoman laughed heartily and glanced over at Aaron and Katrina. Katrina's sense of dread faded as she cozied against Aaron. But Officer Fieldstone departed, her heart sank and the dread came back more acutely.

"Hey, there they are over by the refreshments." Katrina waved at Dan and Coriander.

"Let's eat."

"We really should go apologize first, Aaron."

"Where you lead, I follow, Katie."

Behind him a classmate was singing, *I love you, you love me...* "Oh my gosh, it's Brewster!"

Brewster had cut off the head of a stuffed Barney, and de-stuffed it enough to fit it over his own head! Aaron and Katrina giggled. An arrow between the dinosaur's eyes accented its purple forehead, as if he had been shot from behind. The plush life-size Barney wore a huge name tag that read,

PLEASE LOVE ME, I'M REALLY BREWSTER.

"My favorite color," said Katrina patting the large celebrity dinosaur as she and Aaron pushed their way off the dance floor. , Suddenly, Brewster stepped in and tried to waltz with Katrina. Aaron prodded him out of the way and sang the Barney song to Katrina himself.

Katrina plugged her ears and yelled, "Dan! Correy!"

The four friends approached the buffet tables on the sidelines.

Dan turned his back on Aaron and Katrina and grabbed a handful of orange and yellow candy corn.

"What is so scary about candy corn?" Dan asked a freshman assigned to serving. "I never understood why it's considered a Halloween food."

"What?" the underclassman yelled, unable to hear Dan over the music. Dan shouted his question louder.

Coriander happily greeted Katrina and Aaron, "God, I'm so relieved to see you guys."

"What's with Dan?"

"Don't worry, he'll get over it."

"Hey, why don't you two go for a ride now? McGhoul's right over there. Go on. It's a lot of fun."

"Want to, Danny?"

"Nah."

"Come on." Coriander whispered in Dan's ear.

"Maybe."

"Go ahead, Dan," Aaron said. "Look, I'm really sorry. McGhoul was goofing on us all and acted like he was going to kidnap Katie and me. Because of what we listed on the questionnaire under what kind of entertainment we like. You know, *scary*. Now it's your turn. Go on."

"As you know, Aaron, I despise *scary*." Dan spoke disdainfully. "And I did not list horror movies on *my* questionnaire as my favorite form of entertainment. Frankly, Aaron, this has all been a waste of my hard-earned lawn mowing money."

Peeved, Dan took Coriander by the hand and strode away toward the main door. As he passed by McGhoul, Dan snapped his fingers but did not make eye contact with the driver. McGhoul followed them out.

"What *did* Dan list on his questionnaire under preferred entertainment, then?" Katrina asked.

"Beats me. Maybe chem lab." Aaron stared after them pensively. "One thing's for sure, I've never seen Dan act so mad before."

14

Leaving the thrum of the dance behind, Dan led Coriander to his locker, where he snatched a pen and a sheet of lined paper. Crouching, he wrote quickly.

"What're you writing? Let me see."

"No." Dan cupped a hand over the page.

Coriander rolled her eyes. "Dan, you're acting so weird."

"Come on, let's go for a *test* drive." Dan hid the note in his trouser pocket, then dragged her by the hand to the exit. "I've got a hunch, Correy."

"Okay, Dan." Coriander looked happy again. Maybe they would have a fun evening after all. He'd been such a boor since they'd snogged at the gas station.

Inside the fuchsia hearse, McGhoul apologized for having abandoned them at the gas station and asked where they would like to go.

"I'll direct you as we drive," Dan replied and removed his beard and wig lazily, tossing the gray mass on the seat.

"You kids had a good evening?" McGhoul ventured to ask.

"Just great, thanks," Coriander lied.

Dan was silent for a while.

"Go left here, please. Now right," Dan instructed.

"Danny, this is the way to my house. How will you get home later?" Coriander was psyched. Her parents were out for the evening at an office party. She would have Dan all to herself in her bedroom without the strict *four-feet-on-the-floor* rule imposed by her parents. Not that *that* had ever stopped her from innovating.

"I'm going home now," Dan retorted.

"Now? What for? We haven't even started having fun yet."

"Precisely my point."

Coriander was crushed.

McGhoul glanced in the rearview mirror at them.

"First fight?"

"I would prefer if you would mind your own business, Mr. McGhoul," said Dan plainly and politely. "But thank you for asking."

"What the heck is wrong with you, Danny?" Coriander demanded. "All evening you've been a troll!"

Dan was kicking himself inside. He could not bring himself to say really mean things to Coriander. He did not want to hurt her feelings, not too badly, but just enough. He could not tell her the reasons why he was about to say they were through. He thought about saying that since she became Homecoming Queen she was more stuck-up than ever, but that had always been one of the qualities about her he had found most endearing. Before he said anything further, the fuchsia hearse pulled up in front of the Preston residence. McGhoul flew to the door and opened it, bowing.

"Be sure to read this, Correy," whispered Dan removing the note from his trouser pocket. Coriander looked confused. Then Dan stated loud enough for McGhoul to hear, "Coriander, this'll explain why..." Dan placed the note deliberately in Coriander's palm.

McGhoul watched wide-eyed.

"Why *what*?" Coriander was flabbergasted.

"Why I'm dumping you, Coriander," replied Dan, absolutely dying inside at his lie.

"I don't want your stupid explanations," Coriander screamed at Dan, and threw the note back in Dan's face. Dan grabbed her wrist. McGhoul averted his gaze.

"This note..." Dan looked her in the eye intently. "...will *explain*..." He squeezed Coriander's fingers around the note and gave her fist an extra squeeze, then pushed her out of the hearse. He hoped she would not slug him.

McGhoul tried to be helpful, getting her to her feet. Coriander hid her tears and ran to the house.

"I hate you!" screamed Coriander as she ran to her front door.

"Poor Coriander," muttered McGhoul.

"Poor *Spice Seed*," said Dan with sarcastically.

"Chicks, eh?" McGhoul seized the moment to bro-bond.

"Let's go. I'm tired and I want to go home, Mr. McGhoul."

"Whatever you say, kid."

Coriander fell on her bed and cried herself to sleep before she remembered Dan's note wadded in her sweaty hand. By that time, nearly an hour had passed since Dan had delivered her safely home. She read Dan's note, her eyes crimson-rimmed. She could not believe what Dan had written. Had he gone mad?

"You know the way from here, right, Mr. McGhoul?"

"Sure do." McGhoul smiled in the rearview mirror at Dan. "Mind if I ask you what happened tonight between you two?"

"Interesting question."

"I bet the *answer* is even more interesting," said McGhoul. "So, may I ask?"

"Sure. Doesn't mean I'll tell you." Dan chortled. "Makes me look bad."

"What do you mean?" McGhoul was genuinely interested.

"Well, I guess I'm a bit of a cad. You know. Tried some stuff in the gas station bathroom. She wouldn't let me go as far as I thought she would. So why waste my time? Know what I mean? There are other girls, girls who understand *customer service*. So, I figure Spice Seed's just another experiment. Anyway, she's a bit full of herself."

"You mentioned in your questionnaire, Dan, that you find it entertaining to study human behavior. Surprising difference compared to your friends, who all wrote that horror movies were their favorite entertainment. I didn't quite understand what you meant though..." McGhoul probed carefully.

"Well, I experiment with people, with human nature. I think it's interesting to see how far you can push people. Girls especially."

"Hmmm. *mommy issues*, Dan?" McGhoul resisted the temptation to agree wholeheartedly.

"Yeah, big time, er, *mommy issues*," Dan agreed awkwardly. In fact he and his mother had an excellent relationship. He was starting to worry he was getting in over his own head in his charade. "You know what I mean, Mr. McGhoul? They're disposable anyhow."

"What you're describing sounds very cruel to me. Cruel and... *unusual*," McGhoul said cautiously, suppressing a giggle.

"Yeah." Nauseated, nevertheless, Dan faked a jovial laugh and smiled at McGhoul in the rearview mirror.

McGhoul laughed with him, recalling his own tormented teenage years. Soon the fuchsia hearse echoed with perfidious laughter as Dan connected with a lunatic.

"I think you and I have a lot more in common than you're letting on, Mr. McGhoul." Dan laughed again. "Well, there's my house, up on the left. Boy, I sure am tired. Can't wait to get some shut-eye."

The hearse turned up the rural road leading toward Dan Pritcher's house.

"So, you really think we have a lot in common, Dan?" McGhoul's tone darkened. Instinctively, the wizened predator in him sensed he was being cornered swiftly by a minor, and McGhoul had every intention to side-step Dan's stealthy approach and let the inquisitive boy slam himself into the nearest wall.

"Yeah! *Lots* in common!" Dan faked another evil laugh and leaned forward to reach the door handle, expecting the hearse to stop in front of his house.

But it did not. Nor did the door latch release.

"That's my house, Bob, my man." Dan imitated Aaron's bravado.

"I know," replied Bob McGhoul.

"Where're we going?" Dan asked, trying his best to sound unaffected by fear.

"You're so observant, Dan. I thought you might like to see something. Then we'll know just how *alike* you and I are. Right, you think we're so *alike*? I've always hoped to find a suitable apprentice."

Quietly, Dan tried the door handle again, but it remained master-locked. His heart raced seeing McGhoul's deranged eyes in the rearview mirror.

With that, McGhoul drove right on down Dan's street, back to the main road toward the super highway... That is when Dan heard the nauseating sound of a slow zipper.

Crap, this guy's a pervert.

"Look Dan," cooed McGhoul.

Dan wanted to puke. The *ziiiiiip* sound continued for an unusually long time. And the hearse swerved as its driver attempted to multitask. *Weird*, thought Dan. The *zipping* did not stop until—

"Look, Dan," again McGhoul murmured happily, "C'mon, look what I've got."

That cannot be a trouser zipper, thought Dan with some relief.

"*Voilà!*" declared Bob McGhoul as he reached the end of the zipper of the bright red gym bag next to him on the front seat.

"What's in the ba—?" *Bigger crap*, thought Dan.

"So Dan, is *this* what you mean when you say we have things in common?" asked McGhoul, revealing its contents to Dan.

Through the Plexiglas divider, Dan looked into the red gym bag. The first thing he noticed was a pair of black butterfly false eyelashes... *stuck to a...?*

Dan did not speak. His first thought was that Coriander was safely at home. Dan, however, most definitely was *not*.

15

Dearest Correy,

I'm going to pick a fight with you in front of McGhoul. Sorry. It's to trick him. I have a theory and I want you home safely first. I think he'll fall for it. I'm smarter than he is. Meet me by the stone wall on Pine Street in 20 minutes. Look for my Honda. I'll explain.

Be there, or be square (like me)!

Dan Your Man

P.S. I love you, Coriander Preston!

"Thank God I wasn't dumped!" exclaimed Coriander. *That would be a first.* She shook her head in disbelief, *McGhoul may not be as smart as you, Danny, but he's got way more life experience than all of us combined... and he is a nice man.* So why the heck did Dan have his panties in a twist?

Coriander breathed easily. Dan would have left his house by now and was probably waiting for her already behind the Pine Street stone wall. She checked the time: she was late. Her parents were still out at their office party, so she trotted over to Pine Street, taking the chance that Dan would still be there.

The longer Coriander waited by the stonewall, the more her confidence waned. *It's Halloween night and I am alone... in an isolated area where I know no one... with a serial murderer loose in Westlake... not to mention all the psychos, because the moon's full. And what if—what if McGhoul is a psycho after all? What if McGhoul saw through Dan's little plan? What if he forced Dan to tell him what was really written in the note? Then McGhoul is coming after me now...* Coriander fretted as her imagination did a 180. *But, maybe he's really a nice man who's just eccentric...*

Coriander shivered in her unpopular-girl costume, wishing she had changed back into something fashionable with layers. All the fun had been sucked out of Halloween as if drained by Anthrope himself.

Or worse, she thought, *what if Dan is really in on it? What if the reason Dan says he won't stay out after dark is because he's really the one doing all the... Katrina's paranoia has worn off on me...*

Headlights appeared at the end of the street. Coriander ducked behind the stone wall: no Honda Civic, no hearse. She recognized

Officer Fieldstone as she passed by in her cruiser with her father the detective. Seeing the police made Coriander feel safe, until they turned the corner onto Maple Street. She wished she had flagged them down. She decided to walk home and call the police.

Ducking again behind the stone wall, she watched a marauding group of pirates and ghosts run down Pine Street egging cars and houses. *Crap,* thought Coriander as she watched them disappear around the corner, I'll get blamed if the Fieldstones double back. So she hid. She waited until the coast was clear.

When she stood up, a firm hand detained her.

"Aren't you Miss Preston? The Homecoming Queen?" the man took hold of her shoulder.

Coriander screamed.

16

The rest of the evening was a mix of gory food, cider with candy worms, ice cubes with licorice bugs frozen inside, and dancing with rotting bodies and specters and cannibals and vermin and Aaron.

"You're such a blast, Katrina!" Aaron shouted at the top of his lungs and only Katrina cared or heard over the loud dance music.

Aaron, my love, Katrina thought about saying to him several times. But instead she just grinned a lot and hugged him a lot, afraid to burst the precious moment with bungling words. Even now, after they had gone out together nearly eight months, she still was not really comfortable being effusive, not like Coriander, who, she thought, had rushed into it too fast with Dan.

"Hey, Katrina, I want to do this with you every week. No. Every day!" said Aaron slipping his hand around her lithe waist as they stepped into the neon-lit hallway, leaving the thumping phantom music behind.

"I'm so hot!" Katrina fanned herself with Aaron's vampire cape and used it to wipe off all her sparkly princess makeup.

"Yup!" concurred Aaron.

She missed the compliment. "How 'bout you, Mr. Funny Bones?" She kissed him.

Aaron looked hopeful. "Want to go sit in the hearse? If it's back with Dan and Correy in one piece. Hope he's not still mad at me."

Before Katrina could answer, a twittering skeleton wearing gaudy jewelry and the goat with the tin can necklace stumbled past laughing and darted toward the girls' room. Billy Carlyle chased them in his Frankenstein costume, but the girls slammed the door on him.

"We've definitely got bigger fish to fry," said Aaron, turning his full attention to Katrina. "C'mon, babe. Let's get out of here."

Katrina glowed inside. "Okay, *babe*." A thousand smiles flickered in her eyes.

They didn't have to wait long to pile into the backseat of the fuchsia hearse where they continued their amorous *tête-à-tête*. Their livery soon pulled up in front of the high school. McGhoul was alone, save the red gym bag that seemed to accompany him wherever he went. He got out and waved to Katrina and Aaron.

“Think Dan and Correy are in back?” asked Aaron.

“Or they went home already. Her parents’re out for the evening.” Katrina winked.

Aaron signaled McGhoul with a wave. He rushed obediently to roll out the fuchsia carpet and open the door of the hearse for the teens. He bowed subserviently. And Aaron picked up Katrina—hollering and laughing—and hoisted her over his shoulder.

“Homeward?” queried McGhoul as Aaron placed Katrina gently inside the vehicle.

“With a brief side trip,” Aaron winked mischievously at McGhoul. “And hold the Grey Poupon! Home via the scenic route.”

“Scenic route?” queried McGhoul.

“By the same way we arrived, please.”

McGhoul seemed surprised. “Through the football field?”

“Yes, please, across the football field, up the logging road, through the cemetery—and make it snappy, good sir.” Aaron laughed and McGhoul did too.

“Well, I’m happy to see you kids have finally gotten into the spirit of the day.”

“Yeah, well, with your help, Mr. McGhoul, we finally did,” Aaron assured. “Best customer service ever!”

The fuchsia hearse pulled behind the high school and rolled quietly down the grassy hill with its lights off.

“I’ll turn on the car lights once we’re a ways into the woods. Wouldn’t want to arouse suspicion, you know,” McGhoul said, regarding them in the rearview mirror.

“You don’t mind if I have a private moment with my girlfriend, do you?” Without waiting for McGhoul’s answer, Aaron shut the slide vent in the plastic divider and drew the velvet curtain closed.

Slowly the hearse cruised along the old logging road. For a blissful infinity, Aaron and Katrina felt safe in each other’s arms in the back of the hearse. But, after they had been driving for several miles, the hearse jerked to a halt.

“Hey, why’re we stopping?” Aaron released Katrina and opened the velvet curtain and the vent.

“Out of gas,” McGhoul grunted through the vent. “Sorry, kids, I spaced out about refilling the tank after I, uh, *got rid of your friends*.” He made mock-scary eyes.

Aaron laughed but was concerned about Katrina’s 11:30 p.m. curfew.

“Well, don’t you have a can of gas that you carry in the trunk?” asked Aaron.

"You're *in* the trunk, Sedgewood." McGhoul sighed. "These vehicles were never designed for Route 66 cross-country travel like your Mustang."

"Short hops," mumbled Aaron. "So, what are you going to do about it?"

"So—you want to flip a coin for who hikes back for gas? *Heads* I buy you fly."

"No flipping," insisted Katrina. "Aaron, you're not leaving me here alone," she whispered. "Let him go get it."

"I'm thinking Aaron can run faster than I," wagered McGhoul. "And, there's a shortcut through the cemetery you can take, rather than trekking the seven miles back to the high school football field. It's a nice walk over the hill past the mausoleum. Only about three quarters of a mile to civilization—if you don't mind a cemetery stroll on Halloween night. Flip?"

"Okay, I call *tails*," said Aaron grudgingly.

"Good, because I always take *heads*."

It was in that very moment, as Bob McGhoul flipped the coin, that Katrina noticed the large mole behind the driver's right ear. Earlier the mole had been hidden by his long hair. Now his sweaty ponytail was tucked up under his livery cap. Involuntarily, Katrina raised a finger and pointed at McGhoul's giant mole.

"What is it, Katie?"

"Look behind his ear, Aaron. The mole... from my dream."

In the rearview mirror, Bob McGhoul watched Katrina's lips and licked his own.

17

It was odd there had not been a murder for a whole day after such a rash of them, thought Officer Fieldstone.

"Just wait and see," her father kept saying.

"Maybe the killer went out of town?"

"What, like went on a cruise?" The detective chortled.

"Or moved on?"

"Or, the pre-Halloween murders were part of a pattern, in preparation for something big?"

"But *what?* Now that the prom teens have returned '*wed not dead*' as the news anchors are loving quoting you, Dad..."

Detective Fieldstone's hunch had panned out quite the opposite of what he had suspected. And yet, he had disguised his blunder by praising the prom teenagers for returning home so an innocent person would not be blamed for their demise.

"Yeah, but the murderer didn't flinch," countered Detective Fieldstone. "You'd think maybe he'd pull a copy-catter."

"Halloween night's not over yet." Nancy smiled with pride at her father. "You always get'em, Dad."

It was true, Detective Fieldstone had succeeded in getting the local press to work with him on the case to tone down the gory details of each murder *somewhat*—and somewhat was better than nothing. He did not want the killer to get his jollies reading about the genius of his customer service. And the public had such a primitive appetite for the bloody details. But the sage detective had not counted on the national news picking up the story, and thereby triggering the missing prom teens to feel guilty and come home. He actually believed the prom teens *had* been murdered, even though he had come to the realization that the wad of soiled clothes Nancy Fieldstone had found could not have belonged to the missing prom teens. The clothes were decades old.

After further digging, it became clear that the clothing had been purchased from a local thrift shop. The shop owner identified the buyer as a large man with amber-tinted glasses. This, Officer Fieldstone had noted in her police report. Meanwhile, the prom couple had made it all the way from the Florida Pan Handle back to New England by the time the *USA Today* cover story about them had incited every highway toll booth clerk to call state police with a presumed-positive ID.

"According to Priestly van Swift our forensic pathologist, the knife holes were real," said Officer Fieldstone.

"But then why the red food coloring and no blood?" posited her father.

"Maybe the killer set us up, Dad, on a very deliberate wild goose chase."

"You mean a red herring," Detective Fieldstone corrected his daughter. But why?"

"Why would anyone other than the murderer himself want to throw the police off the trail of the Triborough Murderer?"

"Maybe they're working as a team?"

"Or the opposite?"

The Fieldstones decided to track down the man with the amber-tinted glasses mentioned by the owner of the second hand clothing store.

Scouting Westlake for eggers and vandals, The Fieldstones finished making the rounds at the high school and around the richer neighborhoods that got hammered by sulfurous old eggs this time of year, striping houses and cars, and crazing gorgeous paint jobs with the highly acidic amino acid compound found in the yolk and albumin. The father-daughter law enforcement team usually competed on Halloween to see who could catch the most eggers. That's how Nancy Fieldstone had first fallen in love with the idea of becoming a cop. But this Halloween, though the egg damage caused costly repairs, the father-daughter duo were preoccupied with matters that cost Westlake citizens' lives.

Back at Westlake Police Station, the small cell block was teaming with ghoulish eggers waiting for their parents to come collect them.

"Hey, kids, y'think you're the Easter Bunny?" Detective Fieldstone rapped on the cell bars before turning to praise his colleagues, "Nice work! Our precinct caught over a dozen eggers this year."

"—a baker's dozen, Detective, lucky thirteen," replied Officer Fieldstone as she flashed a smile at a lineup of sad, costumed teenagers before following her father into his office where he played his phone messages.

"Listen to this phone message," he instructed his daughter. She listened intently.

"Chameleon Limousines?"

"Flip you for it?"

"Naw, let's do this one together."

Fifteen minutes later, Detective and Officer Fieldstone arrived at Chameleon Limousines.

"This could be the break you need for that promotion," he chided her, "Since you bungled your second hand clothing *find*."

Nancy was quiet as they parked outside the chain link fence in the parking lot.

"Look, Dad, beyond the fence, the cruiser's headlights captured something."

Outside the cruiser, they took a look with the Maglite at a maroon economy car parked way out back, beyond the high wire fence. Just the nose of the compact car was illuminated.

"Why hide a Honda Civic behind razor wire? It's not like anyone steals *those*."

"Or even eggs'em. Hey, remember the narrow tire marks on the utility road behind Prospect Park the night of Miss Chantal's murder?"

"Looks like we didn't speak to everyone in Westlake with a Honda Civic."

They meandered along the chain link fence. Iris's snarling jaws of death deterred further investigation and drew Paul Reed out of the shadows like a specter.

Is this a trap? Both Fieldstones reached for their gun. The man who approached them wore amber-tinted glasses and his build was sizeable, like in the police report taken from the thrift shop owner.

"Officer Fieldstone? Oh, and Detective Fieldstone, as well! Hi!" Paul Reed hefted his bulk startling them. "Thanks for coming. I'm the one who called you. Come on in this way. Iris won't bite you, don't worry. I've got her."

"Until you let go of her," remarked Officer Fieldstone.

"Show some respect for this concerned citizen, Officer Fieldstone," her father corrected loud enough for Paul Reed to hear, then he winked at his daughter.

Nancy Fieldstone played along. She sensed what her father's intentions were.

Detective Fieldstone's instincts told him not to trust the man with the amber glasses. He wished they had called for backup. And he debated a discrete strategy to send Officer Fieldstone back to the cruiser to get on the CB radio, without spooking Paul Reed.

Paul led the way into the limousine showroom via the side courtyard door. All the while, he kept Iris on a tight leash.

"May I offer you a snack or a beverage?" Paul pointed to a gleaming silver tray on the credenza. Detective Fieldstone's eyes lit up. He popped a grape into his mouth then slathered a cracker with what appeared to be fresh *pâté*.

"Brain food!" extolled Paul and hastened down the hall, "Right back, Officers, there are some things I need to show you."

"*Detective*," corrected Detective Fieldstone, "*She* is the Officer."

"Sorry," said Paul from the hallway. "I'll be right back."

"Oh wow, this is yummy," exclaimed the detective. "Try it, Nancy!"

"I'm on a diet," said Officer Fieldstone taking grapes instead, then whispered when her father dove for seconds, "Dad, please watch your fat and salt intake. I'm already half-orphaned."

As he chewed and savored, he wandered, looking around the showroom, shadowed by his daughter.

Paul returned, and noticed the Fieldstones glancing at the customer service banner over the cars. He smirked.

"Yeah, you think that's weird, Detectives...." Paul deliberately flattered Officer Fieldstone. "...wait till you see this. I found this diary—it belongs to my boss. I clean up around here, you see. I wasn't snooping. Maybe he left them for me to see, I don't know. You know. *A cry for help*? There's a whole box full of these notebooks. Full of stuff like *this*." He pointed out one entry.

Detective Fieldstone's eyes popped at the screamingly convincing evidence that Paul presented. Page after page of documentation: the wino and the champagne flute, Miss Chantal and the classical music, Mr. Samson at the cinema, Farmer Brownell, zounds of others with whom the Fieldstones were too familiar.

"Most of them dead from asphyxiation, Detectives," Paul observed. "Freaky."

Officer Fieldstone leafed through the notebooks, her jaw dropping with each turn of a page.

"Dad, my God!" She finally spoke, then corrected herself professionally, "Detective Fieldstone, there are years and years of proof here describing in autobiographical detail the same kind of murders committed in other towns in other parts of the country, all documented in this..." She studied a page closely. "...exquisitely beautiful handwriting."

"Twenty years' worth of deranged killing," affirmed Paul. "More *pâté*, Detectives? Ah, I see you quite enjoyed it. I'll have to send you home with a jar. I make it by the double dozen. Fresh."

Gladly, Detective Fieldstone took another and pondered the diaries over his daughter's shoulder.

"Maximal customer service with a malicious twist," observed Detective Fieldstone ruefully as he chewed. "Well, the ultimate customer servant... finally slipped up on my watch."

"And *mine*," added Nancy competitively.

Paul Reed could see from the expression in the police officers' eyes that even seasoned law enforcement professionals could become heartsick. Paul was pleased that he had effectively—and rightfully, Paul believed—convinced them of McGhoul's insanity.

"McGhoul must have been tormented ruthlessly as a child to have become such a monster," Officer Fieldstone said, her voice soft with compassion.

"What could the adults in his childhood have done to him to break him?" Paul gently, deftly egged her on.

"Yeah, well, too bad he chose murder instead of psychotherapy," muttered Detective Fieldstone, chewing another thickly laden cracker.

"Yeah, too bad," agreed Paul Reed softly, shaking his head in feigned dismay.

"Yeah... 'cause we're gonna' nail his sorry ass to the wall," Detective Fieldstone barked, his outrage brimming.

"*Language*, Detective," Officer Fieldstone reprimanded her father's lack of professionalism. "And not for nothin', these accounts certainly fit the pattern to a tee. But I still don't see—"

Detective Fieldstone finished his daughter's sentence, "—why the guy kills at all."

"Maybe it's symbolic," offered Paul Reed. "To make up for his failures in life? I don't know, but you're right, Detective." Paul shrugged. "It's definitely a pattern."

Fieldstone did not react to Paul Reed's analysis of the situation. He just listened. Still trying to get a bead on the man with the amber-tinted glasses, though Paul seemed like an alright guy, just a little shy, a little awkward. *Well, heck, that's 80% of the population,* he mused. Still, Detective Fieldstone never fully trusted anyone too soon. Something about this case was too clear-cut, too easy. Too *out of the blue* that all the evidence for which he had been scraping suddenly appeared before him in succinct, neatly written diaries accompanied by delicious snacks. *Man, that pâté was flipping awesome!* He thought a bit, then stuffed one more into his mouth.

Could it really be *that* simple? *Have I been over-analyzing the problem, making it too difficult for myself all along?* Here he had been invited in by a scared employee. *Suspicious? I didn't even have to obtain a search warrant to find all the evidence I need to send McGhoul away for life in the slammer.*

"Call for back up, Officer," Detective Fieldstone said to his daughter. "Have'em seal off the premises. I don't want those diaries tampered with while you go get the search warrant. You'll have to wake the Magistrate to obtain it."

Officer Fieldstone nodded, then she reread the Halloween entry. "And to think, I thought Bob McGhoul was a humorous guy," she said in disbelief. "Met him tonight at the high school Halloween dance after he dropped off the kids. Luggin' that big red gym bag around like a dedicated boxer. The guy's a total *raconteur*—had me laughing my arse off."

"Go!" ordered her father. "We have to act now! Those kids' lives may be in danger."

Nancy Fieldstone disappeared out the side door.

Detective Fieldstone massaged his jaw. "Surprising that *she* didn't have a feeling about the guy. She usually has a feeling about a perp. Got it from her old man." Proudly, the detective winked at Paul.

Paul did not react. Instead, he spoke softly, "I sure hope our Westlake teenagers are safe, Detective. As we speak, they are with Mr. McGhoul."

"She's callin' for backup, Paul, don't you worry, we'll take care of it," Detective Fieldstone said as he headed for the exit.

"May I please go with you, Detective? I think I know Bob McGhoul's pattern well enough by now to be of *some* help," said Paul Reed holding up the lengthy questionnaires the teenagers had filled out. Detective Fieldstone agreed.

As they headed out to the cruiser, Paul handed Detective Fieldstone a small glass jar. The older gentleman's eyes lit up.

"I always make extra," Paul reassured the detective. "Refrigerate it if you're not eating it the same day."

Detective Fieldstone all but forgot about the amber-tinted glasses.

18

McGhoul yanked the small dark, waxy ball off his neck behind his ear and tossed it at Katrina through the vent. She flinched. "Don't worry, it's fake. Aaron told me about your dream. Remember? So I tried to reconstruct it as much as possible. Right down to the mole."

Katrina shot him a dirty look.

"Okay, Aaron, I buy, you fly, man." McGhoul handed Aaron a creased ten-dollar bill and the deciding quarter, *heads* up.

"Whatever happened to customer service at any expense?" Aaron asked, a little put out.

"You've got a good point, Sedgewood. And I'm real sorry for this, but, well, doctor's orders."

"What d'you mean?"

"Why do you think I drive everywhere? I can't walk distances. Asthma." McGhoul fake coughed. "That's why I'm into cars."

"Asthma!?" Aaron grunted. *Wish I hadn't been polite in the first place agreeing to flip a goddam coin.* He had hoped to have Katrina really, truly, *finally* alone on the spacious back seat of the hearse.

Aaron pulled at the door handle. "Locks, please."

"I'm coming with you," Katrina whispered, rubbing her bare arms covered in gooseflesh.

"No, Katrina, you'll freeze. Stay here. I'll be twenty minutes tops," said Aaron, kissing her. "What could *possibly* happen in twenty minutes?"

"You know what happened last time we said that?" Katrina and Aaron broke into morbid, hysterical laughter, recalling the horrible shock of finding Miss Chantal dead.

Bob unlocked the rear door so Aaron could get out.

"Aaron, I've got to leave the headlights off or the battery'll run down." McGhoul sounded apologetic. "It drains it enough using the presto-lock system. But the cemetery exit is just up over the hill."

"Aw, hell, it's really cold," said Aaron.

"Take your cape," Katrina insisted. "You'll freeze. I'll be fine inside the car."

"Are you sure?" She was and helped Aaron bundle up and kissed him good-bye. She shivered without Aaron to keep her warm.

Along the horizon at the end of the narrow cemetery road, Katrina could make out the silhouettes of a mausoleum and several other monuments to death. She was secretly relieved not to have to walk through the graveyard and past that open grave waiting for Farmer Brownell's corpse to be planted forever. In the chill back seat of the fuchsia hearse, Katrina prayed in silence for Aaron's speedy return.

"You girls don't like being left behind, do you?" McGhoul asked rhetorically, patting the big red gym bag on the front seat. Katrina ignored the remark.

Under his breath, she thought she heard McGhoul say something about *his* girl. But she wasn't sure, and she did not feel like getting into a conversation about his personal life. In silence, Katrina watched out the window as Aaron ascended the hill toward the cemetery exit. His billowing cape flapped in the wind—Dracula revisited.

"Cold?" Bob McGhoul asked Katrina, as they exchanged a glance in the rearview mirror. "Sorry the heat doesn't work back there Want to sit up front with us?" His hand patted the gym bag again then he switched on a tiny light in the dashboard. The temperature dropped swiftly without the motor running. And a fresh patter of icy rain prickled the roof and windows.

"No, thanks," Katrina replied, "I guess they never had any need for heat in the back of *these* cars." Katrina intended to end the conversation. She was very tired from dancing and cranky from not having eaten anything but orange marshmallow peanuts. *H.A.L.T* was the acronym she'd learned when her parents went to Alcoholics Anonymous, toward the end when her dad was still alive. She missed him even though he had been a raging alcoholic for a while. And somehow thinking of *H.A.L.T.* gave Katrina comfort because it reminded her of her father when he had been really trying to get well, when he was more appreciative of his daughter for the great human being she always was. But Mr. Phillips' kidneys were already too far gone from the insidious *hand-to-mouth-reflex*, and... *If only he'd learned H.A.L.T. sooner, hungry, angry, lonely, tired, if only he'd quit drinking*. As Katrina understood it, H.A.L.T. meant stop obsessing and call a friend (instead of boozing) when you're any combination of *hungry, angry, lonely*, or *tired*. And right now, Katrina was all four. But she had no way to call anyone from the back of a fuchsia hearse in the middle of a cemetery on a rain-smeared Halloween night.

Bob McGhoul chuckled at her remark. "Good one, '*they never needed heat in these cars*'." He guffawed oddly and kept right on watching her in the rearview mirror. Dim light from the dashboard panel vaguely illuminated their faces in the dark car. Katrina pretended to be interested in anything but Bob's eyes in the rearview mirror.

"You sure you don't want to sit up front? It's warmer with two live bodies next to each other."

Any shred of deliberate suggestiveness nauseated her. And the term *live bodies* made her cringe. Her eyebrow arched a warning at McGhoul in the rearview mirror.

"You mad? You're giving me the hairy eyebrow."

"I pluck them that way. Don't take it personally."

H.A.L.T.-ing in the back seat, Katrina identified herself with the hearse: tank empty, ignition dead, immobile, running off the reserve battery so she'd have a dim little light. She shivered and hunched over, pulling the skirt of her velvet dress up around her arms and shoulders in order to stay warm as best she could.

"So you gonna come up front, or what?" McGhoul urged again.

"Thanks, but my foot hurts. I don't feel like walking around," Katrina fibbed.

"Oh yes, that's right, you hurt it when you kicked the door to my office." There was an uncomfortable pause. Some kind of predatory weirdness alchemized the air. "I could come back there with you," McGhoul offered. "Keep you warm."

"What?" The scorn in Katrina's tone was palpable. "No, thanks!" She changed the subject. "You were changing tires, how do you know I kicked your door? Did Aaron tell you that *too*, that I threw a fit?"

"I was *there* with you, watching you on the security camera." His eyes in the rearview softened. He looked lovingly at her.

The darkness seemed to thicken in every crevice around Katrina as Aaron strode on through the graveyard. Katrina felt defenseless as all the evidence against Bob McGhoul from her nightmare rose through her memory.

Don't overreact, she thought, trying to quell her nerves. *If he were going to kill me, he would've done it already.*

Wouldn't he? Or is this the point when it starts?

"Then why didn't you open the door for us sooner, Mr. McGhoul?" Katrina's voice sounded timid.

"Because I had to watch you. I always like to see how my clients react to poor customer service, like being locked out. The ultimate rejection. Bad customer service makes a person honest. I got to see your true colors. That way, I knew you would be a demanding customer whom I would have to work hard to please. I like that in a client. There aren't enough demanding people nowadays. Without demanding people, there's no need for me. *And I like to be needed, Katrina.*"

She recoiled from McGhoul's reptilian slither.

Affectionately, he patted the bright red gym bag on the front seat once more, caressing it like a house pet. She recognized the bag from his office: the one he had rested from Paul Reed's grip and stowed under his desk. The one he'd slung over his shoulder at the high school dance when he was laughing with Officer Fieldstone.

Customer service, my eye, she thought. The pharmacist never talked to her like that, and everyone said *he* gave great customer service. Cornered, Katrina felt sick to her stomach.

Aaron's form was almost out of sight, all but lost in darkness, obscured by tombstones and drizzle rain. Katrina calculated fast in order to squelch her rising fear at the recognition of the likelihood that she was locked inside a hearse with a lunatic.

I am overreacting—or am I?

"My old girlfriend was very demanding..." McGhoul's voice trailed off as his eyes disappeared from the rearview mirror for a moment. Then, his whining narrative rose to a crescendo, "My parents were very demanding. I learned a lot from them. Nothing was ever good enough for them. Both my parents and my girlfriend... that little b—You know, she dumped me on our prom night and went with someone else. Just up and dumped me. No reason. I had given her the best possible customer service, too. You remind me a lot of her."

Oh crap, thought Katrina.

Bob McGhoul's voice cracked and he began to cry. She was afraid to look in the rearview mirror and see his tears. She was afraid she would feel sorry for him and not escape while she still could. She was afraid McGhoul would read the fear in her face, afraid that he would see through the lie that Katrina was about to attempt to trick him with. She tried the door. It was locked.

Katrina calculated.

"Of Brenda, *Bob*?" she asked cautiously. "I remind you of Brenda Caughin? The beautiful girl in the photo in your office? Tell me about her." She spoke softly, barely trusting herself to sound confident.

"Yes, of Brenda. *Who else?*" he snapped like a grumpy child. "Who else *is* there but *Brenda*?"

"Bob..." Katrina spoke softly like an animal trainer coaxing a new capture to eat from her palm. "...may I sit up front with you now? I'm cold." Katrina couldn't believe her own words. *Stay calm, stay calm, use your head. You can bluff him, you can.*

Magically, the locks opened.

He trusts me, she thought.

She heard McGhoul sniffle. Katrina glanced up furtively and met his teary gaze in the rearview mirror. He watched her so intensely. From somewhere deep within her soul, beneath her terror, Katrina summoned sympathy and compassion for Bob McGhoul and his sickened mind.

"You loved her very much, didn't you, Bob?" Katrina slowly pulled the door handle up, not taking her eyes off McGhoul's in the mirror.

"Yes." He whimpered, then wept openly, yet he seemed mesmerized by Katrina's direct gaze into his wet vulnerable face. Her beautiful visage so reminded him of his dead Brenda.

"*She* understood customer service." Bob's wail was lonely and confused.

"I understand," Katrina whispered soothingly, forcing the tremor out of her throat.

"*She* understood me too... But she betrayed me. So I *had* to kill her. And *him*. He tricked her into leaving me right on prom night. It was not *really* my fault, you know." McGhoul no longer spoke tenderly of Brenda, nor was he in control.

Slowly, Katrina pushed the door open and backed out, keeping her eyes fixed on his in the mirror. Keeping him *there*, riveted. Making him trust her to come up front and sit with him and comfort him.

Outside, cold air swathed her bare arms in ice rain.

"I understand," she whispered. She had to whisper, for she had no voice left. Fear had wrenched it from her. Bob McGhoul read her lips in the mirror. And then he did something odd.

He picked up the bright gym bag from the front seat and hugged it, snuggling his face into the red canvas fabric.

"What's in there?" whispered Katrina, and the moment she asked, she wished she had not.

"Want to see?" Bob McGhoul unzipped the red bag. He was so excited, like a little boy showing off a secret collection of tell-tale treasures hidden under a floorboard. McGhoul cried harder. "I don't know if I can trust you, though," he wailed, his voice trembling.

"*You can trust me*," Softly, she parroted herself over and over and over. "*I understand*."

"Okay!" announced Bob McGhoul, suddenly uncharacteristically chipper. "Okay, I'll show you, then!" Excited, he reached into the bright red gym bag and quickly started pulling out *things*. "I'll show you *Brenda*."

I wish he would not call me Brenda, thought Katrina, and then she realized he had *not*.

Katrina bit her tongue hard to see if she would wake up in her own bed.

Alas.

Even in the very dim light from the dashboard it was unmistakable what McGhoul produced from the bowels of the red gym bag: bones, long and short, brownish, and a skull with dried skin and a long crop of hair tied up in a ponytail. Fresh fuchsia lipstick discolored the full set of teeth. And Katrina's false eyelashes stuck above the orbital bone of each eye.

"Brenda has the cutest little overbite I ever did see," McGhoul planted a peck on the skull's teeth. Fuchsia greased his lips.

This is no joke. It's really happening. Panic surged through her, paralyzing her tongue.

"Well? What d'you think?" McGhoul had lost it. "It's my very own portable Brenda!" he cheered.

Then Katrina noticed the clip earrings attached to the skull's matted brownish hair: diamond and ruby hearts.

My pendant, thought Katrina. Her mood spiraled further downward. Katrina could only parrot herself. "*I understand.*" But she so totally did *not.*

Bob smiled handsomely at her.

Katrina backed out into the night, gathering the full skirt of her ball gown around her so it would not catch again in the door, and in the briars.

She was so tired. Tired of being scared out of her wits, tired of being railroaded into the role of a victim. And now she was getting good and P.O.'d.

"*Bob explains how he killed Brenda and the fellow...*" said Bob McGhoul as if he had suddenly become the narrator of a docudrama about himself. His own memory was too painful for him to bear its weight any longer.

"*Bob tells the girl how he was homesick. Eternally homesick. But he couldn't go home. He wasn't allowed home anymore. Bob tells the girl that he's been in exile. Every town he moves to, he's in exile.*"

Katrina flinched again and again as he spoke. Tears of fear stung her eyes.

"*Oh, why did I ever leave you alone in the bag?*" he wailed, then suddenly controlled, he was again his own narrator, "*But now Bob has her again.*"

Bob kept petting the skull, kissing it, smearing the fuchsia lipstick that prettied it. He knocked off one of the false eyelashes. "You always find fault with me," he shouted at the skull, then his voice softened. "But then, you always make me better. More conscientious. A better customer servant! Thanks to you, I have the best business in town."

"I understand," murmured Katrina. By then, she stood outside the hearse.

Carefully, gently, she closed the rear door so as not to startle Bob out of his trusting reverie.

It was then she heard him snap, "No, you do *not* understand!"

Katrina stood in the dark for what seemed like eons. The pressure was off. For a nanosecond the pressure to escape dissipated. She had succeeded in talking her way *out* of a car with a raving lunatic. The icy air reminded her that she was not yet rid of the monster. She had to flee. It took a few seconds before she got her bearings. In the distance, she could see Aaron's small figure at the top of the hill between the outline of the mausoleum with the angel on its roof and a tall statue like a huge chess piece—then Aaron disappeared completely from view. Silhouetted specters of death became her beacons of safety.

Katrina bolted.

He's got asthma. No gas. He can't catch me. By the time he realizes I'm not getting up front with him, I'll have caught up with Aaron. We'll be safe.

Brambles scratched at her, tearing her stockinged legs, slowing her. But neither they nor the mild ache in her foot deterred her mission.

McGhoul must see me by now. He must be opening his door and starting after me... he can't run... asthma...

As Katrina ran on through the graveyard, the safety she had anticipated eluded her. Aaron was nowhere to be found. By day, the blushing autumn trees might have warmed her spirits. The fall colors were past their peak. By night, however, fear imploded in her chest as death's stony icons glared down at her, judging her attempt to save her own life. The alabaster arms of a decapitated maiden reached out to her. As her eyes adjusted, movement from everywhere seemed to be upon her, approaching her. She gasped. It was just little American flags flapping in the wind, stuck in the ground near the hundreds of Veterans' headstones. Onward, there were wreaths and flowers and stuffed animals strewn over various graves. Ahead of her, acres and acres of corpses lay underfoot.

But none of them actually died here. The thought comforted her. *There won't be zombies or ghosts. Although there could always be a first—me.* Cold sweat beaded on her worried brow.

Use your head, you can handle this, she told herself.

Bob McGhoul still had not left the hearse. That was a huge weight off her shoulders. *I would have heard the hearse door open. I would have heard him thrashing through the brambles, running up the hill through fallen leaves.* He would have shouted insane epithets at her—*wouldn't he?*

Katrina sighed in relief and slowed to catch her breath.

Plus, she reminded herself again, relaxing, *he can't catch me. He's got asthma. I'm totally safe now.*

As Katrina was nearing the crest of the embankment, the unthinkable happened.

19

A motor started. The fuchsia hearse ripped up the hill toward Katrina. Headlights flared blinding her. She gasped.

He's not out of gas! He lied—of course he lied, stupid, he's a killer. They don't reform; they reformulate. Katrina berated herself.

Presto: Fieldstone's meaning became clear. This killer had not changed for the better, he had just made his mousetrap cop-proof.

Think about a thing long enough—you find truth in it, her fleeting thought died.

Lights were on her.

"Aaron?" she whinnied. "Where are you?"

Just then, Dan Pritcher came to and opened his eyes. From his vantage point he saw pale, amorphous shapes illuminated from one side and he heard a familiar motor roaring toward him. And, he heard a girl's voice yelling, "Aaron."

He tried to feel around for his glasses, but he could not.

Have I died? My arms! Did he dismember me? Dan panicked. His head ached. He licked his frozen lips and tasted blood. He saw blurred movement below.

"Katrina! Over here, honey lamb," Aaron hollered back.

"*Hellllp*!" screamed Dan.

Katrina had started toward Aaron's voice, but Dan's cry to her left stopped her cold. She pirouetted—Aaron, Dan, *hearse headlights!* Dan was strapped to a pine tree, six feet up, without his glasses. His face was bleeding. Aaron could not have seen him before in the gauzy darkness without car lights.

Headlights blinded them! She ran, tripping over the footstone of a grave. *RALPH SMITH 1914-1986* blurred before her eyes, and she scrambled off the plot. Something grabbed the hem of her gown. She wailed. *Was it Ralph Smith's skeleton grabbing from the grave?* Her hem was caught; she was dragging a flowerpot of thorny roses that had adorned Ralph Smith's plot. She shook her hem free of it.

Suddenly Aaron was beside her.

"Thank God, Aaron!"

"Take my hand!" He pulled her along.

"Dan's *there*." Katrina pointed toward the pines.

"We'll come back for you, Dan! We'll get help, buddy."

"He's going to kill me *and you*!" Dan managed. His head slumped forward, and he cried from fear and shame at how completely he had misjudged his own ability teach a serial killer a lesson.

Katrina did not need to explain more to Aaron. The speed with which the hearse's headlights catapulted over the lip of the wooded hill made it all very clear. McGhoul had gas, and with it, he planned to kill again.

"Aaron, he told me..." Katrina wheezed. "...he killed his girlfriend. He's got her skull and bones in that gym bag he carries. He's not going to let us get away. I know too much now."

They ducked between gravestones and behind a mausoleum. Shuddering from cold and fear, Katrina pulled the heavy fuchsia velvet skirt up around her bare shoulders, exposing her legs under the crinoline.

"How do we get out of here?" asked Aaron, wrapping his cape around her.

"I don't know," she replied.

"You said you knew the graveyard."

"I said, if I can find my father's grave, I sort of know my way from there back to the entrance. But I can't see, Aaron. My track Coach makes us run sprints on the grass by the entrance, says it's safer than running on the road, said it'll make us appreciate life."

"Does it?"

"Well, let's just say I *really* appreciate it right now."

A sign blocked their way along one of the many narrow lanes, *ONE WAY. DO NOT ENTER*.

"You'd think they'd put in exit signs."

"No one's going anywhere."

They giggled nervously.

"Oh great, he's turned off his headlights. He thinks he can trick us."

"Aaron, he already *has* tricked us, a bunch of times."

"Stay low. The motor..." It purred like a happy cat. They crouched.

"Too bad it's drizzling," Katrina whispered. "The moon *was* full tonight. Wish we could see better."

"What, so he could spot us instantly?"

"*Brenda!*" Bob McGhoul whined from his open window. "Is that you, my dove?"

Along the narrow packed-dirt path, the hearse inched past where Aaron and Katrina lay on their bellies behind a wide family monument.

"He's gotta know the way out. We'll follow behind. Keep back from the tail lights."

"The mirrors, Aaron."

"It's dark. We'll hang back, stay to the side."

They followed the hearse's gradual progression on the dirt road. It was much easier than tripping constantly over gravestones and potted plants and stuffed toy mementos for dead tots. Illuminated by the dashboard light, Bob McGhoul's face was visible in the rearview mirror. He smiled broadly as he called out to *Brenda* his *dove*.

The temperature dropped more and more as the witchy hours tipped toward midnight.

"My mom must be so worried by now, Aaron." He squeezed her hand.

Carefully, they followed McGhoul around the curve of a wold in the earth. There had been no indication that he had spotted them. But suddenly the headlights and taillights glared as the hearse slammed into reverse. Aaron pushed Katrina behind a broad tree to safety. But for Aaron, it was too late.

The crunch of bone breaking seared the chill air.

"Ahhh! He got me!" Aaron cried out in pain, and doubled over beside the chipped headstone against which his shin had been crushed.

The hearse drove forward a few feet, then lurched brutally in reverse again.

"Run, Katie!" shouted Aaron.

She stood frozen by the tree watching Aaron rolled behind the gravestone, dragging his lame leg, just as the hearse caught the edge of his Dracula cape and smashed into the protecting stone, taking out one taillight and fissuring the stone.

"You're making me do disrespectful things to dead people," cautioned McGhoul.

And before reality sank in, McGhoul was out of the hearse and charging at her.

"Run, Katrina!" Aaron hollered from behind a gravestone.

McGhoul grabbed Katrina and enfolded her in his arms. "My love, I knew you wouldn't betray me again," he lied pitifully to himself.

"Let me go!" Katrina demanded, and struggled desperately to release his grip on her cold bare shoulders.

McGhoul forced his lips on hers, then kissed her cheeks all over as his strong, clean hands prevented her torso and arms from moving. Her feet and knees were free to plant one in his groin, but the bulk of the dress and the crinoline made kicking cumbersome. McGhoul lifted Katrina's voluminous dress. Without the velvet obstruction knotting up around her legs and with the added incentive that McGhoul's hands were quickly going in all the wrong places, Katrina channeled every ounce of rage into her right knee. It met Bob's groin with transformative impact.

It's gotta slow him down, she thought.

Bob McGhoul groaned angrily but did not crumble. Infuriated, he slammed Katrina up against Dan's tree. Still her arms were locked by his; his hot breath infected her throat.

"I am so glad your mother let us get the lingerie we added to her shopping list, *Princess*," hissed Bob. "Last time we tried that she said *no*. And you went along with her, you stupid, little..."

Rage met panic in Katrina's blood. She struggled, kicked, screamed, bit, scratched.

Bob did not desist.

"Use your head, Katrina!" shouted Aaron, as he threw a clot of frozen earth that hit McGhoul's chin and crumbled down Katrina's top. "Sorry!" His next clot of earth struck McGhoul's head.

Katrina realized she had been too terrified to think clearly. Aaron's words rescued her. She had seen soccer players do it. And so she slammed the crest of her brow against McGhoul's nose. She'd heard you could actually kill a person if you hit hard enough, by driving the nose bone back into the brain. Blood spurted from McGhoul's nostrils. For a few moments, he was disoriented.

So that's why they're called bangs, she thought, brushing off her aching forehead.

McGhoul keeled backward, screaming and holding his oozing, red nose.

"Aaron, hurry," pleaded Katrina, tears burning her blinking eyes as she put distance between herself and McGhoul.

"My leg's broken. Go get help, Katie!" shouted Aaron. "Get in the hearse and drive! Go!"

"I won't leave you. He'll kill you!" Katrina looked around for Aaron but couldn't see him in his hiding place. Bob McGhoul staggered toward her screaming obscenities at *Brenda*. In slow motion, Katrina felt herself running toward the hearse, toward the driver's side. She opened the door. Got in. Slammed the door praying McGhoul would leave Aaron alone and chase the hearse.

Power locks, where's the power-lock button? Her fist mashed at the console and with it the horn. Four metallic pops reassured her that she was safe. Still, she wasn't certain which four of the five doors were secured. Two front, and two rear, with the hatch unlocked. Or one front and three rear. Or—? One way or another, McGhoul was determined to find an access point.

Now. Key. Where's the key? He's got it? Katrina groped around for the ignition and accidentally hit the light switch. Moth to flame, McGhoul was at her window, pawing, knocking, tugging at the door handle, pleading for her love. His blood smeared the glass as he kissed it.

"Brenda, let me in. I won't hurt you, darling. I love you. *I know you better than you know*. I know you don't want to hurt me. You just have *very* high standards."

Katrina recalled the words he had written on her Advanced Composition essay. His chameleon penmanship had matched hers so closely.

I'm locked in. He can't get at me. Where's the key? Stay calm.

"It's... *Brenda?!*" Katrina gasped, and pushed the open red gym bag away toward the passenger door.

Bob slithered from the driver's door around to the back hatch. Katrina heard it open. Bob placed one foot up to get in. Katrina found the ignition. *Thank God!* The key was still in the ignition. She started the engine, slammed the automatic gear into drive, and tore forward—then, in her panic, accidentally stomped on the brake.

No clutch, it's automatic, that's the brake.

"Very funny, my dove!"

The rearview mirror revealed McGhoul catching up with the hearse and again climbing back in. She floored the gas pedal. Bob fell off again. He got up and raced behind the hearse. On the straight dirt road, Katrina was fine. A curve came and she squeezed the steering wheel tighter. Still her foot crushed the gas pedal.

"Automatic steering," she mumbled to Brenda in the red gym bag beside her on the seat. *Oh no, his insanity's contagious! I'm talking to a bag of bones!*

For a moment she thought she had eluded McGhoul, but the sinewy cemetery roads all seemed to curve around willy-nilly. She found herself back where she started. Bob was waving her down in the middle of the road, calling to her. Blood ran from his nose and darkened his hands.

"Brenda, stop! I love you."

Should I hit him?

She couldn't. She swerved at the last moment and careened a short distance up a grassy bank with evenly-spaced gravestones: the new section of the cemetery. She could not bring herself to kill anyone, not even this loathsome insect named Bob McGhoul. She swerved again to miss a tree and instead hit a small tombstone; there was a disgusting *crack* like the sound of Aaron's femur breaking. One headlight blinked out. There was Bob again, face bloody, at her window. Blindly she hit the power-lock button on the console again to make sure the back door was locked, but instead she inadvertently unlocked the driver's side door. McGhoul knew the noises his car made. The next second, he flung her door open. She hit the gas again, knocking him aside, but without the other headlight she did not see a large gravestone that lay ahead. She had picked up considerable speed.

Ralph Smith again.

Ralph Smith's stone disappeared under the front end of the hearse. She floored it. A threshing gristmill against the carbon steel axel ground the vehicle to a deadly stop. Katrina hit the gas again to dislodge the stone from the drive shaft. She fumbled for reverse but was shaking too hard to shift. The car remained in neutral. She floored the gas pedal again. Nothing, not an inch. The hearse wheezed in a scream of excess energy going nowhere. Still trembling, she shifted very deliberately into drive. Hit the gas. Slowly, slowly the hearse crept forward encumbered by the rock stuck in its gills.

"Go!" she screamed at the car.

That tombstone caught in my chassis.

The hearse moved, but not faster than Bob McGhoul could trot. She secured the power locks. The windshield had steamed up with her rapid breathing and fat cold drops of rain obscured her vision further.

"Get away!" she screamed. Bob pawed at the glass—then suddenly disappeared.

Where'd he go? Katrina searched for him in the three mirrors. The hearse staggered forward. The slow grinding of stone and steel meant lack of speed, lack of defense. She suppressed a fearful wave of nausea.

From the side with the broken headlight McGhoul jumped on the hood of the turtle-paced car, a chunk of broken gravestone clutched in his fists. He smashed it against the windshield. Again and again he battered the glass until a gaping hole revealed his bloodied face to Katrina. Shards of glass flew down Katrina's dress, leaving delicate cuts in the skin revealed by her *décolletage* and heaps of glass in her lap. McGhoul's wrist slashed against the jagged glass. Blood dripped down Katrina's front as Bob reached in and slipped his fingers around her throat. Again, she pressed the gas pedal to the floor. This time the engine reluctantly gave her a little more speed. Bob's bloody visage glowered at her through the windshield hole. Katrina was losing focus as he asphyxiated her. Helpless, she grabbed one of Brenda's bones from the gym bag beside her and stabbed at McGhoul through the hole in the windshield. But he pulled the bone through, tossing it behind him.

He laughed. "I don't even remember the facts of the people I killed," he informed her chattily as he strangled her. "The bag lady, the cinema fellow. *Ad nauseam, ad infinitum.* Everywhere I go. All I know is my stuff is missing, and I end up with a buncha freakin' candy bars. I would've sworn I didn't do it. But others remember for you. And they don't let you forget. But I remember yours, Brenda. And I'm sure going to have the pleasure of remembering this time once and for all," McGhoul huffed insanely.

With every ounce of strength left, Katrina drove on, unaware what lay in her path: hobbled Aaron and the open grave of Farmer Brownell.

McGhoul guffawed his signature asylum laugh as he tightened his grip on Katrina's throat. "I may be crazy? But! They say this happens to serial killers, they forget things. Oh yeah, I've read *all* about it. Damn *near* drove me crazy! You'd think they'd write a self-help book for serial killers, news reporters got so damn much to say about us. I'll just have to go check out my local book store. Perhaps I overlooked it. Or, maybe you and I can co-author it together, *Brenda*?"

With her last breath, Katrina's final effort went into her foot, and she compressed the gas pedal, fighting against the grinding tombstone caught up in her drive shaft.

"You should not have judged *this* book by its cover, Brenda!" Bob McGhoul shouted over the shrieky grinding noise under the hood. "This one is really a philosophical treatise on the human condition..." His bloody face blathered at Katrina.

She closed her eyes for what she feared would be the last time.

Farmer Brownell had not been a big man, given that he'd grown up in privation during the Great Depression, so his open grave, though shorter than most, was just as deep as any. Aaron lay beside it, semiconscious, losing blood. The hearse hurtled toward the open grave. Katrina's last strength crushed the gas pedal. Just before she passed out, she opened her eyes and caught a glimpse of Aaron. The sight of him renewed Katrina's hope. Bob McGhoul glanced around to see what had widened Katrina's eyes with hope and love. As he turned, his sullied hands released her throat slightly.

"*Hit* him!" McGhoul shrieked at her.

The hearse had reached the grave. Aaron was certain to be crushed and dragged into the pit. Katrina braked hard in the soft soil. No longer could she see Aaron. The wheel base of the hearse was wider than the narrow grave trench. But, where was Aaron?!

Katrina braked and skidded to a halt, then threw it into reverse. On impact, McGhoul's arm was ripped by the jagged edge of the hole in the windshield. The sudden pain caused him to release Katrina's throat. A ribbon of flesh from his muscular forearm curled onto the dashboard. Blood ran over the instrument panel. With a painful shout, McGhoul disappeared skidding off the icy wet hood of the hearse. *Butter on a hot skittle,* Farmer Brownell would have said, had he not been so very dead. McGhoul slid directly into Farmer Brownell's grave. And when he hit bottom, the hungry black cat that chased the vole into the pit seized the chance to scramble up Bob McGhoul's side and leap from his head out of the grave. Shrieking McGhoul, however, was not so nimble.

Never had Katrina been so relieved to see a black cat, as it tore up and over her windshield. Katrina sighed. The sight of Farmer Brownell's gravestone leaning against the tree ten feet in front of the hearse brought comfort. Instinctively her hand slammed the horn to wake Aaron. She could not see him or McGhoul. *Had Aaron been hit? Had he crawled away? Where was he?*

"Aaron?" she shouted at a flicker of movement off to the side.

It had to be Aaron. Or, was it McGhoul? She goosed the gas pedal ferociously. The hole disappeared under her. Ralph Smith's gravestone was released from the undercarriage and fell into the pit below. McGhoul howled in pain as the tombstone struck him where he lay in Farmer Brownell's open grave.

Now I'm free, now we can escape, Katrina thought. *But where's Aaron?*

She could not drive forward as the huge tree that supported Farmer Brownell's headstone blocked her way. As she reversed, she tried to maneuver, and accidentally hit the poised rear end of the dump truck full of dirt that was parked adjacent to the grave. Slowly, she backed over the grave. With one headlight out, she could barely see the hole. But she could make out Bob McGhoul reaching up out of it, pulling at Aaron's weakened body. Aaron was semiconscious. His head nodded in the mud. She had barely missed hitting her boyfriend who lay at the head of the grave.

"Aaron!" she screamed. "Wake up!" She leaned on the horn. "Leave him alone, you wacko!"

Aaron lolled on the ground. He was slowly being dragged into the pit by McGhoul. What could she do? She snatched Brenda's skull by the ponytail and prepared to sling-shot it through the broken windshield at McGhoul. But, the hair disintegrated in her hand.

"Ahhhh!" She chucked the matted strands that split from the ponytail. The skull lay on the seat with its bejeweled tufts. That's when Katrina noticed the hole in the back of Brenda's skull.

Must be how he killed her, thought Katrina, reaching again for Brenda's cranium. This time Katrina gripped it like a bowling ball, intending to pelt McGhoul with it. But, it broke into pieces. So, Katrina flung the jawbone, then the skullcap. All missed McGhoul and made a sad splash in a puddle, then toppled into the grave with him.

"I'll get you, Aaron!" she shouted.

But she had to move the hearse out of the way first, so McGhoul could not leverage it to escape the grave.

Katrina threw the hearse into reverse and floored the gas. As the hearse careened backward, she turned the wheel hard to miss hitting another tombstone. Swerving, full-throttle, she was thrown off course, causing the back end of the fuchsia hearse to bash into the front end of the dump truck whose rear had blocked her moments before at the head of the grave. She had driven backwards in a semicircle. The large vehicle was jostled aggressively. Then the hearse stalled out.

The lone skewed headlight caught a red-necked turkey vulture in an oak tree. It flew off. Farmer Brownell's open grave was now in darkness. As she opened the door to go after Aaron, she heard a heavy swishing sound. It was not just the copious freezing rain Farmer Brownell had predicted. The hearse's vigorous impact against the dump truck had caused the truckbed to void its soil out its back—into the hole intended for the belated farmer.

"Aaron!" she shouted frantically, and kneeled down to peer into the hole.

A hand shot up through the grave soil narrowly missing her throat. She fell back.

"Katrina!"

She whirled around in search of Aaron. The heavy cold rain in her eyes made it more difficult to see. She did not know where to search first.

"Katrina!"

She turned toward the muffled voice calling her name but saw no one.

"Aaron?"

She looked at the dump truck gradually pouring, pouring, pouring dirt into the deep grave, where the dirt was mixing with heavier and heavier freezing rain.

"Help me, Katrina, I didn't want to kill you, you left me no choice. You dumped me for that little twerp, I could've made you happy, you would've had everything you want. I had to give you the best customer service, even if it kills me..." Bob McGhoul's monologue was drowned in dirt.

"Looks like you're *dumped* again," Katrina screeched at the talking heap of dirt.

20

Bob's muffled cries for help finally stopped. Katrina slumped, utterly alone. The gravestones surrounding her seemed as innocuous as beach pebbles. Freezing rain had already numbed her into near hypothermia. She caught her reflection in the car window. She thought, *I look as worn out as my mother*. Her breath still came in jags, which quickened now with the realization that Aaron might really be buried alongside Bob McGhoul, dead, like in her dream.

Exasperation shredded her voice as she screamed, "Aaron!"

Another deep breath—she prepared to scream again. But the sound of a motor caught her attention. At first, it was very far away, perhaps in her imagination. Then a trace of light off in the distance, and a faint beam, threaded the trees.

"That must be Gallows Hill Road. In that direction." She was talking to herself. "Now get the boys and go home. Aaron and Dan and... and Brenda and me, we'll just go home now. That's right. Home. Aaron and Dan and Brenda and me. No. I—It's Brenda and I. And Aaron and Dan—Aaron! Aaron! Aaron, where are you, for God's sake, Aaron, answer me, where are you? Don't you be dead, where are you, I need you, please Aaron, answer me, answer me!" Her screaming turned into waves of tears and painful choking sobs like a hungry baby. She stumbled in one direction to search, then in another. She feared she would find him cold and dead.

"Katrina, I'm over here," Aaron coughed from beyond the grave.

A drenched icicle herself, Katrina ran and clung to him before helping him to the hearse. She laid him out in back, just like in her dream, but this time, the only coffin was what remained of Brenda Caughin in the red gym bag on the front seat.

"Don't you dare die on me, Aaron." She knelt by him and kissed him gently.

He tried to sound brave. "It's just a broken leg."

With one headlight askew and one broken, it took longer to find her way back to Dan's tree. She had to stand on the roof of the humpbacked hearse to untie him.

It seemed to take forever to maneuver their way out of the cemetery. They passed lopsided, craggy stones partially sunken into the ground in the old section of the cemetery, and then straight new stones in even rows. Finally, she spotted her father's gravestone, and she said a quiet prayer to him.

"Thank you for looking out for me, Daddy."

Finally they reached the exit and Gallows Hill Road. There, she made Dan take over the wheel.

"But I can't see," Dan protested. "My glasses are somewhere back in the cemetery."

"But I don't have my learner's permit to drive us legally, and Aaron's leg is broken."

"I'll be Dan's eyes," said Aaron. "Okay, Dan, just brake when I say brake, signal and slow when I say to, okay?"

Dan nodded and they drove slowly through frosty freezing rain past the old grammar school, toward the emergency room at Westlake hospital.

In her cruiser, Officer Fieldstone received word over the radio from the precinct. The hospital had alerted the police of the teenagers' condition.

"Okay, thanks," she replied to the dispatcher.

"You say, '*Roger that*'!" Detective Fieldstone remarked from the passenger seat.

"*You* say it, Dad, if it means so much to you. *Thank you* works for me."

"New breed'a cop, you are," the detective grumbled.

In the back seat, Paul Reed rode along with them to the hospital.

Detective Fieldstone grabbed the cruiser radio microphone and spoke to the precinct dispatcher, "That Preston girl Carl picked up for egging houses on Pine Street? She still there?... Yeah, the Homecoming Queen. Have Carl drive her to the ER. Looks like her story holds up. And call these kids' parents, will you?"

As she listened to her father run through his checklist, something nagged at the edges of Officer Fieldstone's subconscious, teasing her memory. Something about amber glasses, like, the amber glasses reflected now in the rearview mirror from the back seat of the cruiser, seated beside the ever-vigilant Iris.

Epilogue

A new grave was dug for Farmer Brownell, short, narrow, and deep. Days later, it snowed, and Dan drove the group in his Honda Civic to visit Bob's accidental grave and search for Dan's gold wire-rims.

"I wonder what'll be on his gravestone," said Josephine Pritcher who had begged to ride shotgun but instead lay across Katrina and Coriander's laps, wedged in the back. With cast and crutches, Aaron had to ride up front. "I bet it'll just say, '*Here lies a cheap scum.*'"

"Or '*Here lies Bob. Customer service was his aim; killing people was his game,*'" suggested Coriander.

"*Rah-rah.* Sounds like a cheer from your championships, Correy," remarked Dan.

"Or his epitaph could be, '*Since a boy misunderstood, now he's dead for the common good.*'"

Giddiness struck. Even Dan snickered.

"Or this," Aaron sputtered, laughing and pounding out a rhythm on the dashboard. "'*Droolin' McGhoul, what a fool, shoulda never gone to school. If he didn't, Brenda wouldn't—be—dead—now.*'"

"Fine attempt at poetic rhythm, Aaron." Dan chortled, adjusting his old horn-rims and touching the bandage on his brow.

"*Poetic rhythm?* Dan, it's this cutting edge new medium called *rap*," Aaron defended his jingle. "Don't you know anything?"

"Apparently not," said Dan, "But, I've got a better one for the creep who was going to kill me after he did you guys in. From Shakespeare: '*McFair is McFoul, McFoul is Mc—*'"

"Old news," said Katrina.

Their laughter petered out as Dan parked his Honda Civic near the grave site, and pointed. There, hunched and sobbing by Bob McGhoul's grave, stood a lanky girl with her head bowed and a bouquet of white carnations clasped in her hands. She wore jeans and a heavy sweater.

"It's Brenda Caughin," whispered Dan, mock-scary. "Back from the dead."

"Shut up, Dan. It is not."

Katrina recognized the girl. She was the age Brenda had been at the time of her death. The girl was Patty Samson, the teenage daughter of the late Triborough Cinema owner. She was crying convulsively.

Undeterred by the sound of Dan's car doors slamming, Patty placed the flowers on McGhoul's grave.

"Patty, why are you mourning his death?" Katrina asked softly, joining her.

The girl raised her puffy eyes. "I am so full of hatred for this man now," she sobbed. "I'm afraid I'm turning into an animal like him. It's making me crazy."

That did not answer Katrina's question. "So why... flowers?"

"I had to do something to start my own healing, or my heart would die. I had to break the cycle of hatred. If I don't take responsibility now for myself, for my own happiness, I'll implode and become like him, *a-a-a* tormented tormentor!" The girl burst into tears.

Stone-faced, Katrina hugged her.

To everyone's surprise, the gravestone just read, *BOB MCGHOUL, NO LONGER SHALL YE TORMENT*, followed by the usual dates.

"So he's frozen in there? Aaron finally caught up with the group.

"Cryogenically preserved," Dad assured.

"What if there's Indian summer and it thaws?" Josephine asked solemnly. "That's what Farmer Brownell predicted for Thanksgiving. That's soon."

"Aww, don't worry, Josie." Coriander comforted the doe-eyed fourth grader.

The teenagers were ready to leave almost as soon as they arrived.

"I'll catch up with you in a second," said Josephine, remaining at the grave site.

Coriander and Dan strayed toward his Honda Civic, assisting Aaron as he made his way on crutches.

Katrina helped Patty to her car and watched her drive away. *She looks less troubled now that she got rid of some of that poisonous hatred,* observed Katrina and vowed secretly to follow Patty's example.

When Josephine was sure the teenagers were not watching, she untucked the torn half dollar bill from her dungarees. Her eyes narrowed as she shredded the half dollar bill. Kneeling, she sprinkled money confetti on Bob McGhoul's sodden grave.

"I hope you're still alive down there!" she whispered, casting an evil glare at the stone. Then she spat.

Suddenly, Josephine bolted to her feet. Guttural laughter surrounded her. *Was it emanating from the grave beneath her feet?* Her eyes searched for the source of the hideous laughter but the grave was quiet. Over by Dan's Honda Civic, her brother, Katrina, Aaron, and Coriander chatted. Shadow engulfed Josephine. She whirled around and ran smack into a man she had never before seen. Amber glasses obscured his eyes. He held out an oversize candy bar to her.

"Want one?" He palmed her a giant Hershey's bar.

Confused, Josephine accepted the candy bar. But the man's heft and tinted glasses intimidated her. She backed toward the tombstone. He paused to give her space.

"Danny! There's a man!" she squealed. She had not heard the limousine drive up from the back road on the other side of Horizon View Cemetery.

"You beat me to it, kid," said the man.

"To what?" Josephine ventured.

"I came to do the same thing you just did, kid."

"Yah, but don't tell on me," Josie implored, keeping a safe distance between them. Just in case he was actually a weirdo, she didn't want to get snatched.

"Don't worry, I won't hurt you, little girl," Paul Reed said, waving to Dan and the others who, by now, were walking over to greet him.

"Hey, Paul, payin' your respects?" Aaron tried to sound serious.

The group remained gathered at McGhoul's grave.

"In a manner of speaking, I guess I have to pay my respects since McGhoul..." Paul shifted awkwardly. "...well, ironically, Bob McGhoul left his business to me in his will. So if you need car service for the spring prom, gimme a call."

"Why'd he leave the business to you? You're the night watchman."

"I guess he felt guilty. You see, he didn't know he had left it to *me*, per se, but he left it to who I used to be. My real name is Paul Caughin, not Paul Reed.

"I'm Brenda's brother. Brenda was my older sister... until Bob McGhoul killed her."

"If you die, Danny," whispered Josephine, "does that mean you'd stop being my brother?"

"Don't worry, I'll always be your brother no matter what, Josie."

"I've been trailing McGhoul since he got released from prison some years back. They let him go on a technicality. My sister's body was never found. He'd stashed it until it desiccated. So, there was no proof. Thanks to you, there's proof."

"Thanks to *us*?"

"Yeah, you got him to open that red gym bag."

Katrina and Dan remembered too vividly.

"It took me until now to gather enough evidence against him to prove he's guilty," Paul continued. "And then I found his diaries. Year after year of his so-called *customer service*. Murder after murder described in detail."

"How could you stand to be around him?"

"I really hated him. I just wanted to see my sister's body parts have a proper burial."

All but that one bone I stabbed McGhoul with, oh, crap, and her skull, thought Katrina, and closed her eyes in revulsion. *I hope Paul isn't gonna' be mad when he finds out most of Brenda is missing 'cause of me.*

"But, over all these years, didn't McGhoul recognize you?" Dan asked.

"Naw. I was a scrawny kid like you when he murdered Brenda. He hardly knew me. He was so obsessed with her, he never noticed her kid brother. Plus, I've had all these years to grow a beard and fill out." Paul patted his ample gut with his candy bar and took another bite. "A couple of times I thought he suspected, but I guess he never caught on. Tinted glasses help, since my eyes are like my sister's. It's only been in Westlake that I got brave enough to get this close to him."

"You mean, close enough to become his night watchman?" Katrina said.

"Yeah, I figured I could maybe drive him crazy in the process in return for what he had done to me and my family by murdering Brenda. I figured if he did recognize me, I'd tell him it was his imagination, just to torment him. And if he tried anything, hah, I'm bigger than he is. Was. I've done everything in my power to bring him down."

Aaron shook his head. "Wow. That's creepy Paul. What did you do before Westlake? I mean before you, uh, got your courage up to come face-to-face with McGhoul?

"Sort of lurked around and followed him everywhere he moved."

"That's weird. That would drive me crazy."

"I *can't* say that it *didn't* drive me kinda crazy," admitted Paul as he nervously creased and recreased a *Chameleon Limousines* business card he held in his fingertips. "It's been like being grounded. But grounded from going home, instead of from leaving home. Makes you homesick." Paul wiped away a tear.

Katrina flinched with recognition at his words; McGhoul had said something similar to that in the hearse. But she let it drop. From hanging around McGhoul, maybe Paul had picked up some of his expressions. Poor Paul had been through enough trouble already.

"Well," Paul continued, I'd better go tally the books. And, I don't think you should have to pay for the other night, though. I'll return your payment."

"Gee, thanks!" Dan especially was excited.

Katrina nudged Aaron. "Okay. Well, Paul, give us your number, or something."

"Same one." Paul handed each of them a *Chameleon Limousines* card with *Bob McGhoul* scratched out and Paul's name inked above it. It's all been so sudden, I haven't had a chance to have my own business cards printed up yet. With my real name, Paul Caughin. I hope you won't mind my name's hand written on the old McGhoul card for now."

"Sure. No big deal."

"You kids can call me anytime, you know, if you want to just drop by for a visit. As you know, I live alone here. I can't move home now. They're all dead or moved away—been decades. And here, well, I haven't exactly had a chance to make friends. It would be nice to finally be able to. You seem like good kids. I owe you a dinner, anyway, or a ride in the Phantom at least."

They all felt sorry for Paul, alone, lonely, with pieces of a dead sister in a red gym bag whose murder had finally been avenged. Of course they would stop by. Of course they would be his friend.

Not, thought Coriander.

On the creased *Chameleon Limousines* card, Paul had written in beautiful cursive:

Paul Caughin. Call anytime!

The sinuous spines of the *a's* curved gracefully into small curly tails, the deft crossbar of the *t* nearly bore through the heavy paper; the sloping exclamation point danced on the card. Heavy of hand, Paul had dotted the *i's* breaking through the paper.

When Paul passed Katrina the bent card, he fixed his gaze on her face and Katrina was reminded of the queasiness she had felt when Paul and Bob had looked at her for the first time weeks ago.

I must just remind him of his sister, she thought, resisting her paranoid gut reaction.

"Beautiful penmanship, Paul," admired Katrina.

"Thanks. I love to write," said Paul, "and I do calligraphy."

"Well, thanks a lot."

"Hey, thanks for listening, guys. And for making my life livable again." Paul breathed a genuine sigh of relief. "And for returning the family heirloom. It was my mother's necklace, Katrina. McGhoul stole it off Brenda's body. Too bad the earrings went astray. I could kill him twice over for *that* loss."

Katrina did not dare fill him in.

"I'd still like to know how McGhoul killed my sister," said Paul. "Then I might have some peace of mind. I gather the forensic pathologist may be able to shed some light on Brenda's final moments on this earth."

Again, Katrina bit her tongue, remembering the hole in the back of Brenda's skull.

"Hey, Paul, maybe Dan and I could drive for you part time," Aaron suggested. "Summer job?"

"You'd make more money selling your cedar skeleton-in-the-closet hangers to the L.L. Bean catalogue, Aaron," Coriander interjected.

"Sell one to Paul. He might like one," added Dan.

Aaron laughed it off. "Paul, you want a skeleton-in-your-closet? All cedar."

"Signed by the artist!" emoted Coriander. Katrina glowered at her.

Paul considered Aaron's request. "It's possible, you boys and girls could drive for Chameleon Limousines. Katrina sure passed the driving test on Halloween, I gather!"

"I have to finish driver's ed."

"We'll talk," affirmed Paul.

"Well, see ya."

"Wouldn't wanna be ya," whispered Coriander.

"Shut up, Correy," hissed Katrina tersely. "The poor guy. Plus, he saved my life. If it weren't for him, that Doberman would've eaten me alive."

The teens watched Paul amble slowly back to the limousine—*his* limousine. As he walked, he took the last bite of an oversize candy bar. Then he creased its wrapper and tossed it onto the car floor as he got in. He brushed a pair of soiled rubber surgical gloves off the seat where he had left them and shut the door. Underfoot, he scuffed aside a handful of stained red wine corks and several blank spiral notebooks he'd purchased earlier that day over in Eastridge.

Katrina thought she heard him sigh, although it could have been a laugh. She shrugged and climbed into the back seat of Dan's car.

"Poor guy. He must be so relieved." Katrina could not help feeling guilty about chucking his sister's bones in the pit along with those heirloom earrings. She looked down at the *Chameleon Limousine* card. Thoughtfully, her finger traced the deft crossbar of the letter *t*. Her thumb beneath the card strummed the dots of the *i's* that broke through the stiff card.

Paul Caughin. Call anytime!

Beneath her fingertips, the sinuous spine of the *a's* curved gracefully into small curly tails. The sloping exclamation point danced on the card. She shook her head thinking of McGhoul's chameleon handwriting with which Bob had tricked her and her mother with forgery: the essay and the shopping list.

One big forgery, just like his life, she thought, *McGhoul's handwriting had no identity of its own. Paul's on the other hand, was so distinctive, so beautiful.* She dismissed the silly thoughts of penmanship.

"Poor Paul," she muttered.
"Yeah, poor Paul," all agreed naively.

At the precinct, Officer Fieldstone studied the evidence, poring over the beautifully written journals of the murderer that had been revealed by Paul. Then she glanced at Paul's typed statement, hand signed in ball point pen with an exquisite flourish,

Paul Reed a/k/a Paul Caughin

A sickening sensation arose in the pit of the young officer's gut. *How'd I overlook that?*

"Hey, Dad!" she hollered at the top of her lungs as she ran down the hall to the Detective's office. "Dad! About that *pâté* you love so much!" Breathless, she flung open Detective Fieldstone's office door. It slammed against the wall. "*Dad, don't....!*"

But she was too late. Feet up, enjoying his lunch, Detective Fieldstone glanced up at his daughter as his pointer finger scooped the last of Paul's home-made *pâté* Paul had so thoughtfully gifted him.

"Who died now, Nancy? I'm eatin' my lunch."

"Cuffs'n coat, quick, Dad!

Bad Dog: A Vampire's Canine

Originally published by Bantam Books' Bantam Starfire, a division of
Bantam Doubleday Dell Group, Inc. New York, NY, 1995

1

"Don't open that door!"

The vampire's shadow glided across the blood-slick floor of the slaughterhouse and lurched through the open garage entrance into the meat-packing company. Yellowed talons of his hairy white hand lifted the blood-encrusted cast-iron latch on the door to the inner sanctum of his abattoir. The sign on the door read,

SLOP ROOM.DO NOT OPEN THIS DOOR.

"Don't open that door!" Screamed the night-watchman again in rampant fear, cowering out of reach of the malevolent specter. The guard's forest-green uniform darkened with perspiration even in the iced air of winter. Worth noting, the old guard wore several flea collars.

Relentless, the vampire ignored the warning and instead skulked inside the inner room that reeked of death and rotting bovine flesh. His cankered hand yanked a filth-stiffened string. Immediately, the room glowed at forty watts. Caliginous light illuminated the vampire's jaundiced teeth that flashed hunger, as his hollow, gleaming red eyes surveyed the meat storage room. The vampire tiptoed around a chunk of fat scythed from a flank steak. His foot slipped in a tract of blackened ungulate offal where a patch of festered entrails and a cow tail lay on the floor.

Apart from those unsavory bits, the slop room had been licked clean. Nary a spare bone remained. From inside the room the patter of damp feet approached, sticky with blood. A fattened dog ballooned past the vampire and out the door. The stout basset hound's long ears dragged in the bloody mire underfoot. The vampire recoiled a moment to watch the dog go. Then, the sanguisuge relaxed, shrugged, and proceeded undaunted toward his hematic feed. His target, a slaughtered side of beef, hung lifeless on a large iron hook at the end of a heavy chain secured to the rafters.

The low slung brown dog soldiered on, its black feet sticking less as it picked up speed to a happy trot.

"*Noooo!*" Cried the watchman. "Don't let the dog out!"

The vampire hissed. "That dog is *nothing* but a bloody nuisance."

Stumbling up a ladder, the night watchman leapt for a crossbeam where he dangled, breathing hard, eyeing the basset hound and the vampire. A clove of garlic fell to the floor from the garland worn by the guard around his neck. A papery sheath of garlic skin fluttered after it like a dying butterfly.

"Do zip it, old man!" The vampire hissed again. "If you want to keep your job..."

"I followed your orders, Mr. Haimatikos," the old man wheezed. "You said keep him in there. I seen what he done to the meat."

"The dog only eats dead meat, you old coward." The vampire sneered. The well-fed basset hound sniffed indifferently at both men. The watchman slipped and fell from the frozen rafter, glancing apprehensively at the vampire and then back at the dog. The old guard felt for the three flea collars to be sure they were still in place on his own neck. Padding on past him, the dog ambled out into the December night through the warehouse delivery dock.

"Uh, Mr. Haimatikos—"

"Do shut up," the vampire screeched in response. An execrable stutter, his scathing words reverberated against the tile walls.

The vampire turned and strode through the small slop room into the vast, refrigerated fresh-kill storage vault. There he fed, sinking his fangs into a cold, dripping carcass of raw beef. In this way, he kept his sangfroid addiction under wraps. *By dining in,* the vampire reasoned, *feeding off fresh-kill cows instead of people, I'm not dining on inhabitants of Westlake, so I can continue to make money off them.*

The black-footed basset hound trundled around the corner of the meatpacking company's warehouse, past a blue police cruiser parked behind a shiny red limousine, and on past a sign that read,

FREE DIRT. HELP YOURSELF.

Snow-dusted shovels leaned against it. Onward, into the cold, past the toxic Haimatikos landfill, and into the late December night, the dog fled its perfidious captor.

2

Right on time, Aaron Sedgewood picked up his lovely girlfriend, Katrina Phillips, in the black Mustang convertible he had received for his sixteenth birthday. They headed to the home of his best friend, Dan Pritcher, to celebrate New Year's Eve.

"Would you please put the top *up*, Garlic Breath?" Begged Katrina as they drove. "I'm freezing."

"C'mon, Katrina, it's romantic. Snow in our faces, wind in our hair." He kissed her gloved hand and ran his fingers through her shoulder-length hair, knocking off her matching lavender wool cap. Her hair fluttered around her face in the wind.

"Come off it, Aaron, shut it! I have icicles on my lips! I'll start to look like a vampire."

"Consider it air freshener. You won't have to smell my garlic breath. C'mon, I like it, babe, and it's a short ride, to Dan's."

"It's creepy out here in the boonies, Aaron. And it *is* nighttime." Katrina crouched by the heater, ducking her head toward the dashboard. Untangling her hair she replaced her wool cap as they sped past the dilapidated sign for *Haimatikos Meatpacking Company*.

"I should've brought my brush-clip. It's the only thing that holds up my hair."

"*Without giving you split ends*," Aaron mimicked the commercial and leaned over to kiss her.

"Pew! You're endangering my life, Aaron."

"*That's* not my breath. It's Haimatikos' landfill," Aaron defended himself. "You saw the local news report on the biohazard pollution Haimatikos dumps in the river."

"Yeah, it slides right off the back of his toxic landfill and into the river." Katrina gasped as the Mustang skidded on a patch of ice. Recovering, she asked, "So what's going on with your parents?"

"Fine. Pregnant."

"That's *so* weird, Aaron."

"It's not *weird*. It just means I'll be a *very* older brother."

"It means I'll never get to see you at all because you'll be changing diapers and teaching *it* to drive a standard."

"No. It means, I'll get a part-time job so I'll have a legitimate excuse to avoid babysitting the little giblet."

"Any leads?" inquired Katrina. "Since your last potential employer got, um, *detained*."

"Buzzy's Grocery Store said I can start New Year's Day."

"Cool. Congrats, Aaron!"

"Yup, I had my training there already. I still have to help Mom muck the stables, though."

"Did you hear Buzzy's got robbed, Aaron? All his garlic was stolen. Powder, bulbs, paste, everything. Even their to-die-for aioli garlic bread in the fresh baked-goods section that you're addicted to *and* the garlic potato chips!"

"Weird to steal that," replied Aaron.

"The fabric store got robbed too. Like a dozen bolts of black fabric—vaporized."

"I understand stealing garlic. But why steal bolts of fabric?"

Katrina shook her head. "The vampire panic has gotten way out of control."

"Well, 'cause missing persons keep showing up dead—repeatedly!"

"You're creeping me out, Aaron," Katrina said nervously glancing up at the consuming darkness.

"Even you, Katrina, will eventually give in to chowing on massive quantities of stinky garlic." Aaron winked.

She shrugged. "So about your *impending* baby. I can't believe your parents got it together to have a kid."

"Yeah, I'm glad they're talking to each other again."

"*Talking?*" Katrina scoffed.

"Don't go there, Katrina, they're my parents."

"Sorry. Do they know what sex it'll be?"

"It's not like they have a choice." Aaron and Katrina laughed as drifting snow flakes gently clouded their faces.

In an instant, the magic moment was shattered.

"Black ice!" Aaron clutched the steering wheel in panic.

The car slid on the icy road as they passed the rancorous Haimatikos landfill. Headlights flashed on a large tree as the Mustang twisted past it in a 360-spin.

Katrina yelled, "Are we dead?" and covered her eyes.

As the car spun, the headlights embraced a tall, narrow form. But this time, it wasn't a tree.

Was it human? Aaron couldn't make out *what* it was. It moved away from the trees and hovered over a snowbank. Suspended in the air, yards and yards of black fabric billowed around it.

Aaron blinked as a powdery blur swept past. Too fast, the Mustang continued to gyrate out of control. Headlights grabbed at more trees and snowbanks as if trying to slow the momentum. *Turn into the spin,*

Aaron remembered from driver's ed. Finally, he managed to steer them out of danger.

"*Whooooa.* Did you see that?" stammered Aaron.

Katrina uncovered her eyes. "Are we alive?"

"We were hydroplaning!" Catching his breath, he cranked the radio. "*Yaaahoo! What a rush!*"

"Lucky we didn't crash!" Heart pounding, Katrina looked out at the snowbank they'd missed burying the car into. Her gaze drifted over Haimatikos landfill. Any snow that had fallen on the vast expanse of wasteland had melted immediately, leaving a bald canker in the otherwise pristine, snow-clad landscape.

"It glows. Look at the landfill, Aaron." Katrina pointed. "I never saw it at night."

"I thought they only dumped recyclables there," Aaron said thoughtfully. "Meat scraps and cardboard. Diapers and crap..."

"That's also where the police found that dead body—the one that looked like our science teacher, Ms. Anthrope." Katrina shivered.

"A body's recyclable," Aaron joked. They giggled.

"But *that* body disappeared *twice*," mused Katrina. "Who steals corpses out of a morgue anyway?"

"Crypt Keeper?" posited Aaron, "Or, maybe *she's* the vampire?"

"Let's get out of here."

The wind in the trees seemed to be making a distinct flapping sound. Aaron backed up the Mustang to get one last look at Haimatikos' glowing mountain of trash. No headlights at all were needed to see it. Without headlights, the teenagers could not see the source of the flapping. It wasn't the wind. In fact, the breeze had gone dead still.

"Looks magical. Snow falling. Earth radiating."

"It stinks, Aaron. Let's migrate."

The sound of flapping increased. Above their heads, the black night pulsed. The impact of a fast air current bombarded them as something large and smelly swooped directly over their heads. Their winter hats lifted off in its wake. Katrina's disappeared behind the Mustang.

"Holy cow! A red-necked turkey vulture!"

"I told you to put the top up, Aaron!"

"Those birds have a gargantuan wingspan."

"As big as a vampire!" She laughed, although she still had the creeps. "Hey, I'm not the one who's been eating garlic on my ice cream like you, Aaron, but I say we get outta' here!"

"Look, Katrina!" Aaron pointed at the landfill. "Bodies walking around on top of the dump."

"Then go! Drive, drive!" She saw nothing through the trees, though she barely dared look. "Go!"

"I'm just kidding." Aaron laughed and pulled his wool cap back on. "Where's your hat?"

"Blew in the back... or, on the floor. Just go, Aaron, I'll find it." She craned her neck around and exclaimed in dismay, "Oh dang, it blew out when that red-necked turkey vulture flew over. Wait a sec, Aaron."

Katrina opened the car door to fetch her lavender hat that lay a mere four yards from the black Mustang. To reach it, she had to trot out from under the trees to the clearing by the landfill entrance. Caught as it was on the *Haimatikos Landfill* signpost near the gate, Katrina paused to read a smaller sign below it.

FREE DIRT. HELP YOURSELF.

A shovel leaned against it.

"I'm surprised no one steals the shovel," remarked Aaron.

"It's so nice of the Haimatikos dude to be so trusting. My mom gets her dirt for our flower beds from here." Katrina glanced at the eerily-illuminated sign.

Aaron turned the volume louder on the radio; its blaring seemed inconsistent with the profound stillness that surrounded them. As Katrina returned under the trees with her lavender cap, Aaron drove forward a few feet. She caught up with the car. Laughing, he sped forward again. Katrina caught up and opened the door. Aaron rushed ahead another ten feet.

"Hey!" This time, Katrina ran faster. "I'm not amused, Aaron. Cut it out!"

"Okay, okay. You in?" He hit the gas again, zooming off before she could get in, leaving her in the darkness under the trees on a deserted rural road—alone.

"You're such a jerk, Sedgewood!" she yelled, laughing as she ran after the Mustang. She could barely hear Aaron's snarky laughter over the loud radio. But she *could* hear the distinctive, flinty pulsing in the air above. Closer it came—directly at her. She sensed it in her bones more than heard it. Again, she dove after the Mustang. Aaron waited, his head back, singing loudly with his eyes shut. Katrina leapt in over the door, without bothering to open it , when...

Swoop! For a few seconds, everything went black... and stinky.

3

Down by the river, in a shack behind Haimatikos' stockyard, a runaway girl shivered under the patchwork quilt she had taken off her canopy bed. Shedding the slightest warmth, a lame Sterno burner licked the polished silver rings she wore. Her sterling silver wristband was engraved: *Kelly.*

I can't go back home now, thought Kelly. *Mom and Dad'll never take me seriously. I'll teach them a lesson and stay out this one night. To scare them.* In fact, Kelly was scared.

Kelly picked a zit.

Serves them right for not letting me go to Joey's party. So what if he got busted for dope. That was practically last year. In fact, it had been *practically last year*, the last week of December, incidentally, on the 28th, so still a fresh wound, as far as Kelly's parents were concerned.

The closer it got to the New Year, the more Kelly thought about the vampire rumors blistering around at school, and the more she wished she could swallow her pride and return home. Ever since that missing body had turned up at Haimatikos' landfill and then it went missing again, many of her classmates had begun accessorizing with garlic. She too had taken an interest in the herb even though she doubted the missing science teacher's double-trouble corpse had actually become a vampire. And despite the fact that Kelly did not like to eat the stuff at all, she still found it cool science-wise. She liked science and nutrition, and loved to have a topic at which she was the know-it-all—especially now, since her parents wouldn't let her hang with pot-heads anymore. Plus, many kids at school had started asking her for her expertise on the benefits of garlic. And she absolutely adored the attention. Her science project for tomorrow's First Night Earth Day fair was a report on garlic's history as a bactericide, and she looked forward to the big day.

Now, as New Year's Eve wore on, Kelly felt more and more alone. She wished she had thought to bring garlic with her—even one clove. Nervously, Kelly scratched again at the enflamed zit on her chin. It bled a little. *Who cares, Joey's not here to see me.*

The sound of the river rushing nearby was abruptly upstaged by a floorboard creaking inside the derelict shack. A stack of broken furniture blocked Kelly's view of the ramshackle door. She huddled tighter inside the dense homemade quilt she'd dragged along and held her breath. What if there *is* a vampire in Westlake? *And here I am all by myself.*

Kelly was afraid to extinguish the Sterno burner. It finally occurred to her how completely misguided she was to leave it on to attract vagrants. How foolhardy she had been to run away instead of settling the pointless argument with her parents. And how little forethought she had used coming *here* to this shack by the river—when she could have gone to Coriander's or Katrina's for sympathy after she had called Joey. Some girl had answered; Joey was probably making out with the *Bimbo Express* right this minute. Kelly sulked. She knew she deserved better.

Another creak, and soft motion jolted her from her angry reverie about Joey and the *Bim. Was it an animal? Was it the vampire?* The Sterno's flickering yellow-and-purple flame cast occult shadows on the ceiling. Picking at her chin zit, the teenager tensed. *Or, is it a homeless wino?*

Kelly felt cornered. In fact... Kelly *was* cornered. Wind whipped outside the shack. The river gurgled past. The unexpected visitor came into view.

Kelly gasped. "Good boy," squealed Kelly hugely relieved, "Good dog! What's a nice dog like you doing in a place like this? Come here. You're covered in snow. Nice doggy. What a friendly guy. Are you hungry? You don't look like you have rabies or anything. Do you?"

With a trembling hand, the sixteen-year-old held out a granola bar for the dog. The happy animal came closer, yet took no interest in the granola bar. His saggy face seemed to smile at her. She parted the multicolored quilt and brushed snow off the dog's strong back and majestic head, then let the basset hound snuggle under it with her for extra warmth.

"Good boy, there you go, fella. You and I will ring in New Year's together. And then I'll take you home with me. How's that strike you?" She patted the noble basset hound which sighed contentedly. "That'll be your reward for keeping me company."

In that instant, Kelly was bountifully grateful for her friendly companion. She felt safe. Now she would be able to brave an entire night in the shack. Now she could really *show* her parents what was what.

"Who says, *diamonds are a girl's best friend!*? Dogs are! Right buddy?" She loved dogs. It licked Kelly's chin, right across her bleeding zit. "What's wrong with your tongue, boy? Let me see. Open up. *Ouch!*"

A flea bit Kelly.

"Gross, do you have fleas? I shoulda' known."

She stripped back the quilt and harshly pushed the basset hound away from her into the cold night air.

"*Bad dog!*"

The basset hound's big black eyes moistened, its sad jowls drooped at Kelly as if waiting for an explanation for her sudden change of tune. Kelly swatted at her clothing, hoping to bat away the clingy fleas.

But it was too late.

A single flea had already found the first opening that Kelly herself had picked on her chin. She'd never been one to listen to her mother and sit on her hands when it came to skin issues. Presently, other fleas swarmed Kelly's nostrils, ears, and eyes. Still others scrambled across her young face, stinging her with eager bites, injecting her with their spittle, and sucking at her capillaries as the critters' vicious heads burrowed tenaciously into her skin.

Kelly screamed and screamed, but not for long.

Moments later, the thirsty basset hound—indifferent to Kelly's screams—cleaned up a slurry of human plasma. Limp and damp, only Kelly's clothes and quilt remained.

4

It smelled like death. Katrina gagged on the stench. The smelly black fabric slapped at her face and entwined her neck. She thrashed to free herself as the creature continued on the course of its flight causing the paint on her side of the car to bubble under its acid heat. The thing flew straight *up*, never venturing into the headlights. At last Katrina's face was free of the snarled, stinking tangle of cloth.

"Drive!" screamed Katrina.

"What?" Aaron opened his smiling eyes and leaned over to kiss his girlfriend.

"Drive!" She smacked his shoulder and snapped off the radio. "Go! It's that *thing*. It just flew by again, Aaron. It got me all... tangled up in its... stinking... *Ugh!* Now my clothes reek!"

"It's just a red-necked turkey vult—" Then he saw it, too. Aaron stomped the gas pedal, but the windshield obscured with a weighty *thump*. A sinister gaping mouth affixed itself to the glass like an eel. Its pug nose pressed flat, its eyes hollow. And yet, the rodent-faced creature had feminine qualities. Its distorted features seemed as though they might have once been a pretty combination. *Once*.

A claw gripped at a windshield wiper, another grasped Katrina's mirrored visor. Rear-lit only by headlights, the creature's features remained largely shadowed. Aaron floored it and the grotesque critter blew off over their heads in a somersault, taking with it a windshield wiper.

"What the...?!"

"Thank God it didn't land in the backseat!" exclaimed Katrina. "Or, did it? Go, Aaron!"

Above the taillights, wings flapped just out of view in the darkness. As it followed the Mustang, it picked up speed.

"It's gaining on us, Aaron. Go faster?" ordered Katrina, jamming her hat on. "Take the river shortcut to Dan's!"

"Tryin' to lose that... what the heck *is* it?" Aaron, swerved down Covered Bridge Road.

But the pernicious airborne monster was nearly upon them. Above Katrina's head, claws grasped at her from wings festooned with billowing black fabric—she ducked.

"Shortcut's dangerous, Katie. No guardrails by the river!"

"Risk it!" Katrina shot back as they neared the water.

5

Dan Pritcher and his girlfriend wondered what was keeping Aaron and Katrina. Dan had planned a small gathering. Just his girlfriend, and Aaron and Katrina, his Science class lab partner, Kenny van Swift, and of course, his little sister Josephine whom he was inevitably stuck babysitting.

"Katrina's never been late for a party," remarked Coriander Preston, Dan's girlfriend the cheerleading captain and Homecoming Queen, as she was wont to mention whenever the opportunity arose. She poured Doritos into a large bowl and sampled the sour cream dip several times.

"This is delish. Thank God I have a high metabolism like you, Dan." She kept on munching.

"Except the Halloween party," noted Dan. Anxiously glancing at his bedroom clock, he adjusted his wire-rims and turned his attention to his science project notes.

"Could you please not do homework on New Year's Eve, Dan?" begged Coriander and kissed him.

Just then, a faint scream from out of doors drew them to the window.

"Josephine!" Dan bolted to his feet.

On the street outside the Pritcher's home, a blue saucer sled skidded under a car's hood. The old woman's four-door slowed involuntarily, then lurched forward. The driver was not excessively drunk—*just tipsy*, she'd have said, *one or two to fend off December cold*, and her sadness spending yet another New Year's Eve alone. In any case, she had drunk enough to *not* notice the difference between snow falling and a ten-year-old girl on a saucer sliding under her car.

From his bedroom upstairs, Dan Pritcher and his girlfriend Coriander heard the desperate little scream and left his science project notes strewn. Before they could see out, Dan had to warm the frosted windowpane with his palm and rub it with the other. It was already dark, yet the strident porch light cut a sharp line down the snowy hill.

"Josephine!" His gaze traced sled tracks that sculpted the curve of the lawn embankment all the way to the road. Snowdrifts obscured the old woman's car from view, but Dan did see on the rural road that headlights illuminated a patch of deep red blood growing around a child's body.

"Call 911, Correy!" he instructed his girlfriend as he sprinted downstairs and out across the snowy lawn in stockinged feet.

From the porch steps, Dan scarcely noticed a fat brown basset hound that stood looking over the mangled body.

"Oh my God, Josephine!" Dan's voice fogged his glasses in the cold air. His younger sister did not answer. Halfway down the embankment he heard the car drive away, on the other side of the high snow drift. He saw the red snow and ice dead center in the rural road: blood on ice; blood on snow. Bright red mittens, a girl's snowsuit, and a hat lay in the street. The blue plastic saucer that Josephine Pritcher had received for Christmas lay unharmed by the side of the road. Dan's heart pitched and sank. Only moments had passed since he and Coriander had heard the scream. The snow melting through his socks did not faze him. Dan's mind raced. His friends would arrive soon to celebrate the New Year and together they were to have baby-sat his kid sister, *who's now dead.*

"Josie!" He murmured. *Where the heck are the police?*

Unsure if he should get closer and inspect the body, he steadied himself and glanced back toward the house. The fat basset hound tripped on its long, brown ears as it sniffed at the snow suit. Dan did not take much notice of the dog. It must have been a neighbor's or a stray. He had never seen it before. What did it matter? His little sister had been killed. Back up the snowy lawn to the house Dan raced for the phone. *Why aren't the police here yet?*

After a mile or so, the disoriented old woman pulled over. Dull grinding in her axle struck her as unusual. The plink of a red plastic saucer replayed in her vaguest memory.

I better check, she thought.

She hobbled around the front of her car, shivering, bundling her shearling collar to her ears.

"What've I done?" cried the woman known even to State Troopers as old *Lead-foot Liz.*

Two small disembodied fingers were bent around the car's grill. Oddly, some fleas hopped from finger to finger, then onto the cold, snow-covered road.

Red froze on her fender. Blood matched the plastic saucer sled that fell out from under her car where it had gotten stuck on impact. The heartsick woman decided she should drive to the police station to turn herself in.

Just as Westlake's Officer Fieldstone was dispatched to the Pritcher residence, *Lead-foot Liz* attempted to shift her car into drive, but she was still too snockered to locate the gear stick.

In the same moment, Dan wept as he fell into Coriander's waiting arms inside his house, "My sister was hit by a car. She's dead,"

Over his quaking sobs, Coriander heard the gritty rasp of nylon approaching from the kitchen. *Maybe Dan's parents were home early from the New Year's Eve part they went to,* she thought.

"Why're you crying, Danny?" a Lilliputian voice asked through a cookie mouthful. "Hi Correy..."

"*Aghhhhh!*" Dan leapt. His glasses slid off his nose.

"What's with you, Danny?" asked a little girl bundled in a floral snow suit.

"Josephine!" Dan hugged his sister, making her spew cookie crumbs. "I thought you were dead, Josie."

"No. I'm getting us cookies." The ten-year-old was offended, "Milk's gone sour. And Mom just bought it. That vampire *must* be real."

"But the blood in the road, and... Then *who's...?*" Dan faltered.

"Why...?" Josephine's green eyes blackened with trepidation. "Penny's out sledding." Penny was having a sleepover with Josephine who had left her alone on the embankment to dash inside to get them cookies.

Officer Fieldstone led the investigation of the hit-and-run of Josephine Pritcher's friend, Penny Griscom. Yet strangely, the fifth-grader's red sled was missing and her body was nowhere to be found. *No body, no crime.* The police kept checking up and down the road for clues.

"Found the kid's red sled up the road a ways," said Fieldstone's beat partner.

"Lady, you're sayin' you didn't stop? Then where's the girl?" Officer Nancy Fieldstone barked. "Snow suits right here! What did you do, put her in clothes no one would recognize? You workin' a child ring or alone kidnapping?"

Old *Lead-foot Liz* cried, "I don't know. I don't recall hitting her. It was icy. I heard *something*, I guess I thought it was a chunk of ice under my tires."

"You *guess!*" screamed Mrs. Griscom in tears, lashing out at the woman. Officer Fieldstone had to restrain Penny's inconsolable mother.

"I never saw a girl at all," the old woman wailed. "It wasn't 'til I saw the two fingers in my grille..."

"Found the kid's boot!" called an officer gravely, "...somethin's in it!" The man gagged and placed the small, frozen red boot in a plastic evidence bag. "The foot's still inside... like it was...

"...ripped off," nauseated as she looked inside the boot, Officer Fieldstone finished his sentence. "The impact must've been pretty strong to do that. What was it this time, *Lead-foot Liz*, 70 or 80 miles per hour on a rural road?"

"Maybe the car tire severed it, Officer Fieldstone?" suggested another officer. "Other boot's empty. Maybe an animal...?"

"Ma'am," Officer Fieldstone continued, her anger tightly controlled. "You're under arrest. While I read your Miranda Rights, maybe you'll remember whether you stashed the girl's body or you were speeding?"

Amidst the commotion, the basset hound sat itself down in the snow, and its hairy pink tongue licked its sated black lips.

6

As Aaron's black Mustang fishtailed along the river road toward the covered bridge, he shifted into fourth gear. Katrina wailed for him to slow down, but he had no choice. The winged monster was gaining on them.

"Either we'll crash or that thing'll slam into the awning of the covered bridge," shouted Aaron as he stared ahead at the blinding snow. Like an Olympic luge, the high snow embankments around the sharp curve funneled the Mustang toward the covered bridge.

From the passenger's seat, Katrina glanced overhead at claws trained on her head. Wings and ripples of black fabric billowed directly above her head. Aaron shifted down-shifted just as a yellow talon hooked at Katrina's eye. A fulsome, sulfurous stench engulfed her again.

"Go faster, Aaron! *Pew!*"

As the talon swiped again at her, Katrina ducked under the dashboard. Lower she crouched, yet the claw struck again. Katrina's lavender wool cap was liberated from her head. A claw mark remained on her scalp. The convertible raced forth slightly faster than the mutant being, and roared inside the covered bridge—*Safe!*

Outside the snow fell harder, obscuring their abysmal view. At the last moment, before the ghoul slammed into the façade of the covered bridge, the creature swirled up into the air. The winged beast dropped away into blackened branches. It seemed to have given up the chase.

Katrina shook uncontrollably. "That thing took my hat."

"Did you get a good look at it?"

"What I saw was ugly, and it stank."

Trembling, Aaron glanced over his shoulder into the night. "I'll put the ragtop up. I just hope we don't get stopped for speeding before we get to Dan's house."

"What about when we go home tonight, Aaron? What if that thing is waiting for us?"

But Aaron wasn't listening. He had lost his chance to put up the ragtop roof. He yelled.

"Duck! It's back!"

He jabbed the gas pedal to the floor.

7

Dan, Correy, and Josephine huddled together watching from a frost-encased window in Dan's room. Josephine rustled each time she moved, still bundled up in her nylon snow suit. In the street below, the Pritchers and the Griscoms tried to get answers. Blue police lights flashed in their faces, and lit up Dan's bedroom.

"I saw her body, Josephine. I thought she was *you*. By the time the police got here, someone, or something, took her body. There was just blood. And that flowered snowsuit like yours. And the boots."

"You think it's the vampire, Danny? Everyone in fifth grade *knows* there's a vampire in Westlake," said Josephine solemnly, and pulled Dan's feather comforter around her snow suit.

"Not possible." Dan stared at his sister for a long time, watching the flickering blue cruiser lights play across her pretty, troubled features. Dried tear salt striped her round cheeks. "There's no such thing as vampires, Josie."

"You're not the least bit superstitious, are you, Dan?" asked Coriander.

"Just in case..." Dan paused, ashamed to admit. "...you both should take one of these every day." From a secret compartment in the back of a drawer in his desk, Dan removed sheets of blister-packed tablets. He handed one sheet to each girl. "Kelly was handing these out to promote her science project. Kenny's and mine will still beat hers, without the cheesy promo."

"What's this?" Josephine asked. "You want to drug the vampire... or feed him vitamins?"

"It's garlic," replied Dan. "In tablet form."

Josephine made a face. "Chewable?"

"No. Don't worry, they're odor-free if you swallow it. No one will know you're taking them."

"Except the vampire?" Coriander was doubtful.

"Exactly. Kelly said that once it gets into your blood stream, even if you're bitten... There's something in the garlic that kills off the bacteria in the vampire's filthy bite."

Josephine stared in wonder at her big brother. "Are you sure, Danny?"

"Yes. I've been fact-checking Kelly's assertions. There's a lot of research available on this," Dan assured. "*Nature* magazine has an article about garlic as an anti-bacterial. And so I figure, a vampire's bite leaves virulent bacteria that quickly infect you and rot away your brain, making you insane, so you become a crazy blood-sucker too. If the bacteria doesn't kill you first," Dan explained, as he stretched out on his bed. Coriander sat close beside him. Josephine stared out the window.

"Rabies," murmured Josephine to herself. "What if Penny's a vampire now?" She was terrified. "She'll come for me 'cause I didn't get back fast enough with the cookies."

"Not unless you invite her in, Josie, you'd have to invite her in for her to get you in the first place. Otherwise, all she could do is hover at your window. That's part of their crazy blood-suckers' ritual. They consider it good manners to wait for an invitation. They like to be treated like guests."

"What you're forgetting, Dan," whispered Correy, "is that they can still nail you if you're outside your house, according to folk lore."

"Unless of course you have garlic in your system."

"How can a vampire know anything about manners?" Josie asked skeptically.

"Just take the garlic, and don't worry. If you're bitten, you won't become infected."

"I won't froth at the mouth and thirst for blood and become a crazy cannibal?"

"Nope," reassured Dan, not entirely convinced himself.

"I sounds like rabies, Dan," said Josephine.

"Rabies is a bacteria, too." Dan pondered. "You could be on to something with that, Josie."

"So you've been taking the garlic pills, Dan?" asked Coriander. "Since when?"

"Since our science teacher disappeared twice. But don't tell anyone. I'll lose my cred."

"They'll think he's superstitious," said Josephine.

"Aren't you?"

"No. I'm scientific about it. Besides, Aaron will make fun of me and try to get me to go to some stupid horror movie with him if he knows I let my guard down about nonsense."

Dan propped his head up with a second pillow to look out the window at the drama below. He saw Aaron's Mustang skid and slow down at the foot of the driveway as the cruisers departed into the snowstorm followed by an empty ambulance.

"Thank goodness they're here," said Coriander.

Josephine started to cry again.

"Try to be strong, Josie, don't think too much about Penny. Okay? Think about all the special holiday snacks we get to eat tonight."

"Way'ta train your little sister straight into an eating disorder, Dan," said Coriander.

The little girl nodded bravely then continued crying anyway as she peered out the window watching her brother's friends rush toward the house.

As they climbed the steps, Katrina and Aaron noticed a dog near the Pritcher's front porch. The stray basset hound lay panting in the snow.

"Can we let him in?" begged Josephine, peeking around her brother as she and Correy stood at the open front door.

Mr. and Mrs. Pritcher were in the driveway comforting the Griscoms who prepared to follow Officer Fieldstone to the police station.

"No, Josie," said Dan shutting the outer glass door just in case, as he watched his friends climb up the steep steps. "We don't know the dog."

"But Danny, I saw that dog before in the street when we were sledding. He's so cute! Look at his big black feet. He must be freezing." Josephine pressed her face against the glass door and waved at the basset hound.

The dog seemed harmless, and Dan's little sister was begging, so Dan agreed and opened the front door to invite in the basset hound.

Just then, Mrs. Pritcher excused herself from the Griscoms to holler over her shoulder, "No strays in the house, Dan! Fleas or rabies are inevitable, and very hard to deal with!"

Mrs. Pritcher had *no* idea how very right she was.

8

Mr. and Mrs. Pritcher came in from the cold and hugged their children for a very long time. Then, Mrs. Pritcher settled Josephine with the teenagers in the den fortifying them with enough delectable snacks to last beyond midnight. Soon after Aaron and Katrina arrived, Mr. and Mrs. Pritcher said good-night, and turned in, too drained from the traumatic event in their front yard to return to the van Swift's New Year's Eve party from which they'd been summoned.

Fireside, Dan, Coriander, and Josephine solemnly explained to Aaron and Katrina what had happened to Penny Griscom. In turn, Aaron and Katrina told of their ghastly car ride. Nevertheless, Dan explained away their "presumed vampire" as a red-necked turkey vulture like those that feed at the toxic landfill dump.

"That's what we first thought, too, a mutant from scavenging toxic waste," said Katrina.

"But there's no way," Aaron affirmed. "That thing was no red-necked turkey vulture. Mutant or not."

"Is Kenny still coming?" asked Josephine hopefully.

"He didn't say he's not," replied Dan.

Watching the fire flicker, they snacked, and the conversation turned to New Year's resolutions.

"Mine's to become a supreme grocer, just like Buzzy," said Aaron wryly. He poked at the embers with a firebrand.

"New Year's Eve with your best friends is the best resolution," said Coriander contentedly pulling a woven coverlet around her as she curled up beside Dan.

"That's not a resolution, Correy," Dan advised his girlfriend. "Who'd guess you've got the second-highest GPA in school next to mine?"

"Dan!" Everyone reprimanded his lack of tact.

Sometimes, thought Dan, *Correy's kind of obtuse.* His skinny hand patted her shoulder. In all fairness, he was still wound up about the sledding accident.

"What's *yours*, Dan?" challenged Katrina, defending her friend whose face betrayed genuine hurt at Dan's correction. "Your New Year's resolution?"

"Oh, nothing too heady or demanding." Dan joked, attempting to dig himself out. "Maybe kill vampires."

The others laughed quietly.

"Aaron, yours should be to learn to change diapers." Katrina sniggered as she placed a knitted pashmina coverlet over Josephine who had fallen asleep on the Persian rug by the fireplace.

"Something you two aren't telling us!?" said Dan.

"Not *me*!" Aaron replied hastily.

"Mr. and Mrs. Sedgewood," explained Katrina.

Dan's eyes bugged.

"Not *us*! My parents!"

"Oh," said Dan. lifting Josephine's sweet little head to support it with her plush polar bear toy.

"Too bad Kenny never showed up," said Aaron.

"He called to say he had to do something in his dad's home lab," said Dan. "Said he'd be late."

"But not this late!" added Coriander. "It's nearly the New Year."

"He didn't miss much," said Katrina. "I mean, we're not exactly a rockin' crowd tonight."

"Anyway, he'd be the third wheel on the tricycle." Dan muted the television. "Did you guys hear *that*... that thumping?"

Aaron, Katrina, and Correy shook their heads.

"Ten seconds till midnight," Katrina whispered. "The witching hour... *nine, eight, seven, six, five...*"

A feeling of quiet gloom embraced each of them.

"Well, don't everyone look so cheery. It's the New Year... we should be full of beans." Coriander's voice seemed loud and abrasive. She braided her superlong hair nervously.

As *The New York Times* ball dropped in Times Square on the TV screen, the silence in the room seemed to gel and condense like clotted cream. They all felt it—a cruel supernatural presence.

"What's happening?" Katrina whispered cautiously. "It's the same feeling I had when that... *thing*... came at us on our way here."

An aggressive thump against the window in the den gelatinized the teenagers' courage. The distinctive sound of thick, leathery wings flapping deafened them with fear.

"It's back," said Aaron knowingly.

"*Shhh*," instructed Katrina in a soft voice so as not to wake Josephine. "Don't open the curtain, Dan."

But Dan was already twisting the wand on the Venetian blinds to peer outside.

"Nothing's out there," assured Dan, separating the slats of the blinds to prove it. "You guys're whacked!"

"Dan—*you* didn't see its yellow claws—" Katrina started.

"You mean bird's feet? Imagine, a large red-necked turkey buzzard near a toxic waste dump! I told you guys to stop watching horror movies."

Just then a flurry of snow rushed at the window. Dan leapt backward and fell on the rug. "*Aghh!*" He needed a few seconds to recover. "It's just the wind. It's the blizzard. We're just getting a blizzard." He explained it away sensibly.

Josephine stirred.

"I wish you had a light on that side of the house," Correy whined, and cuddled Josephine back to sleep.

Whump! Again, the impact came against the glass. This time they saw solid movement, whipping onyx fabric, wings, talons, and then that face with the pug nose. The same revolting face that had pressed itself to the windshield of Aaron's Mustang now sucked up to the window of Dan's den. Fangs and bluish lips shoved hard against the glass, further deforming its features. Too frightened to whisper, the teenagers screamed. It was past midnight. Elsewhere, people celebrated and sang *Auld Lang Syne*. Thankfully, Josephine continued to sleep through the terror in the den.

"Looks like a human animal!"

"It's wearing my lavender hat!"

"Shut the shade, Dan. Shut it. You're egging it on. Give me the coffee table. I'll put it against the window in case it breaks the glass," said Aaron.

"Like one table will keep it from coming in any other window," said Dan but obeyed anyway. His hands shook.

"Two strays in one day. This one I'm *not* inviting in."

"Call Kenny. Tell him to stay put," instructed Aaron.

Dan did picked up the black rotary phone and dialed Kenny. The van Swift's home answering machine recording went on and on. Finally, Dan left a message for his Science lab partner.

"I guess Kenny blew us off and went to that swanky party his parents are hosting at his mom's job."

"Where's that?" asked Katrina.

"Some biotech lab," replied Dan, bunching his black eyebrows into one.

The phone rang. The four friends leapt.

It was Kenny's mom. The blizzard detained her at the party—stranded overnight—and could Kenny stay there overnight at the Pritcher's?

Before Dan could tell her that Kenny never made it over, the phone line crackled and went dead.

Then the electricity failed.

Blackout.

9

Much earlier on New Year's Eve events had taken an unfortunate turn that caused Kenny to be a no-show.

"Way t'spoil New Year's Eve," grumbled Priestly van Swift, Westlake's only forensics pathologist who was, for better or for worse, Kenny's dad.

"You're part of the team, Priestly. You're the only one who can get us results by morning," Officer Fieldstone insisted. "Westlake safety depends on you."

"But it's New Year's Eve! My wife's expecting me."

"By tomorrow morning!" Officer Fieldstone left the forensics laboratory.

Priestly van Swift sighed and glanced at his watch.

"Fine, if I have to work through New Year's Eve," he murmured to himself, "I'm doing so on my own terms in my own lab in my own basement in my own home." The forensics pathologist packed up the evidence in a hazmat thermal case and left for home.

At the van Swift's home, one thing led to another as Priestly hurried to get dressed for his wife's lab party. Already he was late meeting her there.

I'll get up early tomorrow and finish the kid's autopsy, he thought. He left the hazmat case containing the evidence on the steel table in the cleanroom in his basement. He ducked under the wooden sign that his son, Kenny, had made for him in shop class. It hung from the ceiling:

CORONER'S CORNER.

Often, Kenny had watched, spellbound, as his father performed lab work at home. Each time, Kenny followed his dad's cleanroom precautions and suited up in a hazmat suit. And now, Kenny was waiting anxiously for his father to leave the house so he could check out his dad's new *homework.*

"Stay out of the lab, son," warned Priestly on his way out the door. "Hazmat!"

"Right, Dad. I'm headed to Dan Pritcher's for a party," Kenny assured his father.

"Great, and Dan's parents are meeting us at Mom's lab, so either they'll drive you home or Mom and I will come pick you up after."

"Sure, Dad," said Kenny. "Bye."

Kenny waved at the kitchen window until his father's 4-wheel drive was out of sight. Then he rushed downstairs.

As he had seen his father do when performing basic lab tests, Kenny washed his hands well, donned his father's lab coat, and placed a tiny cassette in his mini recorder to tape his observations. The cassette player fit perfectly over Kenny's heart in the breast pocket of his white lab coat. His hands were free to work.

Kenny pressed *RECORD*, and decided to have some fun with it. "Great to be back in the saddle. Been away for a while," Kenny chatted to the tape recorder. He looked over the evidence in the plastic bags he removed from the hazmat ice box. He read his father's notes carefully, then dumped the contents of the plastic bags onto the clean steel slab inside the cleanroom.

"Cool!" Kenny chuckled and nattered like a game-show host. "Okay, folks, it's December thirty-first, New Year's Eve. Dr. Kenneth van Swift, attending physician, coming to you live from Westlake, hippest town on the Eastern Seaboard. And tonight's amusement includes the completion of one autopsy of apparent girl age ten." He read the tags and observed the pieces of evidence. "Not much to go on: two torn fingers, and a boot with..."

Kenny's tone grew more serious as he examined the boot's contents. "...a frozen foot still inside."

He wiped away a renegade tear that slid down his cheek. *A kid. It was a kid... from Westlake.* He checked the ID tag again and read *Penelope Griscom.* Her sister was his classmate. Grief gripped his gut. He had to finish what he had started.

"A clear substance..." Kenny continued, "...has accumulated on top of the flesh in the boot. Looks like gelatinized chicken broth." He poked the jelly with a cotton swab, a precaution he had always seen his father take. "Appears to be protein-based, most likely... or... animal saliva?"

Kenny jabbed the cotton swab into the fluid again, gathering a good dollop as it thawed. Examining it more closely, he noticed several small fleas stuck in the gooey mass. They wriggled free from the goo.

Kenny squished one flea with his bare fingernail. In his haste, he had not bothered to don disposable rubber gloves. Upon closer inspection, he noticed more fleas struggling to escape the goo.

"*Gross.* Fleas. I'm outta here," Kenny grumbled into the recording device imitating his father's style, "It's late. It's New Year's. Time to get over to Dan's house."

Just then, Kenny noticed his fingernail: the one he had used to crush the flea. The nail was already gone, dissolved, exposing moist, new pink flesh. A warm sensation pulsed quickly down his finger into his hand and up his arm. His finger dripped clear, viscous plasma.

Another flea sprang free from the moisture and bit him tenaciously on the neck.

"What the...?" Kenny slapped his neck.

The cassette recorded the phone ringing.

I bet it's Dan, he thought.

Kenny's finger went limp, and fleshy. His hand had no support. Before his eyes, his forearm bent like a hot wax rod. It hung, deflated. The warmth spread upward into his shoulder. He grabbed for the phone, but his hand could not grip. The machine picked up the caller's voice: "Kenny, it's me, Dan. Guess you're on your way." *Click.*

"Hey!" shouted Kenny. "What's going on here? Help! Somebody help me! I don't know what's happening to me."

With his other hand, Kenny picked up the receiver too late and screamed into it. Dan had already hung up. Kenny was alone. He tried to dial the rotary phone. But he collapsed on a steel countertop. He scratched limply at another flea bite. A flea disappeared into his hair, nipping as it went, spreading more of its virulent saliva as it shuttled itself to safety.

"Help me," Kenny wheezed. "I'm not in pain. I'm becoming paralyzed, numb... losing control. Quick, call an ambulance... please... help."

He could not even dial 'zero' to ask the operator to connect him to the police. And dialing '911' was completely out of the question.

Kenny strained to heave his chest as it grew heavier. He forced himself to breathe by throwing out his rib cage with the muscles of his stomach and sternum. The muscles compressed his lungs with a suffocating weight each time he exhaled. Oddly, it did not hurt. He just felt warm and oozy. Too cozy.

Clutching the little girl's red boot, he stumbled to the oxygen tank his father kept in a corner. He dropped the boot and cranked open the oxygen valve, inhaling from its tube. He grew giddy from the pure oxygen. Speaking aloud, he hoped the tape recorder might eventually save him.

"Mom, Dad, if I'm still conscious when you hear this, this is what's going on. Listen to me..."

He opened his lab coat and blue button-down shirt he'd neglected to button. Both garments were drenched in sweat. He could not believe what he saw.

"No CPR," puffed Kenny, his eyes wide with fear as his free hand felt his pectorals and slid down his side to his waist. "Whatever you do, don't... pump... my chest."

The sight of his own heart pumping arrested him—a fist-sized reddish glow through his pale skin. He felt for his ribs but detected none.

Kenny barked, "My chest is collapsing. My ribs are gone. All bones... disapp—"

Gasping, he slumped and reclined, well, actually he folded onto himself on the floor, as he sucked at the oxygen tube. Debilitating warmth spread down his torso to his coccyx.

"It's no use." Kenny recognized paralysis in his legs and remaining arm. "Bones are gone." He choked out the words in horror. "A pool of clear fluid... beside me... oozing out of my fingertips. One foot feels... wet. It smells... safe, pleasant, like your chicken soup, Mom." He giggled, not in fun but panic.

Boneless, essentially a jellyfish, Kenny van Swift lay on the lab floor. His clothes collapsed on his flattened skin. He could no longer speak. The recording device would later play the vague sound of sloshing as the fleas continued to liquefy what remained of Kenny.

10

Dan lit a candle. Hearthside, Aaron stoked the fire. A brittle-crackle fire blazed in the den.

"Are you bonkers?" demanded Coriander.

"I'm not sleeping upstairs either," added Katrina.

Dan spoke anxiously. "But my mom said—"

"We're not going to get pregnant by sleeping in the same room, Dan," advised Coriander haughtily.

"That's exactly how girls end up getting killed in all those horror movies," insisted Katrina.

"Divide and conquer," noted Aaron.

"I wouldn't know," retorted Dan. "I don't *do* horror movies."

"We're sticking together, Dan," said Katrina. "We can't even call the police since your phone's dead."

"Like it's my fault," sniped Dan.

"Chill out, guys," said Aaron.

"We're all sleeping in the same room," Katrina continued.

"And it's going to be the room with the least number of windows," Coriander completed Katrina's thought.

"Pantry!" suggested Aaron. "No windows, one door."

"Too cramped," advised Dan handing Aaron more fuel. "Cellar?"

"Fat chance!"

"No tornado, no cellar."

"If you insist, then to the pantry," Dan conceded.

"No sleeping either," Katrina announced. "We'll keep watch."

"In case that awful thing comes back," seconded Coriander. "And breaks in."

"We need pillows and sleeping bags to keep warm."

Coriander knelt to wake Josephine.

"Let her sleep. We'll be right back," said Dan.

"We can't split up. That's how *it* happens," insisted Katrina.

"In the movies," scoffed Dan.

"I'll carry Josephine," offered Aaron, hoisting the cranky bundle in his arms. She clung to Aaron and awoke gradually.

Dan placed the fire screen in front of the fireplace and fitted it snugly against the bricks so no sparks could scatter embers and cause a house fire. By candlelight, they tiptoed up the stairs to get provisions.

"I feel like we're being watched," whispered Coriander, flicking her ultralong hair.

"I feel like we're being *stalked,*" whispered Katrina.

From every room they passed they heard it: the same vulgar flapping at the windows.

"You'd think the blizzard would blow that gross creature off its course," said Coriander.

The winged beast hovered and slapped and sucked at the windows, melting the ice off the glass. Dan drew the curtains across the frosty panes and the revolting pug face. Silently, the group of five efficiently loaded up and descended the stairs with armfuls of bedding.

"What if it comes down the chimney? Like Santa." Josephine worried.

"Can't. Fire's going," Aaron reassured her.

"Not only that," reminded Dan. "If it really is a vampire, it has to be *invited* inside. Vampires like to be treated like guests. It's *driven to kill* but can't if you don't invite it in."

"You've become quite the expert, Dan," remarked Aaron.

"Aaron, it was my desire to understand what makes your sick mind tick that inspired my initial research at the public library. It's purely academic, believe me."

"Thanks, buddy. That means a lot to me." Aaron laughed. "If I'm lucky, I'll get you to see *Nightmare Matinee* with me."

Dan scoffed.

"He means *Still Life: The Best of the Worst,*" corrected Katrina.

A crash against the glass at the upstairs landing sent them hurtling down the stairs to the main floor. Josephine began to cry and buried her face in Aaron's shoulder.

"*Shhh*. It's okay. We're safe," Aaron reassured her.

"Josie just wanted an excuse to hug you, Aaron," Dan whispered, joking, yet his voice shook.

"*S-s-s-so* they just can't come in, right?" asked Coriander.

"Right." Dan choked out, doubting it himself.

"Oh, I feel one *hundred* percent safe now," Katrina said sarcastically, hugging the heap of blankets she carried in her arms.

Just then shards of frosty glass splintered the air as the bay window in the living room blew in.

11

With a cold wind and a gaping specter at their backs, the friends stumbled to Dan's pantry and piled in. It was a tight but safe hideout. Dan braced himself against the door.

"Needs an invitation, eh, Dan?" Aaron remarked.

For a long time, the teenagers listened. They heard nothing but the wind howling around inside the house. They lay the nest of sleeping bags and pillows on the floor of the pantry. Josephine conked out right away from the stress of it all, then Coriander. Dan and Aaron chowed Josephine's stack of on-order Girl Scout cookies to try to stay awake, taking turns bracing their feet against the door as a barricade.

Next to Aaron, Katrina leaned against a cupboard and nodded off. Their candle burned and the air in the small room quickly grew thick from their exhalations.

"We need air. Hey, quit chewing, Aaron. Did you hear that?" A potent draft raged under the pantry door.

Aaron swallowed and listened. Sure enough, they heard footsteps—inside the house! The door draft stopped suddenly. But then the flapping started anew.

"Oh, my God, the vampire's in the house!" whispered Aaron.

"*Shhhush!*" whispered Dan.

The flapping was approaching the pantry door, then it stopped.

"We've got to make a run for it," whispered Aaron, quietly waking the girls.

The flapping sound continued to draw nearer.

Aaron gently shook Katrina. Coriander was more difficult to wake. Josephine just plain refused.

"Ammunition," said Aaron reaching for a pantry shelf to retrieve a mesh bag of garlic cloves. Beside it, Katrina located an economy-size bottle of garlic powder and dumped half in a mixing bowl for Coriander.

"Will crushed red pepper do the same thing?" asked Katrina, examining the candle-lit spice shelf for additional weapons.

"Doubt it," said Dan.

"Shhh! Whisper Dan!"

The heavy flapping grew louder and more aggressive right outside the pantry.

"It's flying right for the pantry door," whimpered Coriander. From the kitchen, they heard a sigh then a cat's violent yowl. "It's feeding on your cat!"

"I don't have a cat," whispered Dan. Just then the electricity came back on. Light came on in the kitchen, slicing under the pantry door, emboldening the teens.

"Storm blew the windows out!" an angry voice was exclaiming just outside the pantry door. "*Damn stray! Out!*"

"Must be others in the pantry," said another irascible voice in the kitchen. "I hear noise in there."

"We're so hosed," muttered Dan shaking his head.

"There's more than one of'em out there," whispered Katrina urgently.

"Let's get'em!" Aaron yelled at the top of his lungs as he charged out of the pantry followed by Katrina and Coriander shaking garlic powder and screaming. Dan hung back inside the pantry.

"What the heck's going on, Dan? I told you the girls were to sleep upstairs, young man!" Mrs. Pritcher said sternly.

"It's not what you think, Mom," said Dan defensively. "Ask Josie." Sleepily, Josephine confirmed Dan was telling the truth.

"Well, your mother was worried, Dan," said Mr. Pritcher. "The storm woke us. We searched the entire house and didn't find you kids anywhere, so we went looking outside in the blizzard." Mr. Pritcher continued to shake out two long black trench coats whose wet fabric flapped snow in the teenager's faces.

"The bay window shattered in that freak windstorm." Mrs. Pritcher wiped snow and garlic powder off her pointy nose. "Hope no more stray cats wander in!"

"I'll check the cellar for plywood to block that window until Home Depot opens tomorrow," said Mr. Pritcher.

"Sorry we worried you," said Dan, "Happy New Year!"

12

Kenny's mother, Dr. Emily van Swift excused herself from the laboratory party to place a phone call from her office.

"Happy New Year! I've been calling you, Mr. Haimatikos, but you never take calls during the day," she said into the telephone receiver. Her two albino bulldogs stood by her, their pink eyes never blinked.

"I'm a very busy man, Dr. van Swift" Richard Haimatikos lied point-blank. Why waste time on things for which he felt no passion, such as daylight? Despite all the perks—zero accountability, no sitting in rush hour, endless life as a living-dead person, for starters— there were some restrictions involved in being a vampire. Lugging around his guitar case full of soil from his homeland was one of those restrictions.

"Were you even invited to a New Year's Eve party this evening, Mr. Haimatikos?" Emily van Swift asked doubting anyone would have invited such a notorious abuser of the public's good will. His toxic waste dumps were the shame of Westlake, and, most likely, the cause of increased cancer rate in the town. Waiting for his reply, she watched heavy snow fall outside her lab office window.

"I'm rather *indisposed,* Dr. van Swift," Richard Haimatikos spoke softly. From the supple leather seat in the semidarkness of his office, he nursed a bloody tenderloin steak.

Ever since that body had been found at Haimatikos' landfill, his entire empire had been under twenty-four-hour surveillance by local authorities.

They're all so ungrateful, Haimatikos thought grudgingly, *They're the ones demanding the meat and making those mountains of trash everywhere, while I'm trying my best to repurpose all that wasted open space for their brats' use. And, yet I'm considered the villain here.* He was dying to ask someone, *anyone, Who's more virulent? Little old me? Or all of them combined?* But of course, Richard Haimatikos was already dead, and so he muddled along doing whatever he felt like. *There's no justice,* he thought languidly, *There's only winning, survival...* He stared out. His interior office window looked onto his refrigerated prime beef storage room the length of several tennis courts. He picked a crust of blood off his lower lip and popped it in his mouth, crunching like a cracker, as he admired the fresh veal carcasses that dangled in tight rows in the windowed stockroom below.

Slowly, his yellow fangs withdrew into his fetid, swollen gums. He had fed enough for today. His claws strummed the Transylvanian soil in the Stratocaster guitar case that rested on his lap. He rubbed a pinch of his home turf against his cheek and in his hair. He sniffed it, inhaling a few grains of dirt. Unlike most things, it gave him great pleasure, and made him feel safe. *Homeland security*, he thought.

"So how's *S.P.U.D.S.*, Mr. Haimatikos?" Emily van Swift asked Richard. His silence made the doctor chatter nervously. "How's my *Self-Propelled Urban Detritus Slurper*?" she repeated. "My basset hound?" Silence. "Mr. Haimatikos, *how's my dog*?"

The vampire chuckled.

"What's so funny?" asked Emily van Swift.

Richard Haimatikos laughed because he felt the *S.P.U.D.S.* code name—*Self-Propelled Urban Detritus Slurper*—was better suited to *himself* than to the genetically engineered basset hound that Emily had secretly loaned to him from her genetics laboratory. The very same dog that Richard Haimatikos had, that very evening—albeit inadvertently and with utter indifference—set loose upon the town of Westlake.

"What's so funny, Mr. Haimatikos? How's the test run going? Is *S.P.U.D.S.-Y.* eating? Does the dog eat all your beef by-products without any resistance? Are you still having to dump the slaughterhouse floor-scrapings into the river?"

The vampire took his time answering. Richard Haimatikos did not necessarily set out lie, per se. Yet he also really did not want to tell Dr. van Swift the truth about her missing biohazard pooch.

"*S.P.U.D.S* ate," he offered cautiously. "Quite a lot, in fact. Good dog."

"Great, because I'm unveiling *S.P.U.D.S.-Y.'s* sibling-clone as a viable waste cleaner-upper at Westlake High School's First Night Earth Day fair tomorrow."

"Tomorrow?" choked Richard.

"Tomorrow, Mr. Haimatikos, on New Year's Day at the high school, you too can '*Make Earth Day Your New Year's Resolution*'. I'll unveil both dogs together as a team. Believe it or not, *S.P.U.D.S.-Y.* alone is going to make the folks of Westlake very happy with you, Mr. Haimatikos."

Richard did not really care about *their* happiness, but remained on the line to hear out the good doctor merely out of respect for the fact that she *was* a doctor and had devoted her entire delicious blood-pulsing life to staring into a Petri dish. The vampire appreciated discipline only because his own strict—and arguably scientific—bad habits of self-preservation ensured his eternal life among the walking-dead who, in Richard Haimatikos' opinion, otherwise managed to blend rather well with the normal population. It was only when the undead got caught for cannibalism, vampirism, etc., or in his own case, for losing a hazmat-dog, that the importance was underscored of their role in balancing the human population by consuming the consumers. *They're the predators, not us,* thought the vampire, *they're the virus.*

"When I unveil *S.P.U.D.S.-Y.*, you'll be known as a politically correct hero with a conscience, Mr. Haimatikos. Instead of a dithering Eurotrash *dilettante* and social parasite."

"Ouch," Mr. Haimatikos grunted indifferently. He liked the way Emily slung an insult. He'd met his match. And a real doctor could fit in well as his companion. He was sometimes lonely, despite the legion of vampires that he was forming with the help of a recent recruit from Westlake High School's science department.

"Mr. Haimatikos, are you still on the line?"

"Yes, Dr. van Swift," he whispered. He reveled in Emily van Swift's velvet voice and his fantasy of sipping her blood. There and then, he resolved to find out what *that* would be like. He had, after all, known her long enough. She seemed so pure yet had that scathing wit he so adored. Surely she had no communicable diseases that could affect him. The beef carcasses were tiding him over while he was under police surveillance, yet he craved the real stuff. Cow juice just wasn't cutting it. *And, Dr. van Swift, yeah, she's a suitable victim to corrupt and retain forever at my side: pure, brilliant, and married. The total corruptible package.*

It was tough to get a good meal around Westlake these days. Everyone seemed to be on this darned garlic accessorizing kick, especially the most delectable quarry. He and Dr. Emily van Swift could work as a team to elude them all and together provide a sort of check-and-balance to the consumer ecosystem. *Thankfully Emily doesn't reek of garlic like everyone else,* thought Richard. *She's a scientist. Not superstitious.*

For months Richard Haimatikos and Dr. Emily van Swift had worked together to pull off this secret sewage-slurping dog project. For months, Emily van Swift had called Richard Haimatikos every day to check on her laboratory test dog, *S.P.U.D.S.-Y.* Flying solo as Haimatikos was, the vampire had come to look forward to Emily's phone calls. And every day his report had been positive; the dog ate. And ate. And ate. Good dog. Gradually, Haimatikos promised, Westlake's polluted river would be clearing up, all thanks to Dr. Emily van Swift's clandestine *S.P.U.D.S.-Y.* project.

"Mr. Haimatikos, you know what this means for your business, don't you? Let me be clear." *He is so laconic,* she thought. "Get excited! This means you'll be able to announce to the public that your slaughterhouse is no longer polluting Westlake's river. You'll be a real *rah-rah* hero. The citizens will love you."

"Yesss, my *image* will be spared." He rolled his eyes indifferently as he practice putted on the stretch of green Astro Turf on the floor of his sleek office. He glanced at the large wall mirror, but saw, of course, only the reflection of his golf one iron and the phone cord stretched from his mahogany desk to the receiver tucked under his chin, invisible in the mirror. Really, Richard Haimatikos didn't care one whit about being regarded as a hero by the citizens of podunk Westlake, and, in fact, he rather looked forward to seeing what kind of mayhem would result from having carelessly freed the basset hound. *Purely accidental though that was,* he snickered at his own lack of accountability.

He decided that Emily van Swift's response to today's dog-loss incident would determine her rate of compatibility for him, on a vampire scale of one to ten. Still, he wasn't sure how to tell Emily the truth, although he knew he would have to. So... he procrastinated.

"We can then use my other laboratory dogs to clean up your toxic landfills that you're trying to sell off as buildable land for schools and children's playgrounds!"

"That's a secret, Dr. van Swift," Richard purred low, a precursor to a growl, and harbinger of attack. "That's a big, big secret... how I *repurpose* the by-product of others' wasteful consumerism, Dr. van Swift. How did you find out such drivel about me and my real estate?" He was intrigued.

"Just between you, me, and the Freedom of Information Act, it's public record what gets dumped and where, when, and by whom, and who owns said land. Your name is on all the deeds as owner of all the radioactive waste dumps in New England. So, do me a favor, Mr. Haimatikos. Stop selling off parcels of toxic land for children's use, until we clean it up with my bioremediation dogs." She patted the twin albinos leashed beside her.

"I haven't sold any plots *yet*, Dr. van Swift," he lied, impressed by her resourcefulness.

"Ah, but, Mr. Haimatikos, I know you *have* sold an eighteen-acre toxic plot of land," she countered. "For a Westlake grammar school with a very elaborate jungle gym." She left him no wiggle room.

Richard Haimatikos grunted again.

"So *then*, Mr. Haimatikos, once your reputation is restored, maybe I'll finally be able to convince you to make a large charitable donation to my research lab," Emily suggested.

"And you to mine, Doctor," he putted, imagining Emily's pulsing jugular vein against his ancient tongue. He paused mid-putt to ponder how her velvet voice would fade delicately in a wilting scream as he drained her blood. "And you to mine," he whispered again. He putted and quivered watching his Titleist roll slowly across the little putting turf in his office... and... *plunk*. "*Hole in one!*" yelled the vampire. *Oh, she's a fine catch.*

Astounded, Emily van Swift asked, "Mr. Haimatikos, are you... *flirting* with me?" For the first time in months, the vampire had dissolved the courteous distance between them. She so preferred the cordial, even courtly, respect Mr. Haimatikos had displayed until now.

Mr. Haimatikos chuckled infectiously into the phone. *Yes, he was sort of endearing, even cute, but... no.* Emily van Swift frowned and took the lead to clear up any ambiguity he might be trying to create in their heretofore professional relationship.

"Would you like to join my husband and me at our New Year's Eve party tonight at my laboratory, Mr. Haimatikos? I know it's late already, but you're such a night owl."

"Join you? Indeed. I'll escort you, *wine* you, dine you, and *win* you," he promised. "All I require is an *invitation*... And... *Emily*," he ventured her first name for the first time, "...you can call me *Rick*."

Nauseated, Dr. Emily van Swift paused to think before she spoke, "*Richard*, uh, *Rick*." His first name felt awkward in her mouth. Dirty, in fact. For starters, Haimatikos just wasn't a nickname kind of guy. Plus, there was something incomprehensibly deceitful about him that made Emily's skin crawl. "Let me stop you right there, *Rick*, my husband will be pleased to meet you, finally, after all these months. Now remember, it's a masquerade ball. If you're going to be very late, call the front desk, so I can reset the door lock system."

"Doctor?" purred Richard Haimatikos. "Emily."

"Yes?"

"You don't mind if I'm attended by my, er, police escort, do you?"

"No, Richard, I'm well aware of the surveillance. My husband works for the police department."

"I see," he choked. *Yet, she still works with me.*

"See you soon, *Rick*. Don't forget to wear a costume. I'll be the one with the two blond bulldogs on a leash. And *you*?"

"I'll be the one dressed as..." Richard Haimatikos took a moment to consider, then a fetid smile spread his mouth wide. "Oh, I guess I'll come as a... vampire."

13

Even on New Year's Day, whilst nursing a *hair-of-the-dog* hangover, Westlake's dog catcher had a keen eye for detail.

"There's a free-wheeler! No tags, no collar!" Officer Rumpelmeyer spied the poodle in front of Westlake High School. The officer parked beside the school announcement case that read,

NEW YEAR'S DAY EARTH DAY
CONVENTION TODAY 10 A.M.-6 P.M.
MAKE EARTH YOUR NEW YEAR'S RESOLUTION!

The only hound he had caught so far on the morning of January 1st was a healthy brown basset with black feet. The handsome basset howled miserably inside the metal chamber in the back of Westlake's doggie paddy wagon.

Safe from fleas and bites inside his hazmat suit, net in hand, the police officer in charge of impounding Westlake's strays next captured a toy poodle that stood shivering by the high-school sign. The poodle struggled in the net as Officer Rumpelmeyer opened a small wire door to the back of the wagon. From within, the brown basset hound seemed to smile at the poodle. In response, the poodle gnashed its teeth. Dogs *know*.

"That old hush puppy won't hurt you, Miss Poodle," Officer Rumpelmeyer reassured the frantic fluff ball.

The poodle's tantrum caused the officer to lose his grip on the net handle. Kicking and clawing, the yapping creature sprang away to safety. Like a fly swatter, the officer's net slammed down on the poodle just as the basset seized the opportunity to escape out the small wire door. The basset hound leapt out of the wagon, past the net, past Officer Rumpelmeyer, and out of sight behind Westlake High School.

Facing the sunny New Year's Day morn, Katrina and Aaron walked briskly, hand in gloved hand, across the high school parking lot. Many other teenagers herded toward the First Night Earth Day gathering, too.

"Gorgeous dog, Aaron, look." Katrina pointed out the basset hound loping the by the rhododendrons.

"Like the one we saw at Dan's house last night," noted Aaron.

"Look at his cute little black feet slip on the ice. Good dog, come here, boy! Aww, come back!" The stray ventured into the shriveled hedge.

"I always wanted a basset hound. My parents won't let me get a dog," said Aaron.

"Yeah? Me too. Ever since my dog died of heartworm. Well, actually, the medicine killed him right after it killed off the worms. Why can't you get a dog, Aaron?"

"Mom says it'd scare her horses," Aaron replied, "Really, she's afraid she'll get stuck feeding it."

"There he is again, *ooooh*, I'm dying to pet him, he's so *cuuuuute!*" Katrina approached the basset hound. "Come here, boy. Good dog." The basset hound trotted toward Katrina, but was suddenly frightened by the crowd of teenagers and trundled away again under the snowdrift that covered the bushes flanking the high school.

"Bad dog!" Katrina pouted.

"Excuse me, kids, have you seen a basset hound?"

"Yeah," said Aaron. Katrina elbowed him. "*Uhhm*, are you an astronaut or is that a hazmat suit?"

"Hazmat, kid. In case of rabies," advised Officer Rumpelmeyer flexing with his net. "So the dog went...?"

"Thatta' way." Aaron pointed in the opposite direction. "Second yard line."

"Thank you. Be sure to call Animal Control whenever you see strays. Rampant rabies this year!"

"Yup," said Katrina, blocking the hedgerow from the officer's line of sight as he headed off toward the football field.

"Food's scarce in the woods this time of year," Officer Rumpelmeyer hollered back, "So raccoons and skunks come 'round homes looking for tidbits..."

"Yup." *Leave already!* thought Katrina.

"....end up in fights with the family pet. Next thing you know, your dog or cat's got a bite from a wild animal with rabies. Don't want'em biting you kids."

"Okay. Better luck next time," said Katrina.

The officer headed off, and then turned back with an afterthought. "Or worse, kids think the wild animal's tame 'cause it's so friendly. Kid cuddles it. Next thing you know, the kid's been mauled and has rabies, too."

"Thanks for the warning, Officer," said Katrina, rolling her pretty eyes.

"And the shots you have to have are very painful," Rumpelmeyer added before departing for real.

"Should we have told him?" Katrina and Aaron whispered in tandem. "Too late." They giggled and kissed.

"Hey, check it out!" said Katrina.

"Nice limo," said Aaron, as a sparkling red sedan with tinted glass pulled in followed by a police surveillance van. "Sure is red."

"Guess we know who's *not* driving it!" Katrina and Aaron laughed.

The rear limo door was opened by a burly driver for his client.

"Check out the Ray-Ban man."

Out stepped Richard Haimatikos followed by a stout woman with rodent features. She too wore dark glasses and carried a file box stenciled *SUNGLASSES & DIRT*.

"Whooaa, what's Ms. Anthrope doing here?"

"She's supposed to be dead again."

"She's with that skeeve-ball slaughterhouse owner!"

"And he owns every toxic landfill in New England," noted Katrina. "You saw this morning's paper? Dirt bag. He's selling toxic land for people to build homes."

"And an elementary school," a passing student chimed in.

"Find Emily," Richard Haimatikos commanded from behind his sunglasses.

"Where boss?" asked his driver.

"In the cafeteria, you moron. Read the flyer."

"Yes, boss."

"You go to the side of the cafeteria that has windows and I'll cover the side with no windows. Jeez, sun's killin' me."

"Right, boss," said the driver.

"I can't stay out long. So find Emily. *Find her!*" Richard Haimatikos carried his guitar case filled with vampire safety-soil. He resembled a rocker.

"I'm on it, boss." The driver didn't budge.

"What a pain in the neck these day ventures are. I can't go anywhere without my dirt," grumbled Richard Haimatikos. "*Terra firma, mama mia.*"

"Yes, boss, must be terrible for you, boss."

"And what's worse, with the constant cop escort, I'm relegated to sucking cold beef instead of fresh kiddie kill," hissed the frustrated vampire.

"Poor boss. Good we lost'em though."

"Shut up and go find Emily van Swift."

The driver just stood there.

"*Go!* Oh for devil's sake! Show him!" Richard Haimatikos gestured to Ms. Anthrope and the former science teacher angled off to the side door of the school leading the driver, as Richard Haimatikos headed toward the main entrance of Westlake High School.

"You've got your marching orders, Ms. Anthrope," he called after her. "Only the best and the brightest."

She nodded, holding her dark glasses in place with one hand.

Only the best students, too analytical to indulge in superstition, thought the vampire. Suddenly a chunk of slippery tan tofu slapped Haimatikos' ear.

"Bull's-eye!" shouted Billy Carlyle, the football captain. Everyone laughed except seething Haimatikos.

"There he is! There's the Toxic Dumper!" Out of nowhere, banners appeared, waving to protest the dumping of sludge from Haimatikos' slaughterhouse into Westlake's river. From the growing crowd of rioting teenagers and parents, incessant, angry chanting swelled to a crescendo, "*Hazmat! Hazmat! Hazmat! Hazmat!*"

In an instant, Richard's driver drew by his side. "I'll protect you, boss."

"Shielded by an utter moron," groaned Richard. "Go on home, kids! Damned brats."

"You tell'em, boss."

"Kids, listen up! I employ most of your parents. It's because of *me* that you get high-quality meats at a reasonable price. Not to mention the fact that I repurpose *your* waste." *I sell it back to you idiots,* he thought smugly, *when I could just be dining on the lot of you to reduce consumerism-induced landfills altogether.*

Nevertheless, teenagers pelted the bloodsucker and his shiny red car with celery stalks and handfuls of sloppy tofu.

"Wastrels!" sniped Richard Haimatikos. "You're wasting perfectly good food. Send it to kids in underdeveloped countries! Like in Eastern Europe."

"Like Transylvania," added the driver helpfully. *Thwapp,* another celery stalk to the shoulder of Richard's Armani suit. *Whump,* a deep purple eggplant thumped Haimatikos' brow, knocking off his sunglasses. Blinded and squinting, his shades had to be retrieved by his driver. "At least they ain't throwing garlic at you," consoled his only living confidant. "At least that's still a secret–eh, boss? *Howtakeepasecret!* Right? Better not tell Emily or she'll spread that around, too. About you being a *vam*–"

"Shut up, you moron! Stop nattering in public."

"Right, boss."

"Mr. Haimatikos, we're boycotting meat from your packing company," yelled a student ringleader, "...until you agree to stop dumping tons and tons of animal by-products in the river. You've spread bacterial diseases by dumping rotting meat in our water. And..."

And lethal viruses! The imperious vampire suppressed a snicker before he spoke again, "You only know the half of it!" He was now encircled by a throng of peevish protesters. "You children and your parents must be accountable. You must take no responsibility for the waste you create... the waste that I clean up for you."

His burly driver forced a path through the riot toward the high school. Richard Haimatikos wiped another chunk of tofu splatter off his brow with an embroidered linen handkerchief.

"This is all Emily van Swift's fault. Spiteful woman!" he grumbled.

"Well, boss, you did lose her dog."

"*Stop* reminding me of my purported failings, you moron!? She did *not* have to turn the whole town against me? Over a dog! She didn't even give me a chance to find her stupid animal."

"Not like you looked either, boss."

"Shut up! You saw what she did to me last night at her party when I told her about *S.P.U.D.S.-Y.!* For being *honest* with her, I am punished!" Richard Haimatikos complained as if he valued virtues like truth. "She locked me in that tasteless souvenir shop at her laboratory until nearly dawn!"

"Good thing you had your guitar case. You made a perfect Rocker vampire in that costume, boss. And y'know, I really liked the t-shirts in the gift shop. The ones with the doggies." The driver recalled wistfully.

"Stop talking."

"Aww, boss, you're just suffering from *unrequited blood.* Mad you didn't get to drink hers," said the thuggish driver.

"The idiom is *unrequited love,* you idiot. For devil's sake, it's because of Dr. Emily van Swift that I can't even get in and out of my own slaughterhouse today without being swarmed by politically-correct wannabes too lazy to be accountable for their own trash. If not for *this* they'd be bored out of their minds at home watching their parents watch the Rose Bowl Parade and stuffing themselves with junk food!"

"And eatin' your steaks, boss."

"As for you, my moronic servant... do you even have a name? *Driver?* I thank my evil stars that I am not condemned to an eternity of your idiocy, because I shall live forever and *you* shall eventually die."

The driver looked hurt.

Inside the high-school cafeteria the chairs and lunch tables had been cleared away and green booths erected around green display tables, row after row. Table after table displayed students' science projects portending to save the planet from the seven human vices.

"Never saw the cafeteria so packed before," Katrina marveled.

"Guess our generation wants to save the planet," remarked Aaron. "Wow, you'd think it was St. Patrick's Day. Every single banner is green." Aaron helped Katrina off with her lavender parka and kissed her. Content, she smiled.

"Check out the toxic waste awareness quilt." Katrina pointed at the far wall where she and other cool people normally sat at lunch. Framed in green linen, the quilt displayed myriad representations of scientific formulae. "It's beautiful!"

"Yeah." Aaron's inner artist loved it. "But you'd have to have a degree in chemistry to truly appreciate it. Dan must love it."

The hazardous waste awareness quilt was comprised of twenty squares. Each square spelled out the chemical formula for a toxin and its antidote. And each had been hand quilted, appliquéd, or embroidered by students.

"Oh, c'mon, Aaron," cajoled Katrina, "you know *hazardous* when you see it."

"Katrina! Aaron! Over here!" called Dan from the hazardous landfill exhibition that he and Coriander had researched together.

Coriander greeted them with European air kisses.

"*Bonjour!* How are *we* on this New Year's Day?"

"After last night *we're* not exactly ready to run a marathon," said Katrina. Sleeping in a strange room full of strange noises on a rumpled cot sized for a small girl had done little for Katrina's beauty rest. Plus, Josephine had awakened several times crying in the top bunk while Coriander snored incessantly below.

"Hey, Correy," Katrina remarked, "you're wearing part of Kelly's bacteria exhibit too?" Katrina waved her own sock sack of lavender fishnet fabric that hung from her neck. The sack contained a bulb of pungent garlic.

"Fishnet stockings around your *neck*?" Dan asked incredulously.

"Great minds think about garlic," replied Katrina with grin. "That's why I wanted to stop off at home this morning."

"Me too. I'm not taking any chances," said Coriander, waving back at Katrina with her own black fishnet stocking dangling from her neck, a garlic cluster in its reinforced toe. "Not after last night."

"You girls're wearin' it now!" Aaron exclaimed.

"Beats eating it, Aaron, and smelling like you."

"And, our little pouches are fashionable," affirmed Coriander. "Kelly gave us the idea last week in class. She did the history-of-garlic-as-an-anti-bacterial exhibit. Ask her when she gets here. She hasn't set it up yet but all her stuff's there from Friday. See!"

"The indigenous Americans believed in vampires too," remarked Dan. "They wore garlic sacks like this around their necks to ward off evil and vampires."

"A lotta' good it did *them*," remarked Katrina.

"You sure they didn't fill it with spice seeds? Like coriander?" Aaron teased.

"No, Aaron, they used garlic," rebutted Coriander.

"Seems garlic's a universal anti-vampire antidote."

"It's anti-bacterial," confirmed Dan. "Vampires were just people infected by the rabies bacteria, I suspect. Made them go *mad-dog* and become insane cannibals."

"Is that your latest theory on vampires, Dan?"

"Yes. Well, Josephine is to be footnoted as its originator, actually." Dan coughed uncomfortably, having to give credit where it was due. "Nevertheless, I researched it further. Virtually every world culture throughout history had a vampire myth."

"Every world culture had vampires?"

"In the Far East, Central Europe, Africa, the New World. And, guess what... all of'em had garlic."

"Fascinating," Aaron said, deadpan. "What's with the chemistry lab t-shirt, Dan? Homemade?" Dan's t-shirt bore lettering hand-emblazoned with black magic marker.

"Should we guess?" Katrina read Dan's t-shirt aloud, "*CH2-CH-CH2(o)SCH2CH-CH2.*"

"That's the chemical formula for thiosulfinate, the active ingredient in garlic, called two-propenyl-two-propenethiosulfinate. Or, *allicin*," Dan explained.

"You've gone superstitious on me, Dan!" said Aaron incredulously and sang the lyrics from Elvis Costello's song *Alison*, "*...this world is killing me...*"

"Not superstitious." Embarrassed, Dan did not bother to mention that he himself had been popping odorless garlic tablets. Coriander sheltered his secret.

"You just better hope that the chemical formula you wrote on your t-shirt is *the* vampire-resistant ingredient in garlic," said Katrina, "Kelly told me last Friday that garlic has over two hundred active ingredients."

Dan looked worried.

"And you better hope the vampire took chemistry, or you're going to have to break down and eat the stuff," cautioned Aaron as he placed two peeled cloves of garlic over his eyeteeth like fangs. His top lip held them in place as Aaron aimed at Katrina's neck. "*I vant to suck your bloooood.*"

"Quit it, Aaron," snapped Katrina. "Look!"

She indicated the suited man in sunglasses hastening up the crowded aisle in their direction. Followed by his driver, Richard Haimatikos repeatedly knocked students out of his way with his guitar case.

"Rock star comin' through," announced the driver.

A trail of Transylvanian dust wafted in his wake.

"I told you to check the other side," Richard snarled at his clingy driver.

"That slaughterhouse owner's a smarm king. He should wash his hair," said Coriander.

Searching each booth for Dr. Emily van Swift and her biologically-engineered dogs, the two men drew nearer the toxic landfill exhibit booth.

"We saw Ms. Anthrope with them," said Katrina.

"But she's dead," said Coriander incredulously.

"Not dead enough. She called me at home this morning after you girls left," said Dan.

"Ms. Anthrope called *you*, Dan? What for?"

"Her special project. She invited only the best students in the class."

"Well, *lah-tee-dah*," said Katrina with pert sarcasm.

"Why didn't she call *me*?" Coriander was dumbfounded. "What's the project on?"

"*Conversion*," Dan replied authoritatively.

"*Conversion?*" asked Aaron. "*Conversion to what*? The walking dead like her?"

"Some kind of *conversion*... ratio, no doubt. Okay, I don't know," Dan admitted. "She said she'd explain when she saw me in her office. I'll be back in ten minutes."

"Wait," Coriander said. She grabbed Dan to smooch him. "And don't think you're smarter than me just because she invited you and not me, Dan."

Dan laughed and kissed her more just as creepy Richard Haimatikos approached them.

"Children, very good, I see you've championed the issue of toxic landfills. Hooray." The vampire's tone was flat. "Yet you've invested not one drop of ink to chronicle the fact that your very consumerism is the culprit."

"He's got a point," said Dan, wishing he'd thought of it first.

The vaguest aroma of garlic caught Richard's attention. Repulsed, he whiffed away then swooned weakly against his driver. For an imperceptible nanosecond, the vampire's rugged face converted into its nocturnal self. It did not last long enough for the human eye to detect his *conversion* at all. Yet the subconscious minds of the four teenagers instinctively registered terror. In that split second, Haimatikos' open mouth gnashed once at the teens. And his fangs dripped cream-yellow saliva onto the stack of toxic landfill flyers on the table in front of Katrina.

His fit passed, and Richard the vampire stepped back, keeping a wary distance from the four friends. He could not discern who the culprit was.

"I couldn't help overhearing the garlic debate you young dears were having. In fact," Haimatikos informed them churlishly, "garlic thins the blood, so it won't clog up the veins. It's an anti-coagulant. Might make you dizzy, kids. Best you all stay the heck away from it! *Wicked* baaaaaad for you."

Then he pushed past them.

"Thanks for the tip," muttered Aaron, "Weirdo."

"Must be why he got dizzy just now," ventured Coriander. "The old buzzard must be taking garlic. You saw him. He nearly fainted. His blood must be thin."

"I'm not sure what I saw," said Dan. "But I definitely saw *something*."

"Just like we *saw something* last night?" Katrina asked.

"I'm not sure," Dan said. *Bet it was my garlic formula t-shirt that set him off*, thought Dan, and checked his watch. "Now I'm really late for Ms. Anthrope. Back in ten, Correy!"

"*Whatevah!*" Katrina shrugged and leaned against the stack of brochures on their display table. As she did, her hands pressed into the vampire's oozey goo.

"*Eeeeeeww!*"

Thick, yellow drool clung to her palms.

14

Dan climbed two flights then strode down the long gray-and-pink hall to Ms. Anthrope's science lab.

"Hey, guys," Dan acknowledged Berry Fisher and Christopher Woodward in the hall. Dan Pritcher and Kenny van Swift had beaten them for first place in last year's science competition.

In dark sunglasses and turtlenecks, Berry and Christopher shuffled along the smooth hall floor. They each held a plastic baggie with what appeared to be crumbled brownies inside. Under an arm, each carried a bolt of black fabric.

"Hi, guys," Dan repeated. *Deaf, much?*

"Ms. Anthrope's been waiting for you, Dan." Berry's voice sounded stilted, metallic. Berry was usually an adorable flirt, known by the football team as *Very Berry*. Now she seemed like a bitter old shrew.

"Hurry, Pritcher," said Christopher. His voice too revealed a droning metallic quality.

Dan looked twice as they passed him. Turning, he bumped into Peter Peterson, causing Peter to drop what he carried. Dan laughed and apologized, expecting Peter to make a joke, as he normally did about everything. Instead, Peter brushed Dan aside to pick up his black fabric bolt and plastic baggie... *Not brownie crumbs*, Dan observed, *but dirt*. Peter walked on.

"Hey, Pete, I said I'm sorry," said Dan quizzically.

Peter turned. He wore dark sunglasses just like Berry and Christopher. He said nothing, but Dan could feel Peter's glare sizzling into his own eyes.

Dan blinked. "I said, I'm sorry, Pete."

Finally, Peter spoke, "You're late for *conversion*, Dan."

"I'm headed there now." Dan gestured to the science department down the hall. But when he turned back to Peter, all three, Peter, Berry, and Christopher had vaporized.

Geez, they must've flown down that hall, thought Dan, noting that the staircase was about forty gray metal lockers away. He shrugged and walked on along the polished checkerboard floor that seemed to stretch on forever down the hall.

The door to the private office of Ms. Anthrope was open and the classroom was empty. Dan tried the inner door connecting her office to the science lab but it was locked. He retreated down the hall to the next door that led directly to the science lab. He tried the knob but it was locked too. The dark green roller blind was pulled down over the door glass. Dan could not see inside, so he knocked. No one answered. As he withdrew his hand, the green shade pressed against the window and rumpled as if someone were leaning against it, maybe even struggling against it. Dan hoped Ms. Anthrope was all right. He *knew* all the nonsense about her double death had to have been a stupid rumor perpetrated by schoolmates who couldn't wrap their heads around chemistry class.

"Hello?" he called. No reply.

Dan rushed back around through the classroom into to her office. Still empty. He hesitated a moment as he heard the lab connector door open slowly.

"Late for *conversion,*" droned Mark Riley with an accusing glare over the rims of dark glasses.

Dan caught a glimpse of Mark's eyeballs—blood-red and the iris was a sickly yellow. A drop of blood raced out the corner of Mark's left eye like a tear; he wiped it away with the sleeve of his turtleneck shirt.

"Ms. Anthrope's waiting for you, Dan." Mark's zombie tone rankled Dan's soul.

Dan noticed three plastic baggies of soil on the teacher's desk. Each had a name tag tied to it: *Mark*, *Kenny*, and *Dan*. Dan backed away into the classroom and made it to the edge of the hall door just as Ms. Anthrope's sunglasses poked out of the science laboratory into her office. Unaware of Dan's presence, she entered her office chatting to Mark and wiping his blood from her mouth.

"Yours is there, Mark, marked *Mark*. Keep it with you at all times when the sun is up," she reminded. "Okay, next! Kenny's late as usual. Who else has not been tutored in *conversion* with me yet?"

That rodent face, thought Dan. *Conversion! Yeah, conversion into a vampire. I think not!*

Dan backed out through the doorway into the hall and listened another moment.

"Mark!" Ms. Anthrope whistled. "Hey! Did you not hear me? Dirt bag! Take it. To tide you over till you can go and dig your own soil."

Dan backed down the hall, hoping Ms. Anthrope and Mark Riley would stay in her office long enough for him to high tail it back to the cafeteria and get his three closest friends out.

Dan's mind raced. *Have I gone crazy? Has everyone gone crazy?*

As he ran, he pondered the name tags on the three remaining dirt bags: *Mark, Dan, Kenny*. What had happened to his lab partner?

15

Dan leapt off the landing into the cafeteria in search of Kenny's anatomy booth.

"Hey, Bruce, where's Kenny's display table?" Dan leaned over the green-skirted table of Bruce Wartmore's "*Save Our River*" exhibit. He heard grunting under the exhibit table and figured Bruce was arranging his belongings under there.

As Dan lay across the table to peek beneath it, he accidentally knocked off plastic baggies filled with tofu and crushed tomatoes that Bruce was selling for people to throw at Richard Haimatikos. Dan leaned over the display table when he noticed a pair of sunglasses on the floor behind it. "Don't want those to get stepped on." He got off the table and picked them up. Placing them on the table beside him, then Dan leaned down far enough to look for Bruce under the table. The grunting grew louder.

"Oh crap," said Dan. What Dan saw under the table made him gasp in disbelief. *Very Berry* was right on top of Bruce Wartmore! "Uh—sorry, guys! Get a hotel." They seemed not to hear Dan. "Dudes, you shouldn't be doing it in the cafeteria," Dan admonished. "You'll get caught."

And then... Berry raised her face from Bruce's neck to regard Dan. "It's okay, Danny," she said hungrily. "It's *berry* juice."

Dan gagged. Berry's mouth and chin dripped blood. Her eyes were yellowish red. The sickly grin on her face told Dan she was not the sweet, flirty girl she once was.

Dan stood, grabbing the dark sunglasses, and raced on to the next booth. There Christopher Woodward was setting out his hemoglobin exhibit. With trembling fingers, Dan forced Berry's dark glasses over his own gold-rims before Christopher could get a look at Dan's frightened eyes.

"What's up, Dan?" Christopher's sunglasses hid his eyes too. His voice was hollow.

"Hey, Christopher, how's it going? Seen Kenny?"

"No. Want to taste my exhibit?" Christopher pointed at a stretch of intravenous rubber tubing in through which blood bubbled up to a soft drink dispenser.

"Sure, sure." Dan fumbled as he studied his peer's exhibit in horror. "But, I've gotta find Kenny."

"Check it out, man," urged Christopher, lifting the green skirt of his display table. Underneath a half-dead sophomore girl stared up desperately at Dan. "Thirsty?"

"Help me," she croaked. Her jugular vein and femoral artery were connected to the spliced end of a rubber intravenous hose that adhered with surgical tape to throat and thigh, respectively.

"I call my soft drink *Quell. Quell your thirst*, Dan man! Get it?"

"Innovative, Christopher. Back in a jiff," said Dan, cutting a corner and rushing up the next aisle of Earth Day booths.

Dan held his own throat to *quell* a surge of nausea. He passed four more booths where students were setting up exhibits. *Were they all vampires by now?* He wondered and adjusted the sunglasses over his own wire rims just in case. When Dan reached Peter Peterson's extraterrestrial exhibit, a six-foot-tall inflated dummy of an alien grabbed Dan and he nearly passed out from fright.

"Dan," said Peter sternly. "I thought that'd give you a good laugh."

Maybe he's returning to his usual good-humored self? Dan hoped. To be safe, Dan covered his tracks. "Pete, did Kenny make it to Ms. Anthrope's lab for *conversion* like *the rest of us*?"

"Didn't see him. Oh, here comes someone," said Peter, getting ready, hiding behind the alien doll.

Alysha French was just arriving to set up her extinct and endangered species exhibit. Her arms were full of stuffed animals. Dan started to warn her to stay back, but Peter had already embraced Alysha, and littered the floor with a dodo bird, great auk, and minis of a black rhino, gorilla, great panda, Asian elephant, and snow leopard.

"Now she's an endangered species, too," exclaimed Peter through a mouthful of throat flesh.

Alysha fainted without uttering a scream. Tighter, Peter wrapped the arms of his inflatable alien doll around Alysha and dragged her beneath his booth table, out of sight, to continue his feed. In disbelief, Dan witnessed a carnal red spot soil the hem of the table's skirting as it absorbed Alysha's spilled blood.

I've got to mobilize Aaron and the girls. He turned to run. "Ms. Anthrope?!" Dan gagged on her name.

"Where are you off to in such a hurry, young man?"

16

Dangling a full baggie, Ms. Anthrope spoke, "Your dirt, Dan!"

"Oh, hey, thanks." He took the bag and stuffed it in his jeans pocket. "I feel better already. And, uh, I-I-I already met with, with Berry on the, uh, *con-con-conversion* matter, and I'm just on my way to share it with my girlfriend, Coriander Preston," said Dan, jamming the sunglasses frames into his face till it hurt.

"The cheerleading captain," mewled Ms. Anthrope.

"And Homecoming Queen!" added Dan.

"I overlooked her. Be sure you tell two people, and they tell two people and they tell two people, *et cetera et cetera*. That's how we build the *varmy*."

"*Varmy*? Of course, *vampire army*." Dan raced away from her, up one aisle and down another to find his best friends.

But Ms. Anthrope slunk behind him.

"Can I pat it?" asked Katrina tentatively, reaching out for the creature that resembled a pit bull. "It's so cute. You call it *S.P.U.D.S.*?" Katrina read the display sign.

She, Aaron, and Coriander had abandoned their toxic landfill booth to check out the action at the bioremediation booth. Dr. Emily van Swift was still rattled by the loss of her black-footed basset hound, yet she kept right on talking to the group of students that gathered around her exhibit.

"Yes, Katrina," said Emily van Swift. "*S.P.U.D.S.* stands for *Self-Propelled Urban Detritus Slurper*."

"Sounds like a newfangled name for a vigilante vampire," said Aaron.

"Weird-looking animal," said Coriander.

"That's not the kind of dog I had in mind when I said I wanted a dog," said Aaron.

"You can pet it," offered Emily van Swift, opening the crate door. "It cannot bite. It has no teeth, and its jaws cannot clamp. It's a drinker. It's genetically engineered to have insatiable thirst."

"Thirst for *what?*" asked Aaron.

"The fur's so soft," said Katrina as she petted the friendly-faced hound.

"*Eeeeew!* Hey! No saliva! The dog's tongue feels like a soft dish scrubber," she said. The peculiar dog-like animal lapped Katrina with its huge dry, hairy tongue. Katrina had expected the tongue to be wet.

"That's right, kids. No saliva. We genetically engineer utilitarian animals that way at our laboratory. As you see, this model is low to the ground for a reason. So it can do its job at ground level and get into geographically difficult places. Places where regular, mechanical aeration bioremediation units cannot go."

"*That's* a mouthful," commented Aaron. "So what's it eat?"

"Garbage, detritus, polymer-based and petroleum-based waste, toxins, you name it."

"We should use it for our toxic landfill project," suggested Katrina.

"You sure could," affirmed Dr. van Swift.

"No meat?" Dan asked, catching his breath, as he skidded into the group to ditch Ms. Anthrope. He pushed the black glasses up on his narrow nose and glanced behind him. The former science teacher was still approaching steadily at her own pace.

"Aaron, we've gotta get the girls out of here," Dan whispered.

"What?" said Aaron.

"No. No meat. *That* model is, er, uh, still, uh, we are still conducting tests on the viability of a carnivorous *S.P.U.D.S.*," Emily van Swift struggled to explain.

"Aaron, we've got to get out—"

"Dan, if you're going to chatter please leave the area," said Ms. Anthrope behind him. "Show respect to Dr. van Swift."

"Thank you," Emily said to the science teacher.

"Would the carnivorous dog be a threat to people?" asked Coriander.

Ms. Anthrope chuckled behind the group of students. Her rodent face seemed to hover behind Dan. Squinting, Berry joined Ms. Anthrope. The science teacher handed Berry another pair of sunglasses to hide her bloodshot eyes.

"Ostensibly, er, yes," Emily van Swift continued haltingly, "...if a meat-eater existed, viably..." Emily changed the subject to explain the vegetarian model of *S.P.U.D.S.* that she had on display in front of her. "Its fur is recyclable. When it's *retired*, we clip and sell the fur. This one has no tail because it would just get in the way of this perfectly streamlined hazardous waste removal unit. One *S.P.U.D.S.* devours toxic wastes at the rate of eighty pounds per minute."

"Hmmm, that's how much my kid sister weighs," said Dan, glancing over his shoulder.

"So, why don't you donate the meat-eater to Richard Haimatikos at the slaughterhouse so they don't have to dump tons of animal by-products into our river?" asked Katrina excitedly.

"Yeah, a team of your animals could reduce Haimatikos' dumping by a hundred percent," Coriander declared.

Emily smiled. "In fact, we hope to be running some tests in that area... *presently*. We're just waiting for certain, uhmm, approvals."

"Amazing, your dog could eat the cow guts the slaughterhouse is polluting our river in Westlake with," added Ms. Anthrope.

"That's *if* a meat-eating *S.P.U.D.S.* existed," Emily answered with diplomatic care. She smiled uncomfortably and changed the subject, "So, Dan, did you boys have a fun party last night?"

Before Dan could reply and tell Dr. van Swift that her son never made it to the Pritcher's New Year's Eve gathering, from across the cafeteria a loud crash resounded. Ms. Anthrope and Very Berry sniggered knowingly. Dan and the other students looked around but could see nothing over the green-crowned tops of the exhibit booths.

"How does *S.P.U.D.S.* eat all that hazardous stuff and not get sick?" Coriander asked, genuinely interested.

"My *Bio-Clone-Dogs* are genetically engineered to work symbiotically with many hybrid strains of bacteria, and fleas. The three species are interdependent." Emily pointed at an illustrated poster on the wall. "Together the dog, the fleas, and the bacteria in the saliva of the fleas digest and break down waste products into a liquid for the dog to slurp up. The dog then converts the liquid into recyclable pellets. Some of these pellets are used for fertilizer. Those containing heavy metals are recycled further and sold back to manufacturers, who reuse them."

"Great idea. Wish I'd thought of it," chuckled Aaron.

Another crash, accompanied by a scream, got everyone's attention.

"Someone must've knocked over a booth," said Berry, moving in close to Dan—and his neck. Dan looked around nervously, waiting for an opportunity to alert people without tipping off Ms. Anthrope that he hadn't actually done *conversion* yet.

"You've heard of the bacteria that Exxon used at Prince Edward Sound, Alaska, to sop up the tragic oil spills in the ocean?"

"Yes, Dr. van Swift," the students replied.

"Well, our version of *man's best friend* contains a user-friendly hybrid of that bacterium, although unrelated. This is my invention, patented, trademarked, and copyrighted."

"How *user-friendly* is *S.P.U.D.S.*?" inquired Katrina.

"We hope that eventually every family can have one for cleaning up the dinner table and even the baby."

Katrina cringed. "That's really gross."

"I'll get one for my parents," said Aaron.

"What is waste anyway?" Emily added. "Is it because we call it *waste* that we think it is, as you say, *gross*? Really, it is just a by-product of a chemical reaction wherein energy is given off. Food and your saliva and bile make energy and waste. To some organisms that *waste* is delicious and nutritious food and yet to others it is poison."

Emily placed newspaper down in front of her dog that stood in the crate on her display table.

"Oh, please," one student complained. "Is that necessary to do in public?"

Emily smiled. "It's not what you think."

Students leapt back as fleas jumped off the *S.P.U.D.S.* dog onto the newspaper.

"Ouch!" shouted Katrina when a flea bit her on the neck.

"Don't worry. These particular fleas are not carnivores."

"Then why'd it bite me?"

"We've engineered their DNA so they prefer a vegetarian meal, like this newspaper. That flea won't continue to bite now that it realizes you're protein-based. It won't hurt you. It won't even leave a mark on your neck. The bacteria in its saliva are engineered to be incompatible with humans. It will find you a distasteful dish. So the bacteria won't even cause swelling in your skin. They'll simply die off."

In moments the newsprint underfoot on the display table was liquefied by the dog's fleas. The thirsty dog lapped up the grayish remains.

"*Cool!*" Aaron whispered.

"Creepy," whispered Katrina.

Another crash and scream in the cafeteria sent a shiver down the spine of all those who had not been *converted* as Mark Riley dragged away a classmate.

"It's nothing," Mark explained. "She fainted when her volcano exhibit blew up. I'm taking her for a... *drink*."

But the hint of blood on the girl's collar told Dan the *drink* had already been taken.

17

The reverberation of Richard Haimatikos voice distracted the students as he and his driver headed toward Dr. Emily van Swift and bio-engineered dogs.

"Found you!" Haimatikos proclaimed.

Emily looked increasingly fatigued as she spoke to the students. She had been up until dawn calling reporters about Richard Haimatikos and his toxic landfill ruse: a small revenge for his having lost her *S.P.U.D.S.-Y.* basset hound.

"*Rick*," she said sarcastically, "what a surprise."

Dan summoned the courage to interrupt. "Dr. van Swift, Kenny never made it to my house! Just thought you should know. I hope he's okay."

She looked perplexed. "I'll go home and check on him."

Dr. van Swift's mutant albino dogs strained to sniff at Haimatikos' guitar case as she reined in the albinos' leashes. Kenny's mother asked her assistant to remain with the vegetarian S.P.U.D.S.'s exhibition. Emily excused herself and headed out.

Nagging Richard followed Emily. He sought to obstruct her from leaving the high school. Emily's two albino bulldogs growled, low and slow. The bulldogs' pink eyes flashed as they continued to pull toward the vampire. Dogs always *know*.

"I'll get you, Emily van Swift!" Richard Haimatikos threatened. His voice continued to echo even after his stormy departure.

Students cheered Dr. van Swift for standing her ground against the king of toxic waste.

Moments after Dr. van Swift's exit, Berry leapt for Dan's throat just as Peter Peterson came up and lunged at Katrina's. Berry fell flat on the tile floor and chipped one of her canine's when, in the same instant, Dan and Aaron sprang on Peter to pull him off Katrina. Peter had narrowly missed biting Katrina with his quick-release stiletto fangs.

"Get *him*, Berry," instructed Ms. Anthrope. "Get Dan."

Berry made a second attempt at Dan's neck, but Coriander tripped her.

"Stay away from my boyfriend," she hissed.

Pandemonium ensued as healthy students panicked and rushed away. Mark Riley took advantage of the mayhem by dipping his teeth into a junior girl's shoulder. Screaming and wailing echoed throughout the cafeteria.

Dan grabbed Coriander and stopped her from pounding the tar out of Berry.

"That's enough! Let's go!" he shouted. "Aaron, Katrina, we've got to get out of here!"

Every green Earth Day display was collapsing around them. On her feet again, Very Berry swooped her pretty face toward Aaron this time.

"Back off!" Katrina threw a metal folding chair in Berry's way. The four friends forced a path out of the cafeteria. At the exit, Mark and Peter were holding down Beth, the cheering squad co-captain, while new recruit Bruce affixed himself to her throat.

"Save yourselves!" cried Beth.

Unconverted teachers and students fled out every door. Those who remained became part of the bloodbath. Already, Ms. Anthrope had cut the school phone lines, so no 911 calls could be placed.

"Out the back!" instructed Dan. "Hurry!"

18

The police surveillance officer assigned to Richard Haimatikos was asleep at the wheel. Still dozing under the influence of a superburger laced with a soporific, the unfortunate law enforcement professional had been duped by the vampire himself.

"Good call, boss," his driver praised him.

So as not to risk waking the officer with the roar of the car engine, the driver had not started the ignition. Instead, he pushed the red sedan to the incline and coasted quietly down the driveway from *Haimatikos Meatpacking Company*, past the landfill, past the *FREE DIRT* sign. There, the driver had started the engine and driven out to the main road. He observed the speed limit, but only until they were well out of the speed trap zone.

"I can't wait any longer for a protein and iron fix," Richard barked at his driver. "That Emily van Swift is not going to let me near her again, is she? All because of that insatiable dog."

"Look who's talkin' boss. Your appetite's—"

"Shut up. *Bovine schmovine*, I'm so sick of cow blood. Makes me feel I've had a steroid injection after sucking those heifers."

"Cook it, boss, brings out the flavor. Medium rare. Hey, how 'bout *that* one, boss? She looks he right age." The driver pointed at a middle school girl on the curb wearing a fluorescent orange parka. "Innocent and sweet."

"She's a minor, you idiot. Where the hell are the parents nowadays?" Richard Haimatikos recalled his own sheltered upbringing by 13th Century helicopter parents who'd stuck him in a monastery to shield him from plague, pestilence, moral decay, and social uprisings in Transylvania. His only escape, back then, from the confines of a monastic life had been to welcome vampirism, *and rise above it all.* Richard chortled nostalgically, as he regarded they middle school girl in the orange parka just outside his red sedan. "But," Haimatikos mused, "The key word here is *alone.*"

"She *is* alone, boss."

"I know." The vampire licked his fetid, swollen gums that cracked open and his yellowed fangs budded and shot forth. "She'll do nicely."

"You want I get her for you, boss?"

"No, thank you. This meal is going to make me very *happy.*"

He replaced his dark glasses before stepping out from behind the tinted glass of his red limo. Clutching his guitar case, he flung back the hem of his long black trench coat and took a step toward the girl in the poufy orange jacket. In that very moment a brown basset hound with black feet emerged from the bushes. It trotted toward the girl.

"You want I catch the dog, boss?"

"Oh, do shut up!" snarled the vampire. "You're ruining my moment of anticipation."

The girl knelt to pet the basset hound. Hearing the voices of the nefarious men, she turned.

"Is he yours, sir?" she queried politely. "May I pet him?"

Richard Haimatikos stepped closer to the polite girl, his parched lips sealing in his razor sharp canines. A look of consternation grew on his brow as he realized that his long-sought happy meal might now elude him.

"Better not touch that dog, young lady. Rabies!" Haimatikos' teeth flashed impotently at the girl who looked confused.

But the fleas had already sprung to her hair and neck.

"Competition," grumbled the vampire.

The girl did not have half a chance to swat away the fleas. The insatiable dog slurped up her liquid remains as they dissolved in the turbo-powered enzymatic action of the flea spittle. Nothing was spared: blood, bone, hair, nails, guts converted into plasma soup.

"Hey, boss, it's just like that vegetarian dog Dr. Swift was showin' off."

"But worse!" griped the vampire.

"Boss, I thought your dog only ate dead meat," said the driver squatting behind his boss to look at the dog half a block away.

"As you see, that is not the case," he replied testily.

The smiling basset swayed toward them, dragging with it the empty orange jacket since one of its black paws had caught accidentally in an open pocket.

"Awww, boss, look at him. Dog's lookin' for love. He just wants positive reinforcement for doin' his job. C'mere, good dog, good boy."

"Get back in the car, you idiot. That dog is a danger to you, and I'm not through using you yet," snarled Richard.

Disappointed by the demise of a warm supper, Richard Haimatikos backed away debating how to transport the *Bio-Clone-Dog* without his driver, and possibly he himself, getting dissolved and consumed. The basset followed them to the red limo still dragging the girl's orange coat on its big black paw.

"You and I *can* work together, *S.P.U.D.S.-Y.* old boy." Richard leered at the saggy-faced dog.

"How, boss?" asked the driver. "How you gonna work with a dog? You ain't partners with no one. Remember?"

"We'll do lunch and blow town," snarled Richard.

"Whaddya mean, boss?"

"We'll go on a feeding frenzy, stir things up in this backwater, and release my *varmy*. Then announce that the dog is the real killer—not rabid a'tall. No one will even bother eating garlic anymore, once they learn it's the dog and not my teen *vampire army*. People will totally let down their defenses so can feed willy-nilly as I wish. And..." Richard Haimatikos exclaimed triumphantly, "I'll ruin Dr. Emily van Swift's reputation at the same time!"

"Good thinkin' boss."

"Come along, doggity-dog!" Richard blew the dog a repellent kiss. "Good dog."

The vampire prepared to throw his own black trench coat over the basset hound. His intention was to wrap up the dog in a coat enchilada, then sling it into the trunk of the red limousine, alongside the meat stash. That would keep the dog happy until Haimatikos figured out what to do next.

The basset hound, however, did not obey. Impatiently, Richard reached for it. But the dog took a few steps backward, away from the rancid outstretched coat. Peeking over his coat, Haimatikos tip-toed closer to the dog. Cautiously, the dog backed away an equal number of steps.

"You's wicked smart, boss."

"Do shut it, you're destroying my concentration," whispered Haimatikos, his knobby hand now held the coat but one yard away from the basset hound. The process was made awkward by the necessity of his guitar case full of dirt that he had to carry with him at all times during daylight. If he threw the coat now, he might miss. He needed to get just a bit closer...

"I believe in you, boss, I think you'll get the dog and Emily van Swift."

"Get her?" whispered Richard, his eyes trained on the dog. "I'll possess and control her. Make her miserable. And then watch her die. *Hahahahahahahah.*"

The hound tipped its head, understanding neither the meaning of the vampire's jerky movements nor his shrill laughter. Its black feet stepped quickly backward just as the vampire cast his trench coat over the dog.

The basset hound jerked away.

Haimatikos missed the mark, faltered, and lost his balance. His arms flailed as he stumbled. Cussing, Haimatikos fell headlong into a snowdrift, and frightened the dog. By the time he dusted his face, the basset hound had fled, leaving a flattened trail in the snow caused by the orange parka caught on a hind paw.

On the loose, the basset hound spotted a mongrel chained up outside a small house. The ragged little dog huddled out of the wind, gaunt and hungry. It *knew*.

As the purebred approached, the mongrel growled. It ran to the end of its leash and choked, then dashed frantically in another direction. Dragging the orange parka, black feet traced the mongrel's path stealthily. The vulnerable little dog snarled and snipped, leaping in every direction away from the predator. Its leash prevented escape.

"Hey! Leave my dog alone! Bad dog!" shouted a latchkey child arriving home.

The black and tan basset hound stood its ground eager to connect. It seemed to smile at the child. But, in fact, it was just gas from hunger pangs.

The red limo drove along a suburban lane. Richard Haimatikos watched for the black-footed canine.

"I've got to snatch that dog before Emily does, or I'll have no leverage over her," Sullen Richard whined to his driver from the backseat. "Stop the car! That's our pooch!" Haimatikos opened the door even before the car had come to a halt. "Pop the trunk."

"You want I carry the flank steaks, boss?"

"No. Stay in the car, moron." Richard got out carrying his overcoat and guitar case. From the trunk, he grabbed several steaks. "Come here, good dog."

This time Richard approached slowly as he studied the hound. Snow reached all the way up to the basset's low slung black and tan belly.

Richard Haimatikos dropped the steaks in the snow and sat back on the front fender of the red limousine to observe. The Stratocaster guitar case rested on his thighs. His overcoat lay on the car hood, ready to throw over the dog.

"A real *steakout*!" declared the vampire smugly.

"Good one, boss."

"Shut up. I don't need to know I amuse you, *Driver*."

The basset scuffed through the deep snow, approaching the beef slabs and sniffed: *Too good to be true?*

Richard gripped his guitar case and held his long black coat poised to net the dog. Then, he crept up behind it.

"Hey, Mister, you stealin' my dog?" emerging from the woods, a young boy screamed at the vampire. The basset hound had already plunged its gnashers into the bait and was gorging itself happily.

"No, kid, I'm not stealing your dog!" Richard sneered at the boy.

"Sure looks like you're a thief."

"We're a charitable organization that feeds prime rib to stray dogs," Richard lied spontaneously. "When was the last time you gave your dog a Haimatikos steak, *hmmm*?"

"Weirdo," The boy sneered back. "Maybe you should try dognappin' *that* one." The boy pointed up the block at a black-footed basset dragging an orange parka. It wandered into the woods.

"Kid, where do those woods lead?"

"What'll you give me?"

"What? I just fed your *apparently-stray* dog the finest steak in the world!"

"Fine," sighed the boy. "The high school."

Haimatikos chucked his belongings back in the car, and got in. Fuming he smacked his driver upside the head.

"What's taking you so long? My canine and my future are getting away!"

The driver stepped on it.

The vampire smacked him again.

"What's that for, boss? I'm crushin' it."

"For good measure." Glib Haimatikos smirked.

"Yes, boss."

"The sooner I mobilize that dog, the sooner I can fully deploy my master plan.

"I bet it's a great plan, boss."

"First I'll take out the police force." This concept delighted him.

Since the dog's appetite for liquefied flesh did not discriminate against the living, this opened up so many new opportunities for Richard Haimatikos to weaponize the insatiable canine.

Just then blue police lights swept the car. The driver sped up.

"Pull over, stupid," demanded the vampire.

The car slammed to a halt.

"Moron."

"Oh wow, she's really pretty, how 'bout her, boss?"

Officer Nancy Fieldstone, tapped on the tinted glass.

"Mr. Haimatikos, we lost track of you," she said coolly.

"Officer Fieldstone, what a pleasure." Richard reached his hand out.

She declined to shake, not because his nails were filthy. "Manicure too expensive for you, Haimatikos?"

"It's been ages. You're right, I should—"

"Step out of the vehicle, please."

"Little old me, Officer? What seems to be the problem?"

She opened the rear door and took a step back.

"Step out, please."

The vampire complied hesitantly. Out of the car, he towered over the attractive young police officer.

"Mr. Haimatikos, what's in your trunk?" Officer Fieldstone was respectful.

"Ah, let me think, Officer, um, first-aid kit. Spare tire. Odds and ends. *Potting soil*," said the vampire. "Why, ma'am?"

"Are you aware, sir, there is blood dripping from your trunk?"

"Blood? *My* vehicle?"

"Pop the trunk, sir."

"But—"

"Pop it."

"But I didn't *do* anything!" *Yet*, he thought, eyeing her throat.

"Pop the bloody trunk!" She pulled her gun.

19

Katrina caught her breath, and checked that her lavender fishnet garlic satchel was still in place around her neck.

"There's that black and tan basset hound again, Aaron."

"No time for puppy love, Katie," said Dan, helping Coriander into his Honda Civic. "Make a run for it! Meet you guys at Aaron's!"

Dan peeled out fishtailing in the snow. Aaron pulled Katrina by the hand toward his black Mustang convertible.

"C'mon, Katrina, hurry."

"No one's followed us yet. Just wait a sec. C'mere, boy. He's so cute and smiley." Katrina couldn't take her eyes off the basset hound.

"Not half as cute as you, Katrina," said Aaron as he dug out his car keys.

"Comparing me to a dog, Aaron?"

"I didn't mean it *that* way, Katie. But we've gotta' go, babe."

"Doesn't it look like he's smiling, Aaron?" Katrina reached out to the dog with both hands. "And well fed. Look at his big belly."

Panting, the bloated dog waddled out of the skeletal bushes toward the teen couple standing alone in the snowy high-school parking lot.

"See, he's not scared of us now."

"Cause the throng of yard apes is gone."

"He's got something caught on his foot." Aaron bent down to untangle the fluorescent orange parka from the black paw stuck in a coat pocket. The dog whined. Katrina and Aaron squatted next to the basset hound to reassure it. The dog licked their faces with its hairy tongue.

"*Eeew*, Aaron, he's got that same dry, hairy tongue! Like the bio-dog at the Earth Day booth!"

Aaron gently peeled back the basset's plump, bristly black lips to view inside its mouth.

"All gums," confirmed Aaron.

"See if he'll eat this." Katrina held out the orange parka. "Dr. van Swift said they eat petroleum-based stuff. This parka's polyester. Isn't that made from petroleum?"

They tried to feed the dog the orange parka, but the basset turned up its dry nose at the fluorescent fabric.

"Guess not," said Aaron. "I wonder what he *does* eat. Maybe newspaper, like at Dr. van Swift's booth?"

Just then a gray squirrel traipsing along a low branch fell and skidded past them, back to the tree. On high alert, the hound followed, stalking the rodent. But before it could reach the small, fluffy bundle, the squirrel sensed a predator and fled up a maple tree. The dog raced after it, bracing its front paws against the tree trunk to bird-dog the squirrel.

"A squirrel is meat, Katrina."

"You're overreacting. It doesn't mean he actually *eats* meat. It's only natural for a dog to chase a squirrel. Give him the benefit of the doubt, Aaron." She *really* wanted that dog.

"But Katie, you saw the other *S.P.U.D.S.* dog dissolve the newspaper today. This one chases meat. He's a bad dog!"

"We'd be dead already if *this* dog were bad, Aaron. He licked our faces!"

"Okay, then, well, let's take him to my house. He must be cold."

"Will your mom be mad?"

"Burn that bridge when we get to it!"

"What'll we call him?" Katrina lead the dog toward the Mustang. "C'mon boy, good dog."

"Oh crap, Katrina, get in the car now!"

Katrina turned. Bloody-faced leering teenagers rushed out the side door of the school.

Seconds later, Aaron floored the Mustang as the teen vampires glommed onto it. One by one they fell away as he sped away.

"Thank God you put up the ragtop this morning!"

"Let's hope they haven't learned yet how to fly," said Aaron, glancing in his rearview mirror. The Mustang tore out of the high school parking lot as Katrina clutched the basset hound to her chest.

Once they were a safe distance away they breathed a sigh of relief.

"So, what'll we call him?"

"Something menacing, since the poor guy's got no teeth," replied Aaron.

"How about *Fang*? *Gums* wouldn't scare a flea."

"Fang's good. Good dog, Fang."

Painfully, Fang heaved a low-slung belly, shifting its weight on Katrina's lap.

"Looks like he ate too much of something," remarked Katrina as she soothed the basset hound.

Finally, the heater blasted hot air as the 1968 Mustang rumbled up the long driveway of Mrs. Sedgewoods' horse farm.

20

The vampire resisted the temptation to attach himself to Officer Fieldstone's throat, pulled over as he was on a main road with witnesses driving by at regular intervals.

"I'd really rather not open it, Officer," mewled Haimatikos.

"Body in your trunk, Haimatikos?"

"Not exactly."

"Open it. Or my reinforcements will." Sirens and blue lights approached.

"Your back up?"

"None other."

Haimatikos knew he was in trouble. Chagrined, the vampire opened the trunk of his red limo. At first glance, it appeared a bloodbath of carnage. On closer inspection, Officer Fieldstone recognized piled cuts of beef: eye of the round, flank steak, and tenderloin.

"Haimatikos, any idea what happened this morning at the high school?" asked Officer Fieldstone as she closed the trunk.

"Absolutely not!" He feigned offense and diverted her focus. "As for meat in my trunk, eh, sometimes we make personal deliveries from my abattoir to restaurants, or if someone's having a gala dinner in the neighborhood. You know, last-minute orders."

"Except this is Westlake, Mr. Haimatikos, and we don't have a restaurant and nobody has *gah-laa* dinners in this neck of the woods."

"Right. With all due respect, Officer Fieldstone, perhaps you just don't get invited." Haimatikos his haughty snub.

"Actually, Mr. Haimatikos, the safety of my town comes before parties." Fieldstone smiled proudly.

"Martyr," mumbled the vampire.

"What's that?"

"Nothing, uhm, Officer Fieldstone, if there's nothing else, I really must be on my way. I have to make a very special delivery to that swanky horse farm. They're expecting me," he lied.

"Fine..." Officer Fieldstone backed off. "We'll resume your police escort, Mr. Haimatikos—for *your* protection, of course."

"Of course," he concurred sarcastically.

"And, Haimatikos..."

"Yes, ma'am?"
"No more gifting our officers your superburgers."

"Out!" The pregnant woman was in no mood for strays.
"But, Mom!"
"Out! And don't you go spooking the horses with that dog, Aaron."
"But—"
"No, Aaron, he may have rabies. Look how thirsty he is! His nose is dry, for heaven's sake!"
"Hi, Mrs. Sedgewood," squeaked Katrina as Aaron's mother waddled past holding her protruding stomach with both hands as she headed back out to the stables.
"Hi Katrina, sorry, I'm due any day now, and—"
"We'll take Fang to my house, Mrs. Sedgewood. Less complicated."
"You want to use our telephone and call home first?" asked Mrs. Sedgewood before she left through the back door muttering, "I can't imagine *your* mother wants a rabid stray either."
Aaron handed Katrina the rotary telephone receiver.
"No, Aaron, if we just show up with Fang, my mom will have to say yes."
"Let's eat first."
Katrina munched garlic-topped popcorn Aaron poured out of the black and white SmartFood bag into a large porcelain bowl. She offered a handful to Fang, but the dog turned its muzzle away.
"Too dry, Fang? Aaron, what can we feed him?"
Aaron refilled the water bowl for the fifth time in ten minutes.
"Poor thing's dehydrated. Sure hope he hasn't got rabies."
Aaron sneaked a raw rump roast out of the well-stocked refrigerator and placed it on the kitchen floor in front of Fang.
"My mother'll kill me if she knows we fed her favorite pregnancy-craving food to a stray. But let's see how Fang reacts to the real thing."
Fang sniffed the huge lump of meat.
Suddenly through the kitchen door they heard shouting at the front door of Aaron's home. Flickering blue lights reflected off the polished hardwood floor of the hallway. Aaron and Katrina glanced out a window to see his very pregnant mother as she waddled as fast as she could go from the barn. She headed toward the commotion of blue lights and a red limo parked in the Sedgewood's driveway.

"Like I said, *no*," Mr. Sedgewood spoke calmly, "I am not going to invite you in, Rick. I don't give a bee-diddle how cold it is outside. My answer is *no*."

"Haimatikos is practically purple," whispered Aaron from their vantage point behind Mr. Sedgewood.

"Don't try to bribe me with your fancy steaks, Haimatikos. The property you're trying to sell me is a well-known hazardous waste dump."

"Mr. Sedgewood, *my friend*, you're just going to build houses on it and resell it. What do you care if it's hazmat?" Richard Haimatikos implored. "*You're* not going to *live* there with *your* family."

Mr. Sedgewood remained cool. "I read what today's newspaper reported about your land, Rick. I cannot, in good conscience, develop that property. Respectfully, I'm bowing out of the deal."

"Go, Dad!" whispered Aaron.

Richard Haimatikos opened his mouth to continue badgering her husband, but Mrs. Sedgewood stepped in between the two men. With a single raised pointer finger, Aaron's mother faced the vampire dead-on. The vampire ignored both her stern gaze and menacing fingertip. He was transfixed by Mrs. Sedgewood's pregnant gut. Then, the unthinkable happened. He reflexively reached for the huge orb.

"May I?"

"No!" She swatted his grubby hand away from her precious cargo. "Why is it people think they can just come up and cop a feel off pregnant women? This..." She pointed at her stomach. "...is *not* a public invitation to—!"

"Got it. Sorry, sorry, sorry..." mumbled the vampire.

"Mr. Haimatikos, do you realize it's because of *you* dumping toxic waste in Westlake that even for my horses I must buy SmartWater." Her Boston accent revealed itself. Her voice rose. "Children in this town are born with birth defects, and good folks get cancer too often around here."

"Honey, don't upset yourself," said Mr. Sedgewood. "You'll send yourself into labor."

"Why don't you... *invite me in*... and we'll discuss it, Mrs. Sedgewood? Sitting, so *you're* comfortable."

As if the vampire cared about her comfort, yet he attempted a last-ditch effort to salvage the spoiled business deal. Plus, in a primitive way, he had an irrepressible urge to grasp her stomach, to feel the new life nascent within.

Flabbergasted, Mrs. Sedgewood clasped her hands around her stomach like a sling as she lit into him, "Mr. Haimatikos, the hazardous waste dumps you created in our town are deadly not only to future generations, but to us, right here, right now. To my son and Katrina and to my newborn who is due any day now! Don't you feel at all guilty Or, or, even threatened for your *own* safety?"

"In fact, no, madam. You'll see someday soon that so-called hazardous waste dumps will be the galactic gas stations of the future."

"What?" She was floored. "And here I thought you were a nice man because you give away *free dirt* for potting soil!"

"Yes, but it's true. I *am* nice." Stalling, he gazed lecherously at her throat then back at her belly, never making eye contact. "You'll see, it's going to turn out that there really are aliens from outer space who will come down here and save the day by using my hazardous waste dumps to refuel their ships. We'll love them for saving us from our reckless wastefulness, and they'll love us for providing them with a high-octane tank of petrol. Your husband will make a fortune... if he buys now!"

"You really are nuts! And, P.S., I would never, *ever invite* you into my house."

"Go Mom!" whispered Aaron.

Mrs. Sedgewood waddled backward to shut the front door on Richard Haimatikos.

Just then, Katrina glanced behind her at the dog in the kitchen, and gasped, "Aaron! *Where's the beef?*"

But Aaron was too distracted by the drama unfolding on his doorstep.

Richard Haimatikos' steel-toe boot remained wedged in the door jamb.

"I'll put that foot," said Mr. Sedgewood, "with your head where the sun never shines, Rick."

"Aaron," Katrina tugged his arm and pointed at the kitchen floor, already licked clean by Fang.

The sated basset hound pitter-pattered between Katrina and Aaron and swaggered a full belly down the hall toward the front door seeking to relieve itself of its newly-processed *hazmat pellets*.

Fang's pace quickened.

"Make way, Fang might have to pee," announced Aaron.

Fang seemed to recognize Richard. Drooping jowls lifted into a doggie smile.

"Aaron, no! Stop Fang!" Katrina yelled.

The vampire's eyes locked on the girl.

"Why Katrina?" asked Aaron.

"He ate the whole thing! But—" Katrina's mind reeled sorting out why the dog could liquefy the meat, yet had not consumed Aaron and her. *Are we immune?* Instinct told her that others might not be. "Don't get near the dog, Mr. and Mrs. Sedgewood!"

"Mom, Dad, get back!" Aaron charged ahead after Fang.

"Rabies! I knew it!" yelped Mrs. Sedgewood throwing open the door for the dog to pass, and leaping back against the wall behind the door with her husband.

On the landing, Fang leapt on Richard Haimatikos.

"Get this dog off me!" shouted the vampire.

"I'll take care of it." Aaron rushed to Fang, shutting the front door behind him.

Out on the front porch, Aaron reached to pull Fang off Richard Haimatikos. But he was too late. Aaron recoiled. There on the front porch, fleas attacked the vampire. Hundreds of them sprang off Fang and swarmed Haimatikos' face, crawled up his nostrils, bit his eyes, burrowed in every pore. The vampire's ears were nibbled raw. He clawed at his own face and shrieked. He stumbled off the porch and into the snow where he rolled, trying to save himself.

A few drops of pale plasma dribbled off the vampire's face. With a hairy tongue, Fang death-kissed Richard in the snow. Still the vampire's face remained intact. As a member of the walking-dead, he hadn't enough living flesh to interest the fleas. He managed to pick away most of the parasites. And the fleas returned to the safety of Fang's face. There they scuttled and clambered into the dog's ears and nostrils and between stubbly lips.

"*Humph*," sniveled Haimatikos as he teetered back to his car to examine his face in the mirror. "The face of the undead cannot tarnish."

His police escort had encircled him, guns drawn, unsure whether to shoot the dog. They stowed their weapons and returned to their cruisers.

"You okay, boss?"

"Shut up and drive." Haimatikos got in the back.

Blue lights followed them as the red limo headed away.

"Didn't know I had any living protein left in my system." He was chuffed. "Seems I'm definitely overdue for a protein shake, and her name is Katrina Phillips."

21

Katrina unclasped the brush-clip and shook out her sweaty hair. They had hiked for miles through the snow, searching. Snowdrifts camouflaged Fang's footprints in the woods. The stealthy dog eluded them.

"Poor Fang," she murmured, "lost in the cold."

"He'll be okay, Katrina. Dogs survive better than humans," said Aaron, taking her hand. "We'd better get back before it's completely dark out."

In the leucophane light of First Night's sunset, Katrina reluctantly conceded to return to the house without Fang.

"You think it's the garlic, Aaron? We should be soup by now."

"Maybe Fang's fleas are like vampires. Good thing Dan never made it over. He'd be *toast*."

"You mean *soup*."

By the time the Mustang reached the Phillips' house on High Street, darkness plagued every inch of Westlake.

"I'm not letting you out, Katrina."

"Why, Aaron?" she was taken aback.

"Not until you promise not to invite anyone in. Teen vampires are on the loose."

"Can you sneak out later?" She winked. "My mom works ER graveyard shift tonight."

"I'll try, after my parents go to sleep." Aaron kissed her good-bye, and she ran up the stairs into her house. He waited until she was safely inside.

Katrina's bedroom was quiet save for the squeaky floorboard where she was examining her teeth at the lavender vanity table. She had chowed down on toaster oven spanakopita so was still flossing out spinach. As she glanced toward her bed, she heard scraping outside her window. She shut off the light in order to see out. But the glass was frosted over, and it was dark.

She breathed yoga breaths on the frosted pane, but it was so cold outside that only a tiny aperture thawed in the frost. Something shifted right outside, inches from her eye.

"Just a second, Aaron," she hollered at the window as she tiptoed to her private lavender bathroom and soaked a purple hand towel in hot water.

When she cleared the glass with it she still saw nothing and no one outside. A fleeting shadow darkened the lavender windowsill. The scraping sound ensued. She peered through the glass at the pine boughs. Not one branch touched the house. What was scraping?

Her father had clipped away many of the fir boughs that used to enshroud the house; that was before his untimely death early the previous summer. *He so totally disapproved of Aaron's midnight visits to my window,* Katrina reflected, appreciating too late how protective her father had been. Despite his booze-hound issues, she still loved and missed him.

So Katrina knew for sure that it was not the big old pine causing the relentless scraping noise outside her window. January wind was strong enough to toss loose branches about, but this noise was too consistent to be random wind gusts. It was scraping, yet it had the rhythm of someone knocking delicately to *please* be admitted in.

Aaron... She smiled.

She stuck her hair in a brush-clip and wrapped her thick lavender bathrobe over her t-shirt, then hoisted up the window.

"Aaron?" Katrina called, peering out into the icy January night.

"It's me," whispered a male voice.

"Where are you?"

Katrina leaned against the sill and peered over the edge. *No ladder.*

"Where'd you go?"

"Up here," came a whispery voice.

Craning her neck, Katrina looked up into the fir tree opposite her, but saw no one.

"Up *here*, missy."

Katrina unlatched the screen and slid it up. Then, she leaned out the window and turned 180 degrees to look up the clapboard side of her Victorian house. The silhouette of someone's head and shoulders faced her.

I must be dreaming, she thought. *It's impossible for anyone but a bat to be up there. There's nothing to grip.* Katrina gasped: What her eyes focused on was not human. A rack of fangs lunged at her—all power, no mercy. She yanked herself back into her bedroom, but not fast enough. Filthy talons lashed the window frame barely missing her head. A claw ripped away a few strands of her hair. The vampire's strong yellow talons grabbed the lower lip of the window frame so that Katrina could not seal the window shut. Its other heinous claw grasped her hand. It was impossible to free herself from its mighty grasp.

How's it gripping the house? She wondered if it had hooks or suction feet.

Glossy black fabric fluttered around the window.

"Might I succeed in luring you out for a walk, missy? Then there's no need for you to *invite me in.*"

"What do you want from me?" demanded Katrina, *Duh. Blood,* she thought, tugging to free her captive hand. The longer his talons remained entwined in her flesh, the more the revolting feeling grew that her hand was melding into the vampire's tissue, molding and growing into one supernatural being. It felt hot and sticky like Richard Haimatikos' thick yellow drool she had stuck her hand in earlier that day on the booth brochures. She felt the quick throbbing pulse of the vampire's deathly hunger—an incessant thrum coursed up her arm and through her body. As the vampire's evil poison seeped up her limb like an infection, it soured her taste buds.

"You know what I want," replied the vampire.

"I don't, creep."

Katrina's other hand groped along the shelf under her window for anything to spray in its face—hair mousse or freeze-shine, even a nail file to stick it with, a holy cross, or her garlic fishnet necklace that lay... just out of reach on her nightstand. In her desperation, Katrina fumbled with a plastic bottle of SmartWater but dropped it.

"Aren't you going to *invite me in*?"

"Aren't you tired of asking bogus questions?"

"Testing my powers of persuasion."

"Well, they *suck!*"

"Indeed," admitted the vampire enjoying Katrina's accidental pun. "Now come along. All *three* of my canines adore you, Katrina—my two incisors and that infernal pooch. So I need you to help me lure it back."

"Mr. Haimatikos! Let me go or I'll scream." Her eyes adjusted to the ambient light. The vampire hung upside down at her window.

"I've sedated your mother already," he lied. "She's having sweet dreams of me." He had no idea that her mother was working at the ER, nor, in fact, that she was returning early from her shift due to a double scheduling error.

"Blood-sucker!"

"True fact!" conceded Haimatikos proudly, "Guilty as charged!"

"I hate you!"

"You know what they say about sticks and stones, missy."

Katrina's blind hand found it: A plastic shaker bottle of garlic left there from Coriander's last popcorn sleepover. Katrina's thumb found the seam of the flip top. She snapped a nail opening the plastic cap.

She swore.

"*Language!*" reprimanded Richard Haimatikos.

"Take *that!*" She shook powdered garlic into the vampire's sickly gleaming eyes.

Brownish blood dribbled onto the window ledge from his eyes. Richard Haimatikos' crusty maw released an infernal scream and Katrina's hand, but not before he first dug a deep, vicious gash into the back of her wrist. Katrina shook and shook the garlic powder at the vampire until he desisted and fell two stories into the deep white snow.

"I'll get you, *Katrinaaaaaaaa...!*" His words rang in the frigid night air.

"Don't you ever come back here again! *Ever!*" She slammed the window.

Before she could lock it, her limbs and guts revolted. Her wounded wrist ached terribly. And, right before her tear-stung eyes, the gash swelled and festered, blistering into a painful, swollen hash of pus. Her other hand still clutched the plastic shaker bottle of garlic powder. In panic, she darted through the darkness and flung open her bedroom door. Racing down the hall she slammed right into someone. *Bam*!

"Katrina! What on earth was that hideous noise I heard?"

"Nothing, Ma, nothing, I was just..." Relieved her mother was home early, Katrina hugged her hard.

"You're not having those awful nightmares again, are you, dear?" Mrs. Phillips switched on the hall light. "Why's garlic powder upstairs?"

"Uhhh. Popcorn. G'night, Mom." Katrina turned and locked herself in her bedroom. She retreated to her bathroom to nurse her wrist. But nothing in her medicine chest relieved the pain. The swelling grew worse and the skin around the open red slash turned black, blue, green, and yellow. A revolting, unnatural fluid seeped from the wound and it stank like Ms. Anthrope when she dive-bombed the Mustang the night before.

Katrina shuddered recalling Richard Haimatikos' parting words. The garlic had really set him off. Then she remembered Dan's lecture on garlic, Kelly's research. The missing peer's sterling silver bangle had been found by police in the shed down behind Haimatikos Meatpacking Company, alongside the quilt that Kelly's mom had made for her. But no body. *No body, no crime.* Katrina reflected on Kelly's antibacterial garlic report.

If garlic's an antibacterial, and my arm's infected... Katrina reached for the garlic powder bottle and shook it hard over her decomposing forearm. It burned. A lot. But perhaps it would help reduce the violent infection.

Blinking away tears, Katrina noticed snow drifting in through her open window. A bold of black fabric had been shoved onto the sill. A note pinned to the dark cloth read:

You'll be needing this.

Love bites... and scratches,

Rick

22

Darkness consumed New England's rural roads. Aaron drove home from Katrina's, and kept his eyes peeled for Fang.

Wouldn't a dog try to find its way home? But where's home to a genetically-engineered clone dog? Dr. van Swift's lab? Or...? Aaron wondered as he approached *Haimatikos Meatpacking Company.*

Aaron reached the curve in the road at the slaughterhouse when a white pickup truck passed him at high speed.

"Dummy!" muttered Aaron.

As if the truck's driver had heard Aaron's words, she looked back angrily with a face that appeared to have been mummified. She flipped him off with her pointer and middle fingers making a "V" sign.

"V" for Vampire, thought Aaron wryly. He looked again. *Oh no!* Very Berry was driving the white pickup.

Aaron slowed to a crawl and let her get well ahead of him. As he approached the glowing landfill, Aaron saw Berry swerve into it without using her blinker and she drove right up to the glowing heap of trash.

Aaron extinguished his lights, parked, and watched.

Berry leapt out of the cab of her truck and grabbed the shovel that leaned against the *FREE DIRT* sign. Hastily, she scooped dirt from the landfill onto the flatbed of her truck.

Headlights! Aaron ducked and peered over the dash. Mark, Peter, and Bruce arrived in other pickup trucks and pulled in beside Berry. They unloaded wheelbarrows, rakes, and shovels. Aaron shivered in his down jacket.

Soon more *conversion* students arrived to assist in the labor. And shortly, Ms. Anthrope pulled up. Aaron could hear her shouting out a military roll call as all the young, sickly recruits stood at attention by the gloomy yellow light cast by the radiating landfill.

She's built herself an army of suckers, thought Aaron. But he could not figure out why Ms. Anthrope would have the teenagers cart away toxic dirt. *At least they're cleaning up the landfill*, he thought. Afraid to start his engine and draw attention to himself, Aaron shifted the Mustang into neutral, released the emergency brake, and silently pushed the car backward until he reached the curve in the road. Once he was out of sight of the landfill, he fired up his engine. Only after he reached the next intersection did he turn on his headlights. *I'll call Mom and Dad from Katrina's,* he thought as he headed back to High Street. He was so shaken by the bizarre *varmy* gathering he had witnessed at the landfill. He prayed Dan had not already *converted.* It all seemed so out of control. How could Aaron flatten the curve and stop the *varmy* from spreading?

By the time Aaron reached Katrina's house it was too late. He had pulled only halfway up the driveway, and then he saw her.

"No!" he shouted.

He threw the Mustang into reverse.

Katrina was taking flight from her bedroom window, emerging like a shiny ebony butterfly from its chrysalis.

She'll be coming for me, he thought.

Terrified, he sped home to the horse farm and lay awake. All night he waited for Katrina. But she never came.

23

Katrina could barely speak as she lay strapped in the intensive care unit bed, her thin body still wrapped in glossy black taffeta. Rigged to her arm, a saline drip delivered a potent sedative. With it, four types of antibiotics flooded into her bloodstream.

"You go without me, Aaron. Ouch! Don't touch my arm!" said Katrina, cotton-mouthed.

"Katie, you look like you're dying. Your arm looks like you've got leprosy," exclaimed Aaron.

"I have rabies." Her lips were blue, and her arm had turned mutant green. Her wound was severely infected. But at least her fever was coming down a bit.

During the early morning hours of January the 2nd, Mrs. Phillips had felt an icy draft. She couldn't get warm in her bed, so she went in search of the problem. The cold draft, she discovered, was emanating from Katrina's bedroom. She knocked. The door was locked from within. Mrs. Phillips, like every caring parent, had a secret key, just in case, and discovered Katrina's window wide open and her room empty. So Mrs. Phillips had searched outside. In a heap of black fabric in the back yard, she had found Katrina hyperventilating and frothing at the mouth. Mrs. Phillips rushed her daughter to the emergency room where her hypothermia and severely infected arm were treated. Test revealed that the infection was animal borne and resembled rabies.

Aaron stood beside Katrina's hospital bed and reached to hold her hand. In doing so, he accidentally knocked a satchel out of her grasp and a stream of dirt poured from the little bag onto the floor of her hospital room.

"Where'd you go last night?" Aaron was tentative, afraid to know the truth. He bent to examine the dirt. *How do you tell one type of dirt from another*, he wondered.

"No place," sighed Katrina. "Leave that on the floor!" she snapped. "Don't touch it."

"But I saw you."

"Please pull the shades, Aaron. It's so bright in here." The early-morning sun was blinding her. She squinted and pulled a pillow over her eyes. "I'm telling you, Aaron, I'm okay. That creep just scratched me."

Desperate to believe her, Aaron knelt beside the bed to peck Katrina's lips. Sensing his proximity, her mouth suddenly grew more parched, and her tongue thirsted for salt. Aaron lay his head on her shoulder, exposing his neck. He stroked her healthy arm.

"So today you work at Buzzy's Grocery?" Katrina tried hard to sound normal.

Aaron nodded. "Yep. I probably should get going so I'm not late," he said quietly. He burned inside, wondering what to do about Katrina—what to do about everything.

"Westlake's under siege, Katie," he whispered.

"I know." Her throat was so dry.

Katrina's vision doubled suddenly and she felt nauseated. Aaron would leave presently. Could she hold off until he left? That *thirst*, that unslakable thirst gnawed inside her. Her gums ached. The roof of her mouth throbbed. She tasted contagion in her throat as her incisors throbbed. There was only one way to dilute that insidious wave of contagion. Instinctively Katrina reacted. With a wretched shriek, Katrina thrust her mouth toward Aaron's neck.

"You gonna puke on me?" Aaron recoiled.

Then he realized that she was baring her teeth at him. He fell to the floor just as Katrina sank her teeth into her own thigh. Through the bedclothes, she sucked.

Aaron whipped out his vial of garlic powder and shook it on her. Her wave of mania subsided, and Katrina reclined exhausted against the sheet littered with grainy garlic powder. Terrified, Aaron moved to the door.

"Uuuhhh, I gotta go, Katrina."

"I'm okay now, Aaron," she whispered. "I'm overcoming it. Come sit by me."

Blood from her own thigh siphoned out of her mouth and dribbled down her chin. Her eyes rolled heavenward, exposing white orbs laced with bulging veins.

"No way." Aaron hung by the exit. "You're one of them, Katrina."

"I don't know what you're talking about," said Katrina, "It's just rabies. They're treating me for it. I'll be fine."

Suddenly, she jumped off the bed and again leapt at Aaron. Her intravenous tubes ripped from her arm, spewing saline and antibiotics. Just as fast, Aaron leapt behind the bathroom door. She hit it and dropped to the floor in a heap. Intermittently, her thirst for blood re-charged like a high-voltage wire. Like an addiction, she felt a desperate need to strike. She needed to bite, to satisfy her thirst. If she could just keep up her energy until she attached herself to her fist victim. But, Katrina was terribly weakened by the infection.

"Help me, Aaron," she pleaded.

"I'm calling the nurse, Katrina." He pressed the call button. "She'll give you a stronger sedative and hook up your tubes again. You need to keep that antibiotic in your system."

24

The boys examined the heap of vampire paraphernalia spread out on Dan's bed and floor.

"C'mon. Let's do this. Let's go."

"You really think this trap will work, Dan?" asked Aaron, hoisting ropes of braided garlic off Dan's bed.

"If vampires are real, which I doubt, but *IF*, then... yes." Dan wound a long garlic garland around his waist.

"But Dan, your big trap ideas don't always work the way you plan'em." Aaron recalled certain *Dan Disasters* that had nearly cost them their lives.

"This is different, Aaron," Dan assured. "It's not an addictive *nightmare matinee* or a serial killer who's *driven to kill!*"

"No, it's an entire platoon of'em, Dan. It's a *varmy*!"

"No, it's an infection, like rabies. Those who are afflicted are, themselves, victims of a microscopic predator."

"Good thing I found this garlic stash," said Aaron, "I feel bad about stealing from Buzzy's Market, though."

"Theft in the name of world peace is not theft, Aaron, it's *expropriation*."

"Whatever, Dan, I still feel bad. And I stole these too." Aaron held up dozens of white plastic loops.

"Flea collars?"

"In case not everyone's immune to Fang's fleas when we capture him. I mean, I thought Katrina and I were, but... now she's..."

"Double trouble," said Dan.

"Too bad Buzzy's a vampire now," Aaron remarked. "I would've liked to keep my job after school. Baby's due any day now. Crap. I'll be back to mucking stalls and changing diapers."

Dan grunted but wasn't listening. He checked the hallway outside his bedroom for clearance.

"C'mon, Aaron."

They crept downstairs, peeking through the rungs of the stair railing. Dan's parents were immersed in a chess game in the living room. Josephine was nowhere to be found. Dan and Aaron tiptoed to the garage, leaving an accidental trail of garlic skin flaking behind them.

"Mom's going to love this," announced Josephine, indicating the mess.

"*Shhhhh*, Josie, don't tell, okay," said Dan.

"What'll you give me?"

"This," said Aaron smiling at Josephine.

She grinned back adoringly at Aaron. Carefully, Aaron placed a flea collar on the middle schooler and palmed her a bulb of garlic.

"Keep it on you 24/7, Josie, promise."

She nodded, blushing. "I'm coming with you," she insisted.

Dan sighed. "Mom, Dad, we're taking Josephine for, um, hot fudge," hollered Dan. "Back in a bit."

The boys loaded the Mustang with anti-vampire paraphernalia. Josephine assisted.

"Ready, Josie?"

"Ready, Danny."

"You took the extra dosage?"

"Yup. Sniff me."

"Imperceptible," affirmed Dan.

"Is Correy coming too?"

"She's at the hospital keeping an eye on Katrina."

"Bummer." Josephine was secretly happy to have Aaron all to herself without Katrina there.

"They'll probably both come after us for a blood donation," joked Aaron.

"You can't think like that," cautioned Dan. "We have a mission to accomplish. We have to be positive. Those so-called vampires need our help as much as we need them to be well again. Afterwards, we'll fix Katrina. Heavy doses of garlic soup and aioli should do it to supplement those antibiotics she's taking"

As they drove, Aaron asked Dan, "Did you ever get ahold of Kenny?"

"No," Dan answered. "Mrs. van Swift said he couldn't come to the phone. But it was weird–she sounded really upset and hung up on me."

"Maybe he's grounded for telling his parents he was at your party when he was probably out all night smoking dope."

"He doesn't," Dan said skeptically.

"Yah, he does," Aaron challenged. "Just sayin'..."

At the toxic waste landfill, Dan and Aaron strapped more ammunition on Josephine.

"You sure the vampires will come here?"

"This is where they dug their dirt last night," confirmed Aaron.

"Leave the car doors ajar in case we have to make a run for it," instructed Dan.

In the woods, they shivered and lay in wait watching the landfill radiate.

"You still feel brave enough for this, Josie?" asked Aaron. Josephine nodded.

"Go for it, sis."

"And don't worry, Josie," assured Aaron. "Dan and I are right here. As soon as one of them gets near you, we'll be all over it."

In the pocket of her winter coat, Josephine carried a short poplar stake, just in case *Plan A* self-destructed. Bravely, Josephine strolled out from the shadows into the clearing at the base of the landfill. Feeling confident, the ten-year-old sauntered past the *FREE DIRT* sign.

"Over here, Mr. stupid Vampire," sang Josephine quietly.

Sure enough, before she had time to become fearful of the realities of playing human chum, a distinct flapping dominated the air overhead. Josephine panicked and ran up the cancerous slope to hide behind a heap of dead car batteries. But she slipped and fell on her tailbone.

The stumpy wooden stake slid out of her pocket and disappeared in a heap of landfill scraps. Josephine found herself surrounded by a veritable sea of smelly old hot dogs, cold cuts, and beef remains. Pounds and pounds of outdated knockwurst and kielbasa broke her fall. Logs of bologna and Genoa salami bruised her as the heap toppled over her legs. Great chunks of bovine intestine, liver, and kidney oozed through her knitted gloves as she tried to push herself to her feet.

"Help, Danny! I'm stuck!" cried Josephine.

Rick Haimatikos had baited this trap well.

25

Ululation pulsed the air as a vampire plunged out of the sky, dive-bombing Josephine. Aaron emerged from the thicket. His weapon at the ready. Sprinting from the woods Fang bolted ahead of him, leading the way.

"Dan, it's Fang!" cried Aaron running toward Josephine. "Stay back, Fang, it's a trap!"

Lumbering ahead, Fang plunged merrily into heaps of cold cuts and offal not far from where Josephine was stuck.

As Fang feasted nearby, Josephine was pinned violently by the winged viper—*Very Berry*.

"What did you do with my friend Penny?" demanded Josephine, righteously glaring as Berry closed in on her.

"Shoot to kill!" shouted a woman's voice training her weapon on the swooping vampire. It was a police stakeout.

A volley of gunshot just missed Fang and grazed vampire Berry. Another shot punctured her wing.

"Don't shoot!" Aaron yelled, lunging into the fray. "Dan, we gotta get Josephine outta here!"

The vampire dragged Josephine up by the shoulders of her thick down parka. Aaron was the first to reach the struggling girl. He hurled a redundant wooden stake toward Berry's heart. Close up, the vampire got a whiff of Josephine's garlic and promptly released her and ascended, wounded, over the glowing hill.

"I've got you, Josie. Dan, take her, and I'll get the dog," Aaron ordered, glancing around for Dan. But Dan was nowhere to be seen.

"*Hold fire!* There are kids on the landfill," Officer Fieldstone yelled into a megaphone, "Kids, outta the way! We're after that giant rabid turkey vulture."

Frightened by gunshots, Fang had retreated into the woods again and found the Mustang door ajar. The vehicle smelled familiar to the basset hound, having cuddled there with Katrina the day before. The frightened dog clambered in and hid on the floor behind Aaron's seat.

"I repeat..." Officer Fieldstone's voice came again through the megaphone. "...get out of the—"

Just then, bodies sprouted from the landfill like Jack-in-the-boxes.

"What the...? Get back. Get in your vehicles."

"We're outnumbered! Hide!"

"A gaggle of giant rabid turkey vultures! Look out!"

The police force ran.

"Wait! Save the children!" screamed Officer Fieldstone. "Hold your positions. *Damn!*"

Out of the landfill's toxic soil, a *varmy* of teenagers arose like zombies, ululating and keening. Like giant Swallowtail moths, they flapped their heavy wings, testing their strength. Black fabric floated around them like evil banners from a nefarious nation. The ravenous teenage beasts took flight, obscuring the glow of the toxic land. The sky flocked with vampires who dispersed for a night of New England feeding.

Swiftly, Aaron spirited Josephine back to the car.

Where the heck's Dan?

"Those aren't vultures. But I don't know what they are. Call for backup," shouted Officer Fieldstone as she ran to her cruiser parked out past the sign that read, *FREE DIRT. HELP YOURSELF.* As she was closing the door to her squad car, a yellow talon hooked her fist. She cried out in pain.

"*You!*" shouted Fieldstone. "Jailbird!" It was the hit-and-run driver whom Nancy had arrested—Lead-foot Liz, newly a vampire, forever alone. "So that's how you escaped my jail!" Fieldstone yelled and slammed the door on the creature, snapping off its claws. Though disembodied, they twitched on the floor of the cruiser. The hag vampire screeched venomously. Fieldstone peeled out. Her hand throbbed in festering pain from the deep scratch. At Fieldstone's feet, the old woman's broken claws inched their way independently through the coffee-stained carpet toward Fieldstone's pant leg... and up... and up...and... The talons clawed their way onto Fieldstone's seat and buried themselves in the upholstery. As she adjusted her seat she felt their prick and she yelled in pain! She tried to raise her bottom off the seat. But it was too late.

Dan, Aaron, and Josephine sneaked quietly back into the Pritcher's house and up to Dan's bedroom. Dan sent Josephine to the shower, then sat on his bed with his face in his hands.

"Look at me, Dan."

Dan obeyed. Aaron looked him square in the eye.

"Coulda used your help out there, Dan."

"That *was* our plan." Dan cringed apologetically.

"Chicken liver. Your sister coulda died!"

"That sound terrified me. What was it?"

"You didn't *see* it?"

"I didn't *dare* look."

"So you didn't dare *see* the proof you were looking for, so you still don't believe they're real." Aaron shook his head, disgusted.

When Josephine was tucked in, the boys returned to Dan's room. Aaron was still gravely irritated by his friend's cowardice.

Dan and Aaron pored over medical textbooks that Aaron found virtually indecipherable.

"I get the illustrations in *Gray's Anatomy*, but the rest of this is gibberish," remarked Aaron.

"The renderings are as important as the text," replied Dan. "So, Katrina was not actually bitten, right?"

"Yeah, I think she just got the one scratch. That's what she told me, at least."

Dan continued to read. "I knew it! This makes perfect sense." He slapped the textbook in triumph. "Katrina may just be experiencing an immune reaction. Like when you get a rash after an inoculation. She's just having an outbreak. A flare-up."

"What, like acne? Gets worse before it gets better."

"Sort of."

"Dan, are you sure? I mean, you should've seen her. She nearly nailed me in her hospital room."

"Aaron, read here in this medical encyclopedia about bacterial infections."

"But what if it's a vampire virus, and not a rabies bacteria? Let me see this book."

"Careful, it's my uncle's. He's a doctor... Loans me his reference books for my extra credit projects in science class."

"I sure hope you're right, Dan. I really love her."

"I know you do, man."

"So, what do we do?" Aaron was still reluctant to trust his friend's judgement.

"If she wasn't bitten, her blood wasn't drained, so her immune system is not weakened like that of a person who loses a lot of blood."

"No blood loss. So, she's not as weak as someone who lost a lot of blood. Got it."

"So, we should be able to do the garlic routine on her. Bath. Shampoo. Soup. Poultices. All in mega doses."

"All garlic?"

"Pretty sure. It'll be painful, I suspect, and she might have another flare-up."

"And gas," Aaron added knowingly.

"But, I expect that it's the only remedy that'll purge the filthy vampire claw bacteria from her system."

"And if she *has* been bitten?" asked Aaron.

"The cure could kill her if the infection's too far gone—like untreated rabies."

26

At arm's length, Aaron examined Katrina's neck and wrist.

"Barely a scar on your wrist from that maniac," he remarked, doubly relieved he saw no trace of a bite on her neck. Aaron kissed both her hands but kept clear of her mouth. "In case you're feeling nippy." He smiled. "How's your thigh?"

"Fine."

"Thirsty? He held out a glass of tomato juice.

"Really, Aaron, I'm fine." She sipped her thermos filled with tepid garlic soup mixed with Pedialyte.

"You sure you're up for this outing to the genetics lab, Katie?"

Really, I'm just tired," she reassured Aaron. Still he gave her circumspect berth.

"Your room looks like a flower boutique," Coriander remarked in awe as she and Dan arrived. Bouquets festooned Katrina's hospital room. "I didn't know you knew that many people, Katrina."

"They're all from Aaron," blurted Dan.

"Oh," said Coriander jealously. "Well, anyway, Katrina, you look like chilled death. But I love your black-on-black outfit."

The nurse entered followed by Mrs. Phillips. "You're free to go, Katrina. Your mom's got your discharge papers."

"Thank you," said Katrina.

"Brought you fresh clothes, honey. Don't you want to change?"

"No thanks, Mom." For the moment, Katrina still did not feel comfortable in any outfit except the black taffeta given to her by Richard Haimatikos. She had banded it around her legs, torso, and arms like a cat suit. When she moved, the crinkly black fabric whispered. Her hair remained wildly unbrushed. Mrs. Phillips handed her a hairbrush. But Katrina shook her head.

"I need to get the heck out of here and be with my friends, Mom!"

"I understand, darling," said Mrs. Phillips. "And I gather Dr. van Swift is eager to meet with you all at her lab. But please don't over exert yourself."

"I promise, Mom."

As the four friends entered the high white marble halls of the genetics technology laboratory, they spied the gift shop.

"I hate gift shop tchotchke," announced Dan with a superior tone. "I'll wait out here in the hall." He wandered around inside the main entrance and read the display boards that featured a cartoon of a smiling dog-like *Self-Propelled Urban Detritus Slurper* licking up a liquid spill.

A thought balloon over the cartoon dog's head read, "*I eat bad DNA for lunch.*"

Aaron draws better cartoon than this, thought Dan.

Inside the gift ship, Katrina, Aaron, and Coriander looked at t-shirts silk-screened with the same *S.P.U.D.S.* cartoon. The tag on a stuffed plush *Bio-Clone-Dog* said, "*Take Me Home with You. No Care Required.*"

"Lots of *Bio-Clone-Dog* souvenirs!" observed Aaron.

"They have a people section too," said Katrina.

"I like this one," said Aaron, holding up a t-shirt that read, "*I'm not one in a million! I'm one in five point six billion.*"

"This is my favorite. I'm going to buy it," said Coriander. "It says, '*Millions of years of hominid evolution dictate that you pick up the check.*' I'll wear it next time Dan and I go out."

"That's never an issue with Aaron," said Katrina smugly recalling Coriander's jab in the hospital room.

"Hi kids." A stout woman in a white lab coat and tinted glasses entered the gift shop. She carried a purse in which she kept one hand hidden as if her arm was in a sling.

Katrina whispered to Aaron, "I don't understand, Aaron, it's Ms. Anthrope. She's supposed to be *double dead*!"

"I just want to welcome you to our lab. This is where I spend my time when I'm not in school."

"Or not snoozin' in the landfill," Aaron whispered to Katrina.

The teenagers stared at Ms. Anthrope unable to see her eyes through the tinted glasses she wore. They sensed that she was up to no good.

"I've just had eye surgery," Ms. Anthrope lied with a lippy smile. "Forgive my impersonal greeting from behind dark glasses." She adjusted the spectacles on her pug nose. "Dr. van Swift will be with you in a few minutes, so I hope you'll enjoy our gift shop. We have t-shirts and mugs emblazoned with brilliant quotes from famous scientists all over the world. You'll have a chance after the tour to come back here and buy mementos. Don't bother to carry them around with you during the tour. Say, isn't Dan Pritcher the fourth in your group?"

"Yes," mumbled Aaron, suspicious.

"Good," she said and departed. A faint trail of dirt left dust motes in the air behind her. Her purse leaked.

"That was nice of her," noted Coriander.

"Yeah, too bad she's a freakin' vampire," said Aaron.

"You can't be serious," said Coriander.

"Look who she's entertaining," said Katrina.

"*Whom*," Coriander corrected.

"Give it a rest, Correy," said Katrina pointing discretely with her chin at the office across the way.

They watched the rodent-faced woman depart and enter a bright white office opposite the gift shop. There, they saw Richard Haimatikos behind sunglasses, his feet on a desk and his Stratocaster case across his lap. On his greasy hair rested Katrina's lavender winter hat.

"Hey, my hat!"

He wiggled his fingers at the teenagers before the office door swung shut.

"That's the slaughterhouse creep?" asked Coriander.

"Vampire," corrected Katrina.

The shopkeeper looked up from his newspaper.

Dark glasses.

"*Shhh*, the cashier must be one too," whispered Katrina. "I think we've been set up."

"Let's get out of here. *Danny!"* Coriander raised her voice.

"Hush, Correy, be cool." Aaron faked a smile and pushed the girls out of the gift shop toward the main entrance.

Dan ambled over. "What's up? Ready to tour this dog pound?"

They steered Dan toward the revolving glass doors.

"We gotta' leave," whispered Aaron.

As they pushed against the security turnstile, lovely chimes emanated through the grand hall followed by an automated loudspeaker voice.

"*Activating security door lock system*," the automated voice echoed in the grand hall.

Just then, Dr. Emily van Swift stepped off the parking garage elevator and approached the teenagers. Her two albino dogs with pink eyes meandered back and forth, twisting their thick leather leashes impatiently, nearly causing Dr. van Swift to trip.

She should train her dogs, thought Coriander.

Dr. van Swift wore a black outfit and black sunglasses.

"She must be one now, too," whispered Katrina. "She's wearing dark glasses and black clothes."

"Sorry to keep you waiting. I've just come from a funeral. My son was killed."

Oh sure, thought Katrina, thinking Kenny had just found a better party for New Year's.

"Kenny's dead?" asked Dan incredulously.

"Yes. My husband and I are keeping it as private as possible until the police finish their investigation. I'm sorry, Dan, I know he was your partner in science lab."

Dan looked stunned.

"We're really sorry for your loss, Dr. van Swift, but, uh, Katrina's not feeling well and, uhhmm, we have to leave right now," said Aaron, his hand gripping the locked turnstile.

Katrina displayed fatigue in excess of what she genuinely felt, and leaned against Aaron for support. She hoped this would convince Dr. van Swift to let them leave right away.

"Right now?" asked Dr. van Swift.

"Yes, right away," said Katrina.

"What a shame," replied Dr. van Swift.

"Yeah, we're sorry too, Doctor. Sorry to inconvenience you," Aaron added politely. "And we're so sorry about Kenny. He was a great kid." *Probably a vampire now like you*, thought Aaron.

"You were so nice to try to help us advance our education," Dan added.

"Don't overdo it," murmured Coriander.

"Unfortunately, the laboratory is on an automatic lockout timer system for security purposes. You heard the chimes? That was the lockout going into place."

"Meaning?"

"Meaning lock*out* and lock*in*. But that's too wordy. And lock*in* sounds so unfriendly. So we just call it—I guess we should just call it lock*down*. But basically, kids, you're stuck here for two hours. That's why we plan lab tours in advance. No one can get *in* or *out*."

Yeah, like it's no coincidence then that a bunch'a vampires are here with us, thought Aaron.

"So, if you really are feeling bad," Emily van Swift continued tenderly to Katrina, "either you lie down in my office and wait for your friends to return from the tour, or you tough it out."

The idea of being separated from her friends gave Katrina the willies. But she was feeling pretty wretched, thanks to stage one of the mega dose garlic treatment coupled with antibiotics to fight the remaining infection that lingered in her system. On top of it, she feared her gnawing thirst for blood. And she still did not quite trust herself *not* to attack someone.

The infection had subsided substantially, but it was by no means dead yet. Instead, the remaining bacteria were the strong ones that survived the first dosage of antibiotics and strong garlic. Those survivor bacteria were accustomed to the dosage, and therefore, when they reproduced in Katrina's blood, their next generation was stronger. Bacteria reproduced quickly—dividing every 20 minutes in optimal conditions. It was not mutating like a virus to adapt to its new hostile environment riddled with garlic-based anti-bacterials. Bacteria function differently than viruses. But each successive generation of the bacteria was more evolved, stronger, and therefore simply immune to the lower concentration of the anti-bacterial. Ideally, Katrina would be taking a stronger dosage with greater frequency. But she was not. Just sipping garlic soup in bone broth with Pedialyte was not enough to entirely kill off each successive stronger generation of the bacteria. Until her immune system caught up and was back in fighting form, she would have to subject herself to ongoing increases in treatment. Or, risk a full-blown recurrence of sickness. And possibly death.

27

Inside the genetics lab building complex, the steel-and-glass shuttle pod propelled itself through a labyrinth of lateral and vertical conduits. Dr. van Swift's albino hounds meandered as she leading the way out of the steel and glass cube and into a wide corridor. The doors of the transport vehicle slid closed behind the three teenagers.

"Here we are on the top floor of the lab, guys. We'll work our way back downstairs over the next two hours," said Dr. van Swift, directing Dan, Coriander, and Aaron into a spotless laboratory.

"Wow. I wish Katrina could see this," said Aaron.

"Ta-dah, over there is *S.P.U.D.S* model *Z.* Affectionately called *S.P.U.D.S.-Z.*" Emily van Swift smiled and pointed at an animal paddock at the far end of the lab. It contained the same dog the teens had seen demonstrated at the First Night Earth Day fair, consuming newspaper.

"Why *Z*, Dr. van Swift?" asked Aaron. "Like *A to Z*?"

"Precisely," responded Emily van Swift.

"So where are *A through Y*?" Coriander probed.

"Well, the first series didn't work as we planned, so we modified the model until we got it right."

"So what happened to *A through Y*?" Coriander asked again.

"They were, uh, detained for further observation, repurposed, or, um, *deactivated,*" said the doctor.

"She means *killed,*" Coriander whispered to Dan.

"S.P.U.D.S. model *Z* is actually an omnivore, with the exception of certain types of proteins."

"Beans and cheese?" asked Aaron.

"Not beans. Meats to be precise."

"Why's that?" Dan asked.

"We didn't want this model to be a threat to humans. We wanted to clone it and make it available to every household without the worry..." she stopped herself. Her eyes watered.

"...without the worry that the clone would eat entire families?" asked Coriander.

"Thankfully no, um, *entire families* were eaten," she choked on her words.

"But you've got one *S.P.U.D.S.* that does liquefy protein, right?" asked Aaron with feigned nonchalance. "The basset hound with the fleas."

"You know of it?" Again Emily van Swift choked on her words, "We are, um, in the process... of, um, deactivating that model."

"So you found it already, doctor? That's great, cause we tried. Man, that dog's fast."

"No, not exactly, our team is, um, in the process of, um locating it. But we're confident it will be detained momentarily if it hasn't already died of natural causes. These *S.P.U.D.S.* clones are very sensitive."

"Sensitive?" asked Coriander.

"They're used to super clean laboratory conditions, not real world challenges."

"Sounds extremely vague," Dan whispered to Aaron.

"We've really got to get out of here, man," Aaron whispered back.

"So, how's that work exactly, Dr. van Swift, with the internal system of the *Bioremediation-Clone-Dog*?"

"Symbiotes, Dan, the fleas—need to stay on the mammal to stay warm," Emily van Swift explained the intricacies of a *Bioremediation-Clone-Dog's* system, "The dog's scent and heat keep the fleas wanting to stay on the dog until the scent and heat of fermenting waste draws them out. The fleas live in the clone-dog's jowls and inside its ears. Flea breeding goes on inside the dog's ears." She lifted model *Z*'s floppy ear to show that it was lined with masses of tiny viscous white bubbles. "Flea eggs. There you have it! The next generation."

"I think I'm going to hurl," said Aaron.

Emily patted the *Bio-Clone-Dog*. It wriggled with delight at the attention.

"He looks neglected," said Coriander sadly.

"Don't worry, we'll have friends for this one soon. As soon as I can clone a batch of pups." Emily van Swift kissed the dog on the head and gently ruffled its ears. "Let's move on to the next room," she said with a smile.

Signaling the teenagers to follow, Dr. van Swift passed her hand over a palm-print-sensitive locking device and a door opened where a blank white wall had been. In the next chamber, glass terrariums containing insects of various sizes rested on polished black tables along one wall. Inside each case the insects were feeding on a different type of material.

"They're all labeled," explained Emily van Swift. "For example, these are carrion beetles. And those are dung beetles. I nicknamed them the *Gregor Samsa* clan," Emily snickered, "...from the existentialist novella *Metamorphosis* by—um, never mind. Each variety of bug is bred specific to a type of waste."

"So why dogs?" Aaron asked.

"A dog is not only *man's best friend*. A dog is naturally a flea's best friend. A dog is the perfect host."

"Definitely more cooperative than cats," said Dan.

Coriander, Dan, and Aaron watched through a huge magnifying glass as fleas inside a terrarium secreted saliva on the surface of an oil spill. A honey-like substance beaded on the surface of the spill. Then the flea spittle seemed to consume the oil, droplet by droplet, leaving a thin, grayish-black liquid.

"Why use dogs at all if your insects will do their thing all by themselves?"

"Transport," replied Dr. van Swift. "The dog connects the dots, so to speak, renders the system self-sustaining, contained, and portable. Have you ever tried to train a flea?"

"I had a flea circus when I was a kid," said Aaron.

"That's funny, Aaron." Emily van Swift smiled. "Bioremediation dogs have no saliva—therefore they have no enzymes to start their digestion process. Thus, the flea spittle is essential. The two species are engineered to be inter-dependent."

"Interdependence is cool," said Dan. "But in us, our saliva begins the digestion process in the mouth, to prep it for the stomach acids, which work in synthesis with the saliva enzymes." Dan recognized the glazed look in Aaron's eyes, so he translated. "When you swallow your food without chewing long enough, you get a stomachache and bad breath."

"And gas," Aaron added.

He reflected on Fang's dry mouth.

"I'd say it's time we move down to the next floor." Emily politely showed them the way back to the elevator transport vehicle and waited while they climbed in.

"Hit the button marked *Quadrant 4BZ*, please. Oops, darn it, I forgot to shut off the overhead lights in the laboratory. Wait here for me, okay. Hold the transport vehicle door so no one calls it away to another part of the building before I get back."

As soon as Emily van Swift and her two albino bulldogs were out of sight, the three teenagers stepped out of the transit pod. Aaron reached back inside and hit the *Quadrant 4BZ* button, and yanked his hand away before the door shut on his arm.

"She'll think we're at *Quadrant 4BZ* already."

"Let's go."

"Which way?"

"*Any* way! Hide until she leaves this *Quadrant*!"

"Then we'll find a way out."

"*Not* without Katrina," puffed Aaron as they ran.

They made it down the corridor and rounded the corner just as Emily van Swift came out of the lab again. They heard her laugh and mutter something about the teenagers' enthusiasm for getting to the next exhibit. She hit the call button for the elevator and waited patiently. When it returned, the doctor pressed the button for *Quadrant 4BZ* and was gone. The clean white hallways were theirs alone.

28

They tossed Katrina's lavender hat back and forth playfully. The pug-nosed woman ignored the security monitor in her office. She was too busy flirting with Haimatikos.

"My lavender trophy hat suits you, Richard. You taught me well how to swoop."

"You've learned quickly, Ms. Anthrope."

"Richard, aren't they sweet?" she glanced up at the security monitor. "Would you call them *late lunch* or *early dinner*?" She leered at the three teenagers on the monitor as they rushed down a long polished hallway.

"*Late lunch*," responded Richard with a hoary grin.

Ms. Anthrope pressed a control button on her desk and the screen showed a door sliding open for the teenagers. She and Richard smiled.

"You start with them, and I'll finish off Katrina," purred Richard.

The three teenagers followed a corridor and entered the only lab room whose door *would* open for them. All the rest were sealed and seemed to require a matching handprint to spring the lock.

"There must be a fire exit here somewhere," said Aaron.

"Guys take a look at this!" said Coriander in horror. "*A through Y*!"

Coriander pointed at a wall of refrigerated glass cages marked *S.P.U.D.S.* units *A through Y*. The door to case *Y* was open; the unit was empty. So was the one next to it. Most of the rest of the cases contained some sort of mutated animal.

"Oh, my God, they're mutant slurpy puppies," gasped Coriander. "All with symbiote bugs in their ears and around their lips. They're all alive."

"We saw *Z* in isolation with Dr. van Swift," said Dan.

"Check the photographs on the other cages. One of the missing ones must be Fang." Aaron studied the identification card on each cage. "It lists what each one is supposed to eat."

"*W* is empty too. This photo looks like Dr. van Swift's albino dogs. Says here they're *detritophages*?" Coriander read carefully.

"*Detritophages*?" said Aaron.

"Dirt-eaters," said Dan. "Swift's albino dogs with the pink eyes."

"But they've got teeth in this photo," said Coriander.

"The doctor must've screwed up their genetic splicing," observed Dan.

The other mutant creatures were horribly deformed: grotesque imitations of real animals.

"It's like in Greek mythology," remarked Coriander, "But instead of Cerberus the dog with three heads, or Orthrus with two, the *Bio-Clone-Dog* alphabet collection is twisted in other ways."

The collection displayed one mutant with eyes, ears, and pink tongue, but not much of a body. Another looked like an embryo with a hairy tongue. The next was a cyclops with a tail and a huge lolling tongue covered in bristles.

"Good call, Correy," said Dan. Sometimes her genius shone through so brilliantly. "Perhaps Greek mythology wasn't myth."

"Looks like someone royally screwed up," said Aaron suppressing the urge to throw up.

"Maybe Zeus and the royal Gods were just sloppy scientists like Dr. van Swift seems to be."

"But, there appears to be a progression of development," said Dan. "*U, V, W, X... Y...*"

The three teens wandered up and down the wall of cages. They reached the last refrigerated unit. It was empty. A photo of a black and tan basset hound with black feet stared back at them with a big doggie smile.

"That's definitely Fang," said Aaron, reading the identification card on the unit, "*S.P.U.D.S.-Y.*

"You've seen this dog?" asked a female voice.

A moment winked past then Dan and Aaron leapt out of their skin, realizing that Coriander had *not* asked the question.

"It's Rodent Woman," whispered Aaron.

"Children..."

Wide-eyed, the Homecoming Queen faced Ms. Anthrope, while Coriander's lithe hands reached behind her and she lifted the latch on cage *M. I hope this thing'll attack her,* thought Coriander taking a very big risk opening the door for a creature with ambiguous appetites.

The grotesque, pink, slithery creature inside thrust the door wide open and bolted into the room.

"Stand *still,* children," ordered Ms. Anthrope, "...until it passes."

Scuttling past the pug-nosed scientist, the creature from cage M disappeared down the hall.

"Don't worry about *S.P.U.D.S.* model *M.* He'll die if he's out of his refrigeration unit too long. They all would. Though he might take out a few office shrubberies and potted plants before he kicks off."

"Could we please leave now?" said Aaron.

"Yes. Leave the *Alphabet Room*," she ordered brusquely and pointed at the door. "You don't belong in here. But don't run. It upsets the animals. Anyway, there's nowhere for you to run *to*."

On the intercom, Ms. Anthrope tracked down Emily van Swift who soon stepped off the transport pod with a renewed smile. She no longer wore sunglasses.

"Kids! Thank heavens, there you!" exclaimed Emily with a big grin. "I'm sure Ms. Anthrope has taken good care—" She stopped short as a dark shadow crept over the three teenagers.

"Well, hello Emily." Richard Haimatikos appeared from another corridor. In one hand he clutched his Stratocaster case full of dirt. In the other he dangled Katrina by the scruff of her neck, like a lifeless kitten.

Emily's disposition nose-dived when she saw Richard Haimatikos.

"It's *your* fault my son is dead, you murderer!" Enraged, Emily advanced on him with her two albino hounds.

The vampire tossed Katrina to the floor in a lifeless heap. Aaron fell to Katrina's side.

Haimatikos positioned his Stratocaster case across his chest like a shield, and caught Emily by the arm with his other hand to stop her from clobbering him. Richard laughed too close to Emily's face. She recoiled from his repugnant breath. On a tight leash, Emily van Swift's albino bulldogs growled and sniffed eagerly at Richard's guitar case.

"Pretty useless mutant guard dogs," Dan whispered to Coriander. Then they noticed Dr. van Swift's tight grip on the albino *Bio-Clone-Dogs'* leashes.

"What's she waiting for? Unleash'em on the vampire already," Coriander whispered to Dan.

"That photo on their cage shows they've got serious canines," Dan spoke even lower.

Emily van Swift's beating of Richard Haimatikos was pointless. He was stronger, and she was tired and heartbroken. She kept on slapping at him until Ms. Anthrope stole the wind from her sails with a single query.

"Emily, where's *S.P.U.D.S.* model *Y*, the basset hound?" Ms. Anthrope glanced conspiratorially over her sunglasses at Haimatikos.

29

Deflated, Emily van Swift's voice faltered and shook with anger, "*S.P.U.D.S.* model *Y* was on a test run in a supervised, *quarantined* environment. Until *Rick* here, in his infinite wisdom—"

"Mr. Haimatikos knows perfectly well that the basset hound is at my parents' horse farm," Aaron lied, attempting to buy time with a bluff.

"Kids," Dr. Emily van Swift turned away from Haimatikos and regarded the high school students. "Why didn't you tell me sooner? I thought *S.P.U.D.S.-Y* might be dead by now! Normally, these genetically-engineered animals cannot live for long outside of a controlled environment."

"Aaron's lying," interjected Dan, "Sorry man, but that dog would've eaten your thoroughbreds and your pregnant parents by now. In fact, Dr. van Swift, these *vampires* need your dog so they can keep feeding on people in Westlake and blame it on *your* clone-dog... and on *you*, Dr. van Swift. That's their *cover*."

Dr. Emily van Swift was unsure whom to believe. And *since when was Kenny's lab mate anything but scientific?* So she started with him. "Dan, are you okay? I know Kenny's death came as a shock to you. But... superstition is not a scientific approach to..."

"Yeah, well, in fact, Dan," Aaron interrupted, "actually I *have* got Fang safely hidden. I moved him last night to an... *undisclosed location*." Aaron mimicked a term from a thriller he had seen.

"Fang, you call him? Quaint," murmured Haimatikos tendering his canines. "Makes me feel all fuzzy-cozy inside. You named him after *me*, his overlord."

"Not on your life, jerk," muttered Aaron, still holding Katrina's limp body where he sat on the clean, polished floor.

"Look," whispered Coriander. "Katrina's stirring. I saw her eyes flutter and her hand twitched."

"Katrina?" Aaron was hopeful. He stroked her face.

As Katrina plotted what to do next, her gums ached. But less than before. Still, she was dying of thirst, not so much for blood per se, but another liter of Pedialyte would do nicely.

"Richard's not a jerk, Aaron," Katrina barked hoarsely, loud enough for Richard Haimatikos to hear her.

"Don't defend the vampire, you spineless traitor, Katrina. He's the enemy," hissed Coriander.

"Richard's my hero." Katrina's voice was raspy, convincing. Coriander scoffed. Haimatikos was chuffed.

"The dog will die if he's not fed continually," Emily van Swift implored, "Poor *S.P.U.D.S.-Y.* Please, we must get him back, if you know where he is, Aaron."

"Quaint," Haimatikos echoed himself, snorting at Dr. van Swift's raw emotion. "Let's go get *S.P.U.D.S.-Y Fang* and introduce him to our target audience in Westlake... so we can continue building our *varmy*. Short for *vampire army*, Emily, in case you wanted confirmation. Yes, we're real." He laughed raucously at his own joke.

Dr. van Swift's eyes widened in horror.

"Gosh, Richard's *soooo* brilliant," gushed Katrina.

Now, Aaron looked doubly stricken.

"You're really ticking me off, Katrina," snarled Coriander.

"Sedgewood, kid, yeah, sorry, your girl prefers me now. Still, before we drain you, we need you to get us into your parents' house or wherever you stashed the dog." Haimatikos enjoyed Aaron's look of shock, then turned his attention to the science teacher. "Ms. Anthrope!"

"Yes, Rick." She was excited to serve him.

"Drain the brats. Give Katrina first pick."

Aaron glanced at Haimatikos and then at Katrina. She winked discretely at Aaron then set her sights on Dan and Coriander. Aaron was confused.

Katrina steadied herself then lay back down on the floor beside Aaron. Her illness seemed to everyone to be advancing aggressively, consuming her. She licked her chops. It seemed to Aaron that Katrina could not resist the impulse to bite flesh. He knew *she* knew that Aaron was unsavory territory because he ate so much garlic on everything all the time. And Coriander, he knew Katrina knew, wore that fishnet sack of garlic necklace hidden under her shirt. But Dan... Dan, surely *everyone* knew, was not superstitious until now. With the exception of the flea collar Dan had agreed to wear, as far as Aaron knew, Dan took no further safeguards against vampires because Dan doubted their existence as anything but unfortunate crazy people with rabies. Therefore, Aaron figured, Dan would be the only one remaining among them whom Katrina could bite. Dan would be safe, delectable, unspiced quarry for the avaricious vampires. *Vampires*, thought Aaron incredulously, *vampires now control the destiny of my closest friends and me, the town of Westlake, and the entire globe, if their new world order succeeds.*

Sure enough, Katrina's energy surged and she leapt on Dan. With Coriander at his side, it was especially difficult for Katrina. She lunged for his throat, trying to whisper in Dan's ear. But, he quickly wound up to punch Katrina.

"Play along, dummy," Katrina whispered as they struggled.

But Dan's fist was already in motion. It connected with Katrina's head. Coriander seconded his punch. Katrina fell back.

"Oh my God," Dan stammered, "I've—I've never hit a girl." He stepped back rubbing sore knuckles.

Nor anyone, thought Aaron.

Arms pin-wheeling, Katrina leapt again at Dan. Aaron darted to Dan's aid and peeled a screaming, drooling creature that was his beloved Katrina away from Dan. Again, Katrina lunged, this time for Aaron's ear.

"Play along, Aaron!" she whispered.

They fell to the floor and wrestled violently, rolling behind a credenza, out of view of the vampires. There Katrina kissed Aaron for the first time since First Night.

"Sorry," she whispered.

"How'd you keep him off you?"

"I locked the door to Dr. van Swift's office and napped until I heard your voices. Then I faked I'm crazier than he is. Works every time, Aaron." She winked.

"And Emily," Haimatikos continued, "we don't need you any longer since the boy can lead the way to *S.P.U.D.Z.-Y.*" Richard grasped Emily in his arms. "Unless you'd like to join our eternal tribe right now?" He leaned in toward Emily's throat. His fangs brushed her soft skin. He shuddered in ecstasy; finally, what Richard Haimatikos had been waiting for so very long.

"*Noooo!*" screamed Emily realizing that even if Haimatikos was not really a vampire—since everyone knows vampires do not exist—still, he did intend to kill her. "You need me alive, *Rick*! I'm the only one who can successfully clone that dog. And if you want to enact your sick plan, you'll need a whole lot more than one *Fang* to do it."

Annoyed, that it had not occurred to him that he would need more than one *S.P.U.D.S.-Y Fang* to fulfill his mission, Richard the vampire released Dr. van Swift, muttering, "A persuasive variable, Doctor."

"You've already stolen my only son from me, Haimatikos. But, I promise I'll work with you if you'll let these kids go. Name your price," Emily beseeched him.

"Okay, kids," Richard's response was almost poignant, "behave yourselves. And *doctor*, in all fairness, technically, your son's death was due to your own Frankenstein creation. All I did was open Pandora's Box. Just sayin'..."

"Richard's such a prince... of darkness," cooed Katrina admiringly as she stood up from behind the credenza with Aaron.

"I agree," said Aaron in a creepy, hollow tone as he stood beside her.

"Good work, Katrina," remarked Ms. Anthrope.

Worried, Coriander and Dan looked to Dr. van Swift.

"Nevertheless," Haimatikos beamed, "I'm feeling a nostalgic fit of generosity thanks to my hungry little namesake, *arf, arf*. I've got prime rib and eye of round in my trunk. So let's commence our search for Fang right this moment? Together. *Ooooh*, I can't wait to have my own little *varmy* of Fang clones, Emily." He danced in place and laughed like a spoiled child getting his way. He crowed, "*Here Fang. Good dog, Fang.*"

Emily stared at the despicable Haimatikos. His infantile giggling echoed, his face leering, grotesque.

"But what's the price?" asked Dan starting to panic.

"Emily knows my price. And Ms. Anthrope will agree it's the politically correct thing to do. No one feels discriminated against in my equal opportunity *varmy*."

"You want me to become one of your team members," Emily conceded.

"What a vainglorious wench you are, Emily. It's not *just you* I want in my eternal tribe. And don't be jealous, now. It is *she*."

Richard pointed his guitar case at Katrina.

"*Her*," corrected Emily softly, "You want *her*."

"And *she* and *he* and *he*," continued Haimatikos, indicating the other three teenagers.

"And *her* and *him* and *him*," Emily spoke a bit louder.

"*What?*" sneered the vampire.

"You want *her* and *her* and *him* and *him*," said Dr. van Swift softly, pointing at each teenager. "Not—

Their argument was interrupted abruptly by savage yowling that emanated from the parking lot outside the plate-glass window.

Immediately, from other *quadrants* of the genetics lab, all the genetically-engineered clones bayed an eerie reply.

"It's my dog!" cried Emily, recognizing Fang's sound that she herself had engineered. She wept in relief.

"My dog's come *home*!" Emily van Swift wiped her eyes.

"*My* dog's come home to *me*!" declared Haimatikos getting competitive with Emily.

"Well, actually, Fang's in *my* car," admitted Aaron, too scared to lie. "I drove Fang here 'cause he wanted to hide out in my Mustang. Guess he felt safe there."

30

Howling in pain, Fang's breathing was laborious.

"Don't die, buddy."

Aaron let the basset hound out of the Mustang. Its stomach distended beyond recognition, Fang collapsed in the snow.

"Fang's dying?" Richard Haimatikos demanded, "If he dies, can you still clone him to assist my *varmy*."

Ignoring Haimatikos' incessant petty questions, Emily van Swift knelt beside her dog that lay convulsing in the snow. Emily felt betrayed especially by Ms. Anthrope whom she had trusted as a volunteer in her lab. Never had it occurred to her that the high school science teacher was not only an acolyte but a stooge of an indolent narcissist with bizarre fantasies of cannibalism.

Hastily, Emily van Swift opened her first aid kit, and Aaron passed her the items she needed. Fretting, Haimatikos and Ms. Anthrope hovered, watching.

Katrina steadied herself against Aaron's car, then stumbled deliberately to make it appear that her illness was progressing faster than it really was. She sprawled on the hood of the Mustang and gazed indifferently as she gnawed at her own arm.

"I shall recruit the remaining youths presently if we do not *immediately* start cloning my namesake. *Arf! Arf!*" Haimatikos' fangs sprouted as his ire grew.

Keeping a distance from the vampires and the dog, Dan and Coriander watched over Aaron's shoulder. Panting hard, Fang lay exhausted in the snow between a trifecta of vehicles: the red limousine, Aaron's Mustang, and Ms. Anthrope's Volvo station wagon.

Emily finished her examination of *S.P.U.D.S.* model *Y*. She patted her dog lovingly, and sighed. At long last, she responded to Haimatikos' mind-numbing nattering.

"*Rick*, my dog is not 100%. I need to perform procedures on Fang in the lab."

"Will he live?" asked Haimatikos.

"I do not know. However, I cannot start cloning if there are signs of compromised health."

Weird, that Dr. van Swift is not getting attacked by the fleas, thought Aaron. Then he spotted it. *Everyone here who's not a vampire is wearing a flea collar.*

"On second thought, I'm thirsty *now*," Richard Haimatikos announced testily. He leaned in too close to Emily who mistook his proximity for an amorous advance.

"Don't be daft, *Rick*," said Emily, "I'm married. And, I need to concentrate on saving Fang."

"How soft in the head of me to have waited so long. You'll still retain all your scientific knowledge after your *conversion* experience, Doctor. You can still repair *olde* Fang here. Your source of motivation will change substantially. But I'll be by your side to guide and nurture you into eternity. I'll be your spiritual Gandhi, of sorts. Forever your personal Svengali, Emily."

Emily van Swift did not like the sound of that.

"Wait!" shouted Aaron. "Fang's convulsions are coming faster. We need Dr. van Swift."

Thirst overtook reason and Richard Haimatikos drove his incisors into Emily's tender throat. Emily screamed and fainted. Her pink-eyed albinos snarled and growled at the vampire. But that's all they were good for, or so it seemed at the time. Pandemonium broke loose as the teenagers took in the terrifying sight of Fang's rapid wheezing convulsions.

"Oh, no, Fang's coming apart!"

"Blood's gushing everywhere!"

"Wake up, Dr. van Swift, please!"

"Help us save Fang!"

"He's dying of starvation," said Dan. "A bloated stomach is an indication of starvation. Worms breed in the gut and cause it to bloat and—

"Give him the meat," barked the rodent-faced vampire woman, interrupting Dan's ardent science lecture.

Aaron did so and Fang's fleas liquefied the beef slabs, yet Fang showed no interest in the plasma goo. The basset hound whined sharply, convulsing harder and harder on the snowy ground as blood gushed from the dog's nether regions.

After Richard Haimatikos sipped Emily briefly, suddenly he threw his head back and screamed, and spat and spewed her life-fluid over the snowy parking lot.

"*Gaaaaaaaaaaarlic bloooooooooood!*" He shrieked and shrieked again. Haimatikos stuck his finger down his throat to purge the garlic-laced antibiotic blood from his festering system. He collapsed in the snowy parking lot, hacking.

"Ha!" Dan mused, "Even a flea has better sense than a vampire!"

Richard spewed again beside his guitar case as the pink-eyed dogs whined and nudged Emily. Gradually, she came to.

"Hurry, Dr. van Swift, Fang is dying," Coriander cried.

"Quick, get up!"

"Who's next?" said Richard, gnashing his fangs and wiping his mouth, while continuing to heave garlic blood from his system.

"We're not afraid of you, Mr. Haimatikos," shouted Aaron.

"Then you're more naïve than I thought."

"Too bad, we're all on the stuff," Dan said proudly—much to Aaron's amazement.

"We'll see about that!" the vampire approached Dan.

"You wouldn't dare endure *that* again," said Dan.

"You're bluffing," Haimatikos challenged.

"Try us," Dan rebutted, exposing his own neck. "We're as full of garlic as Katrina is."

Richard's face fell. "But she said *Very Berry* bit her."

"Hurry, Doctor, please," pleaded Coriander.

"We're losing Fang. Quickly!"

Emily slowly got to her knees. Then, gradually she crawled toward Fang, bit-by-bit regaining her balance. She had lost a fair amount of blood, which now adorned the parking lot and blended with the vampire's red car.

"Dr. van Swift, *now*!" Emily ignored Coriander, she had an idea.

"Mr. Haimatikos, tell me something," said Emily as she crawled toward the convulsing canine.

"The soil in your guitar case. Where's it from?"

"Transylvania, of course." He laughed at her ignorance.

"May I see it?" she asked without a trace of guile in her tone.

He hoped she was flirting with him. "I'll show you mine if you show me yours, Emily."

"Quickly please, Rick, it may be instrumental to Fang's survival."

He was suspicious but could not imagine that any harm could come from showing off his dirt. In fact, he loved to *show-and-tell* his dirt to inquisitive people. It was like showing off his home. He opened the Stratocaster guitar case. As long as Richard Haimatikos had his home dirt from his birthplace in Easter Europe, he was safe from the corrosive effects daylight had on a vampire. Smiling, he snorted a few grains of his soil and breathed more easily.

Emily reached one delicate hand to gently sift Richard's soil. Her eyes twinkled with intelligence which the vampire mistook for admiration.

"You students recall anything from your science project about bioremediation?" asked Emily as her other hand released its grip on her two albino dogs' leashes.

Dan smiled. He had done most of the research for their hazardous waste and landfill booth. He suspected what Dr. van Swift was hinting at.

As the albino dogs sniffed at the Stratocaster case, Dan excerpted his source material about millions of tons of toxic waste shipped from USA to Bangladesh, China, Hong Kong, India, and *other underdeveloped countries*.

Emily reiterated Dan's last three words and added, "And what year did you decide to leave *your* underdeveloped country in order to grace us with your presence here in Westlake, Mr. Haimatikos?"

"It was a good year...," Richard said slowly, with hideous realization.

"*Dinner time!*" Emily gently spoke the order to her albino bulldogs. Immediately, they leapt into the Stratocaster case of dirt. "As you can see, they haven't had a really good meal since they cleaned up the land at the wood treatment facility out in North Andover last week."

"*Noooooooooooooooo!*" screeched Richard. "Not my Homeland Security!"

But by then it was too late. The dogs had already lapped up the last of Richard Haimatikos' home soil. Then they turned to the dirt-filled purse of Ms. Anthrope. Like sharp incisors, the last rays of sun before twilight pierced Richard's cankered flesh. Fearing for her undead life, Ms. Anthrope ran to her Volvo and burrowed into her trunkful of *free dirt*. She slammed the lid shut, blocking out the albino hounds. She plugged her ears against a desperate vampire's final screams as the winter sun set on Richard Haimatikos forever.

All was silent, except for Fang whimpering in pain and the ugly sound of Katrina sucking her own arm.

"You can quit that, Katie." Coriander was in a foul mood.

"It's safe now. They're gone." Aaron embraced Katrina.

Without having to masquerade overt illness in front of the vampires, Katrina stopped gnawing on her arm and giggled.

"Kind of over-played that one," she admitted observing the purple hickey on her forearm.

"Kinda'. Now, let's please save the dog!" insisted Coriander.

"I thought vampires imploded or dissolved or blew up and made a splatter-mess like in the movies," said Aaron.

"I wouldn't know," said Dan disdainfully, then stared at Haimatikos' empty heap of clothing and dust on the snow. "Say, do you think there's a cure for his *varmy* Dr. van Swift? Like, can you cure mass rabies?

"Doctor! Please!" Coriander shrieked, "Fang is dying! He won't eat the beef slurpy! He's writhing in pain bleeding out! Has he got Ebola? You're a doctor! Do something!"

Dr. Emily van Swift began to laugh uncontrollably.

Oh crap, is she a vampire now? Aaron wondered.

31

Through tears, Coriander wailed, “It’s not funny! We don’t want to lose Fang!”

“We thought you were on our side, Dr. van Swift,” Aaron pleaded.

“We love Fang,” implored Katrina.

“Please don’t die, Fang. Good boy,” whispered Katrina, “Good dog.”

But Emily van Swift kept laughing until she cried tears of joy and relief. It had been a terrible day of loss for her. She had lost her beloved son Kenny. And she nearly lost his friends, her creation the *Bio-Clone-Dog*, and her own life.

Finally Emily got the words out, “I’ve... made... a... *ter-ter-terrible* mistake.” She laughed some more. “Fang’s not...” Emily could not stop sobbing and laughing.

Aaron, Katrina, Dan, and Coriander huddled around Fang who appeared to be on death’s door.

“Guys, you’re witnessing parthenogenesis incarnate,” said Emily at last.

Dan’s eyes lit up. “What do you mean, doctor?”

“The genetic mutation screwed up one of the two chromosomes in the pair of *X* and *Y* chromosomes that made *S.P.U.D.S.-Y* male,” Emily continued, “The one-legged chromosome, the *Y* chromosome that renders a creature male, in *S.P.U.D.S.* Model *Y* the *Y* chromosome appears to have sprouted an appendage!”

“An appendage?” asked Katrina.

“The *Y* chromosome sprouted a leg,” explained Dan. “The *Y* became an *X*, so, instead of an *X* and a *Y*, Fang got a pair of *Xs*.”

“Like my parents, a pair of *Xs*,” observed Aaron.

“Different,” advised Dr. van Swift, “I’ll explain. Since Fang now has two *X* chromosomes, not an *X* and a *Y*, the double X chromosome pair renders Fang a—”

“Fang’s a *mother*!?”

“That’s right, Aaron. Through parthenogenesis, Fang needed no mate to reproduce.

“Immaculate conception?” asked Coriander. “Virgin Fang? Should we name her *Mary*, instead of *Fang*?”

“Puppies?!” Katrina rejoiced in astonishment as she witnessed the miracle of life unfold before her eyes.

Sure enough, out they came: eight slippery little basset hound pups.

"Fang's really more a *Fang* than a *Mary*," remarked Aaron, petting the dog's head. "Good dog."

Soon Fang was resting peacefully, no longer writhing in pain but licking her progeny clean.

"I'm taking one home," announced Coriander gleefully.

"I'll talk my mother into it, too," said Aaron.

"I bet I can train Josephine to feed it," mused Dan. "And walk it, if I housebreak it."

Katrina peered closer. "Won't the fleas kill the pups?" she asked.

"We together have provided quite a shield of garlic essence for starters. Quick, give me your garlic," said Emily impatiently. "You said you were on it. Well?"

"We took it, but... we used it all."

Coriander palmed Emily one clove from her fishnet stocking necklace. The doctor peeled the clove and mashed a bit between her fingers, then massaged Fang's head, ears, and mouth with the natural antibiotic.

"Garlic and a flea collar and she's good to go. It's not like West Nile Virus. These fleas are genetically engineered for a limited number of generations. They cannot reproduce in the wild, so they won't contaminate the gene pool of wild fleas."

"So, *Mother Fang's* not a danger to anyone?" asked Aaron.

"I'll keep her and her puppies quarantined here for observation until I'm sure that everything's 100% copacetic. But you guys can visit anytime. I hope you will."

"What'll you feed Fang now? Meat shakes?" Aaron asked.

"Chicken soup," answered Emily. "Good for the soul, too."

"And you can feed your bulldogs the vampires' *free dirt* from Haimatikos' landfill. Without it, the smarmy *varmy* will have nowhere to restore themselves," Coriander added.

They laughed again and nearly wept with relief. At last, their New Year's nightmare was nearly over.

"We'll stop them from hoarding their free dirt so they can't breed more vampires and spread their *varmy* to other towns."

"Can we start now?" asked Dan. "And sic your albino canines on their dirt."

"Your detritophage dogs could start with Ms. Anthrope's," said Coriander, eyeing the Volvo where the former science teacher lay hidden, burrowed in her stash of dirt in the back of her station wagon.

"We can get Officer Fieldstone to crowbar it open," suggested Katrina.

"Or, give Ms. Anthrope a great big *stake!*" said Aaron with a rakish wink.

Puzzled initially, then one-by-one, Katrina, Dan, and Dr. van Swift snickered at Aaron's pun.

Coriander scowled. "But, vampire's don't eat *steak*."

Party Till You Scream!

Originally published by Bantam Books' Bantam Starfire, a division of Bantam Doubleday Dell Group, Inc. New York, NY, 1995

1

A soft voice spoke within a dark chamber, "What if they don't come?"

"They'll come, you'll see. It's their nature," coaxed a deeper voice in the darkness.

"But what if they *don't* come?" whined a third voice.

"We're stuck here."

And then a chorus of others joined in, "What if we're stuck here forever? What if they don't come? Whom shall we torture if they don't come?"

"They'll come. I'll see to it," promised the first voice in the dark chamber, deep inside a seaside cliff, "They won't be able to resist."

2

On the rocks, the seaside backdrop promised a fun night of revelry. That is what Westlake High School students believed when they first arrived at the isolated party site. Only twenty attended the end-of-school bash because so many had died, or remained unwell since the recent toxic waste landfill debacle.

Fireside, Aaron Sedgewood snatched Katrina Phillips' dental floss.

"Dental floss!" exclaimed Aaron "Katrina, who brings dental floss to a beach party?"

Laughing, Katrina shrugged. "Corn on the cob requires it." She dipped her sandaled foot in a tidal pool and splash-kicked Aaron.

A bonfire to celebrate the last day of school flicked burning shadows across their clothing. Aloft, sparks peppered elongated shadows of laughing teenagers that cast occult movement against the rugged cliff sheer.

Senior boys hoisted a huge piece of drift-wood onto the blazing pyre, shouting, "Heave ho!" The bonfire dimmed momentarily before igniting the behemoth chunk of tinder.

The sudden and brief dimming of firelight allowed an uninvited guest to scuttle unseen behind a huge smooth rock directly behind Katrina. The visitor knew the terrain well, he'd been there a while. And he made not a sound as he leapt from crag to granite crag. He observed the teenagers with interest. It had been an inordinately long time since he himself had been one.

"You never know when you'll run out of dental floss," Katrina explained the random contents of her purse. "So I always carry extra." She set down her plate of cob corn and bright red lobster to kiss Aaron. As she did so, her tiny cup of melted butter spilled across the plastic plate and onto the sea-worn rocks beside her. A few drops of the hot butter splashed the hairy toes of the unwanted visitor who hid among the boulders behind her. The visitor ducked his unkempt head of hair behind the large stone plinth that loomed higher than Katrina's head. With surprising agility, he licked his toes, hoping to taste the butter. He recalled the savory from years past, yet, now, he tasted nothing.

"Yeah, but two packs of dental floss, Katrina? Oh wait, three, no four... no, wait, five!" Aaron laughed as he rifled through her purse, and held up many small white plastic containers. Setting them aside, he foraged in her purse again. "What else have you got in here?"

"Emergency provisions," replied Katrina, laughing at her boyfriend's antics. She continued to munch corn.

"You've got everything in here but the family dog, Katrina. Check it out: four lipsticks, tweezers, five pens, a broken wristwatch, three and a—*gross*—half PowerBar, vitamins, masses of pennies, that incidentally are worth more melted down as copper than as pennies, and... a crumpled piece of paper, and... an empty spring water bottle, a note pad, and—*geez*, Katrina, good thing you never have an emergency. You'd be completely unprepared. How can you find anything in this bag? And there's even more junk in the secret pockets. No wonder it weighs a ton!"

"It's my portable fitness center." Katrina laughed. "Give it to me, Aaron." She snatched her purse from him and dug through it as a spray of brine tickled her face and bare arms. "I carry everything I never use but can't live without. Here!" Katrina withdrew from her purse two steel nutcrackers and two steel picks. "Now we can eat our lobsters."

In the darkness beyond the bonfire, the Atlantic Ocean sloshed and roared threatening imminent attack. Yet, the teenagers felt safe in the sunken spot surrounded by boulders that they had discovered for their private party, shielded as it was from the powerful sea wind. Stars winked overhead, and a single light from a trawler on the horizon hinted at a lobsterman's hard life on the water. New England summer was here.

Aaron smiled at his clever girlfriend. He loved the way Katrina's cotton cable-knit sweater was slung over her shoulders, exposing her bare arms in the firelight. He loved the way her long, straight hair flew about and tangled in the ocean breeze, some catching under the wide strap of her lavender tank top. Aaron could not explain all the reasons he loved her. He just did.

"You sure are resourceful, Katrina. I like that in a woman," Aaron remarked as he cracked a claw of his lobster with the steel nutcracker and poked out the meat with the steel pick.

Katrina smiled and flirtatiously dragged her lobster tail in the pool of butter on her plate. As she stared into Aaron's eyes, a figure behind him caught her eye.

"Hi, Dan," Katrina hollered and waved to Aaron's best friend.

"It's too hot on the other side of the bonfire." Dan Pritcher approached with a plate of red lobster and corn on the cob. "Can I join you guys upwind?"

"Sure. Where's Correy?" asked Katrina.

Dan did not wait to ravage his corn before explaining that his girlfriend, Coriander Preston, had gone walking on the beach. She had left her boom box that now played *Rock Lobster*, a snappy dance tune by the B52s. The three friends bopped as they ate and watched other students dancing.

"*Alone?* Correy went for a walk *alone*?" Katrina asked, concerned. "Did you two have a fight?"

"It's no big deal, Katrina. We're isolated here," replied Dan. "The parking lot's a good mile away. You'd have to be a lunatic to come all the way out here just to kidnap the cheerleading captain."

"Cheerleading captain *and* Homecoming Queen," corrected Katrina snarkily. They snickered.

Peering over the large boulder at the group of students, the odd visitor with the hairy buttered toes picked his teeth, or, rather, what remained of them. Dental floss had not existed when he grew up. Back then, a sweet birch twig was the best available tool for dental hygiene. He gazed down the beach, scanning for Coriander. Still no one noticed his tuft of hair and gleaming eyes poking above the huge rock.

"*Dan,*" Katrina reprimanded, "aren't you the least bit concerned about Correy?"

"Katrina, a kidnapper would have to first know we're here," Dan explained logically, "Then find the *shrouded* entrance to Poison Ivy Lane off Ocean Boulevard—virtually impossible in and of itself, since there's no street sign..."

"...and *enshrouded* by guess what," Aaron interjected. "Poison ivy."

The hideous visitor chuckled at the teenagers' conversation.

"Dan!" Katrina persisted, "Go look for Correy. You're her boyfriend."

"It's fine, Katrina, I mean, if I hadn't been following the convoy, I myself would never have found Poison Ivy Lane. And then find that obscure path that we all had to walk down single file to avoid the poison ivy and briars. Then, climb over boulders. Then the stalker would have to locate Correy on the beach?" Dan mused. *Surely Correy's perfectly safe.*

From his plinth vantage point, the visitor spotted Coriander strolling the beach. Firelight rippled over his ragged features that crinkled into a grin. He ducked again behind the boulder and leaned against the granite ledge to plot his next move.

"Go, Dan," Katrina repeated.

"Wait!" Dan was on a roll. "And *then* the killer would have to drag her away without any of us hearing her scream. Ha! Then, back to the only access road—"

"Dan!" snapped Katrina.

"What?" Dan replied irascibly.

"You've got a piece of corn on your glasses."

"Oh." He wiped his gold wire-rims.

"Unless the kidnapper was already here," offered Aaron with a rakish wink.

"We all know paranoia is incurable," joked Katrina.

"Sounds like Dan's got a plan." Aaron laughed, chucking his empty lobster claws over Katrina's head.

"Yuck!" shrieked Katrina, "they dripped on me!"

"Oops, sorry, Katrina."

The stinky wet lobster shells hit the strange intruder in the face.

"Lost your chance to be gallant, Dan. Hi, Correy!" said Katrina as Coriander Preston approached the bonfire. Breezily, she sat down next to Dan on her superlong hair that protected her new white shorts from the dried salt on the sea stone.

"Hi, guys! Looks like our party's going to get rained out," said Coriander, indicating the thunderhead thickening the night sky.

"No way. You're joking!" said Katrina.

"You can see the storm clouds from the beach," said Coriander. "Not from here. The bonfire light makes it hard to see beyond the flames."

"Gotta love New England weather! If you don't like it, wait a minute, it'll change," Aaron noted.

"Didn't Mark Twain say that?" asked Dan.

Another spray of seawater spritzed them when it hit the rocks that skirted the party. A senior girl turned up the volume on the boom box and shouted, "Let's dance!" More students got up to join the throng, and sang along. Rowdy teens swung long tentacles of slippery green and black seaweed, lassoing the dancers. One couple strayed away, seeking romantic privacy closer to the surf.

"Your lobster will be ready soon, Correy," said Aaron, removing a green, snapping bottom-feeder from a wax-paper bag stamped *Captain Marden's*. "But *first* we relax the lobster. Rub its back. And let it do a headstand. Aaron stroked the back of the lobster gently and made it stand on its head.

The others laughed. "You're such a *goof*, Aaron!"

The heinous visitor grew impatient behind the rock. He had a job to accomplish.

"Does that make the lobster taste better, Aaron?" asked Coriander.

"Aaron's lobster-massage lulls the critter into a false sense of security so its end isn't quite so perfidious," Dan informed.

Katrina pelted Aaron with her empty lobster tail, saying, "Just cook it, Aaron. Correy must be starving."

The weird visitor peeked out from the boulder again and watched Coriander swish her hair. He picked at his few remaining teeth with the spike of a horseshoe crab tail. It was then Coriander glanced again at the fast-moving rain cloud and noticed the intruder. At first, she thought he was an animal hunkered to pounce. She shrieked in terror, pointing at the boulder behind Katrina.

"It's a...!" cried Coriander, her eyes locked on the disheveled visitor, "...a weirdo!"

Lightning struck illuminating the disheveled head of the uninvited guest squatting on the granite boulder behind Katrina.

"Don't move, Katrina!" murmured Aaron.

Menacing thunder rumbled, chasing the lightning.

3

No one moved. For a full minute after the thunder died away, the only sounds came from the Cars' *Just What I Needed* on the boom box. Of course, the bonfire crackled in the effervescent sea air. And frothing ocean waves crashed nearby. A soda can, released from the grip of a terrified teenager, tinkled against smooth rocks as it rolled away toward the ocean. It stopped short, ensnared by seaweed in a tidal pool.

In the gaze of the unwanted visitor, the students didn't dare budge. Katrina studied her friends for a cue. She did not yet turn to look up at what they were all staring at above her head. Maybe the thing hadn't seen her hidden at the base of the boulder.

Without a word, Aaron grabbed both Katrina's arms and yanked her over to his side, away from the rock upon which the grotesque creature observed the young adults. Katrina's linen fisherman's sweater fell behind her as she nestled beside Aaron.

Now, she saw it. *What was it? Animal or man? A ghost?* In the light of the fire it held a weird masquerade-ball mask in front of its face. The mask was a horseshoe crab's shell out of which two eyeholes were punched. The visitor held it up by the crab's six-inch, stiff, spiked tail—sharp as a skewer. The prehistoric shape was dead and threatening. Barnacles clung to its brown carapace, mottling it with a jagged crustacean acne. Talon-like thorns edged the lower rim of the horseshoe crab shell, so it seemed the visitor's jawline had fangs or many sharp beard points.

Suddenly the creature-man shouted from behind the mask, "*Eeeeeeeevil!* This place is *eeeeeeeevillllll*! Escape while you *caaaaaaan*," he warned.

A well-timed bolt of lightning struck the rocks, jolting everyone. The creature dropped its mask. The students gawked at the ugly, angry, leering smile of a man-beast. Then, he disappeared among the boulders. In his wake he left only the essence of burnt salt air and a frenzy of ions. The desiccated horseshoe crab mask teetered on the rock and slid off, cracking against the stones beside Katrina. The subsequent thunderclap jarred the teens into mayhem.

"Only evil thing *here* is him," barked Billy Carlyle.

"Where'd he go?" Katrina picked up the visitor's frail mask to examine it.

Billy laughed with false bravado. "Total geek!"

Sherry James started to cry.

"Hey, quit the tears, babe. The guy's just a weirdo," said Billy, seizing the opportunity to grope Sherry's waistline while he pretended to comfort her.

Sherry pulled away from Billy.

Katrina grabbed her sweater and her steel lobster utensils. "He's just a crazy man, Sherry. Don't let him scare you."

"I bet one of the jocks hired the guy to come to the party and scare us," said Coriander. "Billy? Did you?"

"Yeah, who else would be dumb enough to come all the way out here?" said Sherry softly, consoling herself.

"I didn't," retorted Billy.

"Sure you didn't," said Dan.

"One thing's for sure," said Aaron, "that guy could've used your dental floss, Katie. *Grody teeth!*"

Too close for comfort, *again* lightning struck and the sky broke open. A deluge doused the bonfire. *Darkness!* Dismayed, the blinded teenagers yelled when a huge wave crashed over them, soaking the last embers. The teens herded away from their party circle that was now a tidal pool.

The sky continued to spew.

"Can you believe this downpour?" shrieked Katrina.

"What do we do now?" asked Sherry, crying again.

"Hey, my lobster!" cried Coriander. "Washed away in that jumbo wave."

"Yep, fifteen bucks worth of fine dining sent back to its natural habitat," said Dan offering his girlfriend the tail of his own sodden lobster.

Amidst the whipping summer storm, the uncanny visitor climbed the cliffs, higher and higher, laughing to himself about the trick he'd deployed for millennia:

"Tell a kid, *stay away, it's bad for you,* when you want'em to stick around," he muttered to himself, picking his teeth and sniggering, "*...heh, heh, heh,* now they're dying to find out *what* evil lurks here. Now I can manipulate them to do my bidding."

"My feet're soaked!" whined Coriander.

"You're at the beach, Correy." Stymied by her complaint, Dan offered his hand.

"My lobster boiler! I'm doomed!" Katrina sighed as her mother's eighteen-quart All-Clad was swallowed by the ocean. "I've got to go after it."

"No way, Katrina," said Aaron locking a vise-grip hold on her hand and pulling her away from the receding wave. "Rip-tide will suck you out to sea in the undertow faster than you can say *Hat Rabbit.*"

"Over here, you guys, under here!" a senior boy was shouting. "I found an overhang behind this boulder. We can hide out till the storm passes. There's room for all of us."

A few damp flashlights feebly lit the way to a rocky overhang behind the big boulder on which the strange visitor had made his "*eeeeevillll*" pronouncement.

"Can't we just *go*? Back to our cars where it's dry?" implored Coriander.

"Yeah, right," said Aaron plucking his drenched t-shirt away from his chest. "Correy's got a *death-wish date* with General Electric," joked Aaron.

"Dodging lightning bolts! Too dangerous," said Dan.

"Correy, the parking lot's a mile away," Katrina reminded.

"The storm won't last long," Dan reassured.

But he was wrong.

"Whose idea was this, anyway?" asked a sophomore.

"Billy's," accused Aaron, stirring the pot.

"Shut up, Sedgewood," Billy moved closer to intimidate Aaron.

"Bring it on, man." Aaron challenged.

"Stop it, you two," ordered Katrina.

"Can we all fit under here?" asked Sherry politely as she stood in the pouring rain.

"Oh for God's sake, Sherry, you have to stick up for yourself." Katrina pulled Sherry out of the rain.

"Duck your head as you come under," Dan warned.

"Shine the flashlight over here, will you?" Billy pointed at the back wall behind the group.

Sherry pushed her way back there with Katrina's flashlight and offered it to Billy. The teenagers huddled safely under the cliff overhang and watched in awe as the powerful storm crashed their party.

"Billy, cut that out!" said Sherry quietly as she whisked his roving hands off her.

"What? I thought you liked that," mewled Billy.

"No! I told you," said Sherry shyly. "No."

Billy grumbled.

"She said *no,* Billy," Katrina piped up. "God, you're such a pig."

"*No* means *no,* Neanderthal," Aaron chimed in.

"I hope that creepy guy doesn't come back," said Coriander shielding her boom box from the rain.

"Don't worry, Correy, he's outnumbered, twenty-to-one," said Dan holding her close.

"Yeah, we could gang-tackle him," suggested Billy.

"Who's else has flashlights?' Aaron asked.

Five or six students answered by blinking their beams.

"Don't waste the batteries," ordered Dan.

"Where do you think that guy *went*?" asked Katrina.

"No idea," said Coriander. "He was a real piece of work. Not someone we would've invited to our party."

"He was the life of the party, if you ask me," said Aaron. "I liked his horseshoe crab masquerade mask. Genius idea, wish I'd thought of it for last year's Halloween party."

Another bolt of lightning struck the rocks nearby, like a fuse box exploding. It forced the students farther under the rock ledge. Immediately, a steady stream of electricity sent tentacles of lightning across the sky.

"Whoooooaaa! Close call!" exclaimed Aaron.

"That one shattered a boulder!" Katrina trembled.

"Good thing we're under *this* rock," said Billy as if it were immune from a lightning bolt. He broke into song, "*Rock, rock, rock, rock lobsahhhh...*"

A wave of brine soaked the teenagers' feet.

"Spiders!" Katrina screamed and leapt, grazing her head on the low-hanging rock. "I felt'em in my hair."

Everyone ducked away from the low ceiling. Sherry clung close to Katrina.

"Sorry, Katie, I was just goofing around." Aaron delicately untangled Katrina's hair and flashed his penlight. "See, arachnid-free.

Another gush of water and lightning caused the teenagers to withdraw like hunchbacks as far under the cliff as they could. They clustered against the back wall.

"Hey, check this out!" exclaimed Aaron. "Markings on the rock ceiling." A white painted arrow pointed at the back wall here Dan and Katrina leaned.

"A door!" exclaimed Coriander.

"And a metal detector," said Dan. He picked up the gadget on the yard-long pole.

"And a cooler full of sodas," said Billy, pilfering its contents. "Crap, no *bee-uhs*."

"That crazy guy must be a beachcomber. Left this stuff here," said Aaron.

"You think he went inside this door?"

"Do you really want to find out?" asked Dan.

"No," Coriander replied flatly.

"Ouch!" Katrina yelped. She looked at her shoulder and noticed she had cut it against barnacles that encrusted the iron door against which she had leaned. She rubbed the scrape.

"I bet this is a military bunker," said Dan. "I've always wondered about these seaside caves the military used during the wars. Let's check it out."

Just then, a huge wave emerged from the black night and engulfed the cave, rolling against the back wall, and trapping the teenagers in brine. For a breathless few seconds in head-to-toe seawater, all the students felt death was imminent. Drenched and coughing, they shivered as the wave receded leaving them ankle-deep in saltwater.

"My good leather sandals're wrecked!" cried Coriander.

"Aaron, how do we get out of here?" asked Katrina.

He shrugged.

"And my handbag is soaked!" Coriander moaned.

"Be glad you didn't drown, dummy," muttered Aaron shaking his head.

"C'mon, let's go," snapped Katrina.

"We can't," said Dan. "We're trapped by the lightning. There's nowhere to go once we're out from under this ledge. This is our only shelter from the lightning."

"Dan's right. In this electrical storm," said Aaron. "we'd never make it to our cars. We wouldn't even make it ten feet without getting zapped."

"Well, guys, we'd better do something, because that tide is coming in awful fast," said Katrina, now calf-deep in cold brine.

"In an electrical storm, we shouldn't be standing in water either!" Dan added.

"Let's go in through this metal door and shut it behind us," suggested Aaron.

"We'll drown if we remain here," said Dan.

"No way am I going inside some cave," said Coriander.

"Me either," said Sherry meekly. "We'll drown."

"Fine. Then wait *outside*, 'cause I'm going *inside*," said Katrina. She pushed against the door with all her weight. "It's locked."

"Here, let me try," offered skinny Dan, to no avail.

"You're a woos, Dan," said Billy, flexing. He ushered Dan aside.

Several of Billy's jock buddies helped push the door, but it was immobile. Lightning stabbed at the rocks just outside their shelter. They could feel prickly electricity in the air. Another wave dashed the teenagers against the hard back wall. They were forced to hold their breaths until the surf subsided again. This time, the water level remained above their knees causing Katrina to lose her balance and she was sucked out from under the ledge by bubbly undertow. Wailing for Aaron, she feared sharks would be attracted to the bleeding barnacle cut on her shoulder. The wave deposited her on a heap of driftwood that had been their celebratory *school's-out* bonfire. Lightning blistered the air around her. It smelled as if the sky were charred. Gasping, she scurried back toward the tiny flashlight glow, under the ledge with Aaron's help.

"Pull it, *pull* the door open!" gasped Katrina, wringing out the dead weight of her waterlogged purse as thunder reverberated in her chest.

"What? I can't hear you!" shouted Billy over the thunder and another crack of lightning.

"*Pull* the door open, get inside. Move it. Now!"

Sure enough, the old barnacle-encrusted iron door swung outward with relative ease. Aaron guided Katrina with his penlight. They waded through the shallow water that covered the floor inside a rough-hewn stone chamber. Dan followed, leading a reluctant Coriander by the hand. But, just outside the iron door, Coriander started to hyperventilate. Dan took her boom box from her so she could cup her face in her hands to slow her breathing, and overcome the gnawing claustrophobia that consumed her.

A few other students with flashlights joined Dan inside the doorway. Billy pushed Sherry inside and went ahead.

"We're shutting the door, you guys. You better come all the way in or run for it."

"Before the next wave comes, people! Make a decision and stick to it!" Katrina shouted from the front of the line.

Most of the stragglers obliged the warning just as a wave slammed the heavy steel door shut. Billy held the door fast against the reverse pull of the tidal torrent. Inside, the group shuddered as saltwater seeped away beneath their feet and across a cement hallway floor. Aaron beamed his light at the base of the door where more seawater poured steadily in.

"We'd better go inside as far as possible! Make a run for it." Aaron's breathing was short and quick.

"We'll find another exit somewhere in here." Dan sighed heavily, observing their dank surroundings.

"Who else is outside? Anyone?" Counting heads, a senior girl craned her neck over the group.

"I don't know. No one, I guess," said Dan. "Right Correy?"

"Wait. Listen," said Katrina.

"Billy, quit it!" said Sherry.

"What?" he mumbled grudgingly.

"*Shush!*" hissed Katrina.

As the wave subsided, they heard screaming outside the iron door.

"It's Correy!" shouted Katrina. "How'd that happen? I thought she was with you, Dan. Open the door!"

"I thought she came in with the group!" shouted Dan, forcing open the door.

Before the next torrential wave crashed, Dan dragged a sobbing, gagging Coriander inside the cave. Aaron and Billy held the door shut until water gushed across the floor, chasing them all down a long, low tunnel.

4

Tumbling headlong down a steep wet cement slope, Aaron screamed, "Aaaaagh! *Hellllp*!" Katrina fell after him, pig-piled by the others in a deep puddle on a narrow landing.

"Guess it slopes there," said Aaron, collecting himself and helping Katrina up.

The teenagers moved on. Hunched to shield their head from the low ceiling, they ran farther down, deep inside the seaside cliff, flashlights licking the damp walls ahead.

"Summers, when I was a kid, these condemned U.S. Army bunkers at the shore fascinated and terrified me," Dan was saying as he ran to keep up.

"Don't they terrify you anymore?" asked Aaron.

"What's that, Dan? You sayin' you know a way out? If not, shut up and keep runnin'," said Billy. "'Cause I don't want to have to play lifeguard to save you."

"Maybe I do know a way out. I mean, I don't," said Dan, "but I could probably figure it out. The military built these secret tunnels underground like a groundhog network and they disguised the bunkers with sand dunes and overgrown hillocks and scrub bushes and brambles. One time, my sister and I found an open iron door into one of the bunkers."

The tunnel dipped again suddenly and then leveled off. It seemed they had been running along a slow waterfall before. And now it was like they were running in a flooding streambed. In the lowest section of the narrow tunnel, it was shaped like a trough, so water was up to their knees and it was hard to make haste. As the water rose higher, it entangled their legs and slowed their progress to... to *where* they did not know.

"Now you're going to tell us the exciting part, Dan?" asked Aaron, panting hard as he ran.

"No, but here's the *dull* part. When Josie and I explored the bunker, every room was empty with the exception of an occasional rusty nut or bolt. And all tunnel accesses within were either bolted or rusted shut."

"I guess it's just our luck to find this one with a welcome mat?" suggested Katrina breathlessly as she rushed along.

"Hurry up, you guys, the water's coming' in fast!" shouted a sophomore at the back of the line.

"And rising," noted Dan. High tide was imminent.

They ran onward along the narrow level. Suddenly, Aaron tripped and fell in the water. He reached underwater to determine what had felled him and pulled out a clot of driftwood draped in seagrass and knotted seaweed. A starfish and a crab clung to the gnarled mass.

"A drain." Aaron chucked the clog away from the drain and watched with growing hope as the water level receded gradually down the burping drain hole.

"That's a relief. We won't drown in here when high tide comes all the way up." Katrina sighed.

"More good news," added Aaron, pointing his tiny penlight ahead.

Dan exhaled in relief seeing what lay ahead.

"Looks like a wheelchair ramp for daredevils," Aaron noted.

"Boy, I'd like to ski down a slope that steep!" said Katrina.

"Guys, c'mon, the tunnel goes up here, so when the water rises with high tide, we'll be above it," said Dan.

"Hurry," shouted Sherry from the back of the group.

"My flashlight's barely functioning 'cause of the water and another wave's comin' in fast."

Deep inside the oceanside cliff the air was thick with brine. The faraway crash of a wave urged them on. They hadn't much time before another, larger deluge would wash them away.

Belting seawater rushed at them down the cement riverbed.

"Quick!"

"Run!"

"Didn't we shut that door?" yelled Aaron.

"Tidal pull must've flopped it open," shouted Dan.

Katrina thought of the beachcomber. Maybe *he* had opened it on them. Hastening along, the teens ascended the steep, narrow tunnel. Just as quickly, ocean water rose behind them, soaking their feet and ankles, splashing their backs.

"But I pulled the plug in that drain!" cried Aaron.

"Fact is, water's rising faster than the little pipe in the drain can carry it away," shouted Dan.

"Run faster, you guys!" hollered Katrina.

Dan, Aaron, and Katrina helped the others up over the edge at the top of the slope, the highest they could go before the dark tunnel stopped dead level. Just as the last of the students were leaping over the top of the ramp, a ferocious wave flooded in and filled the space behind them. Sherry's legs were sucked out from under her, and she was pulled away, back down the watery chute. She wailed desperately then disappeared under the black water. Frothing brine filled the void.

"Sherry!" shouted Coriander.

"Sherry's gone!" yelled Billy. "Help her. Someone go in after her!"

"Coward!" Aaron gave Billy a filthy look. "Billy, you're always bragging about your expert abilities as a swimmer."

"That was before my football concussion." Billy lamely avoided eye contact.

"Billy, you're either a chicken or a liar or both. Either way, I'm not about to let Sherry drown." Aaron stripped off his shirt.

"Don't, Aaron. Let someone else go," pleaded Katrina. She couldn't stop thinking of sharks. What if that open door let in a shark?

Before Aaron dove into the dark water after Sherry, he said, "Guys, everyone whose flashlight is still working, hold your flashlight near the surface for me."

"Aaron's a strong swimmer," Katrina reassured herself over and over. *He just needs to know where to swim back to.*

Water consumed Aaron and lapped up over the edge of the landing where the group of teenagers scrummed.

"Hope the tide doesn't come any higher," said Billy afraid only for himself.

Katrina could no longer see Aaron. The flashlight beams did not penetrate deep beneath the surface. But far below, Aaron could see their pale glow so knew which way to swim to the surface.

In Aaron's absence, Billy wasted no time putting his arm around Katrina, advising her, "Don't worry, Katie. If Aaron doesn't make it back, I'll get you home safe."

She shook him off abruptly. "Billy, why is it when I'm near you I always feel like some sort of natural resource you're plundering?" snarled Katrina.

Soon, Aaron resurfaced with Sherry. She was shaken up, wheezing, and trembling, but well enough to soldier onward down the tunnel. The others continued around a curve in the hall. Aaron helped Sherry keep up with Katrina and Dan leading the group.

"I'm okay, Aaron, thank you," said Sherry politely, still a bit winded. "You guys go on ahead. I'll catch up."

"Hey, what's that?" said Katrina.

"What?" said Dan.

"I'm not sure. I could've sworn I saw a-a-a shadow, or... movement."

"Gotta have light to have a shadow, Katrina, and the only light is our dying flashlights."

"Maybe it's that beachcomber?"

"*Hellooooo, Beachcomber!*" shouted Dan.

"*Shhh*, Dan!" whispered Katrina. "Shut the heck up. What if he's another *fair-is-foul-foul-is-fair*–type dude? We're stuck in here with him, remember!"

"Yes, but Katrina, there are twenty of us and only one of him, *remember*."

"Odds and Gods favor us, babe," said Aaron reassuringly. "And I'm sure we'll find another exit."

"What if he's got his whole weirdo beachcomber cult living down here?"

"Katrina, he's probably just a homeless guy or a simple vagrant," said Dan. "A grifter."

Seven fading flashlight beams helped the teenagers assess that they had arrived inside a broad, vaulted room with a high, domed ceiling that dripped water.

"What a dump," griped Coriander.

Katrina grimaced. "I'm surprised it's not crawling with rats."

"I feel like we're inside the fat end of an eggshell," said Aaron, looking up.

"Aaagh!"

"What?"

"Nothing. Just a puddle of water in the center of the floor." He wiped rainwater from his face.

The night air was cooler inside the dome. The teenagers shivered in their wet clothing and stood away from the drippy hole in the vaulted ceiling.

"Must be the lair of the beachcomber." Aaron made evil eyes at Katrina and she stopped him by kissing his face.

"It's definitely a bunker," said Dan. "An army bunker."

"How do you know so much?" asked a jock.

"Because I read history books, dim-wit," said Dan smugly.

A sudden gush of seawater brought Billy and Sherry into the room after the group.

"Hey, wait for us!" shrieked Billy.

The water clawed its way into the room a few feet then subsided weakly.

"Hope we're on high enough ground," said Aaron nervously.

"High enough to *not* drown!" Katrina underscored.

"For the moment," said Dan examining their surroundings, "...it appears we're slightly above sea level. But we need to scope out our options."

"Can't we just rest here until the storm passes and the tide goes down?" Katrina suggested.

"I really think we should keep moving," said Dan.

Dan and Coriander examined the walls with flashlights.

"I don't see any signs of high tide on the walls Do you, Danny?" Coriander asked.

"No. No barnacles, no salt residue, no erosion," Dan replied.

"Nice fresh water." Aaron stood in the puddle in the center of the room and leaned his head back, open-mouthed.

"You better hope it's rain, and not sewage, Aaron," said Katrina.

The teenagers chuckled.

"It doesn't stink," observed a junior. "Maybe we're under a pond."

"So, we're staying?" Coriander asked.

"Then let's party!" cheered Billy.

"I think we should start by building a fire. We need our flashlight batteries, and it looks like there's enough stuff in here to burn," noted Aaron, checking his pockets for his Zippo lighter.

Coriander took her boom box from Dan and turned on the radio. All but one of her tapes had washed away.

"And don't use the boom box. We might need its batteries for light later," added Aaron switching off the radio.

"So much for partying on," groused Billy.

Dan shone his flashlight around the room. "This isn't driftwood. Look at this furniture. This must be the beachcomber's den. He's got it arranged like we do at home. He must have guests coming and going."

"But it looks like the guy shot out his TV." Aaron eyed the jagged glass mane of the face of a big old cathode television set.

"What a psycho to smash his TV," Coriander commented.

"What do you suppose he does all day?" Sherry wondered out loud.

"Entertains guests," Dan joked.

"He'll be ticked if he comes back and finds we've burned his interior decorating job for our own amusement," said Coriander.

"We have to dry off," Katrina insisted.

"Tough nuts to the beachcomber," Coriander snapped. "We're staying. He's got terrible taste in decor anyway. He could use some new accessory pieces. My mother would have a field day redecorating this place."

"Coriander, you're cruel," Katrina scolded. "The guy's homeless!"

"No, I just have unrelenting good taste," Coriander replied.

"This place has character, even though his stuff's dilapidated," said Dan, poking through a row of moldy books on a decayed wood bookshelf.

"At least it doesn't stink in here," said Coriander.

"And there are no rats or mice to—" Katrina was cut off by Coriander's shriek. "What is it?"

"I hate moths!" screamed Coriander swatting at a burly moth.

Dan looked up from the ramshackle bookshelf and laughed. "Yeah, Coriander thinks she was a wool sweater in a past life."

Katrina removed a perfume atomizer from her purse and squirted the moth. It fell.

"Thanks, Katrina."

"Hey, check this out," marveled Dan. "The bum's got all the classics on this bookshelf from Twain's *Huck Finn* to George Orwell's 1984 to G.G. Garth's *Driven to Kill*, and, all the monotheistic and polytheistic religious books."

"So he's a well-read bum," said Aaron eyeballing the line-up that included the King James Bible, the Torah, the Quran, the Dao de Jing, and the Bhagavad Gita.

"Remember we read *1984* in English class this year?" Katrina recalled, "I hated the part where the rats eat right through the guy's head while he's alive." Katrina shuddered at the thought.

"To get a confession out of him," mused Dan.

As they discussed the book, the teenagers built a small fire, sparingly splitting up a chair whose leg was already broken, as well as a rickety coffee table.

"I'm sorry to wreck the dude's home," groaned Katrina. "But I'm so cold."

Most of the couples settled in around the fire. One by one the teenagers stopped shivering. In silence, they watched the smoke twist up to the ceiling and out through the drizzly rain vent high above their heads. The rain spattered a short stack of vacant seat cushions. Sodas were the only provisions that had been salvaged from the surf, so Katrina shared her remaining PowerBars with the group. She ate the old salty wet half herself. Aaron offered to tell ghost stories but was outvoted in favor of knock-knock jokes.

"Too bad we didn't bring the metal detector," mused Dan.

"Why?' asked a junior. "You want to search for money?"

"It would have made it easier for us to find another metal door, like one leading to the outside. Like one that would set us free." *Duh*, thought Dan.

Two musty hallways led off the main vaulted room, creating an abysmal labyrinth interlinking cement chambers and hallways. Everyone watched as Billy led Sherry down the far hallway by fading flashlight, presumably in search of a secluded spot for romance. Katrina arched her eyebrow at Billy. Sherry could not look Katrina in the eye.

Coriander cuddled closer to Dan, but he was deep in restless thought. "I think we should explore our alternatives," suggested Dan. "Plus I'm sick of sitting around."

"Yeah, well, since the entrance is flooded, it looks like we've got *two paths* to choose from," noted Aaron pointing out the second and third hallways that opposed one another at either end of the domed room. In silence, he continued to roast a piece of PowerBar on a splinter of wood over the fire.

"'*When you reach a fork in the road... take it!*' What famous *Yogi* that?" Dan read from a book on the shelf.

"Wait, wait, don't tell me! Paramahansa Yogananda!"

Dan rolled his eyes, "No Aaron."

"Deepak Chopra!" said Katrina. Dan rolled his eyes again.

"Yogi Berra!" declared Coriander with certainty. "Massively famous baseball player."

"That's my girl," said Dan, and kissed her squarely.

Katrina grabbed the sports trivia book from Dan and shuffled through it.

"So, we're at a *fork* in the road, Dan? W*hat* you're saying is that we should...?"

"*Take it.*" Several students chimed in and laughed.

"Dan Positive Man, here's the *fork*," said Aaron, "We explore this army bunker without extra batteries or provisions, *or* we stay warm by the fire waiting for the tide to go back down and the sun to rise."

"By morning, we can walk right out of here the same way we came in," Katrina added.

"If the drain doesn't clog again," noted a senior girl. "Dan's right, we need to explore our options.

"My mother's going to kill me. I'm supposed to be home by eleven-thirty, Aaron," said Katrina.

"Someday," said Dan contemplatively, "we'll all have a portable phone. Each of us."

"Sure we will, Dick Tracy," said Aaron patting Dan on the back. "Katrina, I'll help you explain to your mom tomorrow." He smooched her and pulled her closer.

Gradually, more and more couples paired up and disappeared, seeking privacy. Aaron called after them. "Make sure you don't get lost!"

"Or pregnant!" yelled Coriander.

Dan, Aaron, Coriander, and Katrina remained by the fire.

"I've always wanted to *really* explore one of these bunkers," said Dan happily. "I'm dying to see what they keep inside the locked rooms."

“As you can see, *nothing* but junk,” Katrina pointed out. “What? You think there’s a catacomb or treasure chest in here somewhere?”

“No, but maybe there’s a room for weapons and ammunition,” Dan said excitedly.

“Or a bar and grill,” said Aaron. “...to kick-start this party again.”

Just then, a shrill scream echoed up one of the corridors. Shrieking continued wafting over them like an icy breeze.

5

Piercing screams persisted. The four friends sprang to their feet.

"It's Sherry." Katrina grabbed Aaron's hand and ran. "She's screaming *Billy*."

"Which hallway is the screaming coming from?" Coriander asked, glancing from one hall to the other.

"I know for sure that I saw them go down *that* hall over there," said Aaron, pointing at the wall across the room as they approached it.

Arched rock slabs framed the wide cement doorway to the hall. Raw cement framed the two other doorways in the dome.

"But it sounds like the screams are coming from the hallway behind us," said Coriander, pointing at an opposing hall *without* the rock slabs.

"Maybe there's a secret passageway in the walls that connects the three halls without passing through the main dome room?" suggested Katrina.

"Like a rabbit warren," said Aaron.

"Feels more like an ant colony," Katrina mumbled as she joined Coriander near the sound.

"Hush," Dan said. He stood and leaned his face very close to the damp curved wall of the cement dome.

"What're you doing, Danny?" asked Coriander.

"Shush." Dan's ear nearly touched the wall. He waited for the next scream. "I knew it! C'mon, let's go." Dan bolted across the room toward the opposite door, to the one at which Aaron had originally pointed *with* the rock slab around its doorway.

"What're you guys waiting for? Follow me," commanded Dan.

"So I *was* right," said Katrina.

"But Dan, the screaming is coming from this hallway here," said Coriander. "Not that other one. We hear it right *here*."

"No it's *not*. That's an auditory illusion created by this curved dome ceiling. Even a whisper carries like AT&T across the curved surface. It's an ancient method of confusing prisoners. C'mon, you guys, we have to help Sherry."

Aaron, Katrina, and Coriander ran across the domed room to follow Dan down the hall.

"Watch your step, ladies," cautioned Aaron as they hastened down the hallway. A few broken metal and wood machines lay strewn in their way.

"Looks like old generators or pumps," Dan observed.

The four friends reached a curve and then the hallway splintered into a three-pronged fork.

"*Take the fork*, Wise Man Dan!" said Aaron with mild sarcasm.

"Wait. Let's listen a minute," said Dan. "Katrina, give me your dental floss."

"I left my purse by the fire in the main room," she said.

"Great. Don't budge from *that* hallway that we came from, or else we'll never find our way back to the fire dome."

Aaron shone the flashlight alternately down each of the three forks. The screaming came again followed by the sound of sandaled feet approaching the four-way intersection.

"Sherry?" they yelled.

Wild-eyed, Sherry was blood-spattered and shrieked like a banshee as she approached them.

6

Sherry's face and pretty summer outfit were bloody.

"Are you hurt?" asked Coriander, hugging Sherry around the shoulders, carefully avoiding blood smears on her own clothes.

"Where's Billy?" probed Dan.

Scared speechless, Sherry could not answer.

"C'mon, Sherry, let's get you back to the fire," Katrina coaxed.

Instead, Sherry just moaned sickeningly and bolted past them down another hallway—the *wrong* hallway. Katrina ran after and grabbed her slippery, bloodied arm.

"Sherry! This way," Katrina instructed, forcing her back to the intersection where the three friends waited. Together, they guided the traumatized girl back to the fireside in the dome room. There, Katrina sacrificed her brine-sodden cable knit sweater and wiped away the blood from Sherry's face and arms.

"Your good linen sweater's ruined now, Katie," said Coriander. Katrina ignored the frivolous remark.

"Are you hurt? I don't see any cuts. Sherry, talk to me." Katrina inspected the victim. "Is Billy hurt?"

"*B-B-Bi-Billy,*" blubbered Sherry as she pointed at the blood on her shirt.

"Must be Billy's blood on her," said Aaron.

"What happened, Sherry?" Katrina insisted.

"*E-e-e-evil.* We—we—we've gotta get out of this place!"

Sherry cried as she lunged for the first hallway through which they had first entered the dome. It remained flooded.

"Grab her, she'll drown!" shouted Katrina.

The boys caught Sherry just as she was about to throw herself down the steep cement ramp toward the surf. They brought Sherry back to the fire. Katrina pulled out a long strand of dental floss.

"Are you going to tie her up?" asked Aaron.

"What if she flings herself off again?"

"She's going into shock," said Dan.

"How can we help?" Aaron fidgeted.

"She needs to focus on something positive," said Dan.

"Sherry," said Katrina sternly, "I have an activity for you. I want you to sit here and, and, and..." For a moment, Katrina pondered what she could possibly have Sherry do to keep her mind active. Katrina placed the dental floss in Sherry's palm. "...floss your teeth, Sherry."

To their surprise, Sherry obeyed.

"Correy, you stay with Sherry. The boys and I will find Billy and the others. Okay, Sherry, promise you'll stay here and floss your teeth?"

Sherry nodded obediently and kept flossing.

"Katrina, I knew you were resourceful, but—"

"Aaron, focusing on an activity will help her from slipping further into shock," said Dan knowingly, "Keeps the mind connected to the body. Good call, Katrina."

Briefly, Sherry burst into tears where she sat rocking next to the fire. She rocked and flossed her teeth and stared absently into the fire.

"You'll be okay here with Sherry, Correy?" Coriander nodded. Dan kissed his girlfriend and whispered, "Careful Sherry doesn't hang herself on the dental floss."

"And, Correy, keep this lobster pick handy," said Katrina. "You might need it for self-defense if that beachcomber comes through."

7

Their search for an exit commenced in the bowels of the labyrinth and lasted hours.

"Guys, fifteen of us are unaccounted for," said Katrina as she glommed chunks of lipstick to the cement wall in order to stick a thread of dental floss to it. Aaron reeled out the floss ahead of her and Dan shone a fading flashlight.

"Katie, I'll never tease you again for carrying useless stuff in your purse," said Aaron.

"How're we doing for supplies, Dan?" asked Katrina. "Have we gotten anywhere yet?"

Dan scoffed, "Half a dozen 100-yard packs of dental floss, less the length you gave to Sherry. Won't get us too far. What else have you got in that bag, Katrina?"

Before she could answer, Aaron spoke, "Hey, I smell fresh air. I see moonlight!" he announced. "Come on." They heard the ocean waves crashing just outside. The night rainstorm had stopped. They smelled freedom.

Aaron, Katrina, and Dan bounded down the hallway toward the moonlight, quickly reeling out dental floss until they reached the open door. One full pack of dental floss was spent.

"Dead soldier," said Aaron, tossing the white plastic case out the open doorway.

"We can escape and get help," said Dan. "*Yesss!*"

"I didn't hear the empty floss pack hit the rocks. Did you?" Aaron was crestfallen as he peered over the edge.

Outside, a gibbous moon sparkled on the ocean surface far, far below. They stood on a sheer cliff.

"Bingo! I just heard the floss box hit," murmured Katrina.

There was no way off the ledge.

"*Yooo-hoo!*" came a familiar hollow voice that cut short the three teenagers' retreat into the hallway.

Katrina gasped. "Where's that voice coming from?"

"What did I tell you kiddies about sticking around this place?"

"It's the beachcomber," whispered Aaron. "There's nowhere for us to hide."

8

From the shadowed hallway, the beachcomber blocked the teenagers.

"Oh, so *now* Billy's your *friend*?" challenged the strange man-creature.

"What've you done with him?" demanded Aaron.

"Come with me. I'll introduce you to your true friends. And I can assure you, Billy was not one."

"*Was*? You—You mean he *is* dead?" stammered Katrina. "Did you kill him?" Katrina shouted.

"Come with me if you want to learn the *truth*," said the beachcomber.

The three friends approached him slowly, distrustfully. His grotesque face came into focus in the yellow light of the small kerosene lamp he carried. In his other hand he carried a bulky, black satellite-phone.

"Is that a sat-phone? Dan asked politely. "It's—"

"It's like the one in my dad's car," said Aaron.

"May we please use it, sir?" asked Katrina.

"No," the man replied flatly.

"If we can get his satellite-phone, we can call for help," whispered Dan.

"Not that any of us would know how to use it," muttered Katrina.

"Now keep your distance, or I'll be obliged to extinguish my light," threatened the tattered man. "Follow me. But keep your distance."

Minute after minute, the three teenagers let the stranger lead them away from the cliff ledge and back into the featureless maze. He kept a safe distance ahead of them, warning them now and again not to come too near him. When they reached a four-way intersection in the tunnel, Katrina silently pointed out to Aaron and Dan that this was the spot where the dental floss commenced. The strange man turned down the middle hallway and quickened his pace.

"Hey, wait up!" called Aaron.

"You'll have to hurry to keep up with me," said the man-creature.

Katrina fumbled with her next pack of dental floss and hurried along behind them. As before, Aaron helped her.

"I feel like Hansel and Gretel," Katrina whispered.

"Why are we trusting this guy?" asked Aaron in a hushed tone.

"Can you think of an alternative?" Katrina answered, annoyed.

"Not at the moment," admitted Aaron.

As they walked on, the sound of pitiable moans and blood-drained screams crept over them like lice abandoning a chilling corpse.

"We're almost there," promised the beachcomber gaily. "Soon I'll introduce you to your real friends."

Aaron wanted to call out after the odd man to ask, "And what makes you think they're our real friends?" But the question was hard for Aaron to formulate. In his fear, nothing came out except three words.

"Who are they?"

"Historians," answered the beachcomber enigmatically. Then he disappeared around a bend.

"Historians," remarked Dan. "This could be interesting."

"Screaming historians," muttered Katrina.

She, Aaron, and Dan raced on behind, but the freak had vaporized. His laughter rang in their ears. It seemed to be coming from the other side of a smallish iron door. The door was illuminated by the beachcomber's kerosene lamp left gleaming where he left it on the floor in front of them.

"Nice he left us his lamp."

"We should've tackled him for his sat-phone," Dan muttered.

Katrina reached for the low door before them to give it a push.

"Wait, Katrina!"

"For what, Aaron?" she snorted. "Let's do this so we can get out of here."

"We don't know what's on the other side of that door," he said.

"With that attitude we'll sit *here* forever," said Katrina, pushing the door. It did not budge. "Ah, no mystery." She pulled.

The small door opened. Agonizing howls and screams welled. Dan held the kerosene lamp as he ducked into the small room.

"Empty," he said, confounded.

The screaming was a bit louder inside. Yet the room was empty. And it was just big enough to hold the three of them.

"Look! Over there. Another door," said Katrina pointing at the far end of the small room. "Bizarre, it's so little."

"Do you think we can fit through?" asked Aaron.

"Sure, just crouch down," Dan advised.

Katrina pulled open the next door and Dan held the lantern. They peered through. The screaming was nearer, louder than before, but the next tiny room was also empty.

"Let's keep going, guys," instructed Katrina, undeterred by the screaming.

Ever louder Aaron had to shout over the din, "Ladies first!" He opened the next tiny door for her.

Katrina slithered through on her belly, pushing the lantern ahead of her.

"Guys, it's pretty tight in here," she yelled over the ruckus on the other side of the wall in the room ahead of her—screaming and crying grew much louder now. "One more door ahead, and I think we're in."

Aaron and Dan slid in after Katrina and listened. "It's all happening right in the next room," said Katrina, her voice tremulous.

The ceiling was very low and damp walls squashed the three peers close together. They glanced at each other to see who would open the *next* little door.

"Reminds me of one of those kitchen doggy doors that burglars get in through," said Aaron. "You first, Dan."

Dan cordially withdrew. "No, go ahead."

"I insist," Aaron encouraged.

"That's okay, you go," said Dan, nodding politely.

"You guys are pathetic," snapped Katrina and poked the door with her finger.

It swung open easily and the screaming inside ceased instantly, rendering uncanny silence. An eerie red light illuminated the passageway beyond the erstwhile *doggy* door.

"*Red roooom,*" said Aaron, mock scary.

"Shush, Aaron. It's empty." Katrina went ahead. "There's only a wall on the other side. Not exactly a *room*. And hardly any crawl space. More like an air shaft."

"You're sure?" said Dan. "Push the wall."

Katrina did so. "Solid. Where could the beachcomber have disappeared to?"

She withdrew her hand so the tiny door swung closed, and immediately, the screaming resumed loud and clear as soon as the small door clicked shut.

"What the heck?" Katrina popped the panel open again. The screaming ceased. Again, a red light illuminated the passage. "I don't get it." Katrina's frown was illuminated, again, by red light.

In the silence, she paused a moment.

She shut the door again. The screaming continued, and Katrina noticed that the sliver of red light under the door had switched suddenly to *green*, when she let it shut.

"What's this? Like that *Red Light-Green Light* game we played as kids?" Katrina was baffled.

"You mean the game where *Red light!* means *Freeze!* and *Green light!* means *Run!*?" asked Aaron.

"That's exactly what I mean."

"That so-called historian is toying with us," muttered Dan.

"In a deadly game," Katrina whispered.

9

The executioner saw Katrina's hand pull the door shut.

"*Green light!*" he announced. Then he raised a 12-inch ruler the way an orchestra conductor raises a baton. He snapped it against thirty sets of knuckles in rapid succession, making the fifteen teenagers scream. The brute gave Billy Carlyle a crack with his cat-o'-nine-tails, searing the boy's skin with its nine knotted leather thongs. Billy howled.

"Get to work, boy! You're *my* apprentice now." Beside the executioner stood a row of twenty laconic ghouls. "These are my assistant executioners. But you take your orders from me. Got it, now keep cranking. Tighten the thumbscrews!"

Billy obeyed. His peers screamed in pain.

The executioner kept a black-masked eye on the two lightbulbs mounted on the wall near the narrow corridor where the tiny door let out. The green one glowed like a traffic light.

"When do we get our turn?" a pallid, ghostly adult asked wanly.

"Yessss. When do we gain retribution?" echoed another.

"I can't wait any longer," moaned a third.

The rest of the odd specters grumbled in sullen agreement.

"*Red light!* At ease, boy," the muscle-bound executioner said gruffly to Billy. The green bulb had extinguished and the red one blinked on as the tiny door popped open again. Everyone inside the torture chamber went silent, including Billy, who cowered from the raised threat of cat-o'-nine-tails. The executioner and his band of dispassionate assistants watched in silence as Katrina's pretty hand groped around inside the narrow tunnel behind the tiny door. Katrina's red-lit face stuck through into the narrow passageway. The executioner and his assistants pulled away to hide when they heard Katrina speak. Billy opened his mouth to yell for help, but the chief executioner raised the whip. The boy shut his mouth in silence.

"Aaron, look," exclaimed Katrina. "there's a red lightbulb mounted on the wall down at the end of this weird little air shaft. We can crawl down there." Katrina's words echoed clearly into the torture chamber. The chief executioner smiled.

"We'd better go for help," Dan's muffled words trembled.

"What do you think the beachcomber meant when he said our friends would be historians?" asked Katrina.

"Loud, screaming historians?" countered Aaron.

Hearing this, the hulking executioner tittered and covered his mouth daintily with blood-encrusted fingertips. The whip's nine dangling leather thong tails jiggled as his big body shuddered with muted laughter. His companions smiled weakly.

"None of *you* make a sound," the menacing figure threatened the fifteen trapped teenagers. "Or Billy here tightens the thumbscrews."

Tears slid down Billy's cheeks and he tried to crouch away from the hulking goon, never once questioning the apparent authority of the beastly lout.

"I thought I heard someone talking in there," said Katrina, shutting the door again. The green light came on as the red light extinguished.

"*Green light!*" The executioner opened his mouth, showing mottled gums and few teeth. "*Ooooh*, I love this game."

Billy sneezed.

"No sneezing, boy! For *that, that, that* sign of defiance, you must hurt *them* again," said the big fiend.

Billy continued to cry silently, afraid to defy the orders. Yet, he paused. The executioner cracked his whip, lashing at Billy with the nine leather knots.

"Now!" The executioner cussed under his breath.

Teens' screams commenced with increased terror as Billy followed orders and twisted the thirty thumb screws in rapid succession, all the while the lash was poised to strike him.

"That does it! Someone's messing with us and I'm going to find out which of those senior jocks it is!" declared Katrina.

And she forced herself through the tiny door into the narrow, green-lit cement duct. The green light switched to red and silence fell again.

10

In silence, Katrina waited while Dan and Aaron squeeze through the narrow passage on their stomachs. Inside the red-lit duct, they froze. A sickening realization befell them.

"Oh, crap, there's blood on the floor."

"No way," said Aaron.

"Here, take the lantern and look at this stuff," said Katrina, passing the light to the boys.

She stayed crouched in a small alcove she found to the right of the tiny door. The boys slid in to the left and made their way down the low cramped space ahead of her.

"That's not blood, Katrina, it's probably rust," said Dan, craning his neck to look back at her.

"Oh." Katrina sniffed the thick liquid. She frowned.

"I feel like we're in a wide heating duct," said Dan, blotting sweat off his glasses.

"Good thing none of us is claustrophobic," chuckled Aaron, who, like Dan and Katrina, was having a tough time keeping panic from eroding his judgement in such tight surroundings.

"Dan, I don't think this is rust," said Katrina. "I'm pretty sure it's blood. Smell it."

Katrina pulled a piece of paper from her purse and dipped it in the small gooey red puddle, then passed it to Aaron. He sniffed it and passed the sample forward to Dan.

"Rust has iron in it." Dan held the paper near the kerosene lamp and sniffed. His eyes widened in fear.

By now, Aaron, Katrina, and Dan were already well inside the silent, red passageway. Grunting, the boys maneuvered, leading the way. Behind them, the tiny door through which they'd come clicked shut. And the green light came on. The sound of whiplash and screams ensued.

Dread overtook them. "*Green light*," whispered Aaron.

In the moment that Dan panicked and turned to flee, the head executioner leaned into the low, narrow air shaft and grasped him by the collar. First Dan then Aaron were plucked from the tunnel like whelps.

"*Run Katrinaaaaaa!*" yelled Aaron.

From inside the duct, Katrina watched the boys' feet slide away from her. In the struggle, Aaron kicked over the lantern, spilling kerosene at the mouth of the low opening into the main room. Katrina reached too late to grab the boys' feet. They were gone. Fire flared up between Katrina and her friends. The blaze blocked her view of the interior. The fire spread toward her as the kerosene spill crept down the tunnel. The hot flames and fumes made it difficult to breath.

"Aaron? Dan?" she yelled down the shaft. She had not seen *what* or *who* had dragged the boys out.

"Here, boy, two more. Get cranking on'em!"

Katrina heard the unfamiliar voice of the executioner from outside the cramped tunnel.

"Get help, Katie!" yelled Dan.

"What the heck *is* this?" shouted Katrina.

"It's like a, a, a *nightmare matinee*?" screamed Aaron.

"*Like* it," snarled the executioner, "And if not, we'll do our best to see that it *is*."

The heat inside the air duct was too intense. Katrina had to retreat. On her stomach, she wriggled backward inside the tunnel. It was too cramped to turn around on her hands and knees. After several tries, her toes gripped the handle of the tiny door and she was able to make it open toward her just as an ugly shout came from beyond the flames.

"*Red light!* Excuse me, boys and girls," the executioner barked. "But the game must go on!"

Then a huge hand reached through the kerosene blaze with a wrought-iron meat hook. Blindly, the hook scraped the cement walls, *searching, searching, searching* for Katrina.

Katrina slithered backward out of its reach, forcing her knees at a bad angle through the tiny opening. It reminded her of the time she got stuck in the laundry chute at home when she was nine. Her mother had had to pull her out. But now, Katrina had to figure out how to help herself. The meat hook raked the floor in front of her face. Again, she lunged backward in the tiny space and banged her head. She forced herself through the opening, pulling the small door shut between her face and the terrible hook. *Safe!*

"*Green light!*" Katrina heard the executioner shout. Screaming ensued.

She panted. Safe. Just then, the meat hook caught hold of the cast-iron door handle, and yanked it open.

"*Red light!*" the nefarious behemoth yelled gleefully as the door popped out.

Katrina scuttled backward, away from danger. Behind her toward the egress, Katrina kicked the larger door that led to the next small room. She wriggled backward away from the meat hook that was reaching around inside the small dark room, groping for her, scraping for flesh. She heard its *rasp, rasp, rasp,* and saw a scorched muscular arm silhouetted in red. Katrina was nearly out of reach. She stuffed her hand in her purse looking for mace, but extracted the first item her fingers touched: a safety pin. In one swift movement she unclasped it and sank its point into the muscular hand of the executioner. He cried out in pain.

Relentless, the meat hook swiped at Katrina again, until... Katrina managed to back out through the small door and out of his reach.

"*You*, leave the thumbscrews and find the girl!" roared the executioner, dispatching Billy. "Go out the escape hatch door. Cut her off at the fork."

With that, Katrina learned two useful pieces of information. There was a second entrance to the ghastly torture chamber. And someone or some*thing* would be stalking her. She would be on highest alert.

With insane haste, she withdrew deeper and deeper into the dank cement darkness—through wider and taller doorways, through the small rooms whose walls closed in on her only with darkness—back the way she and the boys had come.

By the time she groped her way back to the first door and clambered through, she realized she had traversed all the way relying on her instincts, without lamplight. She trembled in total darkness and recalled her mother's words to her whenever she was scared as a child, "If I'm not there to do it for you, Katrina, put your left hand on your right shoulder and your right hand on your left shoulder and *squeeeeeeeze*." Katrina hugged herself. Her purse was still slung across her chest. She did not bother to search for a flashlight in it; she knew she hadn't one. Instead, she blindly felt the walls for the dental floss she and Aaron had cemented to the cold cement walls using the remains of her *Fuchsia* lipstick as glue. Gingerly, Katrina's fingertips encountered a thick substance that she recognized as a blob of lipstick. Gently, so as not to loosen the dental floss from the wall, Katrina's fingers followed the thin thread all the way back to the dome room.

There the fire was guttering. Radio music played softly. Katrina quickly broke a piece of furniture and stoked the fire.

"Correy?" Katrina woke her friend.

"It's been so quiet," mumbled Coriander sleepily. "Sherry went crazy, though, I think."

Coriander and Katrina regarded Sherry who sat staring at the burning embers, still flossing her teeth with a frayed strand. Blood oozed from Sherry's ragged gums and coated her lips and chin. There was not much the girls could do to help Sherry at the moment except wrest the floss from her, wipe her mouth, and sweetly encourage her to sleep.

"Sherry, lie down." Katrina helped her recline on a cushion, then looked around for a flashlight.

"Did that guy come back through? The beachcomber?"

Coriander shook her head *no.*

"Are you okay, Correy?" Katrina asked.

"Guess so. What's going on, Katie? I have a bad feeling."

"Glad to know your instincts are working," mumbled Katrina as she pried batteries out of the boom box and slugged them into a dead flashlight. "I thought Aaron told you not to run down the boom box batteries."

"Katrina, what's going on?"

"I need your help, Correy." Katrina darted out to the edge of the ramp hoping they could now use it as a point of egress. The deep trough was still full of seawater. She returned to the fire. "We've got to find a way out to get help. Give me your lipstick," Katrina instructed her friend.

"Why, so you can primp before Aaron sees you?"

"No, in case I run out."

"Like I said," replied Coriander.

"I have one tube of *Fuchsia* left to mark the walls with, and I'm afraid of getting stuck in that madman's maze and not finding my way back *here.*"

"That means you'll ruin all my Dior."

"Yes." Katrina simmered. "That's exactly what that means, Correy."

"Well, I'm not sure—"

"Give it to me, Coriander, or I'll take it from you. This is serious." Katrina threatened her with the nutcracker with which she had cracked open delectable lobster claws a few long hours before.

Reluctantly, Coriander produced one tube of lipstick from her satchel.

"All of'em!" Katrina put her hand out and glanced at the far hallway scanning for the mystery stalker who had been dispatched by the executioner to bring her back. "Hurry up! Dan and Aaron are about to be killed by a meat hook, okay? And quite possibly all our friends. Get it?"

Three more tubes of couture lipstick and two ChapSticks materialized from Coriander's bag.

"Why didn't you say so?" Coriander asked, warming to the fact that their lives were truly in danger. "What else can I do to help?"

"Don't let the fire die, Correy And don't talk to any strangers. Someone's coming after me. And if anyone we know comes back, tell them to stay put. I've used dental floss and lipstick to mark the hallway to the chamber where the screaming's coming from, where I lost Aaron and Dan. When I get back with help, that's how we'll trace our way to them through this nightmarish labyrinth. Got it?"

In search of another exit, Katrina strode to the unexplored hallway closest to the fire, the one with *no* stone slabs framing the doorway.

"If I run into any of our friends, I'll send them back to the main room, Coriander. You'd better be here. And, until you recognize someone, stay hidden, both of you. Hurry! Do it now!"

"What if you don't come back, Katie?"

But Katrina was already gone. Coriander stood to break up more furniture for the fire.

I guess we should hide behind that filthy brown couch, thought Coriander.

"Sherry, we have to— Sherry?" Coriander returned to the fire. But, Sherry was gone. Her footsteps echoed in the domed room. But Coriander could not determine into which hall Sherry had run.

"Sherry?" she yelled.

Alone, Coriander waited for a reply. All she heard was splashing... splashing at the egress through which they had entered the dome room initially. Splashing... and flopping and sloshing. It sounded very, very heavy, and very, very big. When she peered around the curve in the hall to see what it was, she froze.

I've got to find Dan, thought Coriander.

What she saw made her retreat quietly and run on tiptoe across the main domed room, down the blinding blackness of the triple-forked hall. At the intersection, Coriander's hand reached for the dental floss marker.

11

Magenta, *Ruby*, *Pearlized-Grape*, and *Flicker-Red* globs indicated the way to the main cavity. Every few paces, Katrina marked the endless cement walls with lipstick. She saved her last remaining tube of *Fuchsia* for the bitter end.

Katrina tried many iron doors, but they seemed to be bolted shut from within. A harmless water beetle scuttled past her. Hearing its movement, Katrina swallowed hard, hoping it wasn't a rat. And then she wondered why there *weren't* hordes of rats in such a vile place. The beetle was the only living thing she encountered until she felt a door with a steel crossbar.

Brimming with hope, Katrina lifted the crossbar from the iron door. The crossbar hung from a wire that was looped around a screw at the top of the door. As she lifted it from its horizontal position locking the door, she wondered whose hands had last locked it in place. *Maybe the horrid beachcomber? Maybe an important army general? This bunker couldn't have been used for decades.* Cautiously, she opened the door one inch, bracing a leg against it, just in case. Fresh air wafted in. She peered out the narrow gap.

Steps? Nothing but cement steps leading up into the moonlight.

She opened the door another inch. She could see the floor directly in front of her, and a little bit to the left, and then to the right, and...

Boots!

Katrina gasped and slammed the door shut.

Someone was standing there, right on the other side of the door. Katrina had seen the clunky work boots. Panting, she leaned hard against the door and grappled with the crossbar to lodge it in place. Although there was no resistance from the other side of the door, Katrina leaned against the door to reinforce it, just in case the intruder was very strong, or crazy, or both.

Maybe it's not a bad person. Maybe it's someone good, thought Katrina, regaining composure.

"Who are you?" Katrina yelled at the doorjamb. "Can you help me?" She knocked at the door. "Hello?"

No reply. Katrina waited for a long time before she dared to lift the crossbar again. She did so slowly, incrementally, in case the person on the other side of the door was tricking her. With a trembling grip, she opened the door two inches and stared into space... at nothing but the stairwell.

"Where'd you go?" she whispered, tipping her eye down toward the floor where she had previously seen the pair of boots. Then she cried, "Oh my God!"

12

There were the boots. Clunky, worn boots standing right where she had glimpsed them. They were old boots, and... they were empty.

Apparently the boots had been abandoned *who knew how long ago by who knows whom*. Katrina wiped the sweaty, bristling hairs at the nape of her neck. She opened the door all the way, looking right, then left, then right again in case her senses were deceiving her under the stress of the moment. She placed a boot at the threshold to prevent the door from locking her out.

It was a long, pretty moonlit climb to the top of the cement stairwell. But with each step, Katrina felt buds of hope blossom in her heart. *I'm out! I'm free!* Maybe the stairwell would dump her out at the parking lot and she could drive to the nearest town and get help. But she didn't have the keys to Aaron's Mustang. She wondered if she could figure out how to hot-wire a car like she'd seen in the movies. *I could set off Billy Carlyle's car alarm and attract the police. Or, run to the nearest town*—she was a good runner and track star. She wondered if she and her friends would get in trouble for partying in a shuttered U.S. Army bunker. But she figured that under the circumstances they could probably explain their way out of it—if there was anyone left alive to corroborate her story.

Katrina reached the top step. She heard the ocean but could not yet see it from her vantage point. The sky was clean of clouds, spangled with stars. And a delicious butter moon filled her with joy. Beyond the broken outer door, corroded off its hinges, lay a moonlit field adorned with blinking fireflies. Gauzy fog clung to the undergrowth—a magical fairyland welcomed Katrina back to the land of the living. In the distance, the ocean roared. Comforting.

This shouldn't be so difficult after all, she thought greatly relieved. *Pretty sure the main road's in that direction.* Away from the ocean. *Simple.*

Katrina tucked away her near-dead flashlight and ran as fast as she could into what appeared to be high grass and bushes.

"*Ouch!*" She stopped dead in her tracks. Her progress was prevented by thick, wiry military-quality briar bushes. She extracted herself and returned to the cement landing of the bunker. There she considered how to get through the turbo-charged brambles and back to the parking lot. Katrina noticed that the thorns had ripped several shallow gashes in her arms and legs. Blood striped her limbs in the moonlight.

"Oh, you've got to be kidding!" shouted Katrina angrily. Crestfallen, she accepted that she was surrounded by fields of briars on all sides. "*Hello*, can anybody hear *meee*? *Helloooooooo!*"

She stopped shouting when her throat went dry. *I've got to get out of here.* She imagined explaining this to her mother who by now worried out of her mind. *First, I lost your big old lobster boiler, Mom, when the high tide came up because none of us thought to check the tide schedule. Then I blew off your 11:30 p.m. curfew. And I let my friends die 'cause I wasn't resourceful enough to find a way out to get help.*

Going back down into the bunker would be like reentering hell. But the glistening corral of briars was impenetrable. And nothing in her purse would cut them, not even gargantuan toenail clippers she had filched from her father's dop kit after his death.

"What're you, radioactive genetic mutations?" She groaned at the thorns and stowed her clippers back in her bag. Off in the distance, she could hear faint *popping*.

Far away up the coast, Katrina could see fireworks igniting at someone's private beach party. A good time was being had by all, beyond the sand dunes, far beyond the brambles, and lifetimes away from the creepy beachcomber and the *red light green light* meat hook dude with the muscular arm. She longed to be up the beach with Aaron and her friends, roasting marshmallows, dancing, looking up at the stars, and watching the surf crash on the magnificent sea rocks. But right now, there was but one single thing Katrina could do. There was no way out of it. She had to go back down the stairs, back into Hades. Katrina had to make every effort to save her friends. Plus, the mosquitos had found her and were feasting. She had to go back inside the bunker. She debated whether to hide out until dawn with Coriander and Sherry—safety in numbers—and hope, when the tide went out, the water in the trough would recede so that she could get out the same way the group had gotten in. Then she would run for help. She wanted to run now. *But how?* The briar field had to be a solid mile deep!

Mosquitos and movement to Katrina's left drew her attention back to the present. Swatting fiercely at the miniscule predators, she backed slowly into the bunker and watched the bushes for movement. Had the scent of her open wounds attracted more than mosquitos?

In a word, yes.

Into the clearing poked a furry face.

"Oh hello." Katrina knelt down to a small fat ball that trundled into the clearing and up onto the cement slab.

It was a baby bear.

"How sweet *you* are." Katrina's heart was glad.

The friendly creature brushed her leg and waddled past her around the corner of the bunker entrance.

"Hey, where're you going?" Katrina was so happy to have such a friendly, innocent companion; she followed the animal around the corner. "Do you know a pathway out of here?"

Sure enough, the baby bear led Katrina between the outer wall of the bunker and a thinner patch of briars. The bear's dense fur enabled it to plow right into the thick of it. Katrina, however, had to pick her way through with care, but at least there was a small gap leading her toward the ocean. Here she had a better view of the far away fireworks popping up the beach. Maybe the baby bear was leading her to the main path by which she and her friends had arrived earlier.

Katrina had walked only a short distance when she realized that the baby bear had led her to the edge of a sheer cliff. Although the sea breeze wafted mosquitos away from her, this left her with no other option but to return to the bunker. She thanked the bear cub and complimented it, "What a well-trained baby bear..." Katrina cut herself off, thinking, *But this is the wild—Where there's a wild baby bear, there's a—*

Thrashing in the brambles sent Katrina plummeting backward toward the bunker entrance. The faint, thunderous boom of fireworks was upstaged by the growl of a grown bear. Katrina slipped backward, and ran and stumbled down the cement stairwell on jelly-legs. She glanced back and caught the image of the second animal. It was huge. Katrina saw dark fur and fangs and angry mother bear eyes. She ran down and down until her knees nearly gave out. She heard panting directly behind her. A snort from her pursuer landed saliva on her neck and shoulders, and Katrina dove for the last step. *Please don't let anyone have locked the door or I'll be mauled.*

Katrina could not run any faster. She kicked the boot out of her way. She lunged inside. And slammed the door shut, pressing hard against the force of the angry bear. In the darkness, she groped for the crossbar. Her eyes had not yet adjusted while she searched for it. The bear's force continually shoved the door open a bit more. Katrina pushed back hard. The crossbar did not drop into place in time. Sharp claws swiped through the opening at Katrina's shorts, slicing her leather belt in two. Its brass buckle hit the floor with a clunk. And from her sliced shorts' pocket the lame flashlight fell to the floor. Katrina lunged with all her might against the door. The crossbar dropped into place. A frustrated growl was accompanied by sniffing at the base of the door. The bear's hot breath snorted on Katrina's feet through the gap at the base of the door. Then its coarse tongue licked at her toes. Katrina leapt away, tripping over something furry.

Rats! thought Katrina in horror.

13

But it wasn't rats. It was bigger, and much, much worse.

"Get away!" Katrina screamed.

She groped the floor for the flashlight and found that it had rolled across the cement hall opposite the door. Katrina retrieved it and gave it a shake to revive its waning batteries. Just then, she felt another brush of fur against her leg. It was followed by a soft whine right beside her.

In the flashlight beam, Katrina caught sight of the crying baby bear.

"No rats," she sighed with relief. "But what do I do with you, Little Beast?" She spoke softly, "If I open the door to give you back to your mom, she'll kill me. And if I don't, you'll become an orphan." *Hard forks*, thought Katrina.

The little monster barked and moaned, nuzzling Katrina's leg, licking her wounds. Then it ran at the door head-first. It wanted its mother. And the mother bear wanted its baby fiercely.

"Oh, don't do that, Little Furball. You'll hurt yourself." Katrina prepared herself for the fastest sprint of her life. "We'll work this out."

She calculated that she would have about a ten-second head start, just in case—just in case anything went wrong with her plan. *But what can possibly go wrong? If I open the door, the bear cub will flee up the stairs with its mother. Won't it?* Katrina slowly lifted the crossbar on the door and braced herself to dash. Although the mother bear had stopped pushing against the door, she still cried and groaned for her baby.

"Okay, you're gonna' run up the stairs to your mom," Katrina crooned as she lifted the crossbar and pulled away. The bar dangled from its wire and banged the iron door, producing a haunting, hollow echo. "Go!" she gently pushed the baby toward the door and turned to run.

As she bolted at break-neck speed, Katrina shone the dim flashlight on a *Flicker-Red* glob of lipstick down the hall and swiftly passed it, then other markers.

"No!" Katrina realized the round ball of fur was chasing her.

She sprinted faster, as did the angry mother bear.

14

Raced up the hall toward the dome room Katrina shouted, "Correy? Sherry? It's me!" *Oh, God, they're both gone.* Drenched in sweat, Katrina ran on. Breathless she glanced behind her for the bear cub and its angry mother. For the moment, it seemed she'd outrun two bears and lost them two intersections back.

Katrina kept her eye on the hallway with the stone slab doorframe. At least, thought Katrina, had Coriander waited, Katrina could have had a fighting chance. Mother and baby bear had had the briefest reunion, but it appeared that the unforgiving mother was more interested in revenge for messing with her baby. And the bear had relied on scent not lipstick globs and dental floss to follow Katrina back to the central dome. Within moments, there they were, headed up the hall toward the dome room but from the opposite doorway. *They found a back way around to this door*, thought Katrina. *Good to know.*

With two hands, Katrina grabbed a heavy, burning wooden chair leg by its unburned gryphon's foot. Still, it was very hot. She threw it at the threshold of the hall, scattering embers and causing the mother bear to pause and pace back and forth roaring at the firebrands. Katrina had already snatched up a discarded seat cushion and pushed the rest of the small fire and red hot coals across the floor toward that access way. Raging across the pile of coals the mother bear bellowed furiously. With the remaining cushions as her shovels, Katrina came face-to-face with the fire and the bear as she deliberately shoved the burning heap over the threshold at the bear. For a moment, the fire deterred the bear's advances. Katrina wasted no time and ran like the wind down the far hallway on the opposite side of the dome room, back toward the triple fork in the tunnel. *I've gotta get back to Aaron and Dan before the fire dies down and the mother bear comes after me again.* While the bear could not cross into the dome room to follow Katrina, still it could follow its nose and meander through the maze's backchannels in order to track her. *I've bought myself some time*, thought Katrina. But did she really?

Deep in the labyrinth, Katrina reached the familiar cliff where she and Aaron and Dan had followed the beachcomber. There at the cliff's edge, she looked out at the moonlit ocean. She had an idea. She fished in her purse for paper and pen. Katrina scrawled a note begging for help and stuffed it in the empty plastic water bottle that was still in the bottom of her purse. She determined to toss it off the cliff. After all, there was a remote chance someone would find it. There was an even more remote chance that someone would take it seriously. Katrina took the chance and threw it off the cliff. She watched it land in a tidal pool dappled in moonlight.

Help! Please call the coast guard and the police. My friends and I are stuck inside the army bunker thanks to high tide. I am throwing this off the high cliff, in case you're wondering. Please get help. I'm not kidding. This is not a joke. We're in danger. There are some very strange things going on inside here. I think there are some sick adults who have kidnapped almost everyone. And there are two bears. I might be the last survivor. Please help. I'm serious!!!!!! And call my mother at the ER where she works.

Thank you,

Katrina Phillips of Westlake

By buttery moonlight, someone read the note.

"Polite kid. Sounds desperate. Oh well, won't be needing this," muttered the beachcomber as he crumpled the paper note and threw it back into the tidal pool. He kept the plastic bottle, however, for his own purposes.

Far below the cliff, he sat on a boulder to watch the tide going out. The sun had not yet sent its first embers toward the horizon to deliver another gorgeous beach day. The swollen moon sank slowly behind him as gray dawn prickled on the surface of the sprawling ocean at his feet. Katrina spotted him.

"Hey, you!" Katrina's voice cracked in a sob way above the beachcomber's rocky throne. "Can you please help us?" *He's holding my message bottle!*

He ignored her.

To attract the person's attention, Katrina dug a handful of pennies out of the bottom of her purse and chucked them at the rocks below. Abe Lincoln's pretty copper clinking gave her hope.

The beachcomber turned around and leered up. Then he wagged the plastic bottle at her as if he were waving. All hope was lost for her message in a bottle. However, now Katrina knew the tide was ebbing. And she knew for certain that she and she alone was her friends' last chance of surviving that meat hook. Katrina had no idea how much worse it was than *that*.

What she did not know was that the meat hook was tame in comparison to what her friends were currently enduring. What she never imagined was that the meat hook was to the chief executioner what her eyebrow tweezers were to her: merely an instrument for pruning unwanted growth.

15

There must be another way out, thought Katrina. *That beachcomber got out to the water somehow. But how? Then again there are probably a whole bunch of secret passages I'll never discover at the rate I'm going.*

Despondent, she ambled back to the junction of hallways and decided to *take the fork*. She kept her ears sharp for bear snarfles. She'd forgotten about the stalker whom the executioner had dispatched to retrieve her.

From the unexplored hallway Katrina heard someone or something approaching. *Was it the beachcomber already? Had the bear caught up? Coriander and Sherry?* Katrina held a steel nutcracker in one hand. Her pale flashlight brought Billy's bloodied face into sight. His shirt was shredded and black with blood.

Katrina sighed, relieved. "Oh my God, Billy, it's you. You're alive. Are you all right? We thought you were dead."

"Naw, they just gave me a bump on the head."

That's an understatement, thought Katrina.

His voice trembled. "I'm okay. We've got to get out of here."

"And get help," urged Katrina.

"No. Just get out!" Billy cried. "Forget them, they'll never survive."

"Billy, we can't just leave our friends."

"Yeah, yeah, we can." He sounded exhausted, as if he was beyond reasoning.

"I found another entrance," said Katrina. "But it lets out into this impossible field of thorns, and there's a b—"

Before she could warn him, suddenly, Billy kissed Katrina right on the mouth.

Eeeeew! She pulled away.

"Katrina, I've wanted to go with you for the longest time."

This is hardly the time, she thought.

He clasped her shoulders in his strong hands and leaned in again to kiss her. His gesture reminded Katrina of the red-necked turkey vultures that fed at the toxic town dump.

"Stop. No. Look, Billy, we don't have time for this."

She squirmed out from under his arms. But he caught her again, now more insistent. Katrina's mind flashed through a menu of excuses.

None seemed particularly relevant now. She sensed Billy was not dealing with a full deck since he was in shock. Then she remembered the bear.

"Billy, a mother bear is going to be coming down this hall any second now. I swear it."

"Oh sure, Katrina. You're rejecting me.

"Yes. I am. C'mon, let's get out of here. I'm worried about our friends," she said.

"You mean like a rain check?" asked Billy optimistically.

"Sure, Billy." *Better yet, a bounced check*, she thought. "Come on, let's go save our friends." She said it as nicely as she could manage since she feared how Billy might react in his unstable condition, and she was, otherwise, defenseless.

"Okay," said Billy softly, kissing her unresponsive lips.

Katrina was prepared to bite him or employ the steel gadget in her pocket or both if Billy pushed further. Single-mindedly, Billy leaned in again to kiss her. But just then the sound of fast, snuffling breaths approached. It was the mother bear.

16

Katrina shoved Billy away and ran.

"We have to split up or she'll maul both of us!" shouted Katrina, "Run, Billy, run for your life."

Billy saw the loping mother bear and fled screaming down the same hall from which he had come.

"Meet me in the torture chamber, Katrina. I'll go in the back way!" yelled Billy.

Katrina darted away toward the two hallways with which she was familiar: one led to the torture chamber, the other back to the high cliff ledge. She chose the route to the torture chamber. It left her more options, namely iron doors that would close between her and the bear. She did not want the bear to corner her at the edge of the cliff.

Sniffing, the bear paused a moment at the hall intersection, but Katrina did not wait to see which fork the angry mother chose to take.

At last, Katrina reached the little door near the torture chamber and plunged inside. Outside it, the mother bear scratched and growled. Katrina clambered onward until several small doors stood between her and the bear. Katrina lay on her stomach inside the narrow duct. It was then, for the first time, that Katrina beheld the atrocities contained in the green-lit room.

Blood coated the floor. Her friends screamed incessantly. Katrina felt ill and so very tired.

I can't let my friends down, thought Katrina. *Billy must be inside by now. We'll save our friends.* But she didn't see Billy anywhere in the dim green light. She huddled in the tunnel. All options were impossible: go back and dodge the mother bear or—

Katrina screamed as the meat hook came at her.

Unknown to Katrina, Billy chose to abandon his friends. Billy's flashlight batteries were dying as he made his way back toward the main domed room. *Any wild animal would be better than the torture*

chamber, he thought. Billy remembered Katrina mentioned the thorn field. He aimed to find it. Even brambles would beat the torture chamber. *At least I'll be outdoors where I can't get cornered again.* In the domed main room, Billy saw fading embers strewn about the threshold of the far hallway. In the dim light, he approached. He determined he could easily pick his way through the remains of the fire. He reached the halfway point in the room where dawn's pale sky illuminated the open vent high overhead. Behind him, Billy heard snorting.

"So you didn't go after Katrina?" Billy taunted the bear. His boisterous bravado vanished the instant the animal lacerated his torso. The mother bear tore into Billy's stomach. The bloody slice left him in shock. In disbelief, Billy watched his intestines spill out, and drape his knees. One length of gut hit the dirty floor.

"*Aaaagh!*"

The bear continued to maul Billy. Full of adrenalin, he tackled the bear and managed to shove it off briefly. Billy fled, gripping at his entrails that tangled underfoot and tripped him up. Between him and the hall egress stood the bear, so Billy stumbled for the doorway that lead to the deep trough where the teenagers had first entered the bunker. In rash pursuit, the mother bear followed.

Please, let the tide be out, thought Billy, racing around the curve. He stopped short. The water had gone down a few feet. But he would still have to swim *down* a good stretch and then back *up* the *other side.* Even then the door might be lodged shut by seawater or driftwood. *Do bears swim?* wondered Billy, consumed by trauma. No choices remained: the bear was on his heels. Billy dove. His large intestine sailed after him like streamers on a kite. At the water's edge, the mother bear swiped and missed. Suddenly, she withdrew. Instinct told her there was something else in the water. And it was bigger and hungrier than she.

17

Before the executioner could drag Katrina into the chamber, she checked that her lobster-cracker was inside her shorts' pocket. She kept a small steel meat pick between her fingers just in case. Although she slithered backward inside the green-lit duct, the meat hook caught her purse strap hauled Katrina out of the tunnel. The strap of her purse dug into her skin. She dropped the lobster pick in order to grip the hook's point with both hands to keep it away from her skin. Instead, of cutting into her shoulder, it sliced her hands.

Eighteen of her missing pals were obscured in green shadows inside the vast torture chamber. Disbelieving, she watched and listened and threw up as carnage unfolded before her. She did not know which horror to observe first. Nearest was Coriander in a small cage draped with mosquito netting and filled with hairy moths of all sizes. Coriander was huddled in a ball, covering her head and screaming. Katrina gasped, recalling that Coriander was terrified of moths.

At least they're not rats, thought Katrina.

The depraved goon slammed the meat hook into a wooden guillotine block and shoved Katrina deeper into the torture chamber. She skidded to Aaron's side where he lay upon a stretcher rack. But the crack of the executioner's whip kept Katrina from getting close enough to untie Aaron. She jumped away in terror.

"*Green light! Red light! Green light!*" the executioner yelled. "Okay, Aaron, Confess! Confess! Confess! Confess! Confess! Confess!"

"Confess what?" barked Aaron from the rack. His limbs were tied so tightly that his hands had turned as green as the bare bulb on the wall.

The executioner gave the control handle a slight turn and Aaron screamed. Speechless, Katrina's eyes streamed with tears of anger and fear. She could see Aaron too was crying.

"Confess to anything as long as you confess," said the executioner irrationally as he nibbled his nails. "Start with this: denounce your love for *her*."

"Bite me!" yelled Aaron.

The executioner did. Aaron screamed.

"Sign here." The executioner held out a bogus statement written in quill ink on parchment.

"Untie me first!" shouted Aaron.

"Oopsie, can't do that. Just admit to it, kid."

"No way." Aaron spat at the grimacing ghoul. "You'll have to kill me first."

"No!" Katrina screamed. "Why are you doing this? What is this?"

"A spatter party!" screeched Aaron in pain.

"This is not just a party, it's part of your education," retorted the executioner, giggling in a way no decent person should. "Plus, he thought Aaron wasn't tall enough for you, girl, so I'm giving him a *stretch*."

"Just sign it, Aaron, so he'll let you out!" cried Katrina.

"I love Katrina!" hollered Aaron.

The executioner gave the crank another partial turn, sending Aaron's limbs into hellish pain.

"Do it, Aaron, renounce me!" Katrina demanded. "Please."

Through tears of anger and pain, Aaron confessed to the lie.

"Traitor! Heretic! Siding with the enemy! You took orders from the opposition! That earns you another quarter turn!" The evil fiend giggled and applied his weight to the control lever again.

'Stop! Stop, please!" pleaded Katrina.

From the green shadows, the beachcomber joined Katrina and greeted her with a firm, guiding arm around her shoulders. "Ah, lovely Katrina. Now we can really get the party started."

Katrina recoiled, but she could not withstand his surprising strength.

"We've been waiting for you, Katrina, so we could move on to the third *course*. That is to say, the most painful *course*, of *course*. Would you like to start with the thumbscrews like the others and work your way up to the real fun rides?"

"What are *you* doing here?" Katrina demanded.

"You might say I come with the package," the beachcomber explained, passing Katrina back to the executioner.

"Hey, give me back my purse. Stay outta my purse!"

"No," said the beachcomber, riffling through it.

"You're violating my privacy... gimme my bag!"

"That's the whole idea here."

"What?" Katrina was bewildered and frightened.

"We violate your privacy in so many ways in order to confuse you... we make you talk. Now be *quiet*," snarled the heinous fiend.

"You're crazy," stammered Katrina.

"Mad," he corrected her; his lip twisted insipidly.

"What?"

"*Maaaaad*. We all are. We got so *mad* we became *mad*." The beachcomber laughed at the simplicity of his statement. It seemed to please him, but it turned Katrina's stomach. "Enough introductions!" The beachcomber's tone soured.

"Introductions?" Dan screeched hysterically from somewhere in the room Katrina could not yet see. "Katie, did you meet Stalin and Hitler and Attila the Hun and the Spanish Inquisition dudes? Let *me* introduce you."

"Such a name-dropper. Dan!" reprimanded the beachcomber. "But I can top you. You forgot to mention the real barbarians from whom Stalin and Hitler learned. Tiberius, Caligula, Nero, Trajan, Maximinius, Diocletian—and that's all before the Middle Ages. Then there's Ivan the Terrible; Gille de Rais; and James II, Duke of York, a true friend of the thumbscrew! Or didn't you know? But I *have* taken to showing off. Now you must forgive *me* for name-dropping."

The mealy-mouthed beachcomber signaled to the executioner to place Katrina next to a deep stone container. Perplexed, she stood beside the chest-high vessel. The stone was smooth inside, apparently from frequent use.

"Stay there," instructed the executioner.

Like where else am I gonna' go? thought Katrina ducking to avoid his flailing cat-o-nine tails.

"When we're ready, you'll have to crouch down inside the mortar."

"This looks a mammoth version of the porcelain cup we used in chemistry to grind up crystals into a powder," Katrina said as she caressed the glassy interior walls of the container.

"It is," affirmed the executioner with a grin.

"I don't like chem lab," Katrina said nervously.

"I know you don't. And Danny boy hates to cook."

The beachcomber glanced at Dan. It was then Katrina noticed the blaze of burning books below a giant cast-iron frying pan in which Dan stood. Over his head was a metal cage that prevented his escape. An assistant executioner stoked the fire with more books.

"Not *that* one!" shouted Dan. "That's a classic." Dan groaned miserably. His sneakers were starting to melt.

A crash drew Katrina's attention back to the mortar as the executioner violently threw Coriander's silent boom box inside, obliterating it to dust with a four-foot bludgeon made of marble.

"And this's the pestle," explained the beachcomber, indicating the bludgeon.

"Hey, what happened to 'innocent until proven guilty'?" Katrina tried hard not to whine or cry.

"What about it?" said the beachcomber.

"This is America! *Innocent until proven guilty!*" Katrina ducked as the executioner reached out a grubby hand to tousle her messy hair.

"So what? You think you have a right to a *fair* trial? You kids didn't remember *that* earlier this evening when you *judged* me an unsuitable party guest."

"Coriander said it!" yelled a frenzied teenager who was inside an iron maiden that was slowly being shut on him. It was set in sync with the hour hand of a grandfather clock. Instead of nails inside the door of the iron maiden, fifty compass sets with number-two pencils poked at the boy. Inside the box, geometry theorems were painted. The compass and pencil set closest to the hinges was already pressing the boy's arm, but it had not yet broken his skin. He continued to shout, "This is psychological torture! How'd you know I failed geometry? My father will sue you for this!"

"Blood from a stone," said the executioner, shrugging. "And trust me, in a matter of minutes, it'll be more than just psychological torture."

Near Dan's flaming book bon fire, another boy, whom Katrina knew from English class, was wearing a formal suit and tie—all soaking wet. She had only ever seen the boy in hip, grungy clothes. The boy was choking. Katrina noticed the tie was of leather that shrank as it dried. The boy's belt was of the same material, also wet and drying. The suit was made of supple wet kidskin. The only article of clothing Katrina recognized was the boy's baseball cap, which he normally wore backward so you could see its leather adjustment strap. Now the boy wore it with the bill in front. It, too, was wet, but drying. As all the leather dried, it shrank and constricted the boy's head, throat, and stomach. His entire body was compressing within the suit. His attending executioner smiled at Katrina and spoke softly.

"Old Apache method." The words echoed quietly.

The boy gagged. His eyes began to bulge from the unbearable pressure of the shrinking leather.

A swish of dirt in her face jarred Katrina's gaping stare from the boy in the wet leather suit. She looked up just as another spray of dirt fell on her.

"What the—?" She shook beach sand from her hair and face and stepped away from the blazing bonfire.

Dangling from the ceiling was a cage with a wooden floor. In it a junior girl swept sand that poured steadily into the cage from the ceiling above her head. When the girl paused from sweeping to catch her breath, the sand heaped up quickly on the floor of hear cage. That weighed it down, and the pulley from which it was suspended shifted. The weight of unswept sand brought her cage floor closer and closer to the flame of the bonfire. The floor of the wooden cage was already charred black. The more the girl swept, the lighter the cage became. It floated back up on the pulley and the sand temporarily caused the flames to retreat.

The junior girl's death attendant nodded politely at Katrina and spoke softly, "Keeping your room clean is *cool*... literally."

Katrina recalled visiting the girl's home and what a mess the girl's bedroom had always been.

"*Wahhhhh!*" shrieked Katrina. The chief executioner grabbed Katrina by her hair and lifted her into the mortar. She kicked him repeatedly as she dangled in mid-air. He thanked her for her cooperation with a lascivious, drooling grin.

"Now's not the time for regrets," sang the beachcomber. "Nonetheless, none of you challenged Coriander's impoverished thinking. This evening, not one of you invited me to stay and party with you. Herd mentality. So, I fault you all. You hurt my feelings," he said, tossing Katrina's purse into a corner next to Coriander's moth nest.

A ghostly chanting murmur floated up from the dark corners of the room. "You hurt his feelings with your herd mentality." It repeated over and over, and rang like an off-key chorus warming up.

For the first time, Katrina got a good look at the rest of the peculiar, passive adults who had stood quietly in the shadows. A different adult stood behind each of the torture devices, guarding, stoking, tightening... participating in the torment of Katrina's friends. The chant persisted then faded when Aaron spoke up.

"I challenged Coriander's thinking all the time," said Aaron. No one acknowledged him.

"What's wrong with you people? You're like out of another time zone," Katrina said, struggling to climb back out of the mortar. "You're like out of a black-and-white photo!"

"Sepia," corrected the beachcomber, "A daguerreotype." He laughed mildly as he gestured to the executioner to strike Katrina with the pestle.

Katrina held her breath and awaited death as the white marble bludgeon descended toward her skull with the full weight of the executioner behind it. Katrina never dreamed she would die as part of an overgrown chemistry lab set.

18

Inches from Katrina's skull, the pestle stopped.

"Just funnin' ya'," laughed the beachcomber. "We've got time yet before we *really* start with you, Katrina. I thought we'd begin with one of your buddies so you could appreciate the full bouquet of our torture methods. So you'll learn them *really* well."

"Consider yourself lucky, Katrina. You get to learn all the old tricks of the trade from real experienced folks," the chief executioner gloated.

"You're not going to *cr-cru-crush* me?" Katrina cried, still recovering from the pestle fright.

"Not *yet*. We've got a special something reserved for you," the beachcomber said, indicating a curved metal device that rested on a big oak table. "You'll be our best apprentice yet since Billy."

"Is that an old-fashioned Habitrail?" asked Katrina sniffling. She couldn't make heads or tails of the ugly metal device that resembled a wire basket.

"Actually, it's a *hat*." The beachcomber lifted the wrought-iron cage and opened a small door on its top. A smiling assistant handed him a six-and-a-half-inch-thick hunk of cheese. He lodged it inside the cage over a six-inch hole in its floor.

"This block of cheese rests against your skull," he explained. "It attaches like so." He placed the heavy curved cage on Katrina's head while the assistant executioner held her still.

"I don't want cheese in my hair," whimpered Katrina.

"Oh, the cheese won't be there long, don't worry." The beachcomber buckled straps under Katrina's chin and arms and behind her back, securing them with a padlock. "The couture cops will love *le chapeau des fauves* Katrina!" announced the cretin.

Katrina understood only when a second cage was hoisted up alongside the metal *hat*. *Le chapeau des fauves* was a *hat of wild beasts*. A ghostly attendant opened released the door of the second cage and Katrina felt scampering as two hungry beasts lunged headlong for the cheese. The attendant secured the little door.

"*Rats!*" Katrina squirmed away but the executioner detained her.

"Sit still, or *else*," the beachcomber cautioned.

What else could be worse?

"Sit still, Katrina!" yelled Dan. "The more you squirm, the faster they eat."

"Fast or slow, rats eat the cheese to reach the SmartFood."

"SmartFood?"

"Your brain!" blurted the chief executioner.

In the cage attached to Katrina's head, the beachcomber goaded the two ravenous rats by blocking them from the cheese. Repeatedly he shoved them off the cheese with a stick, driving them wild with frustration. The only way out for the rats was through the cheese and, then, through Katrina's skull. Through the thick cheese barrier she felt their full rat weight. She hoped they hadn't any fleas, although, granted, vermin were the least of her worries in that moment.

"Ah! Rat nearly bit me. Must be hungry," laughed the beachcomber pulling his stick away.

Katrina felt the rats' frenetic movement, and heard rat mouths gnashing at the thick block of cheese.

"Why are you doing this?" Katrina cried.

"Indolence, and sloth," replied the beachcomber.

"I'll have you know, I got an *A* on my *1984* book report! This rat cage is not your own invention."

"This method has a centuries-old proven track record for success. Why quit while we're *a head*?"

The beachcomber stroked a gray guillotine blade beneath which a senior girl was manacled and kneeling. Each time she struggled to stand, one of the ghostly attendants kicked her legs out. The senior girl cried and cried as she was forced to slice onion after onion, thin as paper, on the guillotine blade. A sizable heap had accumulated on the block beside her.

Katrina looked around, studying the ambient horror of the dungeon. Sherry and Bethany Price shared a five-foot-high white globe to which they were bound with packing tape. They lay with their backs arched over the globe and their feet hung just above the floor. Now and then their attending assistant executioner would give the orb a spin, and the girls screamed for fear it would roll the wrong way and flatten them in one revolution. Upon closer scrutiny, Katrina realized the globe was painted like a giant volleyball. Both Sherry and Bethany despised the game and had played hooky on gym days when volleyball was scheduled.

One exhausted junior girl raced on what appeared to be an old rusted Stair-Master set at a terribly rapid pace. Another girl struggled on a level treadmill. A sophomore boy, his hands soiled in indigo ink, frantically wrote page after page under the watchful eye of a whip-wielding assistant executioner who wore an 18th Century teacher's frock. The mock teacher threatened to whip him for poor penmanship.

"*Write on!*" shouted the degenerate schoolmarm.

The boy cringed and kept on writing. Each of the torture devices was attended by a ghostly assistant executioner, male or female of any race or size or skin color. They all appeared to be insane, and they were all dressed in costumes from different periods in history.

Katrina noticed one was a pretty woman in a 17th Century gown. The pale woman piled dozens of dead green bullfrogs on top of a wide board. Katrina heard moaning coming from under the increasing weight. It was her biology lab partner, Jayne La Roche, beneath the heap. Katrina knew Jayne had despised dissecting her frog in biology class. The pale torturer glanced at Jayne and then at Katrina and spoke.

"*Peine forte et dure,*" whispered the ghostly 17th Century woman.

"How beautifully you speak French," said Katrina, her voice shaking. "That is French, right?" Katrina noticed a tiny red flower tattooed to the woman's chest just below her clavicle.

"Yes," whispered the elegant woman, "*eet eez Fraaanch. Zat* means she is pressed to *dess*."

"*Dess?*" queried Katrina, wiping away a tear as the rats skirmished over the cheese attached to her head.

"Death!" clarified the beachcomber.

"'*Peine forte et dure*' is pressing one to death in the manner you see before you. Frogs optional."

"Stones do nicely, as well."

Beside Jayne was a senior boy who had missed graduating by four credits. Like Jayne, he lay beneath boards. But instead of gargantuan bullfrogs, an assistant executioner heaped books on him—literature and history from throughout the ages.

The senior boy was screaming, "Okay, okay, I'll read'em! Just let me go!"

"Too late," said his executioner.

"You people look like stage actors. This is all a joke, right?" asked Katrina meekly, fighting the lump in her throat. "Billy Carlyle hired you to stage this, right?"

Dan howled again from the frying pan, "Shakespearean actors, Caesar to Stalin. Hey, I'm talking to you, Goon Man!"

"Shut up, Dan, you'll just tick them off," Aaron advised.

The executioner's nine-thong whip threatened to silence the boys. All the assistant executioners stood at attention, listening.

"Good thing you're in that cage, Dan, or he'd hit you with the whip," said Aaron, craning his neck.

Dan chuckled at the irony of Aaron's comment: One form of torment had protected him from another. First Dan, then Aaron broke out in guffaws. Their laughter was contagious. Soon Katrina was laughing through tears. Then, one by one, the other students joined in. Even the beachcomber hissed out an irrepressible giggle. Oddly, the aberrant executioners all stood quietly at attention, like zombies awaiting orders from the beachcomber. Katrina wondered why they were so docile. She thought maybe this was a cult and they were all drugged. They just stood there like submissive sheep. *Talk about herd mentality*, thought Katrina.

"Where's Billy?" Katrina whispered to a nearby classmate. "Did he come back?" The sniffing and chatter of the two rats in the cage on her head made it very difficult to maintain composure.

"He went to fetch *you*, Katrina," said Bethany dully.

"He went for *help*," Sherry defended, much to Katrina's surprise.

"He can't really swim," said Aaron. "We're hosed."

The thrum of the moths in Coriander's cage made it hard for her to hear the conversation.

"Don't be so negative, Aaron," snapped Dan crouching inside the cage that covered the giant frying pan. His knees ached from bending at an awkward angle as his cage roof was too low for him to stand up straight.

Aaron laughed pitifully. "Look at us. I'm a living rubber band, your sneakers are melting under your feet in that frying pan, and you say I shouldn't be negative? Reality check, *much*?"

"Point taken, dude," murmured Dan, hopping awkwardly from one foot to the other. The bars of the cage were heating up too, so much so that Dan could barely hang on to them for support.

Katrina's angst grew. Sweat dribbled down her face. Slowly, she wiped it away as she glanced around for an opportunity, *any* opportunity. But the executioner was ever watchful.

"Should we know you people?" Katrina asked.

The beachcomber smiled. "You *should* know us. But I don't imagine you *do,* since not one of you reads anything of value."

"I do," yelled Dan.

"Silence, impudent urchin. You know *nothing*," snarled the beachcomber.

Someone knocked from inside a black box beside Katrina's mortar.

"Let me out!" a boy shouted from within.

The beachcomber read Katrina's face. "That's what is known as a sensory deprivation box. No light, no sound. No air, *gradually*. It's a fairly modern invention, really. Right up there with the electrode bath, which I can't wait to demonstrate to each of you personally."

"You're sick," murmured Katrina.

"What's that you say? Did I hear you admit you *are* a heretic? A betrayer of the state? A social pariah?" said the cretin, his shaggy head bobbing at her. "Frankly, Katrina, I don't think you're listening to me, I don't think you give a damn."

What a raving jerk, thought Katrina.

"*You are heretics!*" The accusation by the assistant executioners grew like a rabble-rousing chorus. Over and over they sang it until it became dizzyingly annoying, round after round, again and again. "*You are heretics!*"

"Okay, you get the part. Let's end this audition," snapped the beachcomber, slapping the chief executioner's back. "It's time to move on to the serious torture."

"How's *this* not *serious*?" asked Aaron.

"What the heck's a *heretic*?" snorted Katrina in desperation. "And by the way, I was supposed to be home by eleven-thirty p.m. My mother's going to have my head on a silver platter if I'm late. So if you wouldn't mind..." Katrina lifted one leg over the lip of the mortar to climb out. A pitchfork held by a minor assistant executioner discouraged her.

"Silver platter! Great idea. Funny I didn't think of that one. Have we a silver platter in storage?" asked the beachcomber. The executioner shrugged. "No bother, Katrina, but still we must train you, and to do so we must torture you so that you experience maximum pain."

"So that your soul embraces death," the chief executioner snarled I her face, flexing the muscles of his bare chest at her.

"It's purely educational," assured the beachcomber.

"Trust him," said the executioner.

"Trust?" she coughed.

The scars across the executioner's chest frightened Katrina. She felt helpless and fearful. And *that* made her angry. And her anger made her feel a stirring of traction toward bravery, renewed hope that she could actually help herself and her friends. Fiercely, one of Katrina's eyebrows shot up.

"*Uh-oh*, she's giving you the hairy eyebrow," said the beachcomber, laughing.

"I just pluck them that way. Don't take it personally," Katrina answered, fuming.

The boastful chief executioner thrust out his chest at her again and barked, "Perhaps she's too much of a coward?"

And that was all the challenge it took to rekindle Katrina's bravery.

"Don't you know you're in New England? We have blue laws here that say you can't go parading around without a shirt, mister," she berated the executioner.

The executioner seemed mortally ashamed and stumped. The other adults looked on like pathetic dullards. He attempted an apology but gurgled. *A grotesque sound,* thought Katrina. To her surprise, he looked around for his shirt and put it on. It was too tight. To her further astonishment, the executioner then clasped his giant hands obediently in front of him as if he were awaiting her next order.

"Good," snapped Katrina. "Now we can have a conversation." To her amazement no one, not even the beachcomber, countered her instructions. She took a chance and kept fast-talking. *It was strange,* thought Katrina: The more Katrina chattered in a bossy tone, the more passive the adult assistants became.

"You know, I don't think Amnesty International would be real hip on you guys," Katrina continued in the same self-important pitch. *Maybe if I act like I own the place,* she thought frantically.

"Whose king is that? Of what people, Katrina?" asked one of the assistant executioners. "*Amnesty...?*"

"Sounds impressive," said another assistant executioner, enthralled and attentive.

Why're they so dumb? How can anyone born in the 20th Century not know what Amnesty International is? Katrina glared at the executioners before she spoke. *Gosh, even the beachcomber's authority is in remission,* she thought.

Even the two rats on Katrina's head seemed to be listening for her next utterance; they were suddenly so still. All she could think was that they were having a *rat nap*. The thought of a *rat nap* instead of a *catnap* made her laugh aloud.

Consequently, the group of executioners believed Katrina was laughing at them, at their ignorance. They became even more attentive and eager to please her than before.

"Of *all* people!" Katrina finally answered their question. "It's, uh, he's, I mean, *she is* the queen of *all* people... everywhere!" And then while Katrina wondered what the heck she should say next, she mumbled, "Sort of."

"Could your queen help us? I represent *los desaparecidos,*" said an ill-fed assistant executioner.

"You what?" said Katrina. "Who?"

Just then the rat nap was over and the vermin squealed and skirmished again against the cheese... the cheese that pressed against Katrina's skull. A nauseating rat-scream penetrated Katrina's ears. The beachcomber laughed sickeningly. The executioner tittered and stared at Katrina's head. Then he adjusted his shirt, which was binding uncomfortably above his belly button.

Katrina felt warm liquid gush down her scalp, into her ear, and down her jaw and throat.

"*Wh-Wha-What* is it?" she pleaded and wiped her face.

Smelly rat blood the color of decayed berries glistened on the back of her hand in the green light.

"One down," announced the beachcomber.

"Looks like Mighty Rat was wicked hungry," said an attendant softly.

"*Ooooh*, he's eating his buddy. Watch!"

"Less competition for that cheese." The beachcomber shrugged. "You're next, Katrina."

But it buys me some time, Katrina thought as she cried quietly, imagining rat cannibalism. She remembered George Orwell's *1984*. She'd aced the book report, and had been both horrified and fascinated by the use of hungry rats for torture. In the book, the starved rodents eat straight through a man's head. She feared the remaining rat would chew through hers and out her neck. And with that, Katrina threw up violently. The remaining rat was tossed violently against the ceiling of its cage.

As Katrina heaved and retched, the leather straps that held her rat cage in place loosened a little. The heavy cage slipped. The ferocious rat shriek angrily as it was thrown again and again against its cage. Dead-rat blood spattered the floor. But Katrina gained information. She knew now the cage could slip. Maybe slip off. She had hope. She'd escape the contraption if she could wriggle and... Soon the rat would finish eating its dead mate. And then it would gnaw through the cheese barrier to her skull. Katrina acted fast.

19

From her shorts pocket, Katrina removed a steel nutcracker.

"Raise your hand," she demanded. To her surprise the executioner continued to follow her orders. She pinched the executioner's finger, and did not let go.

"Don't hurt me. I beg you not to hurt me. I've spent eternity in pain."

I wasn't even squeezing that hard, thought Katrina.

The others just stood by placidly.

"You promise not to pick on people?" Katrina demanded in the same authoritative tone that cowed him before. "My queen hates people who pick on others."

"*Yeees*," he wailed.

"Promise!" she yelled and squeezed tighter.

"I promise not to hurt anyone ever again."

As long as the bargaining was good, Katrina persisted. "And promise to free all my friends," she barked and squeezed.

"I can't do that," whimpered the executioner.

"Why not?"

"That they must do so themselves."

"What? What d'you mean? Free *themselves*?"

"I can't ask them to do it. They have to make the choice to do it."

"Shhh," hissed the beachcomber. "Don't give away all out secrets, or there's no lesson to be learned."

"I don't get it. Explain!" Katrina faked a bossy shout as best she could. But her fear was winning even as the rat's activities on her head resumed.

"We're vengeful ghosts," stated the beachcomber. "Now, that's all I can tell you."

"You're what?" Katrina whined. She wanted to go home. "Explain, I command you to explain!"

"We must resume our torture because we haunt these torture devices upon which we ourselves were brutally slain," the beachcomber clarified. "Your government collected these and left us here for eternity. We're part of a collection. A military cache."

"We were pillaged," a pale ghost spoke softly.

"Spoils of war," added Dan's attendant.

"We're from all over z'world," added the French lady.

"We need you to help us free our souls. That's why he lured you here."

"We represent periods from throughout the history of human torture."

Explains the bizarre outfits, noted Katrina, *Not exactly beach attire.*

"Oh, and you all just happen to speak English," snorted Dan.

"We're ghosts, so we translate our energy into your mind. Your mind interprets our vibration. And because you speak English, our vibration comes through in your minds in English. Because we're ghosts we can do that."

"But you can't free your own tormented souls?" asked Dan.

"We are cursed to haunt these torture devices throughout time, until someone with an open mind frees us."

"So, pick on us, 'cause we're open-minded?" asked Katrina.

"Precisely," said the beachcomber.

"May we go now?" asked Aaron. "I don't see how we can help you."

"Not so fast," hissed the beachcomber. A new wave of insanity seemed to overtake him. "We've come so far. We must finish the mission."

Katrina's rat seemed to be overstuffed on its mate now and resting, so she breathed deeply, preparing for another round of insane battle. But she was fresh out of ideas, and just wanted to be home in her own lavender canopy bed between her crisp new purple and yellow striped sheets.

"We need you to help us," the chief executioner explained.

"But how can we possibly help you?" Tired of their charade, Katrina grew petulant.

"By listening," whispered a ghost lady.

"*Yesssss*, by listening," a chorus of specter voices sang. "*Listening*."

"I promised you that you would meet your true friends. And you have. Now let them speak," the beachcomber said, surprisingly calm again. "Let them tell you their story."

"How about you let us out of these monkey suits first?" suggested Dan as his sneakers smoldered.

"Not without a history lesson," said the beachcomber with guileless smile.

"Okay, hurry up," snapped Katrina, "Queen Amnesty International is waiting for our safe return... and, uh, and she will help you if you, uh, *chop-chop*." Katrina snapped her fingers.

The ghosts thanked Katrina, then talked over one another to share their harrowing experiences.

"Torture is what happens when humans have no check-and-balance system," began one of the ghosts.

"It'll make you hurl," said the *desaparecido*.

"My limbs were torn asunder," said a youthful male ghost.

"I was ripped apart by a team of horses," said a woman.

"I was tarred and feathered and burned."

"Me? Disemboweled alive."

"Decapitated," added another.

"Dismembered, then starved," said a man toward the back of the group. "But I bled to death."

"Lynched and hanged from a tree in the center of my village." offered the next.

"Flogged," said another flatly.

"Clubbed."

"Bludgeoned!" yelled a chorus of three.

"Beaten!"

"Burned alive at the stake! But I wasn't a witch."

"Bled to death."

"I was sawed in two *ha-ha-halves*," stammered another.

"I was branded and flayed."

"Hah! I was flayed *and* fried alive like Dan!"

"Well, I was burned at the stake after being drawn and quartered."

"Yeah, well, I was—"

"Is this a bloody *competition*?" hollered Katrina, more horrified by their accounts than by the huge rat on her head that had taken to gnawing on the cheese barrier between it and her head.

"And *you*? How'd you get killed?" Katrina asked the beachcomber.

"All of the above," replied the lunatic ringleader.

"If you guys were tortured, you must have deserved it," said Aaron.

"Shut up, Aaron," whispered Dan. "Humor them, we want to get out of here!"

"Didn't you commit crimes?" Katrina asked.

"*Noooo.*" The ghostly chorus billowed up again.

"Well, then, didn't any of you deserve what you got?"

"I did." The chief executioner raised the stump of his wrist. Katrina had not noticed before that he had only one hand. The rat thrashed on Katrina's head as it struggled to pull the chunk of cheese off the rungs of the iron cage. The executioner continued, "I was a thief. My hand was cut off for stealing. But the bread I pinched was for my hungry family. It was during a famine that our opposition had created to break our spirits so that they could steal our riches and enslave our people."

"Wow, that totally sucks," said Aaron. "So, there are no real criminals among you?"

The beachcomber stepped forward, tapping the heavy black satellite-phone against his palm. "It all depends on who is denying your freedoms."

"And your intellectual explorations," echoed another ghost.

I guess none of them would admit it if they were really bad people, thought Katrina, shifting uneasily in the mortar, praying the cheese would sate the voracious rat.

"You guys should have moved to America. It's free here," said Aaron.

"The witch trials of Salem speak for themselves," said a ghost. "Not to mention what was inflicted on indigenous and enslaved folks."

"The world over, people choose good or evil," said another ghost. "Like you choose a fork in the road."

"Each person is faced with many choices."

"*Choice* is what made each of us what we are in life."

"And I wanna kill everyone who made the *wrong choice*!" snarled the beachcomber, slipping into another fit of dementia.

"But anyone you'd wanna' get even with is dead by now," said Katrina. "So what's the point perpetuating the torture?"

"It's complicated," said the executioner.

"Human nature is not dead," shrieked the agitated beachcomber.

"It is human nature's fault. We must get even with human nature," cried the ghosts.

"But you're perpetuating the problem." Dan urged. His feet were frying.

"We want revenge." whimpered a pathetic ghost.

Katrina was frustrated with the irrational ghosts. "You've got power, so why not do good with it? You'd feel a whole lot better about yourselves."

"Because someone's got to pay. Someone's got to pay for what we suffered!"

"But *you* already paid. Now you're *free,*" Katrina whispered softly.

"You can't convince me you really enjoy torturing us," said Dan. His bluff failed and the beachcomber took it as an invitation to stoke the fire under Dan's frying pan with an armful of encyclopedias. "Okay, I believe you!"

Louder this time, Katrina spoke again, "Now you're free. You're *free!* Go be free!"

"We are?" said the head executioner.

"Well, yes," said Katrina. "You already *paid*, you already suffered. You've spilled your guts to us, now go!"

"You said we just had to listen to what happened to you," Aaron reminded.

The ghosts appeared surprised by the concept and whispered among themselves. Adjourning, the chief executioner pushed a pretty ghost forward in his stead. "You do it," he said quietly. "I'm too shy. You tell them."

The pretty ghost spoke softly, "We hereby agree. We are free to leave you alone... as long as you pick up with the torture where we left off."

"Carry the torch!" hissed the beachcomber.

"Only you can keep up our tradition," said the chief executioner with a sickly grin.

With that, the ghosts formed a line at the wall near the door and prepared to depart. The smell of fried rubber filled the air as Dan's sneakers smoldered.

"Wait, set us free, please!" cried Bethany as the ghosts began to fade into the wall. On hearing her words they got stuck, and could proceed no further.

"What's happening?" asked Katrina desperate to get the rat cage off her head.

The iron maiden clicked shut by one notch. The boy inside cried out as the Number-2 pencil of a compass set jabbed deeper into his skin.

"Let me out! I'll die of lead poisoning!" he shouted.

20

The insane beachcomber laughed flatly. “No.”
“No?” shrieked Katrina. “Hey, we helped you.”
“You can’t just leave us like this!” cried Dan.
“Free yourselves,” snorted the executioner. “Face your own truth.”
“Free yourselves by killing each other. Go on, do it, hurt each other,” shouted the beachcomber.
“But—” stammered Katrina confused and desperate.
“Go on! Torture each other! Turn the crank! Stoke the fires! Crack the whips! *Kill! Kill!* That’s the only way out!” hissed the demented ghosts stuck in the wall.
“Death is the only way out!” the chief executioner echoed.
“That’s how we escaped the pain. By dying,” added the beachcomber.
“But who allowed such horrible things to happen to you?’ Katrina screamed.
“You allow it,” shouted a lunatic ghost. “You!”
“No, we’re the victims here!” yelled Katrina.
“Then you’re the culprit and the victim,” an apparition replied.
“Were all adults as crazy as you people?”
“No. We’re the good guys. We were the unsung heroes that you read about in books, the so-called heretics. We were normal people trying to lead honest lives true to our beliefs for principled peace.”
“Got it. We heard your stories! Now, help us!” shouted Katrina.
“Untie me!” seconded Aaron.
“Do you *choose* to be free?” asked the beachcomber, sounding rational again.
“Of course!” many of the students shouted—those who hadn’t already passed out from fear and pain.
“Then you are... *almost* free. You must simply torture one another to death!”
“Carry the torch. Keep up the human tradition! And kill!” The beachcomber’s colleagues echoed his suggestions.
“It’s not that easy,” said Katrina.
“It is that easy to make the right choice,” said the haggard ghosts.
“Go on, make the choice to kill each other. You’ll just adore dying. As we did. Death is such a relief.”

"But we don't want to," cried Katrina.

"Then I guess you'll just have to sit here for all eternity, as we did."

A full ten seconds of perfect silence passed—except for the sizzling of Dan's rubber sneakers, and the ticking of the grandfather clock, and the flutter of furry moths, and the sweeping, and the choking, and the groaning, and the rat chewing cheese between it and Katrina's head.

"Excuse me, Mr. Beachcomber, this is not acceptable. Is there something you haven't told us?"

"Only that it could take several hundred or a thousand years for you to make your decision. I suppose we could stand by awhile longer as your advisors," said the beachcomber.

"No unlike you, we all have lives to lead," said Katrina.

"And a millennium just doesn't fit in our schedule," added Dan.

"Plus, you got us into this!"

"Yeah, it's your fault!" cried Bethany.

"Don't be argumentative, you two," Katrina snapped.

"And someone *before us* got *us* into it, so *boo-hoo*," sniveled the beachcomber. "Such is cycle of torture. Reap, sow, reap sow..."

"We don't have time for *blame!*" shouted Katrina. She could feel the vibration of the rat nibbling through the cheese. The dried rat blood prickled her neck.

"We've told you what you must do," said the executioner.

"Embrace death as we did," urged another executioner.

"No!" shouted Katrina. Her eyebrow flared. "No! We will not die the pathetic way you did. I won't allow it!"

"Very well," said the beachcomber.

"And thank you," added the lady ghost.

Why's she thanking me? Katrina wondered.

"At last, we're free to go." An echo of ghostly thanks filled the torture chamber as the ghosts suddenly glowed brighter, then dissipated into the wall.

Their iridescent shimmer blended with a supernatural light that shone right through the cement walls of the army bunker. The ghosts disappeared without a trace—all but the beachcomber whose disappearance was taking longer than the others.

The ferocious rat's foot stepped heavily through the gnawed cheese and scraped at Katrina's head. Then, she felt the beast snouting at her hair.

"Please save us. Oh, God. Help!" the teenagers cried out.

"You wanna' to talk to God?" sneered the beachcomber, throwing the sat-phone over his shoulder. "Won't be needin' this where I'm goin'."

Katrina leapt from the mortar and caught the phone just before it could shatter on the cement floor. The beachcomber disappeared in a green sprinkling of starry light.

Dan yelled gleefully, “Get me out, Katrina! You broke the cycle!” Dan struggled to escape the frying pan and unlatch his cage.

Katrina burst into tears as the rat truffled through her hair seeking a pulse point.

“*You* freed us by saying *no*.”

“Aagh!” Katrina yelped as the rat nipped her skull.

She tipped her head, harshly bashing the rat cage against the stone mortar. The weight of the cage pulled her down. She nearly dropped the sat-phone, which had started ringing. The single-minded rat was fearless and scrabbled again for her hair. But Katrina finally wriggled loose and threw off the cage as she detangled herself from all its binding leather belts.

“Nice Houdini move, Katrina,” remarked Aaron. “Me next!”

The cage clanged to the cement floor. For a moment, the rat was disoriented. It sat, glaring angrily at Katrina.

“Sorry!” shouted Katrina and stamped her foot. “Get away, rat! I don’t want to have to hurt you!”

Boldly the rat stood fast, chittering. The sat-phone kept ringing and ringing. Katrina stamped her foot again at the atrocious little beast, establishing her boundaries more firmly.

“Katie, could you please?’

With one hand, Katrina was already unlocking the grill lid of Dan’s frying pan, while holding the ringing sat-phone with the other.

“Nothing magic about freeing ourselves,” said Katrina as she raced about the room helping her peers. “We should never have let them bully us.”

She smashed the glass on the face of the grandfather clock and held the hands in place, stopping time. “Dan, help him out of the iron maiden. And throw Correy some mothballs.”

“Aren’t you going to answer that?” yelled Dan, helping the boy out of the iron maiden.

“Who on earth would be calling *this* phone?” said Katrina, silencing it at last. “Hello?” Everyone was still. Listening. “Who *is* this?” shrieked Katrina, and her eyes bugged in disbelief at what she was hearing. “No, not today thanks, *perv*! And, by the way, I’ve got Caller ID, so you can expect the police to arrive at your house in about ten minutes. Better make a run for it, creep!" Katrina shut the sat-phone off and laughed. "Now, *that* felt great!"

"Who was that, Katrina?" Aaron asked.

"Crank caller. I've always wanted to call their bluff."

"Put the phone down and kiss me," said Aaron.

Katrina kept dialing.

21

Still sore, the teenagers wandered out of the torture chamber back to the main domed room led by Katrina who followed her thread of dental floss. Coriander was still unconscious, so Dan and Aaron carried her.

"Where the heck is stalker-Billy? What else is there to be afraid of?" Katrina wondered aloud.

"Besides psychos and natural disasters?" posited Aaron.

"Moths," suggested Dan, quietly plucking a lone dead moth from Coriander's ultralong hair. "And history repeating itself."

"*Lions, tigers, and—*" Katrina halted.

Sunlight through the roof vent of the domed room illuminated the mother bear who lounged with her cub in the puddle in the center of the main room. She fled when she saw the gang of nineteen students.

"Safety in numbers," observed Dan.

"The Coast Guard dispatcher said they're on their way with a map of this military compound. They thought we drowned. Said they'd been looking for us all night," Katrina informed her friends.

"Couldn't have been looking too hard. Wouldn't they have heard us screaming?" Aaron scoffed.

"Army bunkers' walls are too thick," said Dan. "Anyway, tide's low by now."

"Oh no," groaned Aaron, leading the way out to the landing that lead down to the flooded trough. "Drain's clogged with seaweed." Aaron offered to swim down the dark cavern to unclog it. No one made a counteroffer, so he plunged in.

Several times Aaron resurfaced to get his breath.

"Sorry, guys, that rack might've made me taller, but it did a number on my strength. My muscles ache."

"I'll help you, Aaron," offered Katrina.

"No, Katie. Wait until the water goes down. I'll pull the clog and go flag down the Coast Guard dudes. By the time the water goes down the drain, they'll be here.

Aaron dove after the clog. As he descended into the dark water, he bumped into an object suspended in the water. Harshly he butted it out of his way with a sharp elbow jab, not daring to imagine what it was. He felt a strong current of water eddying around him. The thing that was adrift in the water with him seemed to be swishing the water, displacing it, and throwing off Aaron's stroke. Perhaps it was bigger than he. Aaron plunged deeper. He had to unclog the drain.

At the bottom of the water-filled trough, Aaron groped around for the drain. In the darkness, he hoped he was recalling the area correctly by feel. *It's here somewhere,* he thought. He could feel only a heavy clump of fine weeds tickling his palms. *Gross, must be seagrass,* he thought. *But, it feels like hair*. He unclogged the drain and hoist the clump back up to the surface. He did not want to risk it clogging the drain again if he left it down there. *Man, this thing's heavy,* thought Aaron.

With the weighty wad in one hand, he swam hard to the surface, aiming, he believed, for the outside door. As he swam, again he felt a huge presence swish beside him. With his free hand he felt for it. His hand caressed a vast, cold-blooded surface. He felt a dorsal fin and soon the sandpaper tail of what could only be... a shark.

"I'm going after Aaron," announced Katrina. "It's taking too long. The water'd be down by now if he got the drain open."

"Don't, Katrina, he said we should wait," said Dan.

"Fine, you hunker in your bunker," she said handing Dan the last flashlight, which barely shed any light.

"Just wait another five minutes, okay?"

"Five minutes? Aaron can't hold his breath for five minutes," exclaimed Katrina. *What if Aaron didn't make it? What then?* thought Katrina.

Katrina stepped carefully into the water and edged her way down the cement ramp, deeper and deeper. She took several breaths and stared solemnly at the dark brine.

This is it. Lungs full, she dove. Just then, Katrina's splash revived Coriander, who sat bolt upright.

"Don't go in the water!" screamed Coriander.

Aaron panicked with the realization that he was petting the sandpaper skin of a shark. Nervous, he inhaled some water, making him gag hopelessly underwater. His sense of direction skewed. Still, he forced himself to swim up, up, up in the direction he sensed was the outlet to the far side where they had entered the bunker the night before. Harder and harder he swam. His lungs felt like they would burst.

As Katrina swam through the dark tunnel of water, the shallow wounds on her skin began to itch from the salt. Several of the gashes were still open, and blood laced the water as she swam. By the time she felt the grill of the drain at the bottom of the trough, Katrina feared she would not be able to swim any longer. She didn't have enough air and her limbs were weak and sore. She could feel water being sucked out through the drain, and with it little bits of sea grass and tiny periwinkle shells as they fled between her fingers. *I hope this drain doesn't create a counter current that'll keep me down here,* thought Katrina.

The trough was longer and deeper than she remembered. Katrina swam farther upward toward the main door and swam right into a large, mass that seemed to block her way. Its surface felt like sandpaper. Not a wall. It had form, like a very big fish.

My wounds, thought Katrina as she felt her way, *my blood attracted a shark.*

The current from below was picking up and she swam hard against its force, trying to get past the shark. She needed air fast. Her lungs ached.

A shark is beside me. Terrified, her hands swept over the animal surface and she felt a human body entwined with it. *Aaron?* Katrina felt shoulders, neck, and... no head. *Oh, Aaron, my love...*

Katrina released her last air bubble and forced herself away from the huge, rough-skinned creature. She swam up and up. Then, the drain burped lowering the water in a gulp, and Katrina found she could stand on the cement slope. *Air! Sweet morning air!* Above her head in the narrow space between the surface of the water and the low ceiling, Katrina could breathe again. She could saw sunlight above the end of the steep bunker hall. Water was up to her neck. Would the shark get her?

At last Aaron threw over the edge onto the landing the heavy mass of what he imagined would be sea grass he'd dredged from the clogged drain. Screams met him as the water began to drop. Gasping for air, Aaron labored to clamber up the cement slope to the landing. He'd guessed wrong and ended up back on the inner side by the chamber with the high domed ceiling. To Aaron's horror, and that of his screaming school mates, the tangled mass he had retrieved was the severed head of Billy Carlyle.

"The shark killed Billy," sputtered Aaron, relieved however that he had convinced Katrina to remain where it was safe. He looked around at every teen face looking in shock at Billy's severed head that dripped brine and blood on the cement landing.

"Where's Katrina!?"

Dan pointed at the water. Wide-eyed, Aaron dove back in after her.

But the shark's right behind me, Katrina thought, grabbing breaths of air and thrusting herself forward through the viscous water, lunging toward safety. She knew sharks can attack even in two feet of water. She was still waist deep in water.

Finally she saw the barnacle-encrusted door that had shielded them from the enormous waves twelve hours earlier. She heard another loud gurgle and glanced back once to see the surface of the trough water drop away.

Oh, Aaron, Aaron, she thought in despair. She did not wait around to look for the shark. She aimed to run straight outside into the sunlight and wave down the Coast Guard for help.

The water dropped as fast as Aaron could swim. Soon he was wading hard through water up to his neck.

"Katrina!" yelled Aaron.

"You're alive!" She turned to see her best friend in the whole world.

Katrina and Aaron hugged and ran outside and danced on the rocks to the music of their own laughter. Aaron swept her into his arms and planted a huge kiss on her lips right in front of the approaching Coast Guard officers who were clapping.

With the drain empty, the officials found Billy Carlyle's bloated corpse with a dead shark in his arms.

"Looks like he panicked and tried to swim out," said Katrina ruefully.

"But he saved us from being attacked by the shark," marveled Aaron. "He wasn't such a coward after all. Billy disabled the shark with his bare hands."

"He chose to sacrifice himself to save you," remarked a Coast Guard officer. "That's a good friend!"

Knowing Billy, Katrina seriously doubted that he had martyred himself for anyone, but instead of bashing the dead, she changed the subject.

"Why's there a collection of torture devices inside this army bunker, Officer?"

The Coast Guard officials looked at each other. Finally, one spoke, "Through World War II, the U.S. Navy used this bunker to stash what they brought back from various European museums, including war museums. At this point, the retired bunker is nothing more than a great big warehouse," said one officer.

"Spoils of war," added a second officer.

"Guess they just forgot about all the weird stuff in it?" remarked Katrina.

"See to it another lock gets put on," said the captain.

"I don't think you'll need to bother," said Katrina. "The ghosts are gone. They're free. We freed them... by freeing ourselves."

The Coast Guard officers shrugged. "Kid's in shock."

"Awful to see a friend die," the other officer agreed.

The sun rose higher over the sparkling grey Atlantic Ocean as the officers headed in through the barnacle-encrusted iron door. Katrina stared out at low tide rippling across the horizon. She reached for Aaron's hand. Instead, he wrapped her in his muscular arms.

"C'mon Katrina, I'll get you home," he whispered.

"I *am* home, Aaron." She snuggled closer and smiled up at him. "Hollywood kiss?" Aaron leaned in with a smooth, silent reply, there on the rocks.

Find more exciting titles from

JUMPMASTER PRESS™

www.jumpmasterpress.com

About the Author

New England author, G.G. Garth has authored, ghostwritten, and development edited over 50 books for other authors published by Scala Arts Publishers, Center Street Press/Hachette, and others. Her Young Adult novels *Nightmare Matinee, Driven to Kill!, Bad Dog: A Vampires Canine,* and *Party Till You Scream!* published by JumpMaster Press (2020) were first published by Bantam Doubleday Dell (1994-1995). She graduated from Wells College, Aurora, New York, with a B.A. in German and Spanish literature. In high school she graduated from Holderness School, Plymouth, New Hampshire, and attended Berkhamsted School for Girls in Hertfordshire, England. Extensive travel on four continents inspired many of her stories. G.G. Garth is the proud mother of talented writers, Alden, a comedienne, and Jack, a journalist.

twitter.com/GGGarth
pph.me/GhiaWrite
https://www.facebook.com/ggarth1
GGGarthProductions.com

Made in USA - Kendallville, IN
1216028_9781949184426
12.18.2020 1428